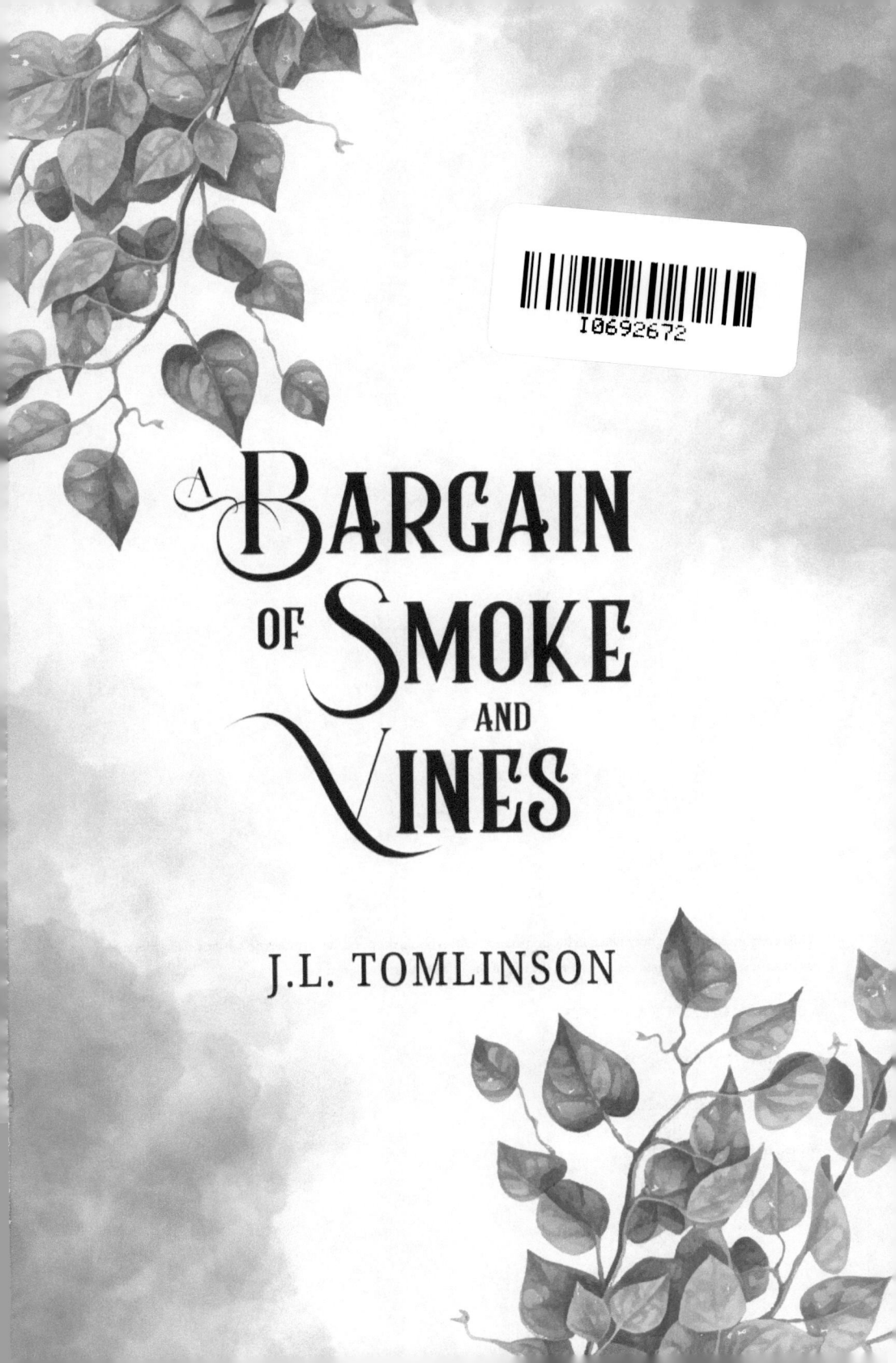

A BARGAIN OF SMOKE AND VINES

J.L. TOMLINSON

A BARGAIN OF SMOKE AND VINES

First edition. November 14, 2024.

Copyright © 2024 Side Eye Publishing.

Written by J.L. Tomlinson.

ISBN: 978-0-473-73098-7

Thank you to my own sister of the vine.

JOR'THALAS

THAL'MORVEN

MOR'THRAVAR

EYR'DROGUL

FYN'ROTHAR

BAEV'KALATH
HOUSE MORDORIN

PARISETH

GRYN'VELCOR

THE UNTOLD SEA

CYRATH
HOUSE ITHRANOR

THE SUNDERED
KINGDOMS

KALE HARBOR

VALORNE
HOUSE MALEDANNAN

LORTHYS
HOUSE CAELITHAR

THE GROVE

RETHMAR
HOUSE VALASTRAL

THYROS
HOUSE TARAMETHOS

CONTENTS

THE BARGAIN

DEAR TOVAR, KEEPER OF THE TENDERS,

Under the sight of the Pale Eye, I, Kaelus, King of the Sundered Kingdoms and Lord of House Mordorin, extend my greetings to you and the people of The Grove.

The dark tides of war advance swiftly, with The Legion of Saints threatening to engulf your lands in fire and despair. In these perilous times, alliances must be forged under the dominion of those with the power to protect and command.

House Mordorin, with its ancient and unparalleled might, offers a covenant of protection to The Tenders. Our forces shall stand as an unyielding shield against The Legion of Saints, driving back their advances and securing your borders. However, this protection comes at a price, for power demands submission.

To this end, a union must be forged between our people through the marriage of your Jewel of The Tenders and my heir, Crown Prince Daedalus Phaedren, and in doing so, bind The Tenders to our will. You shall bend the knee and acknowledge the sovereignty of House Mordorin. From this union, old treasons shall be forgiven, and a new era will dawn, where The Tenders shall thrive under our protection and guidance.

This is the will of House Mordorin. Submit to our rule, and your people shall be spared from the wrath of The Legion of Saints. Defy us, and face the relentless tide alone.

May this letter serve as a testament to our intentions and the path that lies ahead. Join hands and hearts with us, for only together, under the rule of House Mordorin, shall we withstand the trials of war and emerge victorious.

Our ship awaits to deliver your Jewel to the fortress of Baev'kalath and the arms of her adoring future husband.

His Majesty Kaelus Phaedren,
King of the Sundered Kingdoms, Lord of House Mordorin

CHAPTER 1

As the furious black waters crash violently against the hull of the grand ship, a shiver runs through me, and I feel the last warmth of sunlight seep from my skin like a fading whisper. The sky above churns with ominous clouds, and the scent of salt and storm hangs heavy in the air, mingling with my rising anxiety. Each wave seems to echo my racing heart, a reminder not just of the darkness that awaits me but of the fate I cannot escape—marriage to a Fae prince whose ruthlessness and cruelty has left our world in ruins. The weight of it presses down on me like the sea itself, waiting to consume me.

I close my eyes, not to shield them from the biting sea spray that lashes like icy needles, but to remember the warmth. I crave the sun on my skin, the feel of soft grass between my toes, the rustle of leaves in the breeze, and the laughter of the forest children echoing through the trees. With my eyes closed, I can forget the endless expanse of the Untold Sea, the haunting gaze of the crescent moon, and the looming shadow of Baev'kalath's island stronghold creeping ever closer.

With my eyes closed, I am home.

With my eyes closed, I am free.

Suddenly, a firm hand roughly grabs my arm, ripping me back to reality. Although he has never formally introduced himself, I have heard the other Mordorin warriors aboard the ship call him Arax. He looms over me, his armor gleaming even in the storm's dim light—sleek, tiered charcoal plates fitted like the scales of a predatory beast with spiked pauldrons as sharp as the blade at his hip. His helm is a steel shroud, black as ash, smooth and commanding, offering no glimpse of his features within the darkness. He has never removed it, and I have never seen his face.

"You were told to stay below deck," Arax growls. "The storm worsens and the Untold Sea is merciless. It will tear you right off this deck and drown you in its depths."

I glare at him, the hood of my cloak whipping sharply against my face in the unforgiving wind. "I am not a prisoner. I may go where I please."

His chain-mailed hand curls tighter around my arm. "You're lower than a prisoner. You're a human traitor. If I had my way, I'd throw you overboard right now," he hisses.

With grit teeth, I wrench my arm free of his grip, startling him. "That is not the truth, and you know it."

Arax scoffs. "That's right. Your people chose not to fight. You're worse than traitors. *Cowards.*"

When he takes a heavy step towards me, I take a step back, only to find myself hard against the railing of the ship. I glimpse the raging waves crashing below, and realize it would be so easy for him to carry out his threat, but I hold my nerve.

"How do you think your prince will react when this ship docks absent a bride?" I ask sharply, and even in the dark of night, with the wind howling and the rain pelting down, I see the warrior's throat quiver. "Is he a merciful prince?" I ask, already knowing the answer.

He snarls beneath his cowl. "Very well, human. But if you fall, it won't be on my head."

As he turns his back and his heavy black cloak whips up in the wind, I catch sight of the one vulnerability in his imposing armor. There's no steel protecting his shoulder blades—only a web of harnesses that exposes his skin, revealing a maze of tattoos sprawling across his back. These markings are runes, but not the familiar ones I know. They belong to the Mordorin Fae.

I clutch the carved wooden talisman hanging from the leather cord around my neck, my thumb tracing the familiar, timeworn grooves of the rune etched into its surface. Unlike the Fae, who carry their magic branded on their skin, humans—or at least those fortunate enough to be trained—must rely on talismans to harness the ancient power. Where the Fae's runes are a permanent part of them, mine is something I must always wear, a fragile link to a force far greater than myself.

For wearing such inherently Fae sigils, many on both sides deem my Sisters of the Vine and me abominations. Arax's cutting remarks are nothing new to me and I have heard far worse. If he seeks to intimidate me, he is sorely mistaken. I have witnessed the true cruelty of the Fae. Forests reduced to ashes, cities crumbling into dust, women left widowed and children orphaned. Their actions have wrought centuries of immeasurable suffering, yet to them, such a passage of time is merely a fleeting moment in their eternal existence. Let the Fae despise me all they want—the feeling is mutual.

A sudden crack of lightning tears through the starless black sky and the boom of thunder that follows rattles me to the bone. My frozen fingers grip the railing to hold me steady and I feel my knees buckle when another wave pounds the ship. I fight to find purchase upon the slippery boards as water floods the deck, my eyes half shut to spare them from the harsh sting of the rain, but they are open enough to catch sight of a monstrous creature rising from the waves.

Lightning sunders the sky once more, illuminating the serpentine figure with its giant yellow eyes, weaving towards the ship at speed.

"There's something out there," I say, but another crash of thunder drowns out my voice. The creature gains ground, its massive jaws widening to reveal rows and rows of needled teeth. "It's a monster! Turn the ship!"

My eyes dart to the crow's nest, only to find it empty, and where Arax stood behind me a moment ago, now he is nowhere to be seen. In fact, the entire ship appears abandoned. It is only me, alone, staring down one of the ancient beasts the Fae once treated as pets.

My fingers loosen from the railing, but I'm almost swept away when another rough wave hits. I scramble to stay on my feet. What a miserable choice to make; let go of the railing and take my chances with the sea, or count the seconds before the beast reaches the ship and swallows me whole. The saddest part is neither fate is worse than what awaits me in Baev'kalath. I prayed to the Souls for mercy, for an escape from the bargain forced upon me. Perhaps this is my salvation. At least I would die knowing I had denied the wicked prince of The Mordorin a bride.

As the monster nears me, it unleashes a high-pitched shriek. My eyes close once more, and I think of home. The sun, the trees, the soil beneath my feet. *Please let it be quick.*

"Don't just stand there, you foolish girl!" Arax yells as he reappears. He grabs my arm and yanks me away from the railing before tossing me across the deck, where a second Mordorin warrior catches me. "Frane. Protect the human!"

"Yes, Reaper Arax," Frane replies, her voice carrying a soft edge that catches me off guard. In the ranks of The Mordorin, men and women fight and die side by side. I'd find it admirable if I didn't despise them so much.

Frane's dark eyes flicker through the narrow visor of her helm, distinct from Arax's. Hers does not resemble a shroud, instead a fierce bird of prey, sharp and poised to strike.

As I watch her, I catch the murmur of unknown words slipping from her lips, almost lost beneath the din of battle.

Then, with a sudden surge of power, wide, black wings unfurl from her back, enveloping us in a protective embrace. The feathers glisten, their surface smooth and glinting in the light, wrapping around us like an impenetrable shield forged from the very essence of night. My fingers instinctively reach out to touch the feathers. To my astonishment, they are impossibly soft and I can't quite grasp how such delicate things can shield us from the chaos outside.

Another shriek from the sea beast steals my attention and I look up, finding a narrow gap between the Frane's wings where I can see the sky and the glow of the crescent moon. A figure swoops above us, followed by another, and another, all with broad wings pinned back, accelerating through the sky with swift precision.

"Slay the Stormwyrm!" Arax commands. "Take it's head!"

The wyrm's screech slices through the night like razor blades, a sound that gnaws at my very bones. The sounds of battle erupt around me as The Mordorin clash with the Stormwyrm, grunts and shouts mingling with the clash of steel and flesh. Then, after a thunderous splash, an unsettling silence takes hold of the ship.

"Is it over?" I ask, but my question goes unanswered. I struggle against Frane's grasp. "Release me!"

She gives an irritated grunt and her wings unfurl from around us, spreading broad and powerful at her back. I'm reacquainted with the rain as Frane eases me to the ground and I take a moment to adjust the hem of my dress tangled at my knees, but when I glance down, seawater floods over my silk slippers. With each rock of the ship, the water darkens, shifting from blue to deep crimson. For a moment, I wonder if it's a trick of the light, but when I look up, I see Arax lying flat on his back, blood pooling from the gaping wound in his chest.

His brethren surround him, arguing amongst themselves, but they take no action. The ship's railing where I once stood is now rubble. Splintered planks and shattered wood scattered over the deck where a fierce battle has taken place. The beast is gone, and though Arax bleeds heavily, I do not believe all the blood belongs to him. He is the victor, but at what cost?

His warriors stand frozen, their gazes locked onto him as if they await his final breath rather than rushing to his aid. It shouldn't matter to me. This Fae, Arax, has treated me with nothing but disdain since I first boarded the ship. He is no different from the others of his kind—a perfect lapdog to a dreaded master. *So why does it bother me that no one is fighting to save him?*

"Why is no one doing anything?" I yell the question plaguing me into the night, and in reply dozens of dark eyes glare at me.

Frane pushes past me to join the others who hover over Arax.

"Will you not help him?" I ask.

She shakes her head. "There is no saving him. The poison will kill him quicker than the wound."

A crack of lightning startles me, but provides enough light to draw my eyes to the tooth as long as a sword protruding from Arax's wound. At first, it was not visible in the darkness, but now the sight serves as a reminder of the Stormwyrm's rows of needle-like teeth.

"Poison?" I mutter. The warriors continue to argue amongst themselves in their foreign tongue, an urgent rage to their tone. "What are they saying?" I ask.

Frane exhales. "They are deciding who kills him. Puts an end to his misery." Her eyes stare coldly at me through her visor. "Gives him mercy."

Mercy? What do Fae know of mercy? Though it makes sense that they would consider murdering one of their own a gracious deed. Arax lies on the deck, his chest shuddering with short, sharp breaths while his hand twitches at his side. This Mordorin monster may mean nothing to me, but as a Sister of the Vine, I am taught to embody kindness, empathy, and above all, forgiveness—even towards those who may not deserve it.

Frane joins the huddle, and it seems as if the conclave has concluded when I hear the scrape of a blade unsheathing, and Frane takes a slow step towards Arax.

"No," I yell, and it takes a second for me to realize the word has come from my foolish mouth. Frane pauses and glares. "Damn it," I mutter, balling my fist and thumping it against my thigh, but it is too late to stop now. I have already decided.

I stagger toward Arax, my feet slipping on the blood-slicked deck as the howling wind shoves against me, trying to drive me back. Each step feels like a battle, but I push forward, my gaze locked on where Arax lies. As I near him, a wall of broad Mordorin chests rises before me, blocking my way.

To those who face them at the edge of a sword, they are a nightmare you will never wake from. But to the rest of the world, they are the Blades of the Ebon Flight, the warriors of House Mordorin. Their sheer size and presence stops me cold.

"What do you think you are doing?" Frane snaps.

"I can help him," I say, still unsure why my mouth is refusing to stay shut. "Let me through."

I take a step forward, but the Blades close ranks and, with a pulse of energy that throbs in my ears, huge black wings emerge from their backs, blocking out the moonlight.

"You will not touch him, human," a Blade scorns, his hand hovering over the hilt of his sword.

"My name is Amara Tyne. I am Jewel of the Tenders," I say firmly, hoping none of them see straight through me. "And it will not be long before I am the wife or your prince. So I command you to move aside."

The Blade's exchange venomous looks and my heart beats hard and fast in my chest as I wait for their response. Perhaps they will obey. Recognize me as their wicked prince's bride and move aside. *Yes, or they could slit your throat, throw you overboard, and tell their master the sea monster killed you as well.*

Thankfully, they slowly step back, clearing a path to Arax and I am grateful the heavy rain and miserable dark hides the relief on my face.

I drop to my knees beside Arax, the chill of the deck biting into my skin. His breaths rasp painfully in his chest, his gasps escaping the shadows of his shroud helm. My gaze locks onto the jagged tooth protruding from the horrific wound, a grotesque reminder of the Stormwyrm. Swallowing hard, I wrap my trembling hands around it, summoning every ounce of strength to pull. Blood erupts in a violent spatter, and Arax lets out a strained cry, his body lurching forward before collapsing with a heavy thud against the deck.

"That will do nothing!" Frane growls. "You should have let us end him. He will suffer more now."

I block out her words, refusing to accept them as the truth. Death should not be a mercy. Not when I have the power to save. *No matter whose life it may be.*

I place my hands on his chest and his blood seeps between my fingers and soaks through the sleeves of my green dress. This dress, made for me by the elder women, woven from sacred cloth washed in ancient waters that my people gave their lives for when the Fae sought to destroy all who did not bend the knee.

Now Mordorin blood once again stains our hands.

I close my eyes and try not to think about the war that tore our world apart. Instead, I think about the runes carved into the trunks of the old trees and the words only spoken in whispers. A warmth fills me, nestles beneath my skin and wraps around my bones like creeping vines. The threads of power strengthen and soon the whispers of the Souls are deep, bellowing chants that pound in my ears. A soft green light radiates from my chest, and the Blades take a step closer to look upon the glowing wooden rune dangling around my neck.

As the power of the rune courses through me, the light fills my fingertips and I push them deep inside Arax's wound, amongst the torn muscle and severed organs until a luminescent pulse fills the ravaged cavity.

Arax gasps and reaches for his blood smeared helm, wrestling it from his head and tossing it aside where it tumbles with hollow dings across the deck. My eyes flash open and it is the first time I have seen his face. I assumed him to be younger, or at least look younger, like all Fae do. But he reminds me of the men who sit on The Tenders Council, his white hair streaked with silver, rows of deep creases through his brow and circling his eyes, and an ivory beard that sits at his chest. The men on the council are in their sixtieth or seventieth cycle of age, but the Fae age much slower than us. With Arax wearing his age as he does, he could be anywhere in the hundreds, maybe more. If I had known he was older, I might have let him go. The Souls of the Forest have taught me that when it is one's time, they must be freed.

It's too late to turn back now.

Arax reaches out, grasping my arm with an intensity that sends a jolt through me, his wide dark eyes lock onto mine, and I notice a red ribbon marred with dark stains twisted around his wrist. I feel the warmth of his tissue and organs mending, his skin weaving itself back together beneath my hands, until, with one final gasp, he is restored completely.

The Blades whisper behind me and I realize more have gathered to witness the gifts of my people, The Tenders of the Grove. But it is not The Tenders' name I hear spoken amongst them.

"She wields the powers of The Maledannan."

I rise to my feet with a bitterness welling deep inside me.

"This is the will of The Tenders!" I yell, so all may hear. "And I, a human, saved his life while you did nothing but watch!"

It is not until the words have passed my lips that I realize I am scorning a ship full of Mordorin Fae, and that even though I am forced to wed their prince, there is still time to slit my throat and throw me overboard if I test their patience. Their eyes widen and their jaws fall open, but the sound of something massive emerging from the ocean at my back hints that I am not the focus of their attention.

When I turn, I find the Stormwyrm looming over me, its long neck weaving back and forth as it rises taller from the water. I freeze, every muscle stiffened with fear, but I'm aware enough to notice both the monster's giant yellow eyes are missing, along with its front tooth. A chorus of scraping steel slices through the air as The Mordorin draw their swords, but none are fast enough to strike before the beast lunges its open mouth at me.

My instincts sharpen, propelling me out of the way as I roll across the slick deck just in time to avoid the wyrm's massive jaws, which snap shut around the ship with a thunderous crack, splinters of wood showering from the sky amidst the sheets of rain. The Mordorin take to the air, slashing at the monster, but even their fearsome weapons are not enough to penetrate its thick, mottled gray skin. The Stormwyrm thrashes at them, knocking them from the sky as it lashes out at the Blades with its bared teeth.

Suddenly a hand grips my wrist and when I turn, I find Arax pushing the tooth I pulled from his chest toward me.

"Only this can break its skin," he murmurs, barely conscious.

I grasp the tooth with both shaking hands and when I open my mouth and find no words, I simply nod at him and clamber to my feet. The Mordorin continue their assault, and when their steel fails, they use their armored fists instead.

Arax had found a weakness—the Stormwyrm's eyes—and that was enough to make the beast retreat for a time. Yet as it returns, it dances around The Mordorin's attacks with surprising agility, evading them as if guided by instinct. Its blindness proves to be no hindrance. Whether by their raised voices or the vibrations thrumming through the air, the Stormwyrm seems to know exactly where the Blades are.

I stealthily make my way toward the edge of the shattered ship, teetering on a jagged plank. I do not understand why I chose this—why I took the wyrm's tooth and now stand before the beast. Perhaps the isolation of days at sea has driven me mad, or maybe I've finally reached my limit with the Mordorin's taunts. Perhaps the weight of this cursed bargain has pushed me to throw myself at death's feet in a desperate attempt to escape. But when I trip over a loose plank, hitting the deck with a hard thud, the wyrm snaps its head toward the sound, leaving me no time to reconsider.

The beast's head swivels to face me, and I stare with horror into the empty, bloody sockets. Before I can get back on my feet, it opens its gaping maw of a mouth and lunges at me, and my only instinct is to close my eyes and thrust the tooth towards the sky. Suddenly, the rain stops for the first time since we set sail for Baev'kalath.

Since I farewelled my home and my people.

Since I made a bargain to save our way of life and doom myself.

I hear a sickly gurgle above me, and even though the rain has ceased, I feel a wetness dripping across my face. I open my eyes and look up to see the Stormwyrm's head skewered with its own tooth, so deeply that my hands curled into fists are hard against its skin. Its thick, oily blood streams down my cheeks and over my chin, and the smell is so putrid it makes my head spin. I release the tooth, scurrying across the deck on my knees as the Blades watch in silence. After what feels like forever, the beast falls into the ocean with a hollow splash, causing a surge of water to flood over the deck.

I'm shaking as I lay on the cold, wet wood and my chattering teeth sound like thunder in my ears. I can feel the Mordorin's gaze pressing down on me, but they have nothing to say. Neither do I. Only when two armored boots stumble to stand beside me and a chain-mailed glove reaches down do I hear a voice.

"Amara. Jewel of the Tenders," Arax says as he takes my hand. "Let me help you to your feet." He is frail and hunched, but lifts me from the deck easily, my trembling fingers vanishing within his paw-like grasp. "What do you require?" he asks.

I gulp standing before him, my hands soaked in his blood, my face smeared with the blood of the Stormwyrm, my once flawless dress sodden wet. "I wish to go below deck," I reply.

He nods. "Very well, Jewel of the Tenders."

CHAPTER 2

My cabin mirrors the rest of the ship—dark and damp. A flickering amber glow emanates from a lantern, swaying precariously, the tiny candle within struggling to keep burning. *My strife is not so different.*

All my life, I have known only The Grove, a sprawling forest in the province of Valorne, a territory once ruled by House Maledannan. And for as long as I can remember, I have never trusted the Fae. In truth, The Maledannan were not as openly brutal as their kin, but they still made it clear—we were to serve them, and their word was law in Valorne.

Mostly, they allowed us to live in peace. Occasionally, they would visit The Grove, sharing their knowledge, teaching we Sisters of the Vine new runes and amplifying the gifts bestowed upon us by their ancestors centuries ago. Ours was a delicate relationship—tenuous at best. The Maledannan were our lords, and we were bound by oath to obey them. But we, The Tenders of The Grove, took the modest magic we were granted and turned it into something extraordinary.

This made The Maledannan nervous.

Suddenly Sisters of the Vine began to disappear, and we would wake in the morning to find parts of the forest culled to nothing but stumps, the ancient Souls that dwelt there lost forever. The visits became raids, children were dragged away in the night to serve in their castles, and soon The Maledannan were just as vile as every other Fae in the Sundered Kingdoms.

So when the human rebellion known as The Legion of Saints rose against them—against all the Fae houses—and The Maledannan demanded we fight by their side... we refused. Their wrath nearly burned The Grove to the ground. So many died—men, women, children—all lost to their rage. Not because of some grand cause, but because the Fae couldn't bear to share power. The Tenders did not shed any tears

11

when the Maledannan were wiped from the face of the Kingdoms on the last day of the war that would become known as The Betrayer's Battle.

We had no tears left—all spent grieving our own dead.

I was just a child when it happened, more than fifteen years ago. From that moment on, I vowed to protect The Grove and its people at any cost. We won't survive another blaze.

Yet, I could never have imagined that the price of our survival would be a marriage to the only Fae House that emerged from the Betrayer's Battle, while all others lay dead or vanished entirely. And now, to make matters worse, I've just saved the life of a Mordorin who dared call me a traitor.

All I do, I do for The Grove.

When Keeper Tovar struck this bargain, I went along willingly, but now that I am here, amid the Fae, I feel as though I've betrayed everything I once stood for.

How can I protect my people when I'm forced to walk among those I swore to fight?

How can my candle keep burning when the vengeful wind wants nothing more than to extinguish my light?

A wave strikes the ship and I stumble into the wall. I struggle to stay upright as the cot in the corner of the cabin calls to me, a refuge I desperately crave. I barely manage a few unsteady steps before I lurch forward, my hand darting out to grasp the edge of a table. A searing pain radiates from my chest, and I grimace, clutching at the spot with a sharp gasp.

Did the Stormwyrm wound me?

With my dwindling strength, I pull at the leather ties of my bodice until they loosen enough to inspect the source of my agony. The skin just above my breast has turned as dark green as swamp moss, with pulsating tendrils creeping from its center. There is no bite, no blood, no sea monster's poison, and the mark has spawned in the same place as Arax's wound.

Of course.

One of the first things the Souls of the Forest whispered to me was that everything comes at a price, no matter how good your intentions are. That magic, born from dark or light, was not a natural occurrence in humans. It was a rare and powerful artifact and just like anything of value, whether bought, bartered, or traded, there was always a substantial cost. For The Sisters of the Vine, the price to heal is to absorb the affliction. To suffer as they suffer.

I have healed many times before. A village girl struck with fever. A noble hunter ravaged by wolves. Their pain presented upon my body, just as Arax's pain did now. It would pass in time, and eventually the mark on my skin would disappear completely, but for now, I needed to sleep, silent and still, like the trees.

I stagger to the cot as the room spins and the pain burns deep. My vision blurs as I reach the bed just in time, falling onto the lumpy mattress as my legs give way beneath me. The waves crash against the ship, rocking me back and forth like a babe in a cradle and I don't recall the exact moment my eyes close and I fall into a deep, dreamless sleep.

"Jewel. Wake up."

The words don't sound real, and I wonder if I'm dreaming.

But then I remember I have never dreamed. Not once.

"We have docked. Wake up."

My eyes flutter open and I feel as if I've barely slept at all. I find Arax hovering over me.

"Have we reached Baev'kalath?" I murmur.

He nods. "The king and queen await you." His gaze flits over my chest and his face sours as if he's caught the scent of something rotten. He gestures uncomfortably to where my bosom peeps through my loosened bodice. I bolt upright from the cot and draw tight the leather ties to conceal myself. I notice the mark has already vanished from my skin, and the pain is a distant memory.

"Do you have anything you can change into?" Arax asks.

I shake my head. "This is all I brought."

Arax furrows his brow, his wrinkles crawling into his hairline, as if a woman not having trunks of clothes is an oddity. But Tenders do not have possessions. At home I have my Sister robes which I wash and wear every day. Even the dress on my back, now stained with blood and soaked right through, is a gift from the village, so that I might look more like a bride than a child of the forest.

I've even worn shoes for the occasion.

"Queen Lanneth is easily offended by..." Arax pauses. "...soiled things."

"This is the bride they bargained for," I reply, giving the ties of my bodice one last tug that tightens my waist and steals the breath from my lungs. "If I am not good enough, they are welcome to send me back."

Arax exhales, the exasperation spreading across his face like a rash. "Very well. Follow me. I will escort you to the throne room."

"The throne room? Right away? But I'm a mess."

He raises an overgrown brow. "Yes, that much is clear. But King Kaelus and Queen Lanneth wish to inspect you immediately."

"Inspect me?" I scoff, but Arax does not respond, instead staring blankly ahead.

Is there really a point in arguing?

I am in Baev'kalath, far from the shores of home, in a wrecked ship surrounded by hundreds of winged warrior Fae. So I do as Arax says, but before I follow him out of the cabin, I rush to the table to collect the one other thing I brought with me across the Untold Sea, apart from the clothes on my back.

In a wooden bowl cradled by rich, dark soil, a serpentine vine unfurls, its pale green tendrils writhing gracefully, mottled with delicate white patches. Seven arrowhead-shaped leaves sprout from its twisting form, vibrant and full of life. These resilient vines weave through The Grove, intertwining like the bonds of The Tenders and the Souls of the Forest. My Sisters of the Vine gave me this plant before I left to remind me of home.

I scoop the bowl into my arms, holding it close, feeling its heartbeat against my chest.

It may be the last piece of home I'll ever have.

I step onto the deck beside Arax, greeted by the howl of the wind and the sound of waves smashing against rock. The ship feels abandoned once more, not a single Mordorin in sight. But then I catch Arax's gaze, tilted upward, and I follow it to a night sky alive with Fae cloaked in leather and steel, their faces masked beneath their helms as the rain pounds down upon them. Despite the roaring wind, their ebony wings hold steady, unfurled majestically against the backdrop of the stars, a breathtaking sight that sends a shiver down my spine.

Though their eyes hide within the recesses of their helms, I feel their stares piercing through me, weighing and measuring the human who will be their princess. Drenched in my sodden dress, I look less like royalty and more like a drowned rat, an overwhelming sense of inadequacy crashing over me.

The Mordorin do not move or speak. They hover overhead in silence as Arax leads me across the deck toward a ramp lowered onto the dock. His boots thump loudly as we descend, while my ruined silk shoes slosh with water, my feet aching with blisters as I follow.

"Behold the stronghold of House Mordorin. The power in the Untold Sea."

I look up, and beyond the hovering wall of Blades, the gargantuan black fortress of Baev'kalath rises from the jagged peak. Massive floor-to-ceiling arches and long, sweeping balconies jut out dramatically, centered around a vast courtyard bathed in the orange glow of blazing pyres. Towering spires and ornate turrets stretch upward, vanishing into the thick, gray clouds, which loom like restless spirits, threatening to engulf the fortress entirely.

This place is dark, desolate, and seeps despair.

But somehow it is also the most hauntingly beautiful thing I have ever seen. We humans know of Baev'kalath, but very few have actually seen it. Compared to the other Fae houses, the Mordorin stronghold is the most remote and dangerous to reach. The part of me that craves knowledge and discovery stands in awe. But the bargained bride I have become realizes that this wicked place is now my prison, and soon that naïve wonderment will wash away, and I too will seep despair.

Arax mutters in Mordorin tongue and his wings erupt from his back and pound the air. He opens his arms to me, and I'm not sure how I'm supposed to respond.

"I will carry you to the castle," Arax explains.

I frown. "I'm quite capable of getting there myself."

Arax grumbles irritably. "By all means, spread your wings and I'll meet you there."

I reply with an unamused frown.

"The castle is only accessible by air," Arax explains in one long breath. "You will need to be flown. There is no path."

I glance at his outstretched arms, unsure if I'm really expected to let him pick me up. I've been handled by more Mordorin in one night than I have by humans in my entire life. Taking a step forward, I move close enough for his chain-mailed hands to scoop me up—one cradling my back, the other supporting my knees.

I gasp at how effortlessly he lifts me from the ground, but I catch the way he hisses through gritted teeth as his shoulder sags.

"Are you sure you're strong enough to do this?" I ask skeptically, reminded that I pulled a tooth the length of his arm from him not long ago.

He swallows his discomfort. "I have been commanding armies and slaughtering enemies since before you were born. I'm sure I can manage carrying a little girl who asks too many questions."

"Well, make sure of it," I say curtly. "After surviving that journey, the last thing I want is to fall out of the sky and splatter across the rocks because a surly old Fae dropped me."

Arax grumbles as he pushes off the ground and soars into the sky.

It feels as if I've left my stomach on the dock as he flies higher, clearing the jagged rocks of the cliff face, his wings beating the air with an unworldly power that sends a puzzling shiver through me. I hold my vine close to my chest, while my other arm loops around his neck, the sharp steel of his pauldrons pricking at my skin. But I ignore the discomfort. I'm far too busy pretending that being this high in the air isn't absolutely terrifying.

I thought my arranged marriage to the Mordorin prince would be the worst thing to happen to me when I left The Grove. But since stepping foot on that ship, I've had to share the agony of Arax's wound, fight a sea monster and now be slung hundreds of feet in the air, all before even setting eyes on my dreaded betrothed.

At last we reach a grand balcony high upon the castle where the Mordorin obviously come and go from. Arax touches down heavily on the wet stone and the rain lashes my skin. I feel the cold creeping into my bones.

"This way," Arax says, marching forward with his helm tucked under his arm.

I follow him towards the dim light of the castle and standing before the massive structure, I've never felt smaller. It is three times the size of The Maledannan ruins that overlook The Grove. Before we enter, I catch the indistinct murmur of voices drifting up from below, their words blurred by the steady downpour. I wander towards the stone railing, inching closer until my eyes find a circle of Blades surrounding a Fae male who kneels dangerously close to the edge of the wall, above razor sharp rocks and the violent swell below.

Another Fae looms behind him, his black shirt clinging tightly to his form, soaked through by the rain. The leather of his trousers glistens, outlining the sinewy muscles beneath, while wet strands of pitch-black hair obscure his face, shrouding his expression. He raises his hand to the stormy sky, and I watch, breathless, as tendrils of smoke weave between his fingers. Slowly, a brilliant silver sword manifests, its shimmer cutting through the gloom. My heart stops in my chest as I grapple with the realization of what is coming next.

With brutal swiftness, the sword arcs down. The kneeling man's head falls away, his body frozen in a macabre posture. His killer steps forward, his boot pressing into his victim's back before sending him over the edge. I watch, horrified, as the body tumbles through the air before smashing against the rocks below.

A scream tears from my lips before I can hold it back, and the killer's head snaps in my direction. From this distance, I can just make out the sharp angles of his cheeks and jawline and the glow of his slate-gray eyes, along with the broadness of his shoulders rising and falling with each breath.

With a deliberate motion, he curls his fingers into a fist, and the silver sword dissipates into tendrils of smoke that drift into the twilight. We remain suspended in that moment, our gazes locked—mine brimming with horror and revulsion, while his reflects a disturbing blend of curiosity and apathy.

"Girl," Arax snaps. "This way."

I turn to him. "What was that down there?"

Arax exhales, a rumbling in his chest. "The execution of a coward and a deserter. He fled the battlefield when his brother and sister Blades needed him most. For this, the punishment is death."

"That is murder," I strain through grit teeth.

"No. That is Mordorin justice," Arax replies coldly.

I turn back to the scene, my soaked hair whipping my face, but when I look, the man in black is gone.

"The king and queen wait," Arax reminds me.

My chin drops to my chest, rain trailing down my chin as I follow Arax through the archway, my gut twisting with disgust. He may not have spoken his name, but there is no doubt in my mind who the wielder of that blade is.

Ruthless. Cruel. The wicked prince of The Mordorin himself. *My fated husband.*

CHAPTER 3

The coldness in the executioner's eyes follows me as Arax and I enter the castle, and though I'm grateful to be free of the rain, I still hear it pattering on the stone and running down the columns. Arax guides me through dimly lit corridors, where flickering torches cast eerie shadows upon the stone walls. The Mordorin guards stand like silent sentinels, their formidable forms as still as statues, their eyes glinting like embers in the gloom. Each step feels like a journey in itself until we finally arrive at a pair of colossal doors, flanked by black banners emblazoned with the Mordorin crest: a winged sword soaring above a crescent moon.

Arax pushes hard against the dark wood and the doors groan open. The throne room unfolds before us, a breathtaking expanse adorned with intricately sculpted archways that soar high above. Candle light bathes the room in an eerie saffron glow, from the scattering of candles across the stone floor to the elaborate tiered candelabras and gigantic chandelier overhead dripping wax like rain. At the far end of the chamber, behind three thrones hewn from rock, stands a magnificent stained glass window, stretching from floor to ceiling, depicting a Mordorin warrior in full garb; the spiked pauldrons, the flowing ebony cloak, the shrouded helm, and black wings that fill the starry sky backdrop.

I stand behind Arax, my heart racing in my chest, beating so loud it sounds like thunder in my ears, and when a crack of lightning makes the grand room as bright as day, I see two shadowed figures standing on the dais before the thrones.

"Go," Arax says in a whisper that vibrates the surrounding air. "They are waiting."

I nod in agreement, but my feet freeze in place.

He glances at the figures, then back at me and clears his throat. "Girl? Did you hear me?"

I hear Arax's words. I know what I should do, but still I do not move.

Then suddenly someone whispers in my ear. *"You should not have come here! Run while you can!"*

For a moment, it feels as if the Souls have found me. But that is impossible. Their home is the trees. A chill runs through my veins as I turn toward the sound.

Arax meets my gaze, confusion etched on both our faces.

"What did you say?" I whisper, my throat tightening.

He eyes me as if I've lost my grip on reality. "What? I told you to go to the King and Queen."

My brow burrows, mind drifting off. *I could have sworn...*

"They've sent us a mad bride," Arax grumbles under his breath.

"What is the delay?" calls a voice smooth as velvet from beneath the stunning stained glass.

"Apologies, my Queen," Arax says, a grimace crossing his features as he turns back to me. "Move, Jewel. Now!"

My mind goes blank and I wonder if Arax is right. Have I gone mad, hearing voices that belong to no one? But before I find reason, there is a soft popping sound, followed by a plume of black smoke that explodes before me, and when the charcoal slivers fade, a Fae female stands regal in its place.

She is tall and willowy, with long slender limbs draped in iridescent black silk. Her pale shoulders are bare, her skin stretched tight against her collarbone, with a steel choker worked into a lace pattern wrapped tightly around her neck, a shimmering black opal at its center.

Even though Fae age slower than humans, I make out the lines around her eyes and mouth, hinting she must be centuries old like Arax, but she disguises this beneath layers of powder. Her eyes are eerily pearlescent, framed by long lashes and encircled with dark, heavy makeup. Her hair does not resemble that of her raven-haired kin. Waves of silver, streaked with stark white, and crowned with a black tiara, its sharp edges mirroring this forsaken rock we stand upon.

If her appearance is not startling enough, her arrival has me stunned. I have never seen void walking first hand, a Fae ability unique to the Mordorin, allowing them to travel short distances in the blink of an eye. My mind has a million questions, each one longer than the last, but I stifle my curiosity when Arax stamps his foot at me, before dropping to one knee.

19

"King Kaelus. Queen Lanneth," Arax says with reverence. "I present Amara Tyne. Jewel of the Tenders." He glances up at me from beneath his brow and scowls when he sees I am still standing. "Bow," he hisses under his breath.

Even though my body is at last willed into movement, it takes longer than it should for me to take a knee before the Mordorin. After all, it is a sign of loyalty and respect, and for these Fae, I possess neither.

There is a second soft pop, and King Kaelus instantly appears from the smoke at the queen's side, his gray eyes narrowing on me curiously. Queen Lanneth extends her hand to him, and he gently curls his fingers around hers.

"She does not bow," Lanneth laments. "Do they have no etiquette where you come from, girl?" Her eyes skim my serpentine vine. "And look, she brings... a weed."

"Now, now, Lanneth," the king interjects, his gaze lingering on my vine with a flicker of interest. "She's merely unfamiliar with our customs, as we are with hers. Besides, she is Fae nobility now—no need for such rigid formalities."

Lanneth glares at me through slitted eyes. "She is not nobility yet, my love."

Though her voice is smooth, there is a slither to it that puts me at unease, and her disconcerting eyes do not give me a moment's peace. I glance away from her briefly, if only to take a breath from her stare, when I glimpse something in the corner of my eye. A shimmer. A ripple in the air. And it seems to surround the queen.

I strain my eyes curiously. "What is that?"

The king and queen exchange bemused looks before returning their attention to me.

"Are you sickly, child?" Lanneth asks, her chin tilted upward.

"Now, my love," Kaelus sighs, laying a kiss on her knuckles. "She is clearly weary from travel."

He is not wrong. I suppose exhaustion could have something to do with the voices I'm hearing or the strange way the light plays off the queen's skin, and when the shimmer vanishes, I doubt if it ever existed.

"The travel *was* long and difficult," I say to justify my odd behavior, my throat dry and voice raspy.

Lanneth forces a smile over her thin lips. "That is not good. Our prince needs a strong and healthy bride and your Keeper assured us of your quality when the bargain was struck. I would hate to think we were deceived."

A scowl spreads across my face, and my eyes narrow on the queen. "There is no deception. I promise. A wife in exchange for Blades to protect The Grove. So here I am. Have you met your obligations?"

Tension takes hold of the moment. Kaelus glances at Arax, who rises to his feet.

"Twenty Blades were left to watch over The Grove after we escorted the Jewel to the ship," Arax states.

Kaelus raises an eyebrow at me. "Excellent. So we have both made good on our promises."

"Only twenty?" I ask, my eyebrows knitting together. "We will need more than that to defend The Grove."

"And you shall have them," Lanneth interrupts. "As soon as you and the prince are wed."

I hold her stare, even though it stings as much as the blisters on my feet. I do not want them to think even for a moment that I am some naive girl from the forest, easily manipulated. I am very aware of the terms of the bargain, and I will see them met. But for now, it seems as if all is well.

"Very well," I say, nodding my head subtly.

"And the sooner you are wed, the better," Lanneth adds. She runs her eyes over me with distaste. "But we must clean you up immediately. The prince cannot see you like this. Is that... blood?"

"None of it is mine," I reply bluntly, and the queen regards me with a dubious glance.

I do not mention that the prince has already seen me like this.

The same time as I saw him cut off a man's head.

After that little showing, I could not care less how the prince sees me. But I am eager to wash the dried blood from my skin and soak my aching feet.

"If you tell me where to find my room, I will make myself more presentable."

"I will do you one better," Lanneth smiles, an expression I do not trust. "I will take you there myself."

King Kaelus exhales. "Good. While you attend to our Jewel, Arax and I will discuss what happened on the journey from the mainland. I have heard a great many concerning things."

His gaze shifts to Arax, who stands stoic and stalwart. "Yes, my King."

King Kaelus kisses Lanneth's hand once more, then tips his head to me before strolling from the hall, gesturing for Arax to follow.

"Now then," Lanneth starts as the giant doors close with a resounding thud. "Time to prepare you for our prince."

The way she speaks makes my skin crawl, as if I am a gift to be wrapped and presented for his enjoyment. All I want right now is to be shown my room so I can escape her.

We do not leave through the doors as I expect, but through a passageway unseen in the room's corner between two columns. Queen Lanneth takes a torch from the wall and I follow behind her, weaving through a maze of dark, narrow corridors and passing several plain wooden doors before coming to a stop before one in particular. The queen leans into the wood and the door opens to reveal a bedchamber. When she closes the door behind us, I notice it appears as only a wall panel on this side.

I wonder just how many secret doors there are in this place.

"The castle is large, especially as you cannot fly or void walk. These passages will be helpful."

I bow my head and give an appreciative nod, only slightly unnerved that she's followed my train of thought. It's also possibly the least condescending she's been since we've met.

The first thing I notice are the arches that lead onto a wide balcony overlooking the vast stormy sea, with dark shimmering curtains billowing in the whistling wind. Beautifully carved and lavishly dressed furniture decorates the space. There are tables and desks, chaises and sofas and two crimson high-back chairs in front of a blazing seven foot fireplace with an ornate baroque mantle.

It is hard not to notice the enormous bed against the wall with its intricate headboard and wooden posts that twist like a serpent, and the black gossamer curtains draped around its sides. It is a reminder of just what I must do to seal this bargain, and a knot forms in my belly.

"Put your plant down there," Lanneth instructs, gesturing to a round table by the arch.

Her suggestion is acceptable. Right by the open archway, my vine will get the sunlight she needs. I place her down and realize she has been quiet for some time. Perhaps the journey has exhausted her, too.

I glance at the bed once more, its dark covers piled high with cushions and scattered furs, but relief comes as the queen guides me into an adjoining room, away from the reminder that soon I will be someone's wife and bedmate.

The next room warms me with the soft amber glow of a roaring fire. A clawfoot tub sits by the hearth, its water scattered with dried flowers and fragrant herbs and the soothing aroma fills the space, inviting a sense of calm to settle over me.

In The Grove, hot baths are not common. The weather is fine, so we wash in the river where the sun warms the water. You would certainly not find a copper clawfoot tub in the forest. But with my body sore and cold, I can not wait to throw myself into the steaming water and sink to the very bottom.

"Thank you, Your Highness," I say, eager for her to leave.

But she doesn't. Queen Lanneth stands still as a statue. *Staring at me.*

"Let me help you," she says abruptly, pinching the leather ties of my bodice between her fingers and loosening them.

I gasp and take a step back. "I can undress myself."

The flames from the fire reflect in her frighteningly pale eyes as her fingers continue to pull at my bodice. "Nonsense. Mothers bathe their daughters all the time. Did your mother not bathe you?"

I cannot find words as the queen pulls open my bodice and slips my dress off my shoulders. Instinctively, I cross my arms over my breasts and I can feel my skin glowing bright red, but Queen Lanneth seems disinterested in my discomfort. When my dress falls from my shoulders, it catches on my hips and the soft round of my belly, but without a second thought, she balls the fabric in her fists, wrestling it over my curves and down my thighs until it falls in a sodden pile on the floor.

I cross my legs, hoping to conceal my most private area, but still the queen shows no concern for my naked state and how strange this is.

"Well. Get in," she says, as if I'm the one acting unusual.

I rush into the tub. At least if I'm underwater, my body is not on display. I sink beneath the flowers and herbs. At first the water is so hot it stings, but it is not long before I feel myself melting like candle wax, and as my eyes roll back in my head, an overwhelming sense of relaxation takes over me. I'm not sure where my body ends and the water begins. I close my eyes, content to lie here forever, then I feel the queen's breath on my neck and the sound of dripping water.

I open my eyes and see Queen Lanneth soaking a yellow sponge, then squeezing out the excess before gently dabbing at my shoulders.

"There. Doesn't that feel better?"

My unease immediately returns and the words fall awkwardly from my mouth. "Yes. Thank you, Your Highness."

She moves the sponge up and down my neck, along my collarbone and when she dips below the waterline, dragging the porous sponge over my breasts, I squirm.

"Our prince deserves a bride, clean and free of impurity," Queen Lanneth says as she washes me. "Don't you agree, Amara?"

I swallow hard, unable to meet her eyes. Instead, I focus on the water as it turns dark, the grime and blood swirling away from my skin. "Your Highness," I murmur, my voice barely steady. "The journey was long, and I was brought to you before I had the chance to make myself presentable."

Queen Lanneth laughs lightly. "No, dearest. I'm not talking about the filth on your skin. We can wash that away. But there are some parts of us that, once soiled, can never be made clean again." Her eyes search mine. "Do you know what I speak of?" I understand what she is implying, but when I do not answer quickly enough, she speaks instead. "The Keeper told us you are a Sister of the Vine." She lifts the sponge from the tub and squeezes out the excess water. "Is it true a Sister has never known the touch of a man?"

I nod, my stomach knotting with discomfort. "Yes, Your Highness."

She nods her approval as her eyes trail over every inch of my body, like I'm livestock at a market.

"Your face is comely enough. Not beautiful, of course, but pleasant looking." She peers at me coldly. "And you are rounder than I expected, but perhaps such wide hips will be helpful for a human womb carrying a Fae baby." Queen Lanneth gives a tight-lipped smile and rises to her feet, laying the sponge on the edge of the tub. "Let us hope any offspring inherit the fair skin of their grandsires. Not that your tint isn't... delightful." She wipes her hands on a nearby cloth. "I will leave you now to finish up. Your maids await you in your bedchamber when you are ready to dress."

The seconds crawl by, each one stretching painfully until, just as I think I'll finally be rid of her, she looks back. I quickly smooth the scowl from my face before she catches it.

"I am very glad you are here, Amara Tyne," she says over her shoulder. "You will make a fine bride for our prince."

Queen Lanneth closes the door behind her, and I finally release the breath I've been holding tight in my chest. The fire crackles softly, and the steady rhythm of rain drums against the stone, but I let it all fade away as I surrender to the silence beneath the water.

My body sinks deeper, my muscles unwinding as I wonder what would happen if I stayed here, submerged, and never resurfaced.

It would be such an easy escape. But the Mordorin bargained for a bride, not a corpse, and without their protection, The Grove is lost. A single tear slips down my cheek, mingling with the bathwater, vanishing long before I rise from the tub.

CHAPTER 4

The cold and wet had turned my fingers to prunes long before I stepped foot in the bath. Now they are so shriveled, I look more like a mummified crone than a princess. But the warm water has soothed my blisters, and I didn't realize how much feeling I had lost in my toes until I wriggle them on the fluffy rug.

I pick up the heavy black robe hanging on the edge of the tub and swirl it around my shoulders, pulling my arms through the long hanging sleeves and knotting the silver cord at my waist. I could easily crawl into bed now. Fall into a deep sleep and pray this was all a nightmare I would wake from. But the chorus of voices from the bedchamber makes me think the night is not yet over.

I take cautious steps towards the door, unsure of what might be on the other side. I stare at the gilded handle. Surely there can't be anything worse than a sea monster awaiting me. I shrug off my nerves and open the door, and a cluster of cackling Fae maids immediately falls silent. It is hard not to notice they are all beautiful with their sparkling eyes, striking features and pointed ears peaking through their braided dark hair. They quickly shuffle their feet and form a line, then bow before me.

"Good evening, my lady," they say in unison.

"Good evening," I reply, a nervous croak in my voice.

One maid steps forward, her nose slightly sharper, her face slightly prettier if that was possible, and raises her head. "My name is Solena. If you require anything, you need only summon me."

Though she offers her service, disdain drips from her clipped words, and her eyes scan me as if I don't belong here. I choose to ignore it.

"What would I require?" I ask instead.

Solena clasps her hands. "Anything. Draw a bath. Prepare you for bed. Brush your hair."

I frown. "Are these things people usually need help with?"

"Yes. Usually."

"And it takes five of you to brush my hair?"

Solena's lips are a straight line. "If that is what you require, my lady. Now, are you ready to be dressed?"

"Dressed?" I query.

The line of maids part revealing a dark, crimson gown laying across the bed, the bodice encrusted with black pearls, with layers and layers of black lace beneath the luxurious silk fabric. I've never seen a dress so shamelessly joyless and decadent, and certainly not something worn to bed.

"You want me to wear that? Now?" I ask.

"Yes, my lady," Solena replies.

Abruptly the maids pounce and pull at my robe with their nimble fingers, but when I shriek, they stumble backwards.

"You know, I'm quite tired of strangers undressing me tonight," I snap, tightening the cord around my waist. "And I am far too exhausted to put on that ridiculous dress. The hour is late and I wish to go to bed."

"Queen Lanneth commands we dress you," Solena says firmly. "So dress you, we shall. Otherwise..."

"Otherwise what?" I taunt. "What worse things could you Fae possibly have in store for me?"

"Otherwise, the queen has instructed some Blades of the Ebon Flight to dress you instead," Solena replies sharply. "Outside. While the others watch."

My jaw clenches. "You wouldn't dare."

Solena bows. "I dare nothing, my lady. These are the orders of Queen Lanneth."

An ire swells in the pit of my stomach as I grind my teeth. I yank the cord away from my waist and my robe falls open before I shrug it to the ground. "Fine. But be quick about it."

The maids set to their task, stuffing me into a dress which seems far too small and tying the corset so tight you would think breathing was of no importance. The bodice feels hard as steel against my chest, cinching my waist tight and pushing my breasts up and out while the satin clings to every curve of my hips and thighs. Huge, puffy sleeves erupt like wings from my shoulders, and layers of heavy lace flare out at the back, leaving a long, snaking train behind me. With the dress on, the maids attack my face and hair next and it is not until the powdering and combing ceases and they at last give me room to breathe that I behold what a monstrosity they have made me.

Is the reflection in the mirror truly me?

Amara Tyne, Jewel of the Tenders, Guardian of the Grove.

I walk through the forest barefoot in flowing green robes sewn by my hand, with my brown hair long and matted down my back. Now I am imprisoned in a death shroud—prepared, painted, and presented for the Mordorin gaze, a spectacle meant to please their wicked prince.

I struggle to find myself beneath the heavy, glittering black eye makeup and luminescent face powder. My lips painted deep red, almost black, to match the gown, and my wild waves of hair tamed and slicked back into a severe bun.

Solena opens a green velvet box on the dressing table, and I'm practically blinded by the glinting jeweled combs and headpieces inside. The precious gems hold such great value they could feed a village for an entire season. It is far too much wealth to be held by one person, and even worse, just for their hair. Solena takes a set of ruby combs that could buy a mountain of grain and places them on either side of my coiffed hair.

Now I can barely stand to look at myself.

"Maybe we should have braided her hair," a maid remarks to another. "The prince favors a braid."

"You would know," is the reply, and the women giggle behind their hands.

"Perhaps we should loosen the corset," whispers another. "Our prince can be impatient."

The maids laugh again, twittering like little birds. I look at Solena behind me, reflected in the mirror. She does not engage with them, her eyes set solely on fidgeting with the last few details of my hair, but she could not hide that smirk even in pitch black darkness.

They speak so freely about the prince with no regard for my presence. It is clear they want me to hear their bragging. To make me feel embarrassed, helpless and alone.

I will not allow it.

I slam my hands on the dressing table and push myself to my feet, my scowl silencing them.

"You are no longer needed," I say tersely. "Leave. Now."

The maids bow and hasten from the room. Solena is last, bowing before taking a gilded handle in each hand and smoothly closing the doors behind her. But even when they are gone, I can hear their cackles in the hall.

Is this true? Does the Mordorin prince make bedmates of his servants in this awful place?

I knew I was to be the bride of a fiend and a murderer. Of course, he is a lecherous scoundrel as well.

Perhaps it is just this ridiculous corset, but suddenly I cannot breathe.

Why am I wearing this hideous gown?

Why have they dressed me up in the middle of the night?

I hate it here. I want to go home. Far away from these cruel creatures and the horrid fate they have in store for me. But there would be no home if not for this bargain. Mine is a sacrifice that keeps The Grove safe.

I muster my resolve and push such selfish thoughts from my mind, closing my eyes tight and hoping my prayers ascended the gloom of Baev'kalath.

"Souls. Please give me the courage to survive this so my people might live. Please give me hope."

"There is no hope here," a voice replies from the shadows. *"Only sorrow. Only pain."*

I spin on my heels, the weight of the dress putting a stumble to my step. I look into the darkened corner of the room, but no matter how hard I try, I can not make out the figure that stands there, its shape loose and wavering like smoke. The voice I recognize. It is the same voice from the throne room that screamed at me to run. Deep and consuming and haunted by great sadness.

"Who are you?" I demand, desperately clutching the dressing table, my knuckles white. "Show yourself."

"I am the curse of this place. The bones that rattle beneath the rock," the voice replies. *"I told you to run. Why did you not run?"*

The smoke expands, slithering across the room and blackening the walls.

"I thought I imagined you. That my mind was playing tricks on me."

"Tricks would be a blessing," the voice says, its presence spreading through the bed-chamber and casting impossible shadows across the floor that seem to reach for me. *"For Baev'kalath is a place of horrors, and the dark prince is a cursed thing."*

Soon, the shadows are at my feet and smoky tendrils slither up my gown, twisting around my waist and rushing over my chest before encircling my throat.

29

"Why did you come?" the voice scorns, but there is a woeful pleading in its words. *"Do you wish for death? Or did you bring it with you?"*

"I had no choice." I gulp as the ice-cold tendrils tighten like a vise.

The voice whispers. *"Now neither do I."*

The tendrils tighten again, and my breaths sharpen in my throat as I choke.

"Do not fall in love with the cursed prince. It will be your doom!"

Suddenly, the doors of the bedchamber fly open and the smoke retreats to the darkened corner from where it appeared.

"Amara Tyne," Arax says, cradling his helm under his arm. "It is time."

I stagger against the dressing table, gasping for breath.

His silver eyebrows furrow with concern. "Girl. Are you alright?"

I pause to collect my thoughts, straightening my back as I banish the lingering shadows of my imagination. I can't share what I didn't truly see with Arax; he already thinks I'm mad. Yet the words echo in my mind, leaving a chill creeping down my spine.

"Time for what?" I stammer.

"For your wedding," he replies, his tone as gruff as ever.

The words reverberate in my mind, simple yet elusive, slipping through my grasp like water. I can't make sense of them, no matter how hard I try.

"Wedding? Now?" I shake my head vehemently. "No. This is ridiculous. I have only just arrived. You cannot expect me to marry a man I have never met in the middle of the night?"

Arax stands stalwart. "This is the command of your king and queen."

I plant my feet like roots in the earth. "I said no, Arax."

He exhales, his dull eyes staring solemnly at me. "You did me a kindness by saving my life on the ship. Please do not make me drag you kicking and screaming to your own wedding."

"You wouldn't," I mutter under my breath.

Arax's face hardens. "I am a Blade of the Ebon Flight. I have done far worse."

I may not know this warrior of the Mordorin well, but I do not doubt he will carry out his king's orders and I would rather meet my fate on my own two feet than over his shoulder.

I lift my dress above my shoes and march past Arax, my mood sour and my thoughts dark as I spit curses under my breath. Never have I regretted my gift of healing until now.

What fleeting madness made me forget that all Mordorin are cruel?

None deserve mercy or pity, for they would offer neither in return. I should have let Arax succumb to the Stormwyrm's poison or perish on the edge of his kinsmen's swords. If only I could take it back—I would do so in a heartbeat and be happier for it.

I storm into the torch lit hall and take in the long, empty passages either side of me. It all looks the same, dark and miserable, with an endless chorus of rain falling upon rock. Arax closes the bedchamber doors and turns to me, then nods his head to the left.

"Follow me. This way."

He walks ahead, and I reluctantly follow, conveying my anger in every one of my thundering steps. My anger masks the fear twisting in my belly like a barrel of slippery eels. I knew this moment would come. The conditions of the bargain between The Mordorin and The Tenders were very clear. A union forged in marriage between our people. I'm not sure how I imagined it would happen, but not once did I predict a midnight wedding dressed in a blood red gown as lightning tore apart the black sky above.

I can hear my heart pounding in my ears as Arax guides me deeper into the castle, away from the vast balconies and terraces that only those with wings can reach. We come to an abrupt stop in a massive, empty antechamber bathed in dim candlelight, the flickering flames casting dancing shadows along the intricately carved stone walls.

I recognize the banners and the two giant doors before us and remember the breath-taking stained glass window that lies behind them. My stomach twists at the thought of what lies beyond those doors—my wedding. The very idea sends a fresh wave of anxiety coursing through me.

Arax looks at me over his shoulder. "Are you ready?"

I tighten my fists at my sides. "Does it matter?"

Arax turns his face forward and pulls on his helm. His armor scrapes against the door handles when he grasps them, and when the doors open, the weight of my dread crashes down upon me like a landslide.

A sharp silence cuts through the thrum of voices as the room of hundreds takes me in with their gaze. The last time I was here, only the king and queen stood before me. Now, strangers gawk without the decency to hide their sneers—some in armor, some in crisp linens, and others in gowns as dark and suffocating as mine. Fae are so different from The Tenders: pale and splendid, more beautiful than any creature has a right to be. But there is not an ounce of warmth or joy among them.

They are just empty, lovely shells.

The crowd parts, creating a narrow aisle that stretches ominously between where I stand and the thrones at the opposite end of the room. The king and queen sit regally, their expressions unreadable, while before them stands a figure cloaked in black.

Even from this distance, his towering height and broad shoulders command attention, the casual clasp of his hands hinting at a confidence that borders on arrogance. As I take a step forward, the moonlight streaming through the window slices across his face, but the shadows cling to him like a veil, concealing his features from my view. A chill dances down my spine, an unsettling premonition creeping in—the knowledge that whatever lies behind those shadows will change me forever.

Arax steps aside, and without him to shield me, I am laid bare for the Mordorin court to ogle, and they do. I can barely breath beneath the weight of their stares and whispers slither through the heavy silence. It all feels like hands around my throat, starving me for air and the ground turns unsteady beneath me.

"Human weakling," someone mutters from the assembly. "She is far too fragile to be a Mordorin bride. Look. She can barely stand. She is not worthy."

I swallow hard as the words stab like daggers into my back. Here I stand, outnumbered by the remnants of a dwindled house, and they dare to call me weak and fragile? Unworthy?

Old gods be damned. I refuse to let anyone—man, monster, or faerie—cast judgment upon me.

I take a deep breath, pull back my shoulders, and fix my gaze down this forsaken aisle, focusing on the man in black who awaits me at the other end.

With each renewed step, my shoes clap rhythmically against the stone, echoing the tension that crackles in the air. The wicked prince of Baev'kalath grows closer. I hate him, I truly do, yet a part of me is curious about what he hides in the shadows. Surely, he must be beautiful—after all, all Fae are. But then I remember the malice that seeps from him, the ugliness that overshadows any beauty he might possess.

The male I witnessed him murder lingers in my mind, a reminder of the monster he truly is.

Before I know it, I have reached the end of the aisle and find myself under the gaze of King Kaelus and Queen Lanneth. The queen smiles, and the memory of her undressing me fills me with disgust, a wave of nausea rising in my stomach.

The prince stands silent beside me, towering above, my head barely reaching his shoulder. His thick, muscled arms strain against the seams of his black coat. Shadows conceal his face as he stares straight ahead, but between my stolen glances, I catch glimpses of his smooth, razor-sharp jawline framed by loose black waves that curtain his eyes. My gaze follows the hard contours of his rugged features, and when I finally find his mouth—a perfectly sculpted, sensuous bow—I momentarily forget where I am.

Queen Lanneth stands. "Forgive the suddenness of all this," she says. "But this union is most urgent. For both our people."

I am too preoccupied to speak, my eyes constantly darting back and forth at my silent groom who seems to refuse to acknowledge me.

An elder Fae with slicked-back silver hair and a wiry gray beard approaches, his ebony robes adorned with a large solitary eye stitched in shimmering silver thread. As the queen takes her seat upon the throne, the elder addresses the prince and me, his empty white eyes reflecting the queen's unsettling gaze. I fight the urge to stare at those disconcerting eyes, but whenever I look away, that familiar ripple in the air pulls me back to him—just as it had enveloped the queen when we first met.

I don't know what it is or what causes it to happen, but I know it's something unnatural, something I've never seen before now. Frustrated, I shift my gaze to the prince, who stands like a statue, his indifference only fueling my anger. Why do I care if he acknowledges me?

The elder speaks. "Behold House Mordorin. Disciples of the Ebon Blade. High Fae of the Storm and the Sea. On this night, beneath the Pale Eye, our favored prince takes a bride."

The court cheer and the armored warriors among them pound their fists once against their chests in unison.

"This human, Amara Tyne, Jewel of the Tenders, stands before us beneath the Pale Eye and swears to all who witness that she shall serve her Fae masters and graciously submit to her Fae husband, now and forever."

My head flings back and the words spill from my mouth before I can catch them. "I do not!"

The court gasps, and I can see the flash of rage in Queen Lanneth's eyes. The elder's lip twitches, and his deathly white gaze reflects my anxious self back at me. I hadn't meant to speak; I had resigned myself to my fate. Everything I do is for The Grove. A pang strikes

33

my chest, realizing in that moment, my heart had screamed its silent truth. The elder turns to King Kaelus, who glares and releases a guttural growl from his throne, leaning onto his knee.

"Your people swore an oath," he mutters angrily, loud enough for only me to hear, as if to spare himself embarrassment. "You in exchange for our protection from The Legion. You are in Baev'kalath now, girl, and Jewel or not, I will throw you into the sea to *drown* if you dare defy me. But not before I withdraw all my warriors from The Grove and let your precious forest burn. You are ours now. Do you understand?"

The king's words sting, his pleasant demeanor evaporated, and once again I'm reminded of how quickly The Mordorin become callous. My eyes well, but I refuse to give him the satisfaction of knowing he's struck a chord.

"Yes. I understand."

He grits his teeth and leans back in his throne. "Proceed, Archdruid Theros."

The Archdruid shifts his gaze to the groom, and it dawns on me that these are the only words he intends to direct toward me. My consent holds no value in this ceremony; I am merely a pawn in a game played by those with far greater power.

"Favored Prince of the Mordorin. Son of Kaelus. Heir to the Sundered Kingdoms. Commander of the Ebon Flight. Beneath the Pale Eye, will you take this human as your bride, to use her as you will, to breed her so that the blood of the High Fae may prosper, until such time as she is spent."

I can hardly fathom the words I'm hearing. I am not a person in this arrangement. I am reduced to a vessel meant to please the prince and bear his heirs until I draw my last breath. Stealing another glance at the silent man beside me, I find myself curious about his reaction to our wedding vows, wondering if he feels even a fraction of the weight of this twisted union.

That is when he speaks for the first time.

"I do," he replies, in a tone that rumbles deep as the black sea.

"Give me your hands," the Archdruid demands as he draws a jeweled dagger from his sleeve.

The groom's hands are adorned with intricate rune tattoos that snake around his sinewy forearm as he rolls up his sleeve, offering his hand, palm up. The Archdruid's sneer makes it clear that he expects me to do the same. I swallow hard, steeling myself as I pull back the lace cuffs of my gown and hold out my hand. In one swift motion, he slashes our palms, the cut deep enough to send blood streaming freely onto the floor. I bite down on my lip, fighting the urge to cry out.

I would rather die than show fear or weakness in front of this assembly—or in front of him.

I glance up at the Archdruid, then gasp when I see an inverted crescent burnt into his forehead, but I am sure it was not there before. My heart thumps and I close my eyes tightly before looking once more. This time, the mark is gone. I ignore the figment of my imagination.

"By the joining of blood, she is yours," The Archdruid declares, his voice reverberating through the chamber like an incantation. The words hang heavy in the air, a promise woven into the fabric of the ceremony. Each syllable feels like a spell, binding me to a fate I never chose. I can feel the weight of the eyes upon us, the spectators leaning forward in anticipation, as if they are witnesses to a great and terrible moment in history. The mingling of our blood signifies not just an alliance, but an irrevocable claim over my very being. I shudder, realizing that this simple act transforms me from an unwilling participant into a possession.

Suddenly, the statue beside me comes to life, seizing my hand in a rough grip and forcing our palms together. A sharp wince escapes me as my wound collides with his, and our blood merges, seeping between our laced fingers like two rivers converging, pooling at our feet.

The connection strikes like lightning, fierce and unrelenting, as though the world itself has been waiting for this moment. When I was chosen by the Souls to be their Jewel, I felt their power course through me, a sacred infusion of purpose and strength. When my sisters and I stand together, communing with the ancient pulse of the forest, I feel our bond hum like the roots beneath our feet. When the sun slipped from my skin for the last time, leaving me in the cold embrace of twilight, I mourned its loss.

But this... this is not loss. Nor is it power or purpose. This connection is unlike anything I have known. It surges beyond the limits of flesh, deeper than nerves, further even than blood. It reaches into the part of me no blade could ever find, no wound could ever expose. It touches my essence—my spirit—the light within that will one day leave this body and rise to whatever lies beyond.

And it whispers. A truth I wish I could unhear, yet cannot deny.

This Fae is not merely my husband. He is my destiny. My fate. My beginning and my end.

The realization is agony, a betrayal from the one voice I have always trusted: my own. It claws at my soul, demanding I accept it, even as I recoil from its inevitability. For in that truth lies a bond I cannot sever, a fire I cannot extinguish. And I know, with aching certainty, that I am his as much as he is mine.

And as the turmoil within me threatens to overwhelm, he finally turns his gaze to mine. The world narrows, and everything—everything—becomes him.

Moonlight streams through the window, casting a rich glow upon his skin, while his ebony waves of hair fall back, revealing piercing gray eyes that seem to hold the very essence of the storm. They radiate light, a vivid hue that transcends mere color, glowing with an intensity as bright as the moon on a starless night. Yet, there's a haunting darkness beneath the surface—bottomless, fathomless, eternal. The longer I hold his gaze, the more I feel myself sinking, falling helplessly into the abyss of his eyes. Fear grips me, yet my instinct isn't to flee. It's to remain here, ensnared by his gaze, waiting for the darkness to consume me.

He leans closer, tall and broad and diabolically muscled, a looming presence that casts a shadow over me, pinning me to the ground. I can feel his breath against my neck, a tangible weight that deepens my sense of helplessness.

"She is mine," he declares, the words resonating with a finality that sends shivers down my spine.

CHAPTER 5

When I was a child, I stumbled upon a rabbit caught in a poacher's snare.

In The Grove, the earth nurtures us, so I had never encountered a trap designed to catch and kill. The rabbit lay on its side, its brown eyes wide with terror, its chest heaving with frantic breaths. It was the first time I truly sensed fear. I tugged at the frayed noose wrapped around its delicate legs until it loosened. The rope had been so tight that it had sliced through fur and flesh, leaving raw, bloody wounds in its wake.

I expected the rabbit to leap up, bounding back into the safety of the forest, overflowing with gratitude for its newfound freedom. Instead, it remained there, its gaze locked onto mine, almost resigned to its fate. Even when released, it seemed to hesitate, choosing to stay rather than flee.

Now, I struggle to recall whether it ever hopped away or if, after long moments of silent watching, I was the one to leave first. Tonight, I understand what that rabbit tried to convey with its eyes—its fear, sadness, and the profound loss of hope. All I can do now is wait for my own release from this snare.

But the question lingers: *will I have the strength to run when the moment comes?*

The Archdruid interrupts my spiraling thoughts with a harsh, rattling cough to clear his throat, then stretches his arms wide, addressing the court with a voice that echoes through the hall.

"Brethren," he declares. "I present to you Princess Amara and our crown prince, Daedalus Phaedren."

Our names ring out like a proclamation of doom.

The prince pivots us to face the applauding crowd, lifting my hand high, our blood streaming down our arms like a crimson ribbon. A wave of dizziness washes over me. I can't tell if I'm feeling unwell from the warm trickle of my blood pooling wastefully on the floor, or the oppressive weight of the smirking Fae surrounding us. Perhaps the very presence of the prince is causing the nausea to churn in my stomach, although I know if he hadn't looked away from me, I might still be lost in the depths of his haunting eyes.

Suddenly, he brings my hand to his lips and lays a kiss on my knuckles. The soft warmth startles me, and a breath lodges in my throat. When he lifts his head, I see our mingled blood smeared across his mouth. I watch as his tongue slides over his bottom lip.

"You taste as sweet as you look," he mutters and my breath escapes my body in a shivered gasp. "How does the rest of you taste?"

"Enough Daedalus," Queen Lanneth says. She grips his shoulder and pulls us apart. "Why not fetch your wife a goblet of wine or something to eat?"

Daedalus wipes his blood stained mouth on his sleeve and continues to hold me in his unwavering gaze. "I have done my part, Your Grace, and if I am to get through this night, my own goblet will need filling." He bows half-heartedly. "Wife," he calls me, before turning his back and joining his Mordorin court, who have already begun celebrations.

Wife.

The word is like a blade scraping against the walls of my skull. I, who vowed never to tether myself to a man, now stand in the fortress of Baev'kalath, the bride of a Mordorin prince. I have sacrificed my freedom, my independence, even my dignity to protect The Grove.

I look over the raucous assembly as they laugh and sing, red wine spilling from overflowing cups. Suddenly, my eyes find my husband—dear old gods, I cannot believe I am saying this—*my husband.*

He raises his goblet to me, his stare so intense that I can't hold it for more than a second.

He moves with a predatory grace, draped in garments woven from the threads of the night. There is a hunger in the way he watches me, and I am reminded that I am nothing more than a plaything for the prince's amusement. I take a deep breath, shivering even though I feel no chill.

What more must I give?

I remain awkwardly beside the thrones in my atrocious gown as blood runs from my wound and the king and queen not so discreetly whisper about me to each other. Wine and laughter flows easily amongst the Mordorin and the more they drink, the less formal the occasion becomes.

The slender hands of the Fae females caress the charcoal armor of the warriors, male and female alike, removing their helms and putting goblets to their lips. Some of the more regal Fae in their fine linens and extravagant gowns take to the darkened corners, but even in the shadows, I make out bodies twisting and entangling.

As I stand amid the revelry, discomfort washes over me. The air is thick with laughter and the sounds of lips meeting skin. Their whispers and giggles feel like a stark contrast to my upbringing in The Grove, where physical intimacy is shared only in the most private moments.

Watching them entwined—so casual and unrestrained—fills me with a longing I barely understand. It's both intoxicating and frightening. My cheeks flush with heat, making me feel exposed. I want to look away, yet I can't help but be drawn in.

Suddenly Queen Lanneth stands and for a brief moment I fear she has heard my thoughts. But she is only concerned with the court, and when she claps her hands, all fall silent.

"Fearsome Fae of House Mordorin," she begins, her voice resonating through the hall. "I know that for some of you, this match may seem unimaginable. After their ill-fated rebellion, why would we unite our beloved prince with a mere human?" A heavy silence blankets the court, all eyes trained on her, their anticipation palpable—mine included. "But do you not see? This is a time for glorious celebration! While the kingdom was torn apart, it was The Mordorin who stood firm. The other great houses scattered to the winds, while we fought fiercely until the last human bent the knee." She pauses, her eyes fluttering shut as she takes a deep breath. "We are a generous and forgiving people, and what greater demonstration of our benevolence than to make a bride of those who have wronged us?"

I scan the court for their reactions. Some nod and applaud, but just as many exchange glares, muttering behind their hands. To me, the queen's words feel like sheer delusion. Generous and forgiving? I was barely nearing my womanhood when the war begun, but even so I remember the forests on fire with flames so tall they burnt through the clouds and scorched the heavens. The Ebon Blade extinguished thousands of human lives in a massacre of steel and smoke, and for the humans who survived, the choice given was kneel or die.

Some say the price was too high for a failed uprising. That humans are still slaves to the Fae. But of the six houses that once ruled over us, only one remains. The Mordorin.

Whisperings of their dwindled numbers are rife through the human villages, and as The Grove knows only too well, the Legion of Saints still thirsts for vengeance.

Queen Lanneth opens her pearlescent eyes and the thin line of her mouth curves into a smile. "So rejoice House Mordorin. For beneath the Pale Eye, you are fortunate enough to witness our salvation."

The court erupts into applause, but still I can see the discontent lingering with some who return to their goblets and whispers. Does the queen speak the truth? Is this union more than just a bargain? Is it truly the dawn of a new day for Fae and human? I remember the screams from within the burning forest, so loud and horrifying that even with my hands covering my ears, I could hear them.

I still hear them.

No. The Mordorin cannot change. They are Fae. They are murderers. And now I am amongst them.

A server female approaches the queen with her head bowed and hands her a jeweled goblet. Queen Lanneth raises it to the assembly, and I find it curious that King Kaelus sits in silence while she holds court. In fact, apart from threatening me at my wedding, he has barely spoken at all.

"A toast to Prince Daedalus and his bride, Princess Amara," the queen declares. She takes a long sip. "Now. A dance."

My stomach drops to the floor, and I look at the prince. He pretends he isn't listening with his head bowed and his mouth buried in his cup, but his stunning eyes flit up to find me before swiftly looking away. The queen reaches over to King Kaelus, gripping his forearm, and this is enough incentive to get the king on his feet.

"Daedalus," he booms. "A dance with your wife. Now."

The prince takes one last drink from his cup before slamming it onto a table. He drags his sleeve across his mouth and strides to the center of the room, loosening the leather ties of his collar as if it was choking him. The court forms a circle around him and once again, all eyes are on me as they await my response.

My feet stay frozen in place and I'm certain that even the end of the world could not get them to budge. The prince rolls his eyes and extends his arm.

"Wife," he calls. "Come. Dance with your husband."

Footsteps close in behind me and I feel the queen's breath on my neck.

"You do not wish to embarrass the prince, do you?"

I gulp and shake my head, forcing myself to take a step, but my feet feel like lead, weighed down by this enormous dress and the torturous corset that feels like a suit of armor. I manage another step, then another, but each movement feels heavy and awkward, and I am certain I must look like a clumsy fool in front of the lithe, graceful Fae court.

As the distance between the prince and me narrows, he extends his hand, and my trembling fingers reach out to accept his. His grip is firm and calloused, devoid of any gentleness, and before I can fully process what's happening, he yanks me into his arms with such force that I stumble, colliding face-first against his chest. It feels like hitting a brick wall.

When I pull back, my gaze travels down the strong column of his throat to the intricate tapestry of black rune tattoos sweeping across his collarbone and around his neck on a leather string is a shimmering moonstone that appears cracked in half.

A low chuckle escapes his mouth. "Not particularly graceful, are we? Though I imagine weddings in the woods are mostly chanting and naked mud dancing around a bonfire."

I glower, and I'm about to unleash a tirade of insults upon him, when suddenly a duet of violins starts to play and the prince grabs me by the waist while his other tattooed hand wraps around my fingers. He pulls me against him, our bodies pressed so tight I feel his heartbeat and each hard ripple of his abdomen.

With every dark, melodious chord, he moves me back and forth, side to side with such assertiveness that I would be foolish not to follow his lead. Though I feel his gaze, I can not meet his eyes and his every breath is soaked with sweet wine, so strong that I could get drunk just by inhaling. The prince's fingers curl tighter around my waist, and I gulp when his hips press hard against me.

"Do you not speak?" he mutters in my ear. "Are you so well trained, little Jewel?"

His waves of dark hair brush annoyingly against my cheek and I throw back my head sharply. He jerks, giving me space to breathe.

"I speak very well," I snap tersely. "When there is someone worth speaking to."

His eyes widen and a smirk cracks the corner of his mouth. "Are you saying I am not someone worth speaking to?"

I keep the truth I wish to spit at him behind my teeth. "No, Your Highness. I would never."

His lips straighten into a serious line. "Do not call me that."

41

I raise an inquisitive eyebrow. "Then what am I to call you?"

"I'm sure you have plenty of ideas, but Daed will do for now."

I exhale. "If we are doing introductions, then I am Amara."

The hard gray of his eyes seems to soften. "I know who you are."

Whether it's the intensity of his piercing stare or the overwhelming exhaustion setting in, the faces of the court begin to blur, and the room tilts around me. My vision hazes, and I instinctively reach for Daed's shoulder to steady myself. He tightens his grip as I falter in his arms, holding me firmly in place, his presence both a support and a trap, preventing my collapse but offering no comfort.

He glances down at me, his voice flat and impatient. "What's wrong with you?".

"I don't feel well," I mumble, struggling to keep my eyes open.

"Your hand. You're still bleeding." He sighs with annoyance. "Of course you are. You're human."

A sudden swell of cheers and laughter blends with the violins, snapping me back to reality. I find myself draped over my husband, my head slumped against his solid chest, his arms braced around my waist to keep me upright. To the court, I must look like a love-struck bride, but in truth, I'm fighting to stay conscious.

King Kaelus throws his head back and laughs loudly. "It seems as if our princess wishes to honor her wedding vows sooner rather than later."

The court erupts with laughter, and the raucous cackling stings my ears. Just as my knees buckle, Daed sweeps his arm beneath them and scoops me up. I smell the wine on his breath and inhale his salty musk when my head falls on his shoulder.

"Eat and drink until dawn, brethren," Daed booms. "Your prince must bed his bride."

The court grows louder, their fervor intensifying as they close in around us, and I wonder how we can push through them all to reach the door. But at that moment Daed's eyes flash with light and a gust of wind summons giant black wings from his back. After that, everything happens so quickly. He pushes off into the air and we soar straight up with such speed that my body shudders beneath the pressure.

I fight to look up, to see what is above us, and when I sight the solid rock ceiling growing dangerously close, I realize on top of everything else, I've married a man just as mad as I have become.

"What are you doing?" I murmur. "You'll kill us both."

"Nonsense," he replies as we gain speed. "*I* will survive."

Never in a thousand years did I expect my wedding night to end like this. In truth, since I stepped foot on that ship, I've had very little control over my fate. I could muster the strength to fight him. Kick and scratch until he let me go, but then instead of a mess on the ceiling, I'd end up a mess on the floor and as for reasoning with the wicked prince of the Mordorin, time was not on my side. It would all be over in seconds. So I look into his eyes. Resigned to my fate.

"Please keep safe The Grove, Prince Daedelus."

Our eyes meet just before we reach the ceiling. I brace myself and imagine at this speed, the end will be quick and painless. I am partly correct. There is no pain.

Because there is no impact.

A swirl of black smoke engulfs us, thick as treading water and stinking of sulfur. This in-between place is a realm of darkness. I can see nothing, not Daed's face, nor my own hand. But we are not alone here. I feel a presence coming closer. I feel the walls of eternity closing in on me. Then something appears. A single, giant eye and a gaping mouth with a serpent's forked tongue lashing out at me as it screams.

My throat tightens around my horror, not allowing a single sound to escape, but as swiftly as it all happens, a resounding pop deafens me and when the smoke clears, I am reacquainted with the unwelcome sting of icy rain upon my skin.

What is happening to me? Why am I being tormented?

I look up and squint at the bright ivory moon floating in a pitch black sky, and when I look down, I see the fortress and the steepled roof of the throne room that should have been my end. My stomach churns and before I can stop it I expel a sickly stream of vomit that plummets towards the courtyard.

I gasp, then cover my mouth, my eyes wide with shame.

Daed winces. "Charming."

He pins back his wings and descends and I waver in and out of consciousness until I feel a thud as we touch down. Through half-open eyes, I recognize the balcony outside my bedchamber and the billowing gossamer curtains over the arches. Daed pushes them aside and as he strides, I find myself hypnotized by his heavy breaths and the pounding of his heart. He comes to a stop and bends over, and the sinking softness of the bed replaces the ropey muscles of his arms as he lays me down.

"Am I going to be sick again?" I mutter.

"Perhaps. Void walking does not sit well with the human anatomy. But we have not cared to test it thoroughly. It was brief, so you should be fine."

Daed's words patter in my ears like rain as my vision blurs and I wrestle to keep my wits. His hands run over my body as if searching for something, and I recall the bold words he exchanged with his court in the throne room.

Is this truly happening? Am I being bedded here and now... *like this?*

I ball the bed covers in my fists and twist my legs together, but the prince is strong.

He pulls the covers from my hands and pins me to the bed.

"Be still," he mutters. "Before you do further damage to yourself."

My senses fade from me and my mind drifts in and out of waking, but each time I stir, he is still there, holding me down.

"Wait," I whimper.

I wince at the sting of something tightening across my palm, my eyes flashing open long enough to watch Daed walk around the bed towards the door. His shirt is unbuttoned, revealing every smooth, defined line of his torso, from the sculpted planes of his chest to the taut ridges of his abdomen. But I notice part of his shirt ripped away.

The hand he pinned down rests beside my head, and I feel a binding warmth around my palm. I turn and find it bandaged with the missing fabric of Daed's shirt. Slowly, I regain my senses as the haze lifts from my mind, and when I look down, I find my gown intact and my maidenhood intact.

The door handle turns and I call out to him. "You do not...lay with me?"

My cheeks redden and I do not understand why I ask such a thing. I should be happy he did not touch me, ecstatic beyond belief that my husband did not force me to serve him as I vowed.

Daed puts his hands against the door and leans into the wood. "I do not," he replies, his dark hair soaked with rain that drips down his neck, his shirt not only torn in the front but also across his shoulder blades where his wings burst forth. "I am drunk and weary, and your bed does not entice me, little human."

Again, his answer should satisfy, but I persist.

"But is this not *our* room? Do you not sleep here... with me?"

He turns his head enough for me to sight the sharpness of his jawline and a single drop of rain beading at the tip of his nose. "I take my rest in my tower across the courtyard, and I will find comfort in someone's bed tonight, but it will not be yours. Goodnight, wife."

44

He pulls open the doors, strides out, then slams them behind him, leaving me confused and racked with uncertainty. Instead of coldly bedding me, he took care of me, yet had the callousness to throw insults before abandoning me all together.

Comfort in another's bed.

It is easy to guess who that bed belongs to. Pretty little maids eager to fulfill his every degrading fantasy. Would I prefer the alternative? To have my maidenhood taken while out of my mind and against my will?

The king and queen would have found a gleeful widow in the morning if he had dared force himself on me. No matter how many times these villains declare so bluntly that I am theirs—they bargained for a bride, not a body. Then why does this rage burn so bitterly, and why is it tinged with a woeful ache in my chest?

Why do I care that he does not want me?

I roll onto my side and hitch up my knees, curling into a ball, and gazing out the arches to the ink black sky that stretches to eternity. The rain patters against the stone, and when the thunder rolls and the lightning cracks, I do not shudder. Instead, I close my eyes and find a soothing rhythm to the thrum of the storm.

Because I do not dream, I must imagine what dreams are like. Are clouds fluffy enough to bounce upon? If I climb to the very top of the tallest tree in The Grove, can I touch the sun? Would my parents be proud of me? As my heavy eyelids fall closed and I slip into slumber, all I imagined fades from my mind, and the last waking dream I see is Daedalus Phaedren standing over me, devouring me whole with those stormy gray eyes.

CHAPTER 6

My mind stirs and my eyes flicker open. I have always been an early riser, as if my body senses the dawn, but when I glance through the arches of my bedchamber, there is not the faintest hint of sunlight. The sky is gray with dense hanging clouds, and though the rain falls lighter, still it falls.

Does it ever stop?

It is not until the doors open and the maids file in that I'm convinced it is morning. Here in Baev'kalath, the morn is as dark and dreary as the midnight hours.

They rush to the bed, but freeze in their strides when they take in the scene as I lie on top of the undisturbed covers, fully dressed. They look curiously around the room and I know who they are searching for.

"He is not here," I say, putting them out of their misery.

Solena asks the question on the tip of all of their tongues. "The prince did not spend the night with you?"

I roll my eyes. "I assumed you would already know that. At least one of you." Something sour hits the back of my throat. "Or all of you."

They exchange bewildered glances, but I am learning quickly that no one in Baev'kalath is to be trusted and lies fall easily from their mouths, like acorns from an oak. I have no doubt the more enticing bed my husband spoke of belonged to one of these pretty Fae. Solena walks around the bed to stand beside me, then puts her arm behind my back to help me up.

"I'm fine," I say, shirking away her help. I push my hands against the bed to prop myself up, then wince and curse under my breath when a sharp pain surges through my hand.

Solena looks at the black cloth wrapped around my palm. "Are you injured, Your Highness?"

I narrow my eyes at her. It is the first time someone has addressed me this way, and the words feel too big to me. Like clothes I will never grow into. "Just call me Amara."

"Princess Amara," she corrects.

"Fine then. Princess Amara," I reply, and I realize Daed and I had a very similar conversation last night. Both of us unwilling and unwelcoming of the titles forced upon us.

"Your hand, Princess Amara," Solena continues. "Is that from the wedding ceremony?"

"Yes," I grumble. "Is it custom for the bride to bleed out?"

"May I?" she asks. I nod, interested myself to see what it looks like. I wince as she tugs back the cloth of Daed's shirt and the contortion of her face does not fill me with optimism.

I lean over to get a glimpse and find the wound still open and raw, as if freshly cut, like the flesh of the rabbit in the snare.

Solena glances at the maids. "Hot water, towels, bandages, and brew some limmeth tea." They set to their tasks in an instant. "Fae brides heal almost immediately after the cutting," she says to me, her tone dripping with disappointment, as if this is my fault.

I arch an eyebrow. "How fortunate for them. Sadly, marriage alone does not make me immortal."

"Fae are not immortal. We die quite well," Solena retorts. "We just age slower and heal faster than humans do."

"I suppose that makes you superior to us?"

Solena considers me, her face thoughtful, not giving an inch. "It is one reason. Yes."

I nod my head towards the pungent concoction being brewed nearby. "Because of that dirty water?"

Her eyebrows knit together. "Limmeth is not dirty water. The first Fae brought the recipe from the old world. Ancient herbs grown in ancient soil. But Baev'kalath has no fertile land, so we have adapted a plant that grows in the mud on the shoreline."

I cringe. "Delicious."

She leans close, and my body stiffens. "But you have your own remedies, don't you? Word has spread like wildfire of how you healed Arax. So why not heal yourself the same way?"

My skin prickles. Being human was enough reason for the Fae to whisper about me with disdain. My ability to heal will drive them into a frenzy.

She wields the powers of the Maledannan.

Those words spoken by the Blades aboard the ship were nothing I have not heard before. The Maledannan might have been our teachers once, but the Tenders surpassed their knowledge. After the war, Fae considered any use of magic by humans to be theft, especially by those who did not fight on their side. Just another excuse for them to despise us.

I shake my head in reply to her question. "I cannot use the gift for myself. For it to work, I must absorb a beings' suffering. But if I am the one suffering, there is nowhere to channel that pain."

A maid hands Solena a silver cup sloshing with the murky gray brew and she holds it out to me. "Dirty water it is, then."

I gingerly take the cup, and I smell it long before it gets close to my mouth. She glares, her hard stare pressuring me to drink, and I change my mind several times before finally throwing it back in one gulp. It tastes as horrible as I imagined, bitter then gritty as it goes down the throat. I screw up my face and hand her the cup, which she sets down on the table as the other maids bring the hot water, towels and bandages.

"I'm going to dress your wound now," she says before setting straight to work.

With all the delicateness of a wild boar, she unwraps the black cloth. Her eyes linger on the fabric and I wonder if it was her bed Daed visited last night. Perhaps that is why I feel the contempt in her eyes. She wishes to be a princess instead. *Well, she is welcome to it.*

Solena may not be gentle, but she is thorough and quick. She cleans the wound, then takes the bandage and wraps my palm three times over before tossing back my hand with a weary groan.

I furrow my brow, feeling a little worse than when she started as the bitterness lingers at the back of my throat. I swing my legs over the bed and sit upright before the world tilts violently, my vision blurring as the room spins around me.

"Do you still feel unwell?" Solena asks with mild concern.

"I'm just tired," is my response as I pinch the bridge of my nose. I don't believe that's all it is.

There's a weakness crawling through my veins. I feel it taking over, so slowly you might mistake it for an awful night's sleep. But I am in touch with my body enough to know when something is wrong. Perhaps it is just the cut in my palm. Maybe I will feel better in a day or two. I can think of only one way to be sure.

"I want some time alone," I state. "Can you leave me?"

"Do you want us to dress you?" Solena asks, gesturing to the gown I'm still wearing.

"I don't need you to dress me every morning. I've got this far in life confidently dressing and undressing myself."

"Clearly not," Solena quips. "You are still in your dress from last night."

"I command you to leave," I grunt with exasperation. "Is that something I can do?"

"You are the princess now. You can do as you please," Solena says, but even that feels like an insult from her lips. She bows nonetheless and the other maids follow. "If you need anything, ring for us."

The maids file out of the room one by one and as soon as the doors close behind them, I climb to my feet. It takes a moment to get my balance, then I take a deep breath and reach behind my back, yanking at the hooks that keep me bound in this dress. I grit my teeth as I wrestle with the last button, and finally the mass of silk and lace falls in a pile at my feet.

The sleeveless tunic underneath leaves little to the imagination, so sheer that I can make out every curve and intimate detail of my body, but this cinched waist does not belong to me. The hooks of the dress had already pushed me to exhaustion, but I muster a burst of will strong enough to loosen the strings of the corset and rip it from my body with such exuberance that I throw it straight through the arches and over the balcony.

A snort of laughter slips past my hand before I can stop it, the relief bubbling up uncontrollably.

Good riddance.

Finally free, I stride over to the table where my serpentine vine rests, its pale green tendrils twisting in quiet repose. With a soft smile, I gently pour water from the pitcher, watching it soak into the soil.

"Good morning, friend," I exhale, running my thumb gently along her stem. "How was your first night?"

When she remains silent, concern knits my brow, and as I lean in, I spot one of her newly grown leaves lying beside the bowl. I pinch the fallen leaf between my fingers and bring it closer, squinting to focus. Its edges have curled, the tip already turning brown. How could it have withered so fast? It had only just unfurled. I glance through the arch and to the sky, the densely packed storm clouds not allowing even a glimpse of sunlight, but there is no point in finding her a better position. Not a single spot in Baev'kalath is any better.

I return the leaf to where it fell and offer a weary smile. "You don't like it here either," I whisper. "But we must be strong for each other." A soft creaking noise emanates from the bowl and the earth at the base of the vine shifts ever so slightly. The vine grows less than an inch, so little that no one else would notice. But I do. "There you go."

I step away from the vine, finding an empty space in the center of the room. Slowly, I lower myself to my knees, fists clenched and resting on my thighs. My eyes fall shut as I surrender to the silence around me.

When the first Fae arrived in the Sundered Kingdoms, they brought creatures of magic with them. Some were vicious monsters like the Stormwyrm, while others were peaceful explorers like the Elementals.

Legend says that several of these Elementals discovered The Grove, and finding it so beautiful, they stopped to rest and fell asleep. When they awoke, they found themselves changed, their legs transforming into thick roots that held them to the ground, and their arms into twisted branches that stretched to the heavens. Their bodies turned to wood, their mouths sealed shut, but their voices lingered, heard only by those they deemed worthy of their secrets. They became the Souls of the Forest.

When I was six years old, I heard their whispers and followed them to a clearing in the deepest part of The Grove. They told stories while cradling me in their roots, of the first dawn and the long dark, and gods above and below. They whispered I would be the next Jewel of the Tenders, and my lessons with the Sisters of the Vine started straight away. But what my sisters—what no one ever knew—was that I did not just visit with the Souls to learn. I visited them for comfort and friendship and the warmth of the home I lost.

The Souls are not just ancient Elementals. They are my family, and I need them now.

I reach out to them in my mind, my thoughts a desperate plea for answers, for comfort against the weakness that grips me. I beg for some sign that I'll survive this, that I am still tethered to them. But the silence stretches on. Nothing stirs. No voices, no presence, no whisper of reassurance. My eyes snap open, and I swallow hard, pushing back the tears threatening to spill. They are gone. All my life, I had my village, my sisters, the Souls of the Forest. But now, for the first time, I am truly alone.

The realization fills me with panic. I stumble to my feet, an anxious fear clawing at my throat. My mind goes blank, but suddenly, all I hear is that impossible voice that came from the shadows.

"Run!"

My body takes over while my mind struggles to keep pace. I run to the doors, grasp the handles, and throw them open. But rather than finding the freedom I seek, I am face to face with Arax. He stands stoically outside and holds out a stiff arm to stop me in my tracks.

"Princess Amara. You are not dressed." He glances at my sheer undergarments and looks away immediately, then sweeps his gray cloak off his back and drapes it over me. "Where are you going?"

"I..." I calm myself, focusing on slowing my thundering heart beat and soothing the dread churning in the pit of my stomach. "I don't know." I exhale, then look at him with questioning eyes. "What are you doing here?"

Arax rolls his shoulders and I notice his armor is different. It is the simpler garb of the Blades, not the more refined and imposing scaled plates and shrouded helm I remember when first seeing him aboard the ship.

"The king and queen have named me your personal guard," he replies monotone. "I am stationed at your door night and day."

I sigh. "If I do not need maids, I certainly do not need a personal guard. What are you to protect me from in the middle of nowhere?"

Arax does not reply, but I spy a quiver in his throat.

I tap my foot on the ground and gingerly ask my next question. "Where is the prince this morning?"

This time, Arax answers. "The prince's nights are long and strenuous. He spends most of his daylight hours in his chambers recovering."

Recovering? From what? I dread to think.

"Alone?" I ask, not sure if I want to know the answer.

Arax raises an eyebrow. "Would you like me to check?"

I clench my jaw and slam my eyes shut. "No. No, of course not." I take a strained breath, then look at him. "I do not want to stay in this room all day. Can I take a walk?"

"Yes, Princess Amara. As you told me on the ship, you are not a prisoner here."

"I'm beginning to think that is not entirely true."

Arax glances at my attire. "Perhaps you should change first?"

I roll my eyes. "Yes, thank you, Arax...obviously I was..." I continue to mutter under my breath as I shut the door firmly.

He reminds me of Keeper Tovar. Guardian of The Grove, and the closest thing to a father I have. But even the Keeper, in his great wisdom, can grate on my nerves from time to time. So many tasks, so many duties. The expectation that I act mature and poised at all times, when I am barely a grown woman. And the way they spout suggestions.

Perhaps you should change first?

As if that was not something I already knew. If I had secretly desired a break from Keeper Tovar's overbearing guidance, it would have greatly disappointed me to arrive in Baev'kalath and suffer instead at the hands of his twin, Arax.

I march towards a giant, intricately carved wardrobe that takes up the back wall with Arax's cloak still around my shoulders. When I open the doors, my jaw drops as my eyes settle on rows and rows of velvet, silk and lace gowns, all splendidly detailed and finely sewn. There are more dresses and shoes here than I could wear in a lifetime, and it is clear there are only three colors permitted in Baev'kalath.

Blackest black, crimson red and emerald green.

One of the green dresses toward the back catches my eye. Green at least reminds me of The Grove, and with a simple square neck and no train or puffy sleeves, it is the closest I will get to something modest in this wardrobe. I tug the dress from its hanger, pointedly bypassing the row of corsets.

Slipping it on, I'm relieved to find it fits well enough, and when I catch my reflection in the mirror, I don't look entirely ridiculous. With a sharp breath, I pull the combs from my hair, releasing the tension that's been clawing at my scalp since last night. My brown waves tumble free, cascading over my shoulders and down my back, easing the tightness from my brow as they fall.

Yes. That will do.

I throw open the doors and find Arax still there, as he said he would be.

"I'm ready," I announce, tossing his balled up cloak at him.

Arax catches it with one hand, and while he attaches it to his pauldrons, he looks me over again, likely checking that I am not half naked. His eyes linger on my toes, peeking out from beneath the gown.

"You're not wearing any shoes," he remarks, always with something to say.

"Well spotted, Arax—and I am grateful for it," I reply. "Now let us walk."

When I step into the hall, I look down both long passages. I remember the left leads to the throne room, and I have no desire to go anywhere near there. So I step right and begin my march while Arax follows close behind. We pass servants along the way who bow and avoid meeting my eyes and patrols of Blades who move aside for us before glaring at me bitterly. The stone walls are dreary and bare, and the balconies might be stunning if they did not overlook a tempestuous, endless sea below a sky of foreboding gray clouds.

In The Grove, there is always something interesting. A plant, or an insect; perhaps a bird I've never seen. But here it is only long halls of stone that lead to nowhere and seem to go on forever. Then we pass an open doorway and a burst of color catches the corner of my eye. I come to a sharp stop and Arax grumbles when he almost crashes into the back of me.

"What's in there?"

"That is the royal portrait gallery," he answers.

I do not hesitate entering. Inside the room, enormous paintings line the walls, illuminated by an open fire burning in the gallery's center, with the flickering light of the orange flames dancing over the portraits. There are singular portraits of King Kaelus, Queen Lanneth, and Prince Daedalus. Then some of just the king and queen regal at their thrones or arm in arm on a balcony with the Untold Sea at their backs. One portrait shows the king and his son in full battle armor with such ferocity in their eyes I'm surprised the artist did not flee in fear. But the largest of all and positioned at the center is the portrait of all three royals of House Mordorin.

The king and queen stand behind Daed, each with a hand on his shoulder. Daed sits in a stone throne at the forefront, his dark hair slicked back, the sides shaven short against his scalp. His face is hard and pensive, with lines and angles chiseled from rock and polished smooth with those slate-gray eyes of the storm staring straight through me. His hands grasp the ornate, jeweled hilt of a magnificent sword, its silver blade plunging down so its dangerous point meets the floor. But the weapon is not nearly as lethal as his captivating mouth.

I recall how the Archdruid referred to him last night.

The favored son.

This portrait is the embodiment of that title. Here he sits, ruling over all beneath him, his parents presenting him as their champion. As their future. No wonder his ego is so disgustingly large. People shower him with more praise and worship than all the old gods combined.

When I drag my eyes away from his face, I notice that every portrait of the prince shows him as an adult. You would think in a royal portrait gallery, there would be at least one painting to celebrate the birth of the heir to a great Fae house, or even as a child, growing into he who would rule. But there are none. It is strange, but I do not think on it too long.

Who knows why the Fae do as they do?

When I've seen enough, I wander from the room and continue down the hall, with Arax still close behind. Eventually, we arrive at another divergence. Two more long, boring stone halls that stretch further than my eyes can follow.

"What's down there?" I ask, gesturing to both options.

"Nothing of importance," Arax replies. "Would you like to continue walking?"

The four walls of my room were more interesting than this excursion, and I can not even use the need of sunshine and fresh air as an excuse, as there is not a drop of either. I frown. Stranded on a remote island in a dreary fortress full of nothing. I notice Arax looks as bored as I do, but I would much rather be miserable in my own company.

"You do not have to stay, you know? I'm fine by myself."

"No," he replies. "I can not leave your side."

I'm about to roll my eyes at him and his fussing when a Blade patrol approaches. The two towering warriors do not address me straight away, instead I see their mouths twisted as if something sour sits on their tongues. Then Arax glares and demands, "bow now before your princess."

They move slowly as if their limbs are rusted, but eventually I receive the bow that I couldn't care less about.

"Be swifter about it next time," Arax growls. "Now. What do you want?"

I do not hear much of the hushed conversation, but whatever they say is enough to earn a surly grumble from Arax.

"Do not move from here," he says sternly. "I will not be gone long."

Arax flips his cloak over his shoulder, turning in the other direction with the two Blades flanking his sides.

Do not move.

An easy instruction to follow when you are in the middle of nowhere. But when I turn towards the halls, I notice a third option that I swear was not there a second ago. A set of steps leading straight up, right in front of me, veiled by the same translucent shimmer as the queen and Archdruid.

I raise my brow and narrow my eyes suspiciously. I may hear voices and see smoky apparitions, but have I truly gone completely mad? A soft humming reaches my ears, drifting from the top of the stairs. It is the kindest sound I have heard since I arrived. I place my bare foot on the first step, my toes twitching against the cold stone. Leaning forward, I peer up, hopeful to see what is up there without having to get any closer. But all I see are more steps.

I glance over my shoulder in search of Arax, but he has vanished without a trace. My head slowly turns back to make sense of the stairs one last time, but I already decided what I was going to do the moment I set eyes on them.

I begin to climb. Cautiously at first, but when I see no end in sight, my impatience stirs and my pace quickens. Soon I'm jumping two steps at a time, my mysterious fatigue overpowered by my rampant curiosity.

The hum carries on the air, but no matter how many stairs I climb, I am no closer to its source. My legs burn, and the weight of my dress pulls down my shoulders until each extra step becomes a horrible chore. What a fool I was to think this was a good idea. I drop my chin, ready to call this a waste of time, and descend before Arax returns. But abruptly, the humming stops. I look up, only to find myself face to face with a door that was not there before, so close that my nose brushes against the wood.

A hard lump lodges in my throat and my chest fills with a shuddering breath as I reach for the handle. It turns with a click, and the door groans open. The room is starkly empty, without a single piece of furniture and only a blanket of dust across the bare floor. My shoulders slump and I swallow the lump in my throat.

All that climbing for nothing.

But as I turn to leave, I glimpse something in the corner of my eye. I turn, but even with the clarity of both my eyes, it is still just a shadow, a glimmer, a ripple in the emptiness.

My curiosity pulls me forward, but when I place a single foot on the threshold, I am tossed backwards, my back colliding with the wall before I slump with a thud on the steps.

"You shouldn't be here!" the voice cries. *"Why did you come here? Why!"*

I squint up, my eyes half-shut, one hand cradling my lower back as a dull ache pulses through me. The room is still empty. Just me, staring at nothing. Then, out of nowhere, a hand and only a hand, emerges from the nothingness—gnarled fingers stretching toward me in midair. My breath catches in my throat, and I bite back a scream, scrambling up the wall until I'm standing, heart pounding in my chest.

"Run!" the voice wails. *"Run!"*

I linger long enough to note the band of tattoos around its wrist; circles and half circles and crescents in a sequence before I grit my teeth and brace myself for the long descent. But when I turn, I am already at the bottom of the stairs without taking a single step. My heart comes to a hard stop in my chest as I swing around towards the door and the wailing voice that seeps into my skin, but there is no door. There are no stairs. Only the two long, boring halls where Arax had told me to stay put.

My head wavers in disbelief. Impossible. I saw it. I felt the steps beneath my feet.

"Princess," Arax says.

I swing around, my breaths sharp in my chest as I struggle to find reason in what just happened.

"The stairs," I mutter, chewing on my lip. "The voice."

Arax squints at me curiously. "I do not understand."

He is not alone. None of this makes sense. It's this place. This dreadful place is toying with me.

Arax's voice drops low and soft. "Come, Princess Amara. Let me return you to your chambers."

For a moment, I hear Keeper Tovar's concern in his tone, and it is the safest I have felt in a while. I do not argue with him, and rather than have him walk behind me, I stay at his side. I feel safer there.

CHAPTER 7

A rax returns me to my chambers, and there is some reassurance, knowing he is right outside. Whether I imagined it or not, whatever that thing is in that empty room, I am relieved to know it will meet Arax and his sword before it reaches me.

I spend the rest of the day behind the closed doors, having suddenly lost interest in exploring Baev'kalath. But alone with my thoughts provides no solace. I cannot speak with the Souls and this forsaken weakness is spreading. It's making me tired and irritable if I wasn't already. A rumble in my stomach reminds me I haven't eaten all day. It seems like a simple enough thing to remedy.

I roll off the bed, leaving an imprint of myself in the mattress, but I barely take two steps before the doors open and Solena and the maids enter.

"A bath, Princess," she says. "Then we can dress you for dinner."

I groan my disdain. "I told you. I do not need help to dress, and certainly not to bathe."

"And I will tell you the same thing I did last night, Princess. It is us or the Blades. Your choice."

I frown. "What is the occasion? Not another wedding, I hope?"

"Baev'kalath thrives at night and Queen Lanneth holds formal dinners every evening, whether it's four people or four hundred and she cannot stand anything that is..."

"Soiled," I finish. "Yes. I've learned that," I say with surrender, pointing a stern finger at her. "But only I touch the sponge."

The maids giggle into their hands and Solena nods. "As you wish. We will fill the tub."

I sit on the edge of the bed, but I'm not waiting long before Solena signals to me from the adjoining room that my bath is ready. I can smell the same sweet herbs and flower petals that float atop the water, and after the day I've had, they put me at ease almost immediately. The maids remove my green dress and their jaws agape when they discover I am not wearing a corset. You'd think I had another head growing out of my back.

Solena holds up a towel when I climb into the tub, which is more courtesy than Queen Lanneth gave me, and as soon as the water hits my skin, I breathe out a long, blissful moan and sink myself to the bottom. I stay in the tub as long as I can until my fingers crinkle and the water turns tepid. When I climb out, I'm handed my black robe, and the maids follow me to my bedchamber. They present the new dress they have chosen and I hate to admit that I am already adjusting to this routine. Guards and maids. Baths and glittering gowns for midnight dinners. This dress is not as horrific as my wedding gown, but it has a plunging neckline that makes me blush even before I've put it on.

"You will look stunning, Princess," Solena assures me.

The maids descend upon me, tugging the dress over my head and adjusting it meticulously until it clings perfectly to my hips. I catch the word "corset" muttered more than once, and I don't hesitate to cut them off, announcing that it's been tossed out the window, never to be seen again. They dust my face with pale powder, then circle my eyes with a shimmering black paint.

When I glance in the mirror, the plunging neckline of the dress highlights the delicate curve of my collarbone while revealing a generous swath of skin down to the soft swell of my cleavage. The way the fabric clings to my figure draws attention to the contours of my body. I barely recognize the woman staring back at me, draped in these extravagant clothes. What would my sisters think if they saw me like this? My eyes settle on the intricate braid the maids have twisted my hair into, and their whispered words return to me. *The prince favors a braid.*

Solena opens the doors as I stand from the dressing table. I turn and find Arax standing tall and stalwart, his eyes staring blankly ahead.

"Are you ready, Your Highness?"

I wriggle my toes uncomfortably and screw up my face at him. "They're making me wear shoes."

"That is unfortunate, Your Highness," he replies. He bows his head. "Follow me."

I leave my chambers and turn right as Arax leads the way. Through the arches I observe the crescent moon high in the pitch black sky, its sliver of light almost too bright to look at. The rain falls steadily and the ocean crashes fiercely against the rocks that surround the black fortress. I close my eyes for a moment, to recall the birds whistling amidst the rustling leaves, the wind whispering soft secrets in my ear, the sound of sunlight dappling upon my skin. A warmth takes hold of me, like the embrace of an old friend.

"We are here, Princess," Arax states.

When I open my eyes, I pray the sounds linger, that the warmth does not leave me. But as I stare at the giant wooden doors of the dining room, I realize that my dreams and wishes come to nothing here. My throat tightens and I stumble forward, but Arax is quick to take me by the elbow and steady me.

"Princess. Are you alright?"

I nod as I try to settle the rhythm of my heartbeat. "Fine. I'm fine."

He releases me, and I draw back my shoulders to strand straight. It is as if being the prince's wife is not enough for Baev'kalath. It wants to drain the life from me as well.

Arax pushes the doors open, revealing a grand, elongated hall. Stone walls draped in tapestries line the space, while high above, arched wooden beams stretch across the ceiling, curving like the ribs of some great beast.

At the hall's center stands a long, sturdy oak table, its polished surface gleaming darkly in the dim light. High-backed chairs with deep crimson velvet cushions surround it, their presence commanding yet inviting. Silver goblets, brimming with dark red wine, catch the flicker of candlelight from candelabras scattered along the table, their glow casting restless shadows on the walls. Overhead, a grand chandelier hangs, its twisted metal framework adorned with melting candles, wax dripping in frozen trails of light.

Silken black drapes billow in the howling wind that pours over the balcony, allowing the moonlight to bathe the room in an unsettling glow that makes my hosts appear as ghosts at the opposite end of the table. The king sits at the head, his narrow face and hooded eyes turned towards the queen at his side, whose deathly pale skin is almost translucent. She brushes her hand against his cheek and speaks to him, his gaze consumed with every subtle movement of her lips. The exchange is so intimate that I feel I should look away, but I can not.

"Grotesque. Isn't it?" Daedalus whispers to my ear, and every muscle in my body tightens. He presses against my back. "Be grateful you have not had to witness them entangled beneath the Lover's Eye, wearing nothing but moonlight."

"What?" I gasp as his lip brushes my earlobe.

"The moon goes through different phases, and each one holds special significance for us. When it reaches its fullest, we call it the Lover's Eye. During this time, we Mordorin celebrate with feasts, wine, and offerings of flesh. Only the king and queen are expected to take the lead in the ceremonies, but when the air is thick with the scent of carnal pleasure, it's hard not to get swept up in the festivities."

"What are you talking about?" I snap, jerking my ear away from his mouth.

Suddenly, I feel his hand cup the back of my neck. "Are you that innocent wife?" I can hear the smirk on his lips. "They make love before the entire court, beneath the Pale Eye. We watch for a time, but it is not long before all bodies intertwine." He exhales, and my skin prickles under his breath. "I wonder what your body would look like dressed in nothing but moonlight."

"Son. Daughter." Lanneth rises from her seat and beckons to us.

Daedalus steps out from behind me, and I fall under his towering shadow. He wears a black suit cut close against his toned physique, and when he adjusts the cuffs on his sleeves, I notice the silver rings on his fingers and rune tattoos on his hands.

"Come, wife," Daedalus coughs, clearing his throat. "We must not keep the king and queen waiting."

He reaches out and curls his hand around mine. Before I can stop myself, I glimpse up to find him looking down at me, his dark waves of hair curtaining his eyes. Even though I've loathed him since before I set eyes on him. Even though his kind are cruel tyrants obsessed with power. Even though I hate the way I feel when he touches me. Prince Daedalus has a beauty that I will never see rivaled by another. Even if I live a thousand years.

With my hand in his, he guides me to where the king and queen wait for us. He pulls out a chair and I sit down nervously as he takes the seat beside me, and still I can feel the warmth of his skin.

"How was your day, Amara?" King Kaelus asks, gripping the arms of his chair. I notice the soft curls in his dark hair, the same as Daedalus, and the pointed tips of their ears seem to peek through in the same part.

"I took a tour of the castle," I reply.

"Did you?" Kaelus asks. He glances at Arax by the door, who bows his head. "Baev'kalath is old and treacherous, even to those who have lived within its walls for centuries. You should be careful where you venture."

I'm beginning to think their warnings aren't just empty threats meant to frighten me. I've witnessed and heard things within these walls that would drive many to leap screaming from the balcony and plunge into the wild ocean below. Yet, none of it can be real. *Can it?*

I dare not share any of these details with them. I can't let them believe I've lost my sanity or my strength. I refuse to give them the power to control me, or worse, have them cancel our bargain because I am broken.

"I was well looked after," I say, the strain on my face easing when I glimpse Arax.

Daedalus notices the exchange. His mouth sets into a scowl as he snatches a goblet from the table, swirling the wine within. "After what my Blades say you did on the ship, perhaps you should be Arax's bodyguard instead of the other way around."

The king and queen chuckle, but I find nothing amusing.

"You may go, Arax," Daedalus says flippantly.

Arax bows and takes his leave, but I see how his face hardens and his jaw clenches as he closes the doors behind him.

"Speaking of the ship," Lanneth starts, steepling her hands. "I did not know you possessed so much of *our* magic." Her pearlescent eyes are unnerving, but not in the same way the prince's eyes are. I study the sharp angles of her face, the points of her ears, her long slender throat, but nothing sparks of Daedalus in her features. "Who taught you?"

"The Souls of the Forest chose me when I was a child," I reply calmly, meeting her daunting gaze. "And the Sisters of the Vine began schooling me on runes and channeling soon after."

Queen Lanneth tips her chin towards my rune necklace. "And that is your conduit?"

I glance down. "Yes. I need it to channel."

She gives a tight-lipped smile. "How quaint. And what do your parents think of this vocation?"

Quaint? I reply curtly. "They are dead, so do not think much at all."

My candor takes them aback.

The king pinches his squared chin between his fingers. "I assumed Keeper Tovar was your father. He called you his Jewel."

"Keeper Tovar is the lord and protector of The Grove and he guides the Tender Council, but no, he is not my father. He calls me Jewel because that is what the people call me. Jewel of the Tenders," I correct.

Daedalus looks at me over the rim of his goblet. "And why are you so special that you deserve such a title, Jewel?"

My face hardens, and I stare my husband down. "I have never claimed to be more than I am, and even if I was, no one should be raised above others. There is no *worth* in a title unless there is *worth* in the wearer... *Prince* Daedalus."

His eyes flicker with as much ire as intrigue. "You really are a cunning little thing, aren't you?"

"Already bickering," Lanneth sighs, wrapping her bony fingers around her goblet. "You know, passion is the ember that keeps the fire of marriage burning when everything else turns to ash."

"I was always told trust is the strongest foundation of a marriage," I blurt blankly, recalling what the crone sisters would tell the maidens after a match was made.

A deathly silence suffocates the room and the Mordorin royals narrow their eyes on me. Since everyone else is partaking of the wine, I reach for my cup, and that's when I notice my fingers are trembling.

"How... sweet," Queen Lanneth says with a curled lip.

King Kaelus nods with disinterest, his tongue rolling in his cheek, while Daedalus remains silent, staring into the bottom of his cup.

A flurry of activity cuts through the awkward silence when the doors fly open and a line of servants carrying silver trays enter single file. One by one they place their offerings on the long table, and when they lift the domed lids, the air floods with the aroma of roasted meats, succulent fruits and vegetables, and hearty loaves of bread.

Without saying a word, the servants stab and scoop at the morsels, piling our silver plates high with a feast fit for a small village. They leave as swiftly as they arrived, but one servant remains holding a giant jug of wine with both hands, ready to replenish our cups on command.

I study this servant curiously. Like Solena, what makes these Fae serve while others rule? Were all Fae not magical, ethereal creatures? You would think I would strive to keep my mouth shut after the trust comment, but I speak out regardless.

"What is the hierarchy of House Mordorin?"

Daedalus' eyebrows knit together, but his gaze stays fixed to the bottom of his cup. "Why would you ask such a thing?"

"I am a Princess of the Sundered Kingdoms now, aren't I? Shouldn't I know these things?" I reply bluntly.

At last, his eyes lift to look upon me, and a warm shiver radiates down my spine. His lips part to speak, but before he can utter a word, Queen Lanneth loudly skewers a slice of rare beef with her fork.

"The only thing you need to concern yourself with is filling that womb with an heir as quickly as possible." She nods towards my belly, then lifts the beef to her mouth and bites down hard, the bloody juices of the meat smearing across her lips.

My cheeks flush red, and I turn my head to look at anything but her.

She chews her food tightly, then swallows. "Especially if the rumors are true. That the newly wedded couple spent their first night as man and wife at separate ends of the castle?"

Now is the time I choose not to speak. Although I was grateful for it, it was not my decision to sleep separately. It should be Daedalus who responds to his mother.

Daedalus sprawls across his chair, a picture of nonchalance as he rolls his eyes with exaggerated impatience, making it clear that this conversation is a tedious chore for him. He leans back, arms crossed behind his head. "She was a sweaty, sickly mess. She could barely stand. She vomited all over me."

I cringe and my shoulders shrink. *Souls, I did do that, didn't I?*

Lanneth chews her food, unperturbed. "And all these things prevented the consummation of a marriage the king and I bargained at great cost?"

Daedalus looks to his father, but the king offers little support, seemingly more interested in a slice of bright yellow squash on his plate. His upper lip twitches as he snarls at his parents, then he quickly snatches my bandaged hand and holds it out on display.

"We forget that frail human bodies do not heal as ours do. Look..." He shakes my hand at the king and queen as if to prove his point, but we both spy the blood seeping through the white bandage at the same time.

I wince at the sharp pain when he closes his hand around mine and hides it under the table just as Kaelus and Lanneth lift their eyes from their meals.

"Look at what?" the queen asks.

"Nothing," he says through a long breath. "Only that the princess failed to arouse me last night."

He did not just say that.

My jaw clenches and a bitter rage claws at my neck. He hurls insults at me while still clutching my hand under the table, and after whispering in my ear of bodies tangled passionately in the moonlight. A sharp retort sits on the tip of my tongue, but the tense narrowing of his eyes—so at odds with the relaxed sprawl of his body in that chair—quells me into silence.

"You appear paler than when you first arrived," Queen Lanneth remarks.

My anger lulls when I'm reminded of the queen's intimate knowledge of my body.

"You must eat more meat," she states.

"I do not eat meat," I snap through grit teeth as I try to wrestle my hand from the prince's grip, but he does not release.

"Ridiculous," Lanneth sighs. "Fine, eat something else then."

I yank my hand, but still Daedalus does not let go.

"I'm not hungry."

Lanneth leans her bony elbows on the table. "I did not ask if you were hungry. I *told* you to eat."

"I may be trapped in this horrible place, married to your awful cad of a son, but I and I alone will decide what goes in and out of my body!" I shoot Daedalus an ice-cold glare as I finally free myself from his grip. "In all aspects."

Lanneth leans back in her chair, her lips straight as a line. "Very well, then. If you do not eat with us, you do not eat at all." She nods her head at the servant, who puts down the wine jug and rounds the table to take my plate and carry it away.

"Is that really necessary, my love?" Kaelus sighs, leaning his forehead into his hand. "We cannot very well let our princess starve to death."

Lanneth stabs a cube of beef with her fork, holds it to her mouth and clenches her teeth around the meat. She chews so slowly I can hear every slosh as it moves around her cheeks, and does not look away from me until she is done.

"Hunger is cleansing. Hunger will remind our beloved princess that she is no longer frolicking in the forest. She is in Baev'kalath. She belongs to our prince, and that despite our kindness and generosity, we, Mordorin, are the nightmare behind the void. The horror that keeps humankind on their knees. It will serve her well to remember that."

"You do not give yourself enough credit," I hiss under my breath. "I have not forgotten. No human has forgotten. That is why we hate you so much."

"Brave words from someone whose home so desperately needs our protection," the king says sternly. "Retire now to your chambers, Princess Amara, before you say something you'll regret."

I've not even begun. I can feel the tirade building at the back of my throat, ready to be spat in the arrogant faces of these miserable Fae, but I am surprised when the prince speaks before I can.

"Come, wife," he commands.

Daedalus pushes against the table, his chair scraping the stone as he rises to his feet. He runs a hand through the hair hanging like a veil over his eyes, sweeping it back amongst the thick waves, then cocks his head to the side and looks down at me.

"You know how to make an impression, don't you?"

He offers his hand, but he is not giving me a choice. I keep my bandaged hand close to my side, assuming that Daedalus' efforts to keep it hidden mean he does not want the king and queen to see that it is not healing. I accept with my other hand, and he effortlessly lifts me to my feet. I meet his broad chest dressed in smooth, black silk, and I can't help but inhale his rich, musky scent.

He leads me away, his stride slow and cavalier, as if not a single weight rested on his wide shoulders. We reach the doors and Daedalus pushes them open, but before we leave, the king calls from his seat.

"And enough of this dallying. The dawn's first light will find you both in that bed. Do you understand me?"

I look at Daedalus' face for his reaction and it is as sullen as I expected.

"Of course, father. There is nowhere else I would rather be."

His words are so forced I can not imagine his parents believe him. I certainly do not. But I will take any excuse to leave that dining room. When the doors close behind us, Arax is there. He pounds his chain-mail glove against his armored chest and bows.

"My, Prince. Would you like me to escort the princess to her chambers?"

I assume the answer will be yes, but when I take a step away from him, Daed's grip around my hand tightens, and he pulls me back to his side.

"No. You are dismissed for the night," he replies frankly.

I imagine the bemused look on Arax's face mirrors my own.

"My, Prince?" he questions.

Daedalus looks down at me, storm clouds swirling in his eyes. "I am all the protection my wife needs tonight."

I pray he does not notice my throat quiver when I gulp.

"Very well, Your Highness," Arax replies.

He glances at me, as if to ask something, but stays silent before turning on his heels and vanishing down one of the darkened halls of the castle.

I glower. "Is this the part where you fly me up into the air and we vanish in a puff of smoke?"

"And have you shower Baev'kalath in the contents of your stomach once more? No. We will walk."

He lets go of my hand, instead looping my arm through his, as we walk side by side down the hall.

"And then what? You take me to my room, lock the door and fly out the arch?"

"And earn my father's wrath? Not likely. Besides, he will have eyes on the sky no doubt," Daedalus replies, looking straight ahead, the moonlight striking his face each time we pass an arch.

"Really?" I scoff. "What is the worst he could do to you?"

A single dry laugh escapes his throat. "How adorable. You mistake him for something other than a sadistic monster who has had centuries to perfect his tortures and torments." Daedalus turns his head to me. "Do not be fooled. There is a reason he rules the Sundered Kingdoms. Over all the other Fae houses. His is a legacy written in blood."

A chill sweeps over me, and I'm sure I'm shaking, but I will not allow Daedalus to frighten me. That is what he wants.

"So what is your plan, then?" I ask firmly. "How do you convince them you have spent the night with me? Your wife, who is neither *enticing* nor *arousing*?"

"I will convince them of nothing," Daedalus replies. "They will see it with their own eyes."

He comes to an abrupt stop and I realize we stand outside my chambers already. I'm shaking again, but this time I do not have the strength to hide it. Daedalus unhooks his arm from mine and throws open the doors before strutting inside, pulling his thick, muscled arms free of his form fitting coat and tossing it on the bed.

I stare agape. "What... what are you doing?"

"Taking my wife to bed," he replies, as if it was a completely normal thing to say. He stands at the end of the bed with a wide stance, a sly grin on his face as he pops open the buttons of his shirt. "So close the doors and come here."

I hesitate, spinning on my heels left and right, even considering running across the balcony and leaping over the edge. I don't acknowledge the fact I would smash into a hundred tiny, bloody pieces upon the rocks below. All I know is it would get me away from here. I realize although his rejection and repulsion of me summons a melancholy I do not understand, the thought of him actually wanting me, desiring me, touching me, is more frightening than anything else.

But Daedalus, my prince, my husband, grows impatient.

"Now, wife," he demands.

I step inside the room and when I turn my back on him to close the doors I feel splintered, as if I have left a part of myself outside in the cold, dark hall. The only part of me with the will to resist him.

CHAPTER 8

W hen the doors close, we are alone. The Mordorin prince and his human bride
with nothing standing between us but a giant bed dressed in scarlet covers.

I watch him through the black, gossamer bed curtain, his pacing like that of a caged
predator. Back and forth he stalks, his fingers grazing the buttons of his shirt, each one
popping open with excruciating slowness. The shimmering dark fabric slips free, revealing
the sculpted perfection beneath.

Moonlight filters through the scattered clouds and drifts through the archway, casting
a silvery glow over his chest. Each ridge and valley of his physique is sharply defined,
his smooth skin a flawless canvas for the intricate black runes etched across his neck
and collarbone. They twist downward, following the taut lines of his abdomen before
vanishing beneath the waistband of his belt.

Heat swells within me. He is beautiful to look upon. Unlike any man I have ever seen.
Because he is not a man.

I must remember this, no matter how my body betrays me in his presence. I am
bewitched—there can be no other explanation. When his blood mingled with mine, it
must have cast some dark Fae spell, forging a bond both forbidden and unrelenting. So I
ignore the yearning, focusing instead on the runes, forcing logic to take control before I
melt into a puddle on the floor.

"Your runes differ from ours," I say. "I noticed the ones on Arax's back as well."

Daedalus raises an eyebrow. "Runes. That is what you're thinking about right now?"
His hand slides to grip the back of his neck, and every muscled ridge of his body tightens.

I think about sitting with my sisters and weaving for hours until my fingers bleed. The
Tender Council, old hunched men with long wiry hair sprouting from their ears. The
taste of milk left out too long in the sun. Anything to distract me from Daedalus and my
uninvited need to reach out and touch him.

"What else would I be thinking about?" I ask with disinterest, and even I am impressed with how believable I sound.

His eyes drop, and his shoulders slump. If I didn't know better, I'd think he looked almost dejected.

"These are runes of the First Fae," he says.

"Is that what makes them special?"

"Yes, it does, along with the ink that is used."

"What is special about the ink?" I continue.

Daedalus furrows his brow. "Why do you ask so many questions?"

"It is in my nature. Always has been. Keeper Tovar says I have an inquisitive mind." I grasp the rune around my neck and return to the subject at hand. "We do not wear our runes on our skin."

"As you shouldn't," Daedalus says sharply. "Such a thing is heresy and would see a noose around your pretty neck."

I ignore his attempts at scaring me. "If I take off this necklace, my power to heal goes with it. Do you brand yourselves so you are powerful always?"

Daedalus smirks. He straightens and parts his open shirt to his hips. "These runes are for flight, for void walking, for regenerating, for beserking in battle. But none of them makes me powerful."

Suddenly he vanishes before my eyes in a burst of slithering smoke, then in an instant I hear the sharp boom that signifies he has appeared elsewhere, but before I can turn I feel his warmth against my back and my skin prickles.

"I am powerful on my own," he mutters in my ear. "In all manner of things."

I close my eyes as he lays his callused hands upon my shoulders, his fingers kneading at my flesh. His breath is hot as his lips brush against the curve of my neck.

"Why do you do this?" I utter breathlessly.

Daedalus freezes. "What do you mean?"

"Which Mordorin prince are you?" I gulp. "The one who takes pleasure in insulting and frightening me, or the one who whispers his needs and wants so softly in my ear?"

"Which do you prefer?" he asks, his nose against my nape.

It takes all the will I have to not surrender to him. To instead remember the reason I am here. Something far more important than whatever fleeting moment of empty desire he offers.

"I want the warrior who will protect my people from the Legion of Saints," I reply firmly.

His hands slip from my shoulders. I feel the intensity of his eyes as he circles me, but I cannot look at him. If I look at him, my resolve will crumble.

"Do you know when I first learned of the bargain?" Daedalus asks.

I am only brave enough to give him a fleeting glimpse and shake of my head.

"You were already on the ship to Baev'kalath when the king and queen informed me I was to be wed," he answers. His face hardens. "The deal you made is with them. *Not with me.*"

The ire snapping at my heels breaks the hold of his charms. "I do not care which of you fulfills the bargain. All I know is a price was paid."

Daedalus' throat quivers and smoke rolls within his eyes. "What could you possibly understand of prices to be paid? The Tenders of The Grove," he scoffs. "Holding hands and singing songs in the forest. Praying to beings you call gods who were no more than pets to the First Fae."

"Do not assume to know anything about me or what I have suffered," I hiss under my breath, my hands balling into fists at my side.

"Suffered?" The prince throws his head back and bellows an arrogant laugh that fuels my anger. "Because of humans like you, humans who refused to fight alongside us after centuries of peace..."

"We were your slaves!" I snap bitterly, not allowing him to think for a second we were anything else. "Toys to be played with and broken and disposed of whenever you pleased. All we wanted was to be left alone. For you to keep your war far from our forests."

Daedalus lowers his chin at me and glares. "Do you know how many Fae died? Some with souls so ancient they could still recall the faces of the First. Their lights extinguished, their bodies left butchered and bloody on the battlefield, crushed under the filthy boots of the Legion of Saints as they marched onward."

I grit my teeth and turn from him.

Is he expecting me to feel sorry for him?

But before I can widen the space between us, he snatches my wrist and yanks me back. I gasp, flinging my indignant gaze at him over my shoulder, only to find the smoke no longer contained in his eyes. It drifts and singes the air around him.

"House Velastral; burnt to the ground. House Caelithar; all dead." His bitter glower finds my necklace. "House Maledannan, guardians of nature and healing, wiped clean from his plane."

If he is trying to prise some sort of guilt response from me for the fate of these Fae houses, he is truly delusional. Instead, I go for the throat. Matching cruelty for cruelty.

"It is a shame only three of the six perished," I say coldly, my lips a tight, straight line.

He snarls at my audacity. "Driven from their lands, lands infused with the souls of the First, I do not expect House Taramethos and House Ithranor to last long wherever they are."

"We humans can only hope the same fate falls upon House Mordorin," I spit with venom.

Daedalus' broad hand closes around my wrist and he drags me closer to him, and even though I plant my feet, he shifts me with ease. I keep my head down, pressed against my chest, but he pinches my chin between his fingers and lifts it sharply to meet his stare.

"Why, in my domain where no one can help you, alone with me in this room, knowing that I could tear you to pieces with my bare hands, would you *dare* speak to your prince like that?"

I do not look away from him now. Instead, I meet his gaze eagerly, and I hope my eyes convey the oceans of hatred that storm within me.

"Because if you will not help my people as promised, then you are not what I believed you to be. Even though I doubt your honor, I have never doubted that you are a fearsome warrior, but if you will not protect The Grove, then all my family will die, and I have nothing left to live for." His grip loosens from my chin and I free my wrist from his grasp with a jerk. "So go ahead. Tell me nightmares. Tear me to pieces. I am not afraid of you. There are worse things than you in the Sundered Kingdoms."

Daedalus paces backwards away from me, but his eyes do not leave mine. "Really? Like what?" he scoffs.

"The Legion of Saints and the one who commands them," I mutter, inspecting the redness looped around my wrist. "He is the sole reason The Tenders agreed to this bargain."

I grimace and rub at my wrist, then realize Daedalus has fallen silent. I look up to see the fire in his eyes reduced to a smolder and his jaw clenched as he mulls over my words. Is he offended that he is not the only monster in the Sundered Kingdoms?

71

"The Golden Son," he says at last. "You saw him?"

I furrow my brow. "Yes. He stormed through the forest like it belonged to him, his men crushing the undergrowth and slaughtering rabbits and deer that had never been hunted."

"And you are sure it was him?" Daedalus persists.

I nod, as condescending as his tone. "Yes. I am sure. He said as much when he demanded we bend the knee and join his ranks." Then I pause and chew my bottom lip. "I suppose I did not see his face. He wore..."

"A golden mask," Daedalus sighs. "No one has ever seen his face. They say he is so horribly burnt he hides his hideousness behind the mask. But they also say he was killed in the Betrayers' Battle, so who knows if that really is him or if someone else has donned the mask?"

"All I know is whoever he was, he promised to burn The Grove and everyone who dwells within to ash if we did not swear an oath to the Legion. That is when Keeper Tovar sent his letter for aid to Baev'kalath."

"And the Golden Son did nothing to stop this?"

I tighten my fists enough that my nails prick my skin. "You like to tease that we Tenders are nothing but singing, dancing idiots, but we are not as helpless as you think. He did not have the full power of the Legion behind him, only a scouting party. We told him no and fought him back with everything we had and when the rain came and the soil turned to mud that swallowed them up to their knees, they retreated on the promise they would return."

"You told him no?" Daedalus asks with mocking disbelief.

Suddenly the raw ache around my wrist vanishes, the mysterious weakness that starves me for breath and strength disappears. All I am left with is the reminder of that day and an unyielding pain that will stay with me forever, like glass lodged so deep in my heart that it will never come free, but torture me with agony for as long as I live.

"Yes," I mutter, my words barely a whisper. "And forty-nine men, twenty-one women, and six children of The Grove died for our defiance. But even that is hundreds less than what we lost in *your* Betrayer's Battle. So ask me again, Prince Daedalus, if I understand what paying a price means."

He dips his chin, glowering from beneath his heavy brow as he stalks towards me. I refuse to believe the heat building inside me stems from anything but my anger and

72

loathing, but the feline way he moves and the slow, rhythmic thump of his boots as he crosses the floor has me hypnotized. As his open shirt sways around his strong, sculpted hips, suddenly I'm reminded of every perfect, hard ridge of his body and how breathtakingly beautiful he is.

An unsteady step backwards is my only defence, but I come to a halt when I feel the end of the bed press against my legs. Daedalus continues his approach with agonizing carnality until he towers over me, trapping me in his shadow.

I cannot move. I cannot scream. But I do not know if I want to.

His warm, rich scent sends my head spinning. Now I am sure this must be Fae magic. How else could a smell frenzy me the way his does?

His chest heaves before he releases a long, rumbling breath, and I notice the shimmers of color in the cracked moonstone around his neck. "Tell me, Princess Amara. Would you like to continue trading trauma tales, or should we do what we came here for?"

I grit my teeth and slowly shake my head in vehement defiance. "I came here for the protection of the Grove. If you cannot give what you promised, I have nothing to give to you."

He chuckles gruffly. "Oh, there will be no giving, my spirited wife. Only taking."

Every nerve of my body comes alive when he lightly presses his finger to my chest and traces the line of my sternum down the deep, plunging neckline of my dress.

I shudder. "Prince Daedalus…"

"I have told you once. Call me Daed. Don't make me tell you again."

When the neckline of the dress ends at my ribs, he grumbles his disappointment before sliding his hand across my stomach to grip my waist.

Through the thin fabric I feel his warmth, and when he curls his fingers to hold me tighter and his nails dig into my flesh, I imagine he could rip this dress right off my body if he wanted to. But I do not want him to. He is a liar and a murderer and if he will not fight for me—he is also a coward.

"Let me go. Please," I murmur, my eyes falling closed.

If I can not see him, I will not want him.

"So polite," he whispers, and I can hear the grin playing on his lips. "I like it when you say please. Say please again."

"Please," I say as his other hand glides along my shoulder before cupping the back of my neck.

His thumb traces the line of my jaw and sweeps across my trembling lips. "Please let you go, or please don't stop?"

His deep voice fills my head and I can't remember what I want any more. My eyes flicker open and when I meet his piercing gaze, I almost speak the words that my body is desperate for me to cry out. But something behind him catches my eye. Bright and vibrant and green, something so utterly unknown to Baev'kalath that it shines like a beacon in the darkness. My serpent vine on the table, and at that very moment, I watch helplessly as another of its new leaves falls.

Tears well behind my eyes, threatening to fall as achingly as the leaf, but I do not allow it. My anger returns to me, and I need it. It is all I have in this place. To remind me of what I am here for. What I will die for. The rage gives me the strength to look into his eyes and not falter beneath him.

"No," I say through grit teeth.

"No, what?" he asks, cupping the side of my face.

"No to you," I snap back, batting his hand away from my cheek. "No to this. No to any plans you or your strange, horrible family have for me and my body." I slip myself free of the grip he has on my waist and he scowls. "If you will not fight, then I will. I am Jewel of the Tenders, not a Mordorin broodmare."

Daed's tongue rolls in his cheek. "On that, we agree. A broodmare understands when to keep her mouth closed and her legs parted."

The back of my stiff hand flies at the side of his face, but Daed catches my arm before it can connect. The cuff of his sleeve slips down his forearm and I spy the tattoo around his wrist.

A band of circles and half circles and crescents.

Identical to the tattoo on hand that reached for me from nowhere, in the room that doesn't exist. The hand I am still trying to convince myself was a figment of my imagination.

Daed stares deeply into my eyes and the intense heat between us is thick enough to cut with a knife. He glances at my bandaged hand, blood seeping through the bandage.

"That should be healing, human or not. Why isn't it?"

I tug my arm from him, but he does not release. "I do not know."

"Do not let the queen see," he warns. "She will think you are..."

"Soiled? Impure? Weak? Why should I care what she thinks? She is nothing but scheming and vile, rivaled only by her son."

"Do you hate me, Amara?" he asks, his jaw clenched, his chest heaving with breath.

The words flow from my lips with ease. "Yes, Daed. I hate you."

A grin pulls at the corner of his mouth as he releases my arm and I watch the tattoo sink beneath his sleeve.

"Good. That makes this all so much easier."

He puts his hand behind his back and I feel like a fool to be so unprepared for the genuine possibility that tonight my Fae husband murders me in our bedchamber. But he does not draw a blade to slit my throat, instead he drops his head and dips forward, bowing before me, and when he straightens, I have no clue what will happen next.

"Sleep well, wife," he says calmly, and when he walks straight past me and his shoulders rise and fall, it's almost as if he's relieved.

Daed does not go to the door, or the balcony, but instead to the secret wall panel. He pushes against the wood in such a familiar way that this is clearly not his first time, and the hidden door falls open, revealing the darkened passage way within.

A half grin escapes my lips. "That was your plan all along, then? To make your parents believe we would spend the night together, but then slip out a secret door?"

"I didn't have a plan," he sighs over his shoulder. "You and I could be tangled in that bed right now, naked and slick with sweat, with your legs wrapped around me." A breath catches in my throat. "But I would rather spend the night somewhere else." He glances at me with a sideways look. "With someone else. Good night, Amara."

He steps into the passageway, the secret door sealing shut behind him. Instantly, the air turns colder, the rain's relentless rhythm drums louder, and the walls feel like they're closing in on me. I block out the noise and the worry, wandering to the wardrobe and shedding layers of velvet and lace that pool at my feet. As I slip on my nightgown, the sheer fabric glides over my skin, a fleeting echo of the twilight breeze in The Grove.

It would be easy in my sadness to let the dark creep in and allow myself to surrender. But for my people, I must endure. Endure this place. Endure the prince. Endure the weakness plaguing my body that shows no signs of stopping. I hold up my bandaged hand and spy drops of blood seeping through the binding. It's getting worse, I feel it. I glance back at my serpentine vine. Another day passes in Baev'kalath. Another leaf falls. She can not survive here. I can not survive here, and that is when I chide myself for being so stupid. This place. This horrid place is killing us. There is no sun. No soil. No hope.

My stomach growls as I'm harshly reminded of my hunger. It seems each day the Mordorin find new ways to torment me. But I will starve to death before eating the flesh of an animal. I pull back the heavy covers and crawl into bed, the mattress curling around me with a warmth and comfort that feels foreign in this place.

As I stare up at the intricately carved scene on the dark wood frame, I'm transported to a world of rolling ocean waves beneath a full moon and a sky brimming with stars. The full moon. The Lover's Eye. A shiver runs down my spine, and my stomach flutters with a mix of longing and dread. I wonder how many others have lain in this bed. Gazing up at the stars and moon and waves while the prince... I squeeze my eyes tight, erasing the idea from my mind.

No matter how hard he tries to draw me into his web, I refuse to succumb to the intoxicating darkness he wields. I've made it through another night, still a maiden. His repulsive advances are only another attempt to scare me. Not for a second do I truly believe that he wants me, not when he has his pick of beautiful Fae. Why instead would he desire a lowly human?

As for my fleeting attraction, he only needs to remain his insufferable, arrogant self, and keeping my walls intact should be effortless. At least, that's what I tell myself.

When my stomach growls again, I cradle my belly, trying in vain to soothe the ache. I'm tired of thinking about the Mordorin and weary of my hunger, so I force myself to push both aside and focus instead on the carved scene above me. I imagine the waves rolling gently, the rhythm syncing with the distant crash of the ocean outside. In my mind's eye, I picture a ship riding the swells, the steady rise and fall bringing a welcome sense of calm. But then, without warning, a monstrous creature erupts from the depths, coiling around the vessel and dragging it into the abyss, lost forever. I exhale a weary breath. It seems not even my own thoughts are safe from the torments of the Mordorin.

CHAPTER 9

Baev'kalath may be cold and unwelcoming, but this bed is anything but. The covers hold me in a snug embrace, and the warmth enveloping my skin is so comforting I never want to wake. I roll over, still wrapped in a blissful haze, only to realize my cheek isn't resting on the pillow, but against something firm.

My brow furrows, though my eyes remain closed, and I lazily reach out, my hand exploring the smooth lines beside me—the ridges of a toned abdomen, the hard plane of a chest, the sharp angle of a jaw. My eyes snap open, and there he is—Daed, watching me with a crooked grin tugging at his lips.

"Good morning, wife. Do you know how loudly your stomach is growling? Very unladylike."

I recoil slower than I would have liked. "What are you doing here?"

Daed tips his chin towards the balcony. "It's dawn. Your maids will arrive soon, and how will they believe we spent the night together if they do not find us in bed?"

I glance over my shoulder and although my body feels the dawn, I see the sky is dark and dreary as always. I turn back to Daed and narrow my eyes on him.

"You came through the secret door?"

He nods, stretching his arm and putting his hand behind his head on the pillow.

I glimpse his bare chest. "Why don't you have a shirt on?"

"I never sleep with a shirt on," he replies. "And being half naked is more convincing." He inspects my nightgown. "Maybe you should take your clothes off, too."

A breath hitches in my throat, but he does not remain straight faced for long, throwing back his head and laughing. I clutch the bed covers and pull them up to my neck.

"To make this truly believable, maybe I should look unsatisfied and disappointed?" I say.

My sharp words cut through Daed's laugh like a blade, and he falls silent, but before I can enjoy watching the color drain from his face, the doors fly open. Solena enters first, followed by the other maids, and when they raise their heads to greet me, I almost hear the collective thud of their jaws hitting the floor.

"Your Highnesses," Solena gasps, dropping her chin. "I am sorry to interrupt. I did not think..."

"Think what?" Daed snaps, bolting upright and narrowing his eyes on Solena. "That you would find a husband and wife in the same bed? We are fortunate your only duty is washing soiled sheets and emptying chamber pots, if that is the caliber of your thinking."

Solena shrinks, her chin tucking in tighter to her chest, and I can't help but stifle a grin. Daed throws away the bed covers and lunges to his feet, taking a long, black robe with silver embroidery from the end of the bed and swinging it around him, but not before I catch a glance of his muscular legs and sculpted hips. He strides towards the maids and lurches over them.

"Take good care of your princess," he instructs. "Be gentler with her than I was."

Daed exits the room with a smug swagger, but not before flicking his hand to release an arrow of smoke. The dark wisps coil on the bed beside me, swirling for a heartbeat before dissolving, leaving behind a silver tray piled high with shiny red apples. My eyes widen, and my stomach clenches in response, already imagining their sweet, crisp bite.

The moment the doors shut, a silence falls over the room. It's the first time I've seen the maids at a loss for words, unable even to exchange their usual whispers. Whether or not it's all a ruse, I decide to play along. If it spares me from their teasing and rude remarks, then it's a game worth playing.

I grab an apple from the tray, sinking my teeth into its crisp flesh with a satisfying crunch. Chewing, I glance at Solena and, with my mouth still full, say, "I'm ready for my bath."

She blinks away her thoughts, which I hope are unpleasant. "Yes, Your Highness. Right away."

The maids hurry to their tasks, drawing my bath and sprinkling herbs and flower petals over the water. They guide me, and I step in without hesitation, unashamed as I stand bare before them. Daed's reprimand has sparked a surge of confidence, one I'm eager to claim. I'm so satisfied with their discomfort, I push aside the creeping dizziness, the way my limbs feel weaker than the day before. Even as they lift me from the tub and seat me before the dressing table, I pretend not to notice the pallor of my skin, or how my hair and eyes have lost their usual luster since arriving in Baev'kalath.

They comb my hair, weaving it into a long braid that cascades down my back. As they layer face powder and rouge on my skin, I can't shake the feeling that they, too, are aware of my fading color. Next, they lead me to the wardrobe, and today, in a surprising turn of mood, I permit them to lace me into a corset, and I indulge in two more apples while they fuss with the strings. As they deliberate over which dress to choose, I take joy in solving their dilemma myself.

"Only green," I say firmly. "I will only wear green dresses from now on."

The maids nod, brushing past anything black or crimson until they pull out a stunning gown of emerald green. Its simplicity, free of lace and beading, feels just right for the day. As they slide it over me, I catch a glimpse of myself in the mirror and am taken aback by how comfortable this all begins to feel.

When their tasks are complete, Solena claps her hands to dismiss them, leaving her and I alone in the room, but for the first time the idea does not fill me with dread.

She gestures to the dressing table. "Would you mind sitting, Your Highness, so I can redress your wound?"

I catch a glimpse of my hand, momentarily distracted by a shimmer of happiness, only to realize the blood seeping through the bandage hasn't stopped. With a nod, I wander to the dressing table and take a seat. Solena fetches a bowl of warm water and fresh bandages, then pulls up a stool to sit beside me. As she unwinds the bandage, each layer brings a fresh wave of pain, and I wince. Solena notices, her gaze curious, but when the last layer falls away, I see her throat bob with a swallow of concern.

"What is it?" I ask, peering down at the wound myself.

The cut across my palm remains open, as raw and bloody as if it had just been inflicted.

Solena shakes her head in disbelief. "I don't understand. Even a human should heal faster than this." She rises. "I'll brew more limmeth tea."

I quickly shake my head, and she hesitates, slowly resuming her seat. "That didn't help the first time," I say, my voice firm. "I'd rather not have to swallow it again."

Solena says as she scrutinizes the wound. "What could cause this?"

I don't tell her that I think Baev'kalath is poisoning me. I can't let anyone know that this nightmare world, with its lack of sun and soil where nothing can thrive, is the reason I can't heal. I've always been one with life and the power of nature, and this place disrupts my very essence. If the Mordorin discover I am vulnerable, they'll see me as weak enough to control.

"I have no idea," I reply. "Please, dress the wound and you may go."

Solena studies me for a moment, and I can't shake the feeling that she sees right through me. But she says nothing, focusing instead on cleaning the deep cut, navigating the raw flesh and washing away the blood. Be it a little gentler than the first time. Once she binds it firmly, she tidies up and stands before me with her head bowed.

"Will that be all?" she asks.

"Yes. I will have no need for you until the evening."

Solena nods, then leaves the room in silence, and though I reveled in the maid's displeasure, the satisfying feeling is fleeting. I realize it will take me longer to be as comfortable being unkind as they are. I wander to my vine and it is a small blessing that no leaves have fallen today, though her coloring is just as somber as mine.

I trail a finger down her smooth skin. "Will you not speak to me, friend?"

She doesn't reply, and her silence sends a pang of ache through my chest. Though I've only been here a few days, the absence of the earth and the voices of the Souls makes me feel utterly isolated. Their whispers are usually a constant presence, a comforting hum in the back of my mind. My chest tightens. My spirit, my health, and now my connection to what I treasure the most.

Baev'kalath continues to take from me.

Now that I'm dressed, my stomach so overly full of apples that my corset presses uncomfortably against me, I find myself at a loss for how to spend the rest of the day. The thought of climbing imaginary stairs to rooms that don't exist and encountering floating hands again doesn't appeal to me. I'm still unsure if that was real or just another trick played by this meddling fortress. But if I linger here too long, will I invite the attention of the haunting apparition whose cryptic whispers seem laced with ill intent?

When there's a knock at the doors and Arax enters, I'm pleased for the distraction.

"Your Highness. The king and queen wish to inform you that after forgiving your behavior last night, you are now permitted to eat," he decrees.

My eyes subtly glance at the silver tray on the bed, but thankfully I have eaten the evidence.

"Will the king and queen be there?" I ask with a scowl.

Arax shakes his head. "The king and queen are late to rise. But food has been prepared for you in the dining hall."

The offer is suddenly enticing. This room and its four walls are suffocating, and if I do not have to endure the king and queen, I will gladly eat a second breakfast.

"Very well," I say, doing my best to focus through the sickness that clings to me like a heavy fog.

Arax bows before turning on his heels and guiding me through the hushed halls toward the dining room. As we pass by the tall arches, I catch a glimpse of the sky, perpetually gray, with sheets of rain cascading down, drumming against the fortress in a steady rhythm.

As I walk behind him, my gaze roams over Arax's armor—the sturdy pauldrons resting on his shoulders, the plated vambraces encasing his forearms, and the chain mail that shields his hands. His long, flowing cloak with silver runes etched along its edges is the same gray of the clouds that veil the sunlight. When he turns a corner and the wind catches the fabric, I catch a glimpse of the webbed harnesses across his back and the rune tattoos that mark where his wings would burst forth.

Again, I am reminded that this was not the armor he wore when I first met him.

"The Mordorin armor," I start, my thoughts finding a voice. "Are there different kinds?"

"Yes," he replies in a low grumble.

"What kind is yours?" I ask, even though his tone is not inviting of more questions.

"This is the armor of a Blade. Worn by the brothers and sisters of the Ebon Flight."

I tilt my head to the side. "Yes. I see. But it is not what you wore on the ship. What armor was that?"

He comes to such a sudden stop I almost crash into the back of him. "Why do you want to know?"

I take a deep breath. "Because I am bored beyond belief and with each day that passes, I fear I am losing little pieces of my mind with it. If I don't have a normal conversation soon, I'll scream."

I see the hint of a grin in the corner of Arax's mouth, but it is a promise he does not fulfill.

"Very well. The armor I wore on the ship is a Reaper's armor. They are the elite of the Ebon Flight, and serve as lieutenants in battle."

I think over his words. "And why do you no longer wear that armor? It sounds far more important."

Arax looks straight ahead, and I watch his shoulders rise and fall with a heavy breath. "It is."

"So why do you not wear it?"

Arax is silent for what feels like an age, and I feel myself falling in line with his steady stride until at last he speaks. "Because I allowed you to save me."

My heart thumps hard in my chest, and I swallow a lump in my throat. "You did not allow me to do anything. You were dying. What I did was my decision and mine alone."

"That's not how the king sees it," Arax replies, a hint of bitterness in his voice. "To him, I would have died a warrior's death. Instead, I escaped my fate like a coward. So now, I'm deemed unworthy of serving my House as a Reaper. I serve only as a Blade." He glances back at me, his expression hardening. "And a bodyguard to the one I allowed to dishonor me."

My chest tightens. "I was trying to save you."

"It makes no difference," he replies as we approach the doors of the dining hall. He grips the handle and pulls a door open for me. "I will wait here."

I drop my chin, fidgeting with my fingers to avoid his gaze. In his own way, Arax has shown me moments of unexpected decency in Baev'kalath, reminding me of Keeper Tovar with his steady presence. It's a stark contrast to the heartlessness I faced on the ship and the contempt of every other member of his House I've encountered. If it weren't for this, I might find some satisfaction in his downfall, as I did with Solena and the maids. But knowing what I do about the Mordorin and the reverence they hold for their warriors, this must be the ultimate punishment—being deemed a lesser warrior in their eyes.

"Arax. I..."

He shakes his head with a firmness that leaves no room for argument, his gaze fixed straight ahead. "There's nothing more to discuss. Now, please—just eat."

I glance up at him from beneath my brow, but he stands as still as a statue. Biting my lip, I walk past him, feeling the coldness radiating from him as it pushes me away. I wander slowly into the dining room, which feels smaller in the daylight, stripped of the flickering candles and shadowy corners that once held sinister royals glaring from the far end of the table.

The breakfast feast sprawled out before me is a vibrant array of fruits, assorted cheeses, and freshly baked bread—such a stark contrast to the meager handful of berries and nuts I'm used to. I start cautiously, picking at the tiny morsels. After all, I've practically eaten an entire apple tree. But with each delicious bite, my appetite surges. With no one watching, I soon find myself shoving fist-sized portions into my mouth. I'm unsure of how much time passes, but only when my belly strains against the tightness of my corset do I finally pull back, and as I do, a burp erupts from me like thunder, startling me into silence.

A cough floats in from the doorway, and I spin around to see Arax watching me curiously.

"What is it? What's wrong?" I ask.

His lips are a straight line. "Nothing, Princess. Have you finished, or are you just coming up for air?"

"I'm finished... for now." I rub my swelling belly through my corset. "But I think a walk is in order."

Arax bows. "Very well. The rain has eased. We may be able to venture outside."

The thought sends a thrill through me. No rain. Could it be possible that the sun might peek through today? The warmth on my skin could be just what I need to start feeling like myself again. Not to mention being outside might offer some safety. After all, all my nightmares have come to life within these stone walls.

"Yes. Let us go," I say eagerly.

He turns and leads me down the hall, past the stoic line of guards, ducking in and out of the shadows as we walk by the arches that look out across the vast balconies to the Untold Sea. He's right. I can not hear the rain. Just the crash of the waves as they hit the rocks and the hollow whistle of the wind rolling over the endless ocean. But as we approach the largest balcony that overlooks the courtyard, I hear something else. Steel striking steel and voices raised in fury.

"What is that?" I ask nervously, recalling the last time I heard something from the courtyard was when I watched a Fae lose his head.

But Arax's lack of concern is almost comforting. "The Flight is taking advantage of the weather and sparring."

His response has me even more curious.

"May I watch?"

He nods. "But remain silent."

I walk closely beside him as the clang of steel against steel fills the air, the noise so loud it stings my ears. When we reach the railing at the edge of the balcony, I rest my hands on the weathered stone, still damp even though the rain has finally stopped. I doubt anything is ever truly dry in this place.

Peering over the edge, I'm awestruck by the sight of hundreds of Mordorin warriors below. Few are clad in full armor; most wear only leather trousers and tunics, some men standing bare-chested, their rune-inscribed skin glistening in the rare rays of sunlight that break through the clouds. My gaze drifts to the women among them, their hair tightly braided against their scalps, their muscular bodies moving with a strength and agility that stirs a quiet envy within me.

The Blades practice in formations, wielding swords, polearms or even their strapped fists, their shouts mingling with the rhythmic thud of boots on stone. When I look up, some of the Mordorin soar through the air, their movements fluid as they spar, while others hone their skills in void walking, disappearing and reappearing in an instant. Blood splatters across the courtyard as they grunt and roar, showing no mercy to one another, and it would be easy to confuse this so-called sparring with a vicious battle, the atmosphere so thick with the thrill of combat.

As I watch, there is no doubt in my mind that they are masters of warfare, fully deserving their reputation as the fiercest warriors in all the Sundered Kingdoms. Among the throng, I spot four Mordorin wearing the distinctive shrouded helms of the Reapers. They stand at the edge of the sparring ring, watchful and resolute, their mere presence commanding respect.

Suddenly, a male among the ranks loses his footing, stumbling into those around him and earning sharp glares and muttered curses. In an instant, a Reaper void-walks across the courtyard, reappearing behind the clumsy male. With cold precision, the Reaper unleashes a brutal beating, leaving the male crumpled in a bloody heap. Meanwhile, his brethren continue their training, unfazed, as though nothing had happened.

My throat tightens, but Arax's shiftless expression confirms what I assume. This is common.

"Is that part of a Reaper's duty?" I ask with a hint of disdain in my voice. "Beating your own men?"

"Better by us than the enemy. Here they will learn, so that on the battlefield they do not die."

I turn to look at him, but his face stares straight ahead. "And how many have you beaten?"

"Not nearly enough," he grumbles, his voice rough like gravel. "If I'd prepared them better, perhaps fewer would have fallen in the Betrayers' Battle."

Who are these creatures that see pain and suffering as a rite of passage? Whose only joy comes from battle and violence and cruelty? Humans could never have defeated the Mordorin in the Betrayers' Battle. We do not know the depths of their depravity.

Arax's expression remains stone cold, but I sense the torment simmering beneath the surface.

"It sounds like a heavy burden to be a Reaper," I say, and my words finally coax the faintest flicker of emotion from him.

"It is a great honor," he replies defiantly, his jaw clenched. "But one that comes with great sacrifice. A sacrifice of the flesh. A sacrifice of the spirit. A sacrifice of the heart. You may never take a mate, and your line ends with you. You swear an oath to serve and to kill until your last breath."

"You have no children?" I ask. "No wife?"

He sneers, his expression hardening into a fierce scowl, but I once again notice the red ribbon he twists around his finger. "I'm done with your endless questions," he snaps. "I'll speak of it no more."

Suddenly, I recognize something familiar in Arax—sacrifice.

It's a word both of us know intimately, though it steals far more from us than anyone could ever understand. When Keeper Tovar told me I would leave The Grove to marry the prince, I didn't utter a word of protest. It was my duty. But that doesn't mean my heart didn't shatter that day, or that I didn't, for once, wish I wasn't the Jewel of the Tenders.

I imagine for a Mordorin, a warrior born from a line of fierceness and strength, it must be unbearable to know his legacy ends with him. The unwavering loyalty to your people, weighed down by the quiet ache of your own desires, is a burden no one sees. But I see that same heaviness resting on Arax's shoulders now.

A raucous from the courtyard pulls my attention, a chant rising from the crowd—*Rook. Rook. Rook.*

I glance over the railing, and in the heart of the chaos, there he is. The wicked crown prince of the Mordorin Fae. His leather trousers cling to his powerful legs, and a black harness crisscrosses his chest, each strap taut against the sweat-slicked ridges of his muscles. Runes pulse across every inch of his skin, shifting with each graceful, predatory step he takes toward his opponent.

Daed sweeps back his damp hair, bending low with a wicked grin, storm clouds brewing within his eyes, and a slow, simmering heat coils deep in my belly, spreading down my thighs. I force myself to focus, painfully aware of Arax standing just feet away. Thank the Souls he can't sense the unraveling inside me.

Rook. Rook. Rook. The Mordorin continue to chant.

"What does that mean?" I ask Arax, my voice escaping as a breathless gasp.

"Smoke," Arax replies, his voice hushed, as though the word itself carries weight. "He says on the battlefield, royal titles hold no meaning. Out there, we are all the same. So when he fights, we call him *Rook*."

CHAPTER 10

D aed circles the courtyard below, his movements a calculated prowl. His bare chest gleams beneath the overcast sky, every ripple of muscle accentuated by the sweat glistening on his skin. His runes pulse faintly, a reminder of the raw power humming beneath the surface. There's a feral intensity to his gaze, sharp as a blade and just as cold, as he sizes up his opponent, unhurried but certain, like a wolf savoring the chase before the kill.

And I, watching from above, feel it—the pull, the quiet terror, the strange, undeniable attraction. My breath quickens, a flutter in my chest like the rabbit I freed from the snare as a child. That rabbit had stared at me with wide, terrified eyes, unable to move even when I released it. Trapped not just by the rope but by the fear of what awaited it beyond.

I wonder if I'm that rabbit now, caught in a different kind of snare. Am I paralyzed by the same mix of fear and fascination? Or am I just waiting for the moment when I'm too far gone to run?

My eyes stay locked on Daed as he charges, a force of lethal grace. In the blink of an eye, he vanishes, dissolving into a twisting cloud of black smoke, only to reappear mid-stride. His fist connects with his opponent's chin with a sickening crack, the warrior staggering back, dazed. Before he can fall, Daed is on him again, his movements too fast to track. He vanishes once more, reappearing behind the Fae, grabbing him by the throat. With a savage strength, Daed lifts and throws him over his back like he weighs nothing.

The warrior crashes to the ground, his face quickly masked in crimson, a pool of blood blooming beneath him. But Daed doesn't stop. He straddles him, his expression a dangerous calm. With a smooth, almost casual motion, he reaches to the sky. Smoke coils from his hand as he manifests a dagger, the blade solidifying in his grip, the jeweled handle gleaming in the faint light.

"Where do the weapons come from?" I mutter to Arax, struggling to find enough breath in me to speak.

"The void itself," Ajax replies.

"Can all Mordorin do that?"

Arax's voice drops, a low, reverent murmur, as if speaking too loudly would disrupt some sacred truth. "No. There is none among us as attuned to the void as the prince is. He doesn't command it. He is a part of it."

Another question lingers on my tongue, one that must seem obvious to the Mordorin, yet remains a mystery to me. I swallow my hesitation. "What *is* the void?"

I feel the chill radiating from Arax's skin as he speaks, his voice low and steady. "The void is the realm of the Father Below. While our faith lies in the Pale Eye, the Mother Above, the Father offers us gifts we cannot refuse." His gaze narrows, holding mine. "Void walking. Berserking. Our strength and speed... but they come at a cost."

The weight of his words settles heavy in the air between us.

"Venture too deep into the void, and you'll be lost. Meat for the beast. And the beast is *always* hungry."

Fear rattles within me, threatening to topple my already shaky resolve. If I weren't struggling to stay upright, Arax's demeanor would surely send me crumbling to the ground. In The Grove, everything is simple and serene; we worship the great trees and the winding vines, honoring the Souls of the Forest with peace and grace.

But to place faith in such a dark entity?

It's no wonder the Mordorin are steeped in corruption if their power is tethered to a force that thrives on chaos and hunger. The very thought sends a shiver down my spine, igniting a dread that twists in my stomach. I cannot fathom how they navigate this treacherous line, walking so close to the abyss, yet calling it a source of strength. I can almost see it in their eyes, the flicker of something unsettling, a shadow lurking just beneath the surface. The thought sends another wave of dread coursing through me, each heartbeat a reminder of the chasm that separates my world from theirs.

Daed looms over his opponent, poised and ready to strike, the dagger glinting at the male's throat. To my surprise, the warrior beneath him displays no fear, even in the face of death. I know that this merciless sparring is a brutal part of their training, yet a nagging doubt lingers in my mind. I remind myself of the ruthlessness I witnessed when he severed a head from its body as if it were nothing more than a branch to be snapped. And yet, in this moment, I cling to a sliver of hope that he is not entirely devoid of mercy.

I gulp, my fingers instinctively curling around Arax's forearm. "He isn't going to kill him, is he?"

I don't intend to touch him, but when Arax doesn't immediately pull away, I find a strange comfort in the connection. My heart sinks, though, when he replies, "If it pleases the prince... then yes."

The weight of it all is suffocating. The sunless sky and the relentless rain, the centuries-old hatreds mixed with resentment and regret. But more than anything, I am exhausted by the death that permeates the air—putrid and overwhelming. It surrounds me. From the smoldering fires in my forest to the wars that have left both humans and Fae alike as bloody, mangled corpses, side by side on the battlefield.

My heart pounds in my chest, and anguish threatens to spill over, tears pooling in my eyes. I fight them back, summoning every ounce of strength as I call out, "No! Stop!"

My words slice through the thrum of the courtyard, silencing the last echoes of the *Rook* chant. The Mordorin warriors freeze, their movements halting as they turn their gazes upward toward the balcony. I grip the railing so tightly that my knuckles turn white, my breaths coming in ragged gasps, each one a desperate plea for an end to the violence surrounding me.

Daed rises and two Blades hook his fallen opponent under the arms and drag him away. The dagger vanishes from Daed's hand in a plume of smoke before he grins at me, in the same devastatingly alluring way I have come to fear.

"Arax," he calls. "Bring me my wife. Will you?"

Arax frowns before swiftly shoving his helmet over his head to hide his annoyance.

"Princess," he says to me, the only courtesy I receive before he effortlessly scoops me into his arms. His wings burst free from his back, revealing black feathers streaked with gray, mirroring his hair and beard.

With a powerful beat, he lifts a foot onto the railing and pushes off. We soar into the air as the wind rushes around us. I instinctively bury my face in his chest to shield myself from the biting gusts. Suddenly, he shifts direction, diving toward the courtyard with alarming speed. My stomach lurches, the raisin bread I devoured for breakfast threatening to resurface. I manage to swallow it back down just as Arax lands with a solid thump that reverberates through my entire body. He gently sets me on my feet and steps aside, standing tall and silent, his eyes staring blankly ahead through the visor of his helm as Daed strides past him.

The prince stalks toward me, his chest heaving with exertion, and I feel the familiar tension in the air crackle between us. His expression is a cold, disinterested glower.

"You're the first human to witness the Blades spar," he says, wiping the sweat from the back of his neck, his voice steady yet edged with curiosity. "What are your thoughts on the display?"

Despite the magnetic pull he exerts on me, I can't ignore the brutality of it all.

"Barbaric." The word slips from my lips, dripping with disapproval. "What do you gain from beating each other half to death? It's as if I'm watching beasts tear one another apart. This is nothing more than mindless violence."

The collective chuckle of the Reapers and Blades catches me off guard, and when Daed's deep laugh joins in, heat floods my cheeks. I try to hold my head high, but the way they're laughing—mocking, really—makes me feel small and exposed, like a deer in a clearing.

"Why, thank you, wife," he says, dragging his hand across his mouth in a mocking gesture. "But tell me, is this not the mindless violence you bargained for to keep your precious Grove safe from your own kind? It isn't the Fae threatening your borders, but bloodthirsty human rebels who forget their place. Without us *'beasts'*, your people would be left to fend for themselves against their own, would they not?"

I can feel the sharp glances of Fae eyes piercing through me, each one a reminder of my status as an outsider. But I refuse to shrink before them, and even more I refuse to allow Daed to spread vicious lies.

"We are not part of the Legion," I hiss through clenched teeth. "They're more like you than they are like us." I enunciate each word, ensuring there's no room for misunderstanding. "Cold-blooded killers."

A hush blankets the gathering of Mordorin, their eyes now fixed on Daed. He stands unfazed, an air of calm arrogance surrounding him as if nothing could rattle his composure.

"They sound marvelous," he drawls, almost stifling a yawn. "Perhaps I should have married one of them instead."

"Perhaps I should have bargained with the Golden Son instead of you," I shoot back, my tone sharper than I intended. The weight of my words sinks in too late.

Daed's eyes blaze with a fierce intensity, the first fracture in his icy demeanor.

"Perhaps," he breathes, his gaze so penetrating that I struggle to hold his eyes.

Daed's gaze drifts to the sky just as the encroaching storm clouds swallow the last remnants of sunlight. A crack of thunder precedes the sudden downpour, rain cascading over the chiseled planes of his chest. He closes his eyes, tilting his face upward, as if savoring the cool rush that dances over his skin. Water trails down the contours of his body, accentuating every sharp angle, and when he finally turns back to me, he runs a hand through his damp hair, sending droplets flying in every direction.

"In any case, this has merely been a sample. It is the first night of The Warrior's Eye moon. My Blades and I depart for the thrall house of Eyr'Drogul." The Blades erupt into eager cheers and applause around him. "So, I'm afraid, wife, I will be denied your company for a time."

He looks at me with that soft haze masking his hard edge, and I will not allow myself to fall under his spell.

"I'm sure you will manage," I reply curtly. I turn to Arax. "I think we are done here."

I turn my back on my husband and stride toward the sanctuary of the castle, rain drenching me with every step. I don't dare look over my shoulder. Arax follows close behind, but we both freeze when a sharp, chilling cackle echoes from behind us.

"She has you on a short leash, Arax."

We turn as the Reaper pursuing us removes their helmet, revealing Frane smiling beneath. I know for certain she was not a Reaper aboard the ship. She was a Blade, like the rest. But something has clearly changed since then.

"It looks good on you," she taunts. "Babysitting this human. Do you nurse her from your breast as well?"

"Watch your tongue, Frane," Arax growls. "She may be human, but she is still a princess of the Mordorin, and just because you wear the armor does not make you better than me."

Frane grits her teeth as she steps into him. "No. Being better than you makes me better than you. What say you, old one? Care to spar, or has the human made you weak?"

Arax looks over at me, his eyes narrow, his face calm. "Get out of the rain, princess. I will join you soon."

Frane's gaze is like standing too close to fire. I feel it hot on my skin, and if I linger too long, I will surely get burnt. I nod reluctantly, hurrying into the fortress and seeking refuge from the rain.

I shake the dampness from my dress, wringing out the soaked strands of my braid. Just as I'm about to find some solace, a flicker of movement catches my eye in the shadows. There, I spot the unmistakable shroud helm of a Reaper tucked beneath one arm, while the other wraps possessively around the waist of a slender female. They are lost in a passionate, breathless kiss, oblivious to the world around them.

When I gasp, they pry apart. The female's hand shoots to cover her mouth while the Reaper quickly pulls his helmet on, but not before I glimpse his dimpled chin, wide set jaw and long raven hair knotted at the back of his head.

"Your Highness," he says gruffly as he bows, then swiftly walks past me to rejoin the Mordorin in the courtyard.

I'm left alone with the female who I know too well, her dark eyes welling with fear.

"Solena," I say.

She gulps. "Your Highness... I..."

Arax appears behind me and takes in the situation. "What are you doing here? You are not allowed near the courtyard."

Solena's lips tremble, and I stand in front of her, blocking her from Arax.

"She was looking for me," I say, sparing her Arax's wrath.

Arax furrows his brow suspiciously, but I blurt something out before he has time to delve too deep.

"I want to return to my chambers straight away. I am soaked to the bone."

Arax bows his head. "Of course."

He strides ahead of us and Solena touches my arm as I follow him.

"Why?" she whispers, her eyes brimming with confusion. "Why lie for me?"

"I thought seeing you unhappy might bring me some joy, but I've realized it doesn't. No matter how much this place tries to change me, I refuse to lose myself here. I know who I am, and that person does not take pleasure in the suffering of others. I understand the laws of the Reapers, but I have no desire to see them enforced."

Solena bows her head. "Thank you, Your Highness."

She lifts the hem of her dress and breaks into a run, and I watch her disappear around the corner.

I quicken my steps to catch up with Arax.

"So, did you fight her?" I ask. "Frane?"

"No, I did not," he replies tersely.

"She doesn't like me," I say.

"No, she does not," Arax agrees.

"Do you like me, Arax?" I ask, tilting my head.

He stops in his tracks, turning slightly to reveal the weary frown that's becoming all too familiar. "You are not completely unbearable."

A laugh escapes my lips, and the rare sound eases the tension in both our shoulders. "Well, that's high praise coming from you."

He grumbles. "Hurry along now."

I don't take my eyes off Solena as she fumbles around my chamber, her flushed cheeks and trembling hands betraying her nerves. She drops nearly everything she touches and every so often, her gaze flickers toward me, only to dart away before our eyes can meet. Despite my assurances that I have no interest in exposing her relationship with the Reaper, I can see the doubt etched on her face. She's bracing for the other shoe to drop, waiting for a threat or some personal gain to emerge from the knowledge I've gathered.

Perhaps, in another person's hands, such knowledge would be weaponized. But not in mine. I've had decisions made for me before, often under the guise of good intentions, and I refuse to impose that on anyone else—even on someone who could be considered my enemy. That is not who I am, or who I want to become.

Solena helps me out of my damp clothes and into something dry.

"That will be all," I say, but the sound of her restless shuffling lingers.

"Is something wrong?" I ask, knowing clearly there is.

"I need to explain what you saw. It's a misunderstanding." Solena clasps her hands, her knuckles tight with anxiety. "Orios was only comforting me. We've known each other since childhood and..."

"I may have spent my life in the woods, Solena, but I'm not naive. Besides, I've already told you—your secret is safe with me."

But I can see the doubt lingering in her eyes. I remind myself who I'm dealing with: Fae. Scheming, meddling, deceitful Fae. Of course, she doesn't trust me; she's used to that kind of game.

"But why? Why show me such kindness? There must be something you want," she presses, her tone tinged with suspicion.

I shrug. "Perhaps one day I will need your help, and you can remember that, in this moment, I chose kindness."

Solena nods, but I can tell she is still not entirely convinced. If she wants to live with that threat looming over her, so be it. But if it means she doesn't glare at me as much, then I'll let her believe what she likes.

I take a seat on the edge of the bed. While she is here and amenable, I might as well have her answer some questions plaguing me.

"The Warrior's Eye," I begin, "Do all Mordorin celebrate it?"

"Only Blades," she replies. "And the warriors of the thrall houses. It's hosted by a different house each year. This year, it's House Eyr'Drogul."

"And what do they... do?" I press.

"Get drunk and beat each other to a pulp," Solena sighs. "It's believed the Pale Eye blesses the strong on this night and protects them in battle. So they fight for her favor."

"And for how long will they be gone?" I ask, glancing around the room, feigning indifference, but Solena's smirk hints she sees right through me.

"A few days," she replies.

"Good," I say quickly. *Too quickly.* "I will happily be rid of the prince for a while."

She nods. "Of course, Your Highness."

Souls, I wish I was a better liar. I push up from the bed, but immediately wince. "Damn it!" I shout, cradling my hand.

Concern flickers in Solena's eyes. "Your wound isn't improving. We should tell the king and queen. They should know if you are unwell."

"My hand is none of their concern." Solena eyes me suspiciously as my chest heaves. "Please, Solena."

At this moment, I wonder if she too, might choose kindness.

"I will not speak of it again, Your Highness."

I swallow the lump in my throat, creating just enough space to finally exhale.

CHAPTER 11

Tonight, The Warrior's Eye cleaves the moon in two—one half glowing bright, the other swallowed by shadow. I never paid much attention to the moon before. In the forest, it was always hidden above the thick canopy, and at best, we'd catch glimpses of scattered light filtering through the leaves. But here I see it every night, and in this world of darkness, it's the only light that guides me.

Suddenly howls and cries from outside beckon me to the balcony. I shiver beneath the evening's cool touch as fresh rainfall soaks through my nightgown and when I reach the railing I see hoards of Mordorin warriors perched on the walls of the courtyard dressed in leathers, seeming more ready for merriment than battle.

One by one, they leap off the wall, their wings bursting from their backs as they soar high into the night sky, the moon illuminating them like giant birds of prey, and I can hear their laughs long after they vanish into the dark abyss.

As the last of the Blades leaps from the wall, I wander back inside and sit down in the high-back chair in front of the fireplace. What will Daed be doing these next few days? It may not be The Lover's Eye, but drinking and fighting seem to be an aphrodisiac to the Mordorin, regardless of what moon is in the sky. Who could he be with? One of the fearsome yet beautiful female Blades among his Ebon Flight? They seem more suited to him, with their brutality and strength, than I do, with my endless questions and penchant for inappropriate outbursts.

Will he make love to one of them?

There's a knock at the door, and when I say to come in, Arax steps inside.

"Good evening, Your Highness," he says. "Is there anything else you need from me tonight?"

I shake my head, my thoughts scattered. Then I tilt my head curiously. "Is this part of your punishment? Not joining the others to celebrate the moon?"

Arax exhales, a hint of fatigue in his eyes. "The Warrior's Eye is a young Fae's game. I'd much rather have a quiet night with a good book and a proper cup of tea."

"Not limmeth tea," I add with a cringe.

His face mirrors mine, disgust flashing briefly. "Old gods, no. Not that dirty water."

A laugh escapes me, and I catch the faintest hint of a smile tugging at the corner of his mouth. "Good night, Your Highness," he says, his tone softer.

"Good night, Arax," I reply.

In Daed's absence, and with King Kaelus also away celebrating The Warrior's Eye, each meal alone with the queen feels like a subtle interrogation, her questions prying into my thoughts with unnerving precision. Her gaze is heavy on me, studying every word, every shift in expression, as if searching for cracks beneath the surface. I respond with vague answers meant to satisfy while revealing nothing. Still, whenever I am with her, tension coils in my chest like a taut string on the verge of snapping.

Now, in the mornings, Solena is the only one to rouse me. Without the chaos of the other maids bustling about, it's easier to breathe, to move without feeling like I'm being pulled in a hundred directions at once. Solena's demeanor has softened, too—well, softened by her standards. Her words are still clipped, her instructions brusque, but there's a noticeable shift in the way she looks at me, her eyes less judgmental, more... understanding, perhaps. She gives me herbs to ease my constant headaches and takes care of my hand that has not improved.

We often linger in the quiet of my chambers, our attention drawn to my serpentine vine as it sits on the table, its once-vibrant leaves now faded and thinning. I try not to let it get to me each time a leaf detaches, fluttering softly to the table.

In the quieter moments, I wander the fortress with Arax, who, despite his stoic demeanor, has become an unexpected source of solace. I've even managed to draw rare laughter from him—a low, reluctant sound that he promptly denies ever happened. But I take it as a small victory. And thankfully, the ghostly apparition leaves me be and the elusive stairs to nowhere remain just that—elusive. I start to feel that I'm not going mad after all.

But no matter how hard I try to focus on the light, the shadows loom large. I spend hours on my balcony, staring out at the restless ocean, my thoughts a tumultuous tide. With every crashing wave, I reflect on the chaos of the last few weeks—the uncertain future that stretches before me, but when I scan the horizon, I know I am not looking for answers. I am seeking wings, a glimpse of him soaring back to Baev'kalath, yet the skies remain stubbornly empty.

Until the fourth day.

At sunset, the sky bursts with a flurry of black wings as the Blades return, a dark wave against the fading light. Before I can stop myself, I'm already on my balcony, fingers curling tightly around the railing. I watch as they touch down one by one in the courtyard below, the air soon buzzing with the low murmur of voices. I try to convince myself I don't care—yet I notice immediately Daedalus isn't among them.

I linger longer than I should, hoping against hope that he'll arrive late. But as the minutes stretch into an hour, he still doesn't appear. When the rain begins to tap gently against my brow, I finally turn away, damp and frustrated. Perhaps he stayed longer in Eyr'Drogul, or maybe I missed him in the flurry of wings.

Two more days pass, and there's still no sign of him. At breakfast, I keep my tone casual as I ask Kaelus why Daed hadn't returned with the others. The king's response is simple: Daed's wanderlust makes it difficult to keep him anywhere for long. But his words only tighten the knots in my stomach.

That night, after dinner, I sit in my chambers, trying to steady my thoughts. If I can survive a Stormwyrm, I can endure the turmoil building within me—this conflict between reason and an attraction that's grown impossible to deny. But then, a flicker of light catches my eye, pulling me from my chair. I step through the archway, my gaze drawn to Daed's tower. His window is shrouded in darkness, as empty as the past few days have been.

Just as I'm about to turn away, a faint glimmer breaks through the gloom. Candlelight. My heart stutters, caught between curiosity and disbelief. Someone is there.

It's the curiosity that propels me forward, overriding any semblance of logic.

Has he returned? How long has he been back in Baev'kalath?

I can't explain why I find myself at the door, fingers brushing the cool metal of the handles, heart pounding against my ribs. But just as I'm about to pull them open, reality catches up to me. Arax will want to know where I'm going, and I have no desire to endure an awkward conversation about my tangled feelings for the prince. I doubt Arax would want that conversation, either.

After a brief hesitation, I turn sharply and head to the hidden door in the wall across from my bed. The decision feels reckless, impulsive—yet the need to see Daed overwhelms any sense of restraint.

I stare at the panel for a while, my eyes searching for the secret notch Daed used to open it. I feel along the molding and find a spot that appears more worn than the rest, as if rubbed over and over until the hard ridge has rounded. A smile cracks my focused expression as I push the notch, and I can't help but laugh excitedly when I hear a click and the secret door creaks open.

The line of lamps along the wall gives the passage a soft glow, enough to easily guide me through the sharp turns. I pass several doors, with no idea which one will take me to where I need to go, but after walking for what feels like an age, I choose one, leaning into the wood and pushing it open.

It is almost completely black in the hallway I stumble into, with no light but the pallid moon beams that slip through the narrow slits in the walls that serve as windows. There are no open arches, no balconies. It is more confined and claustrophobic than the secret passage. I recall the shape of the fortress from the outside, and how Daed's tower seems so isolated and shut off from everywhere else. Perhaps I am here, on the other side of the castle. I strain my eyes, peering to my left and right for any sign of where I might be. To my right, I spy a pair of darkened stairs leading up. Daed's tower is the highest point of the fortress. If it is anywhere, it will be up.

Each step I take up the narrow, spiraling staircase feels like it echoes through the silence, a sound too loud for the suffocating dark that presses in on me from all sides. The stone walls are cold and damp, brushing against my shoulders as if the tower itself is closing in, trying to swallow me whole. My fingers skim the rough surface, searching for something solid to hold on to, but all I find are jagged edges that bite into my skin, making me flinch.

I can almost hear the stones whispering, telling me to turn back, to run while I still can, like every other otherworldly voice I hear in this place. But I can't. Not now. Not when I'm so close.

Close to what?

The fear gnaws at me, twisting my thoughts into dark shapes. What if I find him—what if he is waiting for me at the top? The thought of seeing him makes my heart stutter, but it also fills me with dread. Is it Daed up there? Or something else? I'm not sure I'm ready for the answers, but the uncertainty is worse. I have to know. I have to see him.

Finally, I arrive at the top. With trembling hands, I reach for the ring that serves as the door's handle. It is slick with moisture, or maybe sweat from my own clammy palm, and for a moment, I hesitate. The fear is a living thing inside me, clawing at my insides, begging me to turn back. I take a deep breath, steadying myself as best I can, and pull the door open.

There is only a flicker of candlelight inside, barely enough to see my face in front of my hand. I take the candle from the table by the door and hold it up. There is no sign of Daed, or anyone else. Just a cold, empty room and a balcony with lightning tearing the black night sky outside.

Even with the candlelight, my steps are unsteady and uncertain. I reach out, gripping the furniture and using it to guide me safely around the room. I feel the edge of a green velvet chair and as the candlelight expands, a grand ten foot fireplace comes into view. It looms with dark, towering stone columns, the hearth yawning open like a maw and framed by jagged arches. I gasp into my hand when a flash of lightning illuminates the sinister stone gargoyles perched on the mantle, their twisted faces leering from the shadows.

I take another deep breath to steady my racing heart, lifting the candle higher when I catch the glimmer of a gilded frame. The candlelight spreads, bathing a large portrait over the fireplace in a dull, amber glow. A beautiful Mordorin female draped in a thin lilac gown that holds tight to every sweeping curve of her body. Her hair is a mass of tight, dark curls that cascade down her back, the warmth of her violet eyes emphasized by her glorious smile. She sits in a chair, a green velvet chair, this chair, and she cradles her swollen belly in her hands. Who is this female, and why would a portrait of a pregnant Fae hang above Daed's mantle?

A pang strikes my heart and asks of it a question. *Is the female... a wife?*

A crash of thunder sends me stumbling backwards, and the candle falls from my hand. I drop to my knees to pick it up before I set the damned chair on fire.

"What are you doing here?" a guttural voice questions from the shadows.

I gasp and look up, both hands wrapped around the candle. I squint to make out the figure sitting in the corner of the room. "Daed? Is that you?"

"I said, what are you doing here?" he repeats, his voice rougher.

"I saw a light," I gulp. "From my balcony. I came to see who was up here."

"Don't lie to me," he mutters.

My body shivers. "I'm not lying..."

The slivers of charcoal cloud shift and a shimmering shaft of moonlight beams through the arch and hits the corner with a hazy, pallid glow. He sits with his legs wide in the chair, a hand resting on each knee as he hunches forward. The runes tattooed on his knuckles are enough for me to know it is Daed, but that is all I recognize about him. His voice comes from someone else. A deep, rumbling growl that is as frightening as it is alluring and the way he speaks to me...he has always been callous, but it is as if he doesn't even know me.

"There is only one intruder here, and it is *you.*"

He leans forward from the shadows, the sharp angles of his face bathed in ivory moonlight, his hair soaking wet and slicked back. But his voice is not the only thing that is different. His eyes. His eyes are not gray, but solid black, reflecting the candlelight like onyx mirrors.

"You are not yourself," I gulp, my throat quivering as I move to stand.

"Stay on your knees," he commands, and another crash of thunder echoes his words.

I freeze, my chin dropping against my chest. "Daed... please."

"Please what?" he asks, his voice a low rumble. "Please do not hurt me? Please let me go?"

I hear the wood of the chair groan as he stands, and his heavy steps trek towards me, but I do not look up. The fear searing through my veins has me silent and still. Suddenly he hovers over me, his leather trousers as damp as his hair, with rain dripping onto his boots.

"Well?" he says tersely. "Do you want me to let you go?"

"No." The words tumble from my mouth. I grimace and close my eyes tight. "I mean yes. Yes, let me go. I'm sorry. I shouldn't have come."

Suddenly swirls of smoke encircle my arms, and I gasp when they pull me to my feet. I have no choice now but to look into those soulless black eyes, and when I do, I see my fear staring straight back at me.

"At last you understand. No. You shouldn't have come. But it is too late now." The ropes of smoke tighten around me and pull me closer to him until his lips are against my jaw, his heavy breaths sending my heartbeat into a frenzy. "I must take you and make you mine."

100

Daed inhales me deeply while dragging his lips down my neck. The smoke curls around the neckline of my nightgown, slowly inching the fabric off my shoulders and down my arms, and when the moonlight falls upon the top of my breasts, the sound he makes is almost feral. My skin feels like it is on fire.

Fire. I remember the candle is still in my hand. I shove the flame towards his face and it's enough to startle him. The tendrils of smoke release me and I hurry toward the balcony. He turns slowly, his eyes tracking my every move, and when he takes a step towards me, I hold out the candle again.

"Stay back," I stammer. "You are not yourself. You don't want me. Remember?"

His black eyes narrow. "Lies. I want you so badly I will die if I can't have you."

My heart is as loud as a thunderclap in my ears. I wrap both hands around the candle, but I am not foolish enough to think the tiny, withering flame is enough to keep Prince Daedalus Phaedren at bay. He holds out his palm and when he curls his fingers into a fist, the flame extinguishes, and when he turns his wrist, the candle itself turns to ash in my hands, crumbling to the floor.

I've not felt such fear since The Golden Son marched through The Grove and demanded we fight and die for him, but I will not allow myself to crumble. I did not give The Golden Son that satisfaction, and Daed will not prise that surrender from me either.

He stalks towards me, the smoke he commands a cloak at his back. There is nothing of him in those black eyes. Not the warrior I bargained for. Not the Fae who consumes my thoughts, even if I don't want him to. This is the monster they warned me about. The wicked, heartless murderer who slaughtered any worthless human who dared oppose him. This is the Rook who will rule the world.

But he will not rule me.

I take a step backwards, through the arch and onto the balcony, where the icy rain hits my skin like shards of glass. I look over the railing to the courtyard below, and beyond that to the jagged rocks and the furious sea. I take a deep breath, shuddering as I muster my strength.

"Try to touch me and I will jump," I say calmly, my face stern.

Daed pauses, a grin sliding across his mouth. "You lie."

"Do I?" I snap. I take another step toward the railing.

He snarls. "You are mine. It is my right to take you if I please."

"No. Not like this. I will not allow it."

101

"You are not brave enough to die," Daed mocks.

I gulp, the words cutting like a knife. "I don't need to be brave enough to die," I say, taking another step. "Just brave enough to jump."

"Enough of this!" he yells, and he charges at me.

I turn toward the railing and feel my body go numb, then close my eyes, allowing myself to fall into whatever is waiting for me. But I hear the sound of Daed turning to smoke, then feel his icy hands. His arms circle around my waist, pulling my back against his heaving chest. He presses his lips to the nape of my neck, sending every nerve in my body into shock.

"No. Don't," he breathes into my skin. "I will not take you. Not until you ask me to." The softness of his kiss turns to teeth scraping against my shoulder as he groans in pain. "Not until you beg..."

He groans again, keeling over behind me. I turn to find him with his head in his hands, his face twisted in agony as he pulls his hair at the roots.

"Get out of here. Now!" he yells.

I can hear my prince's voice again, fighting with whatever has a hold over him. My hand shakes as I place it on his shoulder.

"Daedalus," I mutter. "Husband."

Suddenly, his head jerks back and his mouth opens, sharp fangs emerging from his canine teeth, his solid black eyes wider and rounder, horrifyingly distorted.

"Leave! Now, Amara!" he roars.

I do not hesitate. I run past him, snatching up the hem of my nightgown and holding it around my knees to keep it free from my sprinting feet. I throw open the door, skipping stairs and slamming into the tower walls as I race down the staircase. My bare feet scrape against the stone, my toes crushed on every corner, but I do not stop. Not even when I reach the bottom, not even when I'm down the hall, not even when I burst through the secret door and barrel through the passageway.

Not until I emerge in my chambers do I stop to take a breath, but only long enough to get behind a small cabinet and lean into it with all my might, pushing it in front of the secret door. When it slams into place, I collapse on the cold wooden floor, struggling to remember the rhythm to breathing, the air rushing in and out of my lungs so quickly and coarsely it stings my chest.

As my heart beat settles, I slump against the cabinet, exhaustion taking hold as my adrenalin wanes. As my senses return, so does the pain, and I hiss, holding up my hand to see fresh blood seeping through the bandage. Suddenly the room starts spinning around me and I stagger to my feet, reaching for the bed. I just need to lie down, just for a minute, just until everything stays still.

When my fingers find the mattress, I dig my nails in and drag myself onto the bed before collapsing. I manage to fling myself onto my back, staring up at the rolling ocean carved into the wood above me. For the first time, I'm grateful I cannot dream. If Daed finds me there, in a place where I can be someone else—free from my duties and responsibilities, free from sense and resolve—everything changes.

In that dream, my body would respond to his scent, to his touch, to the vile words that drip from his beautiful mouth. If we were in that dreamscape, and he looked at me with those piercing eyes and told me I was his, I wouldn't run. I would let him grab my hair, grip my throat, and do all the things I know his body was capable of, and I would never want him to stop.

As my eyelids grow heavy, my breaths become shallow, and my heart beats loudly in my ears, I find myself teetering on the edge of consciousness, caught between desire and reality. In this moment of vulnerability, I surrender to the seductive pull of my thoughts, longing for a world where freedom and submission intertwine, even if just for a heartbeat.

Then my eyes close, and I brace myself for the long, empty dark of a dreamless sleep. But it is not dark, and it is not dreamless. Daedalus is not here, but something else is... and it whispers my name.

CHAPTER 12

A hollow thrum of voices in unison floods my slumbering head. Am I dreaming? Impossible. I do not dream.

That is the only way I know that all these nightmares are real. That means the voices are real too. The language is old Fae. No doubt the same tongue as the runes on Daed's body that I do not understand, and when spoken, the words are a string of guttural hisses and whispers that send chills down my spine.

My eyes flutter open, only barely, just enough to see the world around me through a thin, blurry haze. Faceless figures draped in garments of stars and midnight surround me, their heavy hoods keeping any features hidden in shadow. They chant their solemn, haunting tune, the same words hard and monotone, over and over again. The stone floor is ice cold beneath me, its uneven surface prodding at the softest parts of my skin. My head falls to the side and my gaze falls upon a luminous blue line drawn on the ground, its brilliant color dimming and brightening with a hypnotic pulse. I take a moment to realize it is not just a straight line. It curves around my splayed arms and legs. A circle, and I am trapped within its boundaries.

My throat burns dry, and I gulp as my senses slowly return. I can barely feel my body. It takes all my strength for my fingers to respond when I try to move them, and when they weakly twitch, I'm immediately struck with a slice of pain. My bandage is gone and the blood from the wound that refuses to heal drips onto the stone floor, seeping through the cracks in the stone like veins.

Fear takes root in my gut, rushing over me in waves and ensnaring my heart with a vice grip. I struggle against my paralysis, panic escaping my lips in murmurs, but the chanting continues. My head flops back, and now I stare at the ceiling with its wooden rafters. I can not move. I can not scream.

What is this place? Who are these people?

Suddenly, a speck of black appears on the ceiling. An imperfection in the wood, or something in my foggy vision. But it grows, spreading across the ceiling, and I realize it is not a speck. It is smoke. A pool of smoke expanding above me, and inside is an endless, black void that feels like staring into eternity. The void continues to grow, swallowing up the stone and wood until it fills the room, bringing the darkness of the night sky within these four walls.

Something is coming.

From the dark abyss, I see a shape, a mass with dozens of thick, writhing tentacles propelling the creature forward. I gulp back my fear, powerless, hopeless, with no choice but to lie and wait for the monster to reach me. Its mouth is the first thing I see clearly. A gigantic maw with row after row of pointed, razor-sharp teeth that seem to go all the way down its throat and a long, red forked tongue that whips and thrashes and reaches for me.

The chant that has rung in my ears changes. It has been a continuous, emotionless vibration, but now a single word rises above the rest, spoken with such passion and reverence, that I have no doubt it is the creature's name.

Gygarth. Gygarth. Gygarth.

I grit my teeth, forcing my fingers to fold into fists, ignoring the pain searing through my hand. My body tightens and I clench every muscle, desperate to wrestle myself free from the invisible bonds that pin me to the stone floor. Very few could say they have been here before. Looking into the darkness and watching as a beast whose eyes scream with hunger tear towards you. But I have already defeated a monster with plans to devour me, and I will survive this too.

I will not die in Baev'kalath.

No voice passes my lips, but inside me it screams. Screams at my bones, my blood, my limbs and demands they obey me. This is my body. I decide what is done with it and I alone.

Move!

My arms spasm as if awoken by my plea. I close my eyes tight, my face twisted in a desperate effort to fight my fate. My arms are heavy as sacks of grain, but I pull them to my chest, and when I hold them out towards Gygarth, it feels as if they hold the weight of the world. I have to find my strength. Shut out the noise and hear only the voices of the Souls of the Forest. I have to raise the power buried deep inside me. I feel it, a flicker of warmth amidst the cold dread, a tiny spark that grows stronger the more I focus on it.

Gygarth is almost upon me now. It shrieks and I feel its hunger, its desire to devour, to destroy. But I refuse to give in. I swallow my fear and force my hands to steady as I reach deep within myself, summoning the light that has always been there, waiting for me to call upon it. A light used to mend and to heal, but now, in this moment, used to fight.

Warmth spreads through my chest, growing brighter and more intense until it's almost unbearable. I can feel the energy building, the rune around my neck pulsing with life and power, begging to be released. The monster lunges, its massive jaws opening wide, ready to tear me apart. But I do not flinch. Instead, I thrust my hands forward, willing the light to surge from within me, to banish the darkness that seeks to engulf me.

A beam of brilliant, phosphorescent green light shoots from my hands, blinding in its intensity. It cuts through the void, striking Gygarth with a force that shakes the very fabric of the surrounding darkness. The beast shrieks, a sound so horrifying it tears at my ears and gouges my eyes, but I hold my ground, pouring everything I have into that beam of light.

Gygarth recoils, its form writhing and contorting as the light sears, driving it back, back into the abyss from which it had emerged. The void trembles, the shadows tearing apart as the light consumes them. With one final, desperate roar, the darkness swallows Gygarth, dragging him back to the depths, his white eyes flickering out as he sinks from sight and the portal of smoke shrinks and withers until it closes completely, leaving only the untouched ceiling and wooden rafters.

A soft glow of the light lingers around me. With a final, shuddering breath, I let the light fade and my arms fall exhausted at my sides.

All is silent. The pulsing circle around me falls still, now nothing but smudged blue stains on the floor, and the chanting is only a memory, something to add to the waking nightmares in my head. The circle of shrouded figures remains, lurching over me with an eerie quiet.

Will they kill me now? Do I have the strength to stop them? Before I have time to weight up my odds, a loud crash, followed by a terrifying, savage roar, breaks my captor's circle. They scatter and I hear screams and desperate pleas as a flurry of black robes whip around me. Then two strong hands scoop me off the floor and draw me close to the warmth of a broad chest. I nestle close, eager to chase the icy chill from my bones.

That smell. I know that smell. The smell of the night, and the air and the sea.

His hand brushes away the hair veiling my face, and when I feel his fingers drifting from my skin, I find the strength to reach out and grab his hand to keep him with me. I have faced a demon tonight, but I do not want to suffer the pain of losing his touch.

"Daed," I mutter.

He does not speak, but I hear the deep rumbling of his breath, I'm sure of it. His lips brush my forehead in the softest kiss, a touch so gentle it sends a shiver through me. My heart flutters, caught between the dreamlike haze and the startling reality of his touch. I lose my grip on whatever force has kept me lucid this long, but the sensation of his kiss lingers through my dreamless sleep, a powerful, unspoken promise that leaves me breathless.

The smell of dawn rouses me, but when I open my eyes, the sky over Baev'kalath is gray, as always. My memories flood back in a barrage of painful flashes, and I pinch the bridge of my nose to dull the sting. A conclave of hooded strangers, and a circle painted on the ground. A portal of smoke and shadow and a monster born from absolute darkness. Two strong arms saving me, and a kiss that is burnt into not just my mind, but my skin.

I bolt upright with rapid, shallow breaths. "Daed?"

There is no answer. I am alone in my chambers. I look over my nightgown for any sign of dirt or blood. Too much happened last night for there to be no evidence. But the fabric is pristine and pure white, even around the hem, which I know I dragged over stone and through ash. My hand. I raise it to my face, expecting to find the bandage missing and streams of dried blood along my arm. But the bandage is in place without a single drop of blood in sight. My head snaps towards the secret door.

The cabinet should be... no.

The cabinet is against the wall as normal, not in front of the secret door where I know I pushed it after escaping Daed. Or did I? Souls? Did I even see him last night? Or did I fall asleep and imagine all of this?

I shake my head in disbelief and when I do, my head throbs so much I wince. It could not have all been a dream. I do not dream. But what other explanation can there be?

I stumble out of bed and my fingers crawl along my chest to find my rune necklace. The source of my healing gifts. I hold the rune tight and close my eyes even tighter, trying to make sense of all this. The light within me has only ever been used to heal those in need.

107

Never to fight monsters. I shiver. But it wasn't just a monster. It had a name. Souls, why can't I remember?

Suddenly the doors fly open and I spin on my heels, staggering backwards until the dressing table jabs me hard in the back. I wince as Queen Lanneth enters the room with a small army of maids at her back. She eyes me curiously from the doorway as she strokes her chin with her long, bony fingers.

"Did I startle you, daughter?"

The sound of that word on her lips fills me with disdain. I do not speak, only shake my head to keep myself from saying something I shouldn't.

"You look so pale," she remarks, strolling slowly towards me. "Not that I mind. I prefer it actually. But compared to the hue you arrived with, it makes you look noticeably unwell." She narrows her colorless eyes at me. "Are you unwell, Amara?"

I glimpse my serpent vine on the dressing table behind me, another leaf has fallen, and only one remains. I subtly slide across the dressing table to keep the plant from Lanneth's suspicious gaze. The vine and I share the same sickness, our spirits polluted by the gloom that rises from the depths of Baev'kalath.

"I am fine," I say, forcing my back to straighten even though all I want to do is lie down.

"Good," she replies. Her gaze flits around the room vacantly before returning to me. "And how did you sleep?"

"Fine," I lie. That seems to be the only word in my vocabulary at the moment.

"Well, I have excellent news. Your beloved husband has returned."

"I know," I reply lazily, my eyes half closed.

"You know? How do you know?" she asks.

Her question snaps me awake. Do I tell her I went to this room last night and threw myself out of his window? That his eyes were solid black? Or would that only reaffirm how insane I am becoming?

"I don't know," I say quickly, rubbing my fingers against my temples. "I'm not quite awake yet."

"Well, there is no time for rest now," she says. "The prince is back and you must attend to him."

The queen glides towards me with an eerie grace, each movement slow and deliberate. Then she extends her long, bony arm, the pale skin stretched tight over knuckles and sharp joints, fingers tipped with talon-like nails curling in the air. A breath lodges in my throat when she reaches for me and an icy dread settles in my bones when she lays her hand upon my belly.

"If the Pale Eye is kind, you will give our prince an heir. That is why I must be sure you are healthy and well." She scrapes the point of her thumbnail across my stomach and I shudder. "Human wombs can be ever so fragile."

"Thank you, Your Highness, I appreciate that," I reply, forcing the words through my teeth.

"Isn't this nice? This is how I wish it to be always between you and me. You are not alone here, Amara. Even though it can feel that way sometimes. I am here for you."

I nod half heartedly, but her eyes beckon me to speak. "Thank you, Your Highness," I say again to appease her.

"Mother," Lanneth says curtly. "Call me mother."

My stomach churns and I try to keep the bitterness from my tone. "Mother."

"That is what you will call me tonight, when the thrall houses come to banquet." Lanneth snaps her fingers and the maids rally into action, some charging the wardrobes and pulling out a selection of dresses while others begin filling the tub.

I notice Solena lingering in the back, avoiding my gaze.

"Banquet?" I ask as I am flanked by maids eager to get my nightgown off. I shrug them away.

"Only our court was present at your wedding. It is time for all Mordorin of the Untold Sea to set their eyes on you. Now that The Warrior's Eyes has passed, we can host our own celebration." She arches a curious brow as I gaze vacantly. "You look lost, daughter. Bad dream?"

I meet her eyes, narrowing my gaze, wondering if she can read minds.

"Dreams in Baev'kalath can be treacherous things," she sighs. "It is impossible to know in the endless night what is real, and what is not." Suddenly, Lanneth grabs the hand behind my back and yanks it to her. Her eyes fix on the bandage, her thumb smoothing out the bumps in the fabric, and when her sleeve inches up, I see the band of lunar tattoos around her wrist. "What is this?" she asks.

I mumble nonsense, not sure what to reply as she unravels the bandage. When the last sliver of cloth comes undone, my skin anxiously prickles with the anticipation of how Lanneth will react when she sees my oozing wound, but when she expresses nothing, I look as well.

The cut has healed. But there is no silvery line scarred into the skin. In fact, there is nothing at all. The skin is smooth, untouched, as new as the day I was born. But how?

Queen Lanneth furrows her brow. "Remarkable. Not even a scar?"

"Limmeth tea, your highness," Solena calls from behind. "I prepared some for her after the wedding. It seems to have quite a miraculous effect on humans."

Lanneth nods with interest. "Indeed. I will need to mention this to the druids." She holds out the bandage and a maid quickly relieves her of its burden. "Now you must prepare for tonight. It will not be easy. The thrall houses will not take kindly to a human bride. But they are loyal to their king and their prince. Be silent and smile. Allow Daedalus to win them to our side. Do you understand?"

I don't, but I nod. Anything to get Lanneth out of my chambers. At last she releases my hand and I can not wait to climb into the bath and wash her from my skin.

"I will see you tonight, Amara," she says as she departs.

Solena closes the doors behind her before joining me at my side, our eyes agape and staring in awe at my healed hand.

"Is it truly the tea?" I ask, flipping it left and right, inspecting it at every angle in case I've missed something.

Solena shrugs. "Perhaps it is. But the wound was doing so poorly, and at the very least, it would leave an angry scar." She exhales. "It's a miracle."

"I do not believe in miracles," I respond, my bottom lip clenched between my teeth. "Only magic."

The hours that pass are a whirl. I am bathed and dressed and escorted to the dining hall for breakfast. The king and queen are absent, far too busy with preparations for the banquet, and Daed does not make an appearance either. I eat alone and once I'm finished, I return to my chambers and go straight to the balcony. I do not even notice the icy taps of rain on my bare shoulders anymore. It has become as common to me as the wind through the trees of The Grove.

I grip the railing and my gaze finds Daed's tower across the courtyard. His balcony is empty, and my human eyes see no movement within the darkness of his room. But I can feel him. I feel his eyes watching me. Or is this another delusion? It is impossible to know the truth here. The smoke and shadows bend reality, making me question everything. Even things I know in my heart to be true.

What if it *was* a dream?

Not just the demon from the darkness, but that happened in the prince's tower as well? I wish Daed would step onto his balcony. I wish he would summon his mighty black wings and fly to me. I wish he would look at me with his eyes of the storm and tell me it all happened just as I remember it. Then I realize the confession I crave most. That it was him last night with his hands all over me, hungry for my skin, hungry for all of me, and my secret desire to have him break his promise.

His promise to not take me until I ask.

CHAPTER 13

Solena delicately moves the last strand of hair into place, then reaches into the jewelry box and selects an emerald comb. She slides it through the crown of braids atop my head, being mindful of the sharp tines, and does not let go until it sits precisely right. A hint of a smile cracks her focused expression.

"Perfect," she mutters.

I rise from the dressing table and stand before the mirror to take myself in. Not long ago I would have called this monstrosity, disgustingly opulent, almost grotesque. But now such careless words would be an insult to the maker of this stunning gown. The emerald green fabric, rich and lustrous, clings to my skin like liquid silk. The bodice is daringly fitted, its sweetheart neckline plunging low to reveal the curve of my collarbone and the swell of my chest. Tiny emeralds and diamonds trace intricate patterns along the fabric, catching the light with every movement. Delicate, off-the-shoulder sleeves leave my arms bare, draped in thin, jeweled chains that sparkle against my skin. Cinched at the waist, the gown flares into a skirt that flows like a waterfall of green silk, heavy with the weight of countless jewels and the hem is adorned with intricate beadwork, forming swirling patterns that cascade to the floor, with a train that sweeps behind me.

Solena spent a long while braiding my brown hair into coils and pinning them in place, but leaving a curtain of soft waves to frame my face. With a spattering of white powder and a sweep of heavy black eye makeup, I am ready to meet my unwanted subjects.

"You are beautiful, your grace," she says, an admission that she does not give easily.

But there is a softness to her voice, and she was so gentle while doing my hair and makeup. I'm so nervous about tonight, and a kind word would not go a miss. Is there enough goodwill between us?

"The queen says the thrall houses will not welcome me. What does that mean? What will they do?"

112

Solena is reluctant to speak at first, and I fear our relationship is unchanged. Formal and unfeeling, but then she exhales. "Most thrall houses are loyal to House Mordorin and will take up their swords when called. But there are some that do not want to go to war again. Their own houses have already dwindled in numbers after The Betrayers' Battle, and Fae children, especially High Fae, are not easily conceived. It can take years for a couple to produce a child, far too long to replenish an army." Her eyes scan the room as if searching for prying ears. "House Mordorin needs all the thrall houses to swear an oath to battle if they are to defeat the Legion. That is what Orios says."

My jaw falls open. "You mean the Blades they have in Baev'kalath are not enough?"

Again, Solena's eyes dart around my chambers. She leans toward me, her voice dropping to a whisper. "Protection for The Grove. That is what they promised you, isn't it?"

I nod, hanging on her next words.

Solena's head dips and she looks up at me from under her brow. "They barely have enough to protect Baev'kalath, let alone your lands."

My head shakes in soft disbelief. "But that means... if the thrall houses do not accept me..."

"Then both our homes could fall to the Legion," Solena finishes.

"But I have seen the power of the Mordorin," I say emphatically. "I have seen Daedalus turn to smoke. I have seen the Blades soar through the air and fight like beasts unleashed."

"Orios says not only have their numbers waned but also their gifts. Even with runes, some can no longer void walk, and there are even those whose wings refuse to spawn when summoned. He says it is a punishment from the void for their weakness."

A hundred more questions sit on the tip of my tongue.

But they retreat when Arax opens the doors.

"My princess. Your guests await you."

Solena curtseys and turns to leave, but I grab her wrist before she can escape. "You will come with me to the banquet as my handmaiden," I say, my tone firm, but only because I do not want her to refuse me if given an option.

Her head jerks back in surprise. "Your Highness?"

I lean closer, urgency threading my voice. "I know nothing of Fae politics. I don't know who anyone is or what I'm supposed to say or do around them. I need you."

For a moment, her glare softens, vulnerability flickering in her eyes. "You... need me?"

I nod, my heart pounding. "Please, Solena. Come with me to this banquet, so I don't make a fool of myself."

In this moment of desperation, I lay myself bare before her, vulnerable and exposed, waiting for her answer.

"We would not want that," she replies. "I will need a moment to make myself presentable."

A wave of relief washes over me. "Take your time. I am in no hurry."

As Arax and I wait for her return, I decide not to spare him from my anxiety either. "Will there be many there tonight?" I ask, fidgeting with the jewels adorning my dress, their cool touch doing little to calm my nerves.

He nods, his gaze fixed ahead. "Hundreds."

My shoulders slump at the weight of his words. "And they all... hate me?"

"Not all," he says, and for a brief moment, my shoulders lift in hope. "Just most."

That hope fades as my shoulders drop even lower. Why I thought Arax would be a sympathetic ear, I'm not sure. But slowly, he glances at me from the corner of his eye, his expression shifting.

"Do not fear. You are strong. Fae respect strength."

A smile cracks the thin line of my mouth. "You think I'm strong?"

"I don't think. I know."

"Thank you, Arax," I say softly, and he grumbles in response, his focus returning to the distance. Yet his words linger, a small kindness that distracts me from my rising nerves and encourages me to stand tall.

Moments later, Solena returns in a soft ivory dress, the lightweight silk draping gracefully to the floor. The fitted bodice accentuates her slim waist, and delicate lace trim adorns the neckline and sleeves. The forest green apron tied neatly around her waist perfectly complements my gown. Her black hair is styled in a simple yet elegant updo, with a few loose tendrils framing her face, and a delicate silver hairpin adorned with small green stones glimmers in the light.

"You look beautiful," I say.

Her chin drops to her chest, a rare moment where I leave her at a loss for words. "It was hard finding green accents."

"Well, you did an excellent job," I reply.

I rush to Solena's side, though the weight of my dress keeps me from reaching her as swiftly as I'd like. When I meet her in the center of the room, I link arms with her, clinging to the contact as if she's my only anchor in this sea of uncertainty. She looks taken aback by my sudden familiarity, but I remember my wedding and the crushing loneliness I felt among the Fae. I don't trust Daed to make me feel any more at ease now than he did then.

Comfort is a concept I doubt he understands.

Arax leads us toward the throne room, and it seems every Blade has been summoned to line the halls. As I pass by the arches, I catch sight of ships docking in the harbor, their sails billowing in the evening breeze, while the sky is filled with Fae wings as more arrive by air. I grip Solena's arm tighter, my heart racing with each step, and I'm surprised when she squeezes back.

I look at her and manage a smile, and when she returns it with a clipped grin of her own, I can't help but wonder if we are finally starting to understand one another.

We arrive at the antechamber where groups of Fae gather, waiting to be announced. The Fae of Baev'kalath stand apart with their dark hair and steely eyes, but the other Fae here are just as distinctive. Some have red eyes and long, thin sheets of hair that hang below their knees, while others are draped in heavy furs, their heads shaven to the scalp with only a braided top knot remaining. These must be members of the thrall houses.

"House Sylthara of Thal'Morven," Solena whispers in my ear, gesturing toward the Fae with red eyes. "Their Lord Sarberos is one of the oldest High Fae. See their runes?" She tips her chin, and I notice the Fae's pale throats adorned with intricate black tattoos. "They use those runes to conjure ice and sleet. Their runeweaver is exceptional—the lines are flawless."

"Runeweaver?"

"Those tasked with tattooing the runes onto skin. There are many levels of mastery." She smiles coyly. "I was a runeweaver before I came to Baev'kalath. So was my mother, and her mother before her."

"You don't runeweave anymore?" I ask, hoping I'm using the term correctly.

"Baev'kalath boasts dozens of artisan weavers. I'm merely a novice in comparison. Perhaps one day I'll return to it, but for now, mastering your unruly hair is challenge enough."

I furrow my brow as Solena stifles a giggle, and for the first time, I don't mind her teasing.

115

Arax grows weary of waiting, storming forward and extending his arms, forcing everyone to make room for me at the front of the line.

Although they move, not one amongst them is happy to do so. They scowl and whisper to each other. But just as I have grown accustomed to the constant rain and decadent gowns, so too have I accepted that I am despised by all Fae. Luckily, this dress protects me as well as a suit of armor, and even though Solena and I make a strange pair, it is nice to feel as if I am not alone for once.

The doors fall open and a wave of music, laughter and chatter floods the foyer. The room is dense with Fae and I can not even see the thrones on the dais at the other end of the hall. Arax pauses, and I can hear his surly grumble as he taps his foot impatiently. When we still receive no attention from the jabbering assembly, he pounds his fist hard against his armor chest piece and roars.

"Lords and ladies of Mordorin. Make way for Princess Amara Phaedren."

My chest tightens. It is the first time I have heard his last name attached to me. But I have no time to digest it. The crowd falls silent and turns in unison, peering over shoulders and shuffling for a better position, all scrambling to get a closer look at the human bride. I am glad I can not hear their thoughts. They move towards the sides of the hall, revealing a grand banquet table that stretches the length of the room, all the way to the stone thrones before the stained glass window.

Silver candelabras rise from the table, casting an ethereal light over the twisted branch centerpieces. The branches, blackened and bare, entwine with roses so dark they could be soaked in the same blood as the wine, their edges dusted with frost. The air is thick with the scent of roasted game glazed in honey, mingling with the sweet, spicy aroma of exotic fruits and the earthy fragrance of wild mushrooms. Platters overflow with rich, decadent foods—meats spiced and roasted to perfection, velvety soups garnished with flowers that seem too beautiful to eat, and desserts that glisten like treasures, dusted in silver and wrapped in webs of spun sugar. It's all so enchanting, but as always, there's something menacing in the opulence.

Arax cuts a path through the guests. I stay close in his shadow with Solena at my side, not daring to stray too far, and once or twice he glances over my shoulder to be sure I am still there. I feel the weight of the Fae's eyes upon me, inspecting and criticizing every inch of me as I pass them by. They say nothing, but they don't need to. Their upturned, pointed noses and subtle shakes of their elegant heads speak volumes.

"They're all so beautiful," I mutter to Solena, taking in their silken hair and impossibly stunning features, despite the sneers directed at me. It feels as if I can sense the power radiating from them, the light bending and shimmering in their presence.

She scoffs. "Some of them, but most glamor themselves to appear more attractive than they truly are. It's a terrible waste of powerful magic—transforming your eye color or smoothing out a few wrinkles."

At the end of the table, King Kaelus and Queen Lanneth rise from their thrones on the dais in perfect unison as I approach. Kaelus is dressed in a midnight-blue tunic of heavy silk, the fabric adorned with bold silver embroidery that swirls in intricate, ancient patterns, like storm clouds rolling across his broad shoulders and cascading down his sleeves. Beside him, Lanneth is draped in shimmering ivory satin that clings to her long, gaunt frame. A dazzling diamond choker encircles the creamy skin of her neck, while her face is caked in thick white powder. If her goal was to resemble a nightmarish specter, she has certainly succeeded.

I notice something different about the dais tonight as the moonlight filters through the stained glass and dapples the stone with swirls of color. A fourth throne to the side of the king and queen, positioned next to Daed's throne.

But my husband is not here.

"Princess Amara," Kaelus says, his arms unfurled.

Solena carefully slips her arm from mine, and Arax steps aside, allowing me to join the king and queen on the dais. As I stand before King Kaelus, I hesitate, unsure of what to do. We have never embraced, barely even spoken. This gesture, I suspect, is purely for the benefit of the guests.

Doing what is expected, I let Kaelus pull me into his arms. The hug is warm but awkward, and I have no idea where to place my hands. Thankfully, it's over before I can dwell on it. With a stiff pat on my shoulder, he sends me toward Lanneth.

I endure the queen's icy, skeletal embrace as her arms wind around me, every jutting bone poking and prodding against my body. The moment is mercifully brief, and she gestures toward the second throne at her side, releasing me from her grasp.

"For you, daughter," she says, her pale pink lips curving into a smile.

I walk to the throne and pick up the edges of my gown, then sink into the hard, cold stone. It is just a chair. A silly chair of no real importance. I tell myself this to keep calm and stop my heart from beating straight out of my chest.

But it is not just a chair. It is a throne. A throne for a princess of House Mordorin, a title none of the Fae staring daggers at me believe I should wear.

"Where is Daedalus?" I ask, swallowing hard. I wish he were here for many reasons, but mostly because his love of attention and ability to command a room would shift the focus away from me.

But the way Kaelus and Lanneth exchange sidelong glances and release weary exhales makes it clear they don't know their son's whereabouts either.

Kaelus leans on his knee and hisses at Arax. "Find your prince," he orders.

Arax bows and takes a heavy step forward, but before he can move any further, the grand doors swing open.

I sense him before he even enters the hall—the dark presence I know all too well.

There he stands, draped in black from head to toe. His finely tailored jacket clings to his broad shoulders, the fabric so dark it seems to swallow the light. Golden stitching weaves along the edges, intricate and regal, glinting in the night. Each step he takes is measured and confident, his heavy leather boots echoing on the stone floor, a rhythm that quickens my pulse despite myself.

Daedalus strides towards the dais, moving with a predator's grace, each stride purposeful. The air around him seems to hum with a dangerous energy, drawing the eyes of every guest he passes. I can see it in their faces—male and female alike—how they can't help but be captivated by the dark allure he exudes, as if they're caught in the pull of something they can't quite name. He owns the room without a word, without a glance, and I despise and admire him for it in equal measure.

As he approaches the throne, I force myself to meet his gaze, even as my heart pounds harder in my chest. There's something about the way he looks at me; a proprietary glint in those gray eyes that makes my blood run both hot and cold. I hate him for the power he holds over me, for the way his presence alone sends a shiver down my spine.

Kaelus's shoulders sag with relief as he rises to greet his son. They clasp each other's forearms before pulling into a firm embrace.

"Son," Kaelus breathes. "Welcome." The king glances at me, his eyes wide with urgency. "Amara. Come."

I rise from the chair that I fear will never feel comfortable and wait to hear what I'm supposed to do next. But instead of instructions, Daed extends his hand to me. I look at his stern face, but he does not meet my gaze. He splays his fingers impatiently, so I slip my hand into his grip and he closes his grasp.

"Kindred. Brethren. Fae of Mordorin," Kaelus booms. "I welcome you to Baev'kalath, seat of our ancient house, and ask that you join us to feast and celebrate the union of our prince. Heir to the throne of the Sundered Kingdoms. Commander of the Ebon Flight. Daedalus Phaedren and his bride, Amara, Jewel of the Tenders."

A tense silence settles over the assembly, the kind that prickles against the skin. No one dares to speak, but their bitter expressions radiate outrage.

This can't be the first they've heard of our marriage, can it?

I think back to our hurried wedding. At the time, I had no idea what thrall houses were, but now I realize everyone present that night must have been Mordorin of Baev'kalath.

I swallow hard. *Souls. The others here don't know.*

"What is the meaning of this, Kaelus," asks a tall, willowy male with red eyes like hot embers. "You could join your son with any of our daughters, but you choose a human?"

Kaelus raises his hand. "This is not the time, Sarberos."

Two women, with identical features and shaven heads, wearing heavy, sable fur cloaks, push their way to the front.

"This is an insult," one shrieks, baring her sharpened canine teeth. "The humans are traitors!"

The second snarls. "Our glorious dead rot in the ground and you expect us to feast with this... thing?"

"Vashar. Vasheeth," Kaelus says, acknowledging the twins with a nod of his chin. "The war is over. The battle is won. If our houses are to survive, we must make allies of the humans. A long journey starts with a single step." Kaelus offers me a smile. "Amara is that step for House Mordorin." He returns his attention to the assembly. "For all our houses!"

Another Fae steps forward, young and handsome with a shock of copper hair and bronze, bottomless eyes. There is a charming playfulness to his wide grin, an easiness to his bearing that I've not seen in the Fae I've met. He does not address King Kaelus, his eyes immediately settling on Daedalus instead.

"And you, prince," the bold Fae calls. "What do you have to say about your human bride?"

The question draws a half smile from Daed's lips. "Lord Reon. It has been many moons since I have seen you at banquet. Isn't this all too boring for you?"

The knowing smirk on Reon's lips hints to me he and Daed know each other beyond the formalities of their titles.

"I thought the Warrior's Eye would be my excitement for the phase, but I am glad I left Eyr'Drogul this evening. The banquets are suddenly far more interesting than I remember," Reon replies. "So tell me, Rook. What makes this human so special that we should bow before her?"

My heart thumps hard in my chest.

Daed still does not look at me, as if he is making an effort to ignore me. I am not expecting any emotional outpouring on my behalf. In fact, given his sullen mood, I wouldn't be surprised if he threw me to the wolves.

I hear the deep breaths rumble in his chest and notice his upper lip twitch, revealing his sharp canines. His grip tightens around my hand, but this thumb unexpectedly smooths over my skin.

"Lords and ladies," Daed calls to the assembly, and all fall silent. "This is not a mere human before you. She may not have the blood of the Fae running through her veins, but she does not need it. What she does possess is more than enough; honor, dignity, bravery, more than some of you have." The room stirs with discontent, and even Kaelus and Lanneth shift in their thrones. "So, good Lord Reon, when you ask me why you should all bow before her, you mistake my intent. I do not expect you to bow before my wife. *I expect you to crawl.*"

Gasps and outcries erupt through the assembly, a chaotic swell of disbelief. But amidst the uproar, I catch a glimpse of Lord Reon. He simply grins, a glint of amusement in his eyes, as if the chaos itself is nothing more than an entertaining spectacle.

Daed does not speak to silence the raucous. Instead, he reaches skyward, his fingers curled as smoke seeps from his skin, weaving like a serpent between his fingers. From this slithering murk, his blade takes shape. The hilt emerges first, gleaming silver. Then the guard, encrusted with jewels, encircling a moonstone that seems to hold a tiny storm within, its facets shifting and gleaming in the moonlight.

As the blade fully forms, its edges are impossibly sharp, and the silver so pure and flawless that it reflects everything around it; the assembly of cowering Fae, the anxious king and queen, even the terrified princess. But most of all, it reflects Daed. This sword is not just a weapon—it is an extension of the darkness that summoned it, the darkness within its wielder. Vicious. Furious. Bloodthirsty.

120

The warrior I had been waiting for. The one who would save us all.

The Fae fall silent, submitting to the power of the blade, and I hear them whisper its name with reverence.

Death Singer.

Daed twirls the mighty blade in his hand before driving it hard into the dais, blinding sparks flying when the blade strikes stone and the sharp clanging noise stings my ears. His eyes narrow on Reon.

"Does that answer your question? Lord of Eyr'Drogul?"

Reon smiles and bows. "Yes, it does, my prince. A little theatrical, but I get the point."

Daed replies with a smirk. "Excellent," and as if it had never existed, the sword vanishes in a wisp of black smoke. "Now. Who is hungry?" The only replies are a few sheepish murmurs. Daed nods. "Then let us feast." He turns to me at last. "Shall we, wife?"

I'm so in awe of the power and command he wields, I stutter like a fool, and when he smiles softly at me, I feel myself falling, even though I am standing perfectly still.

Daed grips my hand, then goes to leave the dais, but Kaelus roughly grips his shoulder before we descend.

"Be careful son," he whispers near his ear. "Poke these animals with a stick too often and they will bite back."

"They are thrall houses," Daed mutters curtly. "They serve us."

Kaelus' upper lip curls bitterly and he goes to speak, but stops with his mouth half open when he remembers I am here. He swallows whatever it was he was going to say. "Just be careful," he says again.

Daed pays the king no heed as he leads me down the steps of the dais. We stand beside the banquet table and I realize there are no chairs.

"Where do we sit?" I ask.

He chuckles arrogantly and I frown. *How am I supposed to know why Fae banquets have no chairs?*

"We stand," he explains. "We move up and down so we can try everything and mingle with each other."

I scrunch my nose up at anything on the table with a face, but the fat red berries look especially tempting. Daed notices my interest.

"Eat them," he says.

I look around for silverware but find none. "With my hands?" I ask.

"You could try your toes, but it feels a little unseemly for a princess, don't you think?"

It doesn't happen often, but when Daed is content, his eyes soften, and the stone gray changes to swirls of silver clouds. A dramatic change from the black-eyed beast whose hands roamed over every inch of my body last night.

I give half a smile as I snatch up a berry and pop it into my waiting mouth. When my teeth break through the firm flesh, the juice bursts in waves of flavour that have my eyes rolling with bliss.

Daed's teeth graze his bottom lip as he watches me react. "Good, is it?"

I nod as I chew, reaching for another, and that is when Daed takes note of my hand.

"Your bandage," he says. "It's gone." He flips it over, dragging his thumb along where the cut once was, sending a shiver through me. "How is this possible? Not even a scar?"

I want to tell him about the dream—to ask if what happened in his tower was real, or just another trick of my imagination. But before I can speak, his pointed ears prick, his head snapping toward the doorway just as the massive doors swing open. A sudden commotion follows, the air thick with cursing and the scuffle of bodies as the banquet's latest arrivals force their way through the crowd. Their brashness is jarring amidst the elegance of the gathering, their movements disruptive until they come to an abrupt halt. Their eyes lock onto Daed and me at the table, and the entire room seems to hold its breath.

This house is a ragged lot, their clothes a haphazard mix of worn leather, threadbare linen, and tattered cloaks, all in dark, muted colors. Their hair is wild and unkempt, some having braids that have long since frayed, while others wear loose, tangled waves framing faces marked by scars.

There is a raw, menacing energy about them, an air of barely restrained violence. Their weapons, crude and wicked, hang at their sides and as the Fae male at the head of the group stares at us in silence, I feel the tension rising. His long coat, probably once a rich crimson, is now faded and worn, patched with scraps of dark leather. The coat flares out as he moves, revealing a belt bristling with daggers. It is hard to make out the color of his eyes beneath his unkempt curtain of wavy, dark hair, but I know for certain he is watching me.

Daed does not acknowledge him, instead he pinches a berry between his fingers and tosses it into his mouth.

"Prince Daedalus," the male says, his voice low and gravelly. "Is it true?"

"Is what true, Modok?" Daed sighs, eating another berry.

I feel Modok's empty eyes burn through me.

"That this *thing* is your wife," he spits with venom.

Daed releases a long, heavy breath and rolls his shoulders. "I would not say such things if I were you."

He reaches for another berry, but this time Modok grabs him by the wrist. The surrounding guests gasp and fall back a safe distance, as if knowing the consequences of such an action against the Prince of the Sundered Kingdoms.

Daed's composure shocks me. I already expect Modok's decapitated head to be rocking side to side beside the sugared yams, but Daed has not moved a muscle, which is even more unnerving.

"House Merrin of Mor'Thravar can not abide such... perversion."

I notice Daed's other hand twitch under the table, his fingers writhing as he summons wisps of smoke to work his will. I remember Death Singer, the share size of it, and now I take a step back in case the sword suddenly appears.

"Enough!" Kaelus yells as he descends the dais with Lanneth at his side. "You will release your prince, Modok!"

The Fae from his house swaps glances, and I wonder if they're weighing up their odds of escaping this dining hall alive if they do not obey the king.

"Now, Modok," Kaelus repeats, his teeth bared.

Modok grunts and pulls back his hand.

Daed's jaw clenches as he rubs the skin around his wrist, the smoke he commands slowly fading to nothing. "I have killed for less than that," he snarls.

Modok glances in my direction, his face twisted with disgust. "This is not right. Mor'Thravar will not fight for a human."

Kaelus grits his teeth. "Bring your people, Modok. We will discuss this in private." He taps Daed's shoulder. "You too."

Kaelus cuts a path through the guests, his arm linked with Lanneth as they lead Modok and his cronies through the archway of an adjoining room. Daed lingers behind.

"Stay here. Talk to no one," he says firmly. "Arax is close by if you need him. His heart may have softened in his old age, but his blade still cuts through bone with a single stroke." Daed looks me deep in the eyes. "If anyone tries to disrespect you, command him to make them bleed. Do you understand?"

Though I'm sure he's trying to reassure me, I'm more nervous now than I was before.

"I will return to you soon," he says. His eyes roam over my face, a gentleness to his gaze. "You look beautiful tonight, Amara."

I gulp and I'm sure my heart stops beating all together.

Daed leaves me at the table, joining his father and the others departure through the arch. My appetite leaves me similarly. Solena said that Baev'kalath alone cannot defeat the Legion. That it will take all the thrall houses, including this Modok from Mor'Thravar. I can not just stand here while those who care the least discuss the fate of The Grove. I should be there too, convincing them to fight for us.

I must know what is going on in that room.

I know what I must do, and as I discretely slip away from the table, avoiding Arax's seeking eyes, I already regret it.

CHAPTER 14

The shadows are my cover as I slide along the walls and behind the dais to keep hidden from sight. Fortunately, the thrall houses are too preoccupied with gossiping about me to actually care whether I am present or not.

I approach the arch where Daedalus vanished, only to be blocked by a Reaper stepping into my path. At first, I think Arax has found me, but when the helm is removed, I find myself staring into Frane's piercing violet eyes.

"Are you lost, Princess?" she asks, her voice laced with a hard edge.

"No," I reply, straightening my shoulders and feigning confidence. "I'm just exploring."

"Hasn't anyone told you that wandering through Baev'kalath is dangerous? This fortress is so vast you might vanish forever, or tumble off a balcony and plunge into the ocean if you're not careful."

"I'm aware," I snap, irritation bubbling to the surface at her attempt to intimidate me.

Her eyes skim over me, a look of distaste crossing her face. "I don't understand what all the fuss is about. Of all the humans he could have chosen, what makes you so special? Was there really no one else?"

"I thought the same when I learned you'd taken Arax's place with the Reapers. Mordorin stock must be in dire straits if you're the best they can muster."

Frane's fist clenches, the metal of her chain mail grinding ominously. She speaks through gritted teeth. "I should have thrown you off the ship when I had the chance. I may not be a lord, but I stand with their concerns. You will be the downfall of House Mordorin."

I tilt my head, a smile playing at the corners of my lips. "We can only hope. Now, will you move aside? Or would you prefer I summon my husband, the prince, so you can voice your concerns to him?"

Frane swallows hard, her glare faltering beneath her helm as she pulls it back over her head. She bows sharply, then turns on her heel, rejoining the banquet.

I release the breath I had been holding, though it sputters out, the corset squeezing me tight. I return to the archway and find a heavy, deep blue tapestry draping over the doorway. At the center of the fabric, a large ivory eye watches over several winged figures kneeling in prayer. The Pale Eye, no doubt.

Fae gods are mysterious things. To some, the Fae themselves are fit to be gods with their strength and their magic. So a being who can bring them to their knees must be a magnificent thing indeed. The Pale Eye and the moon are connected, I've deduced that much in my time here, and as she resides in the sky, she must be the Mother Above. Then who is the Father Below? Arax called him that. But did not give him a name.

My stomach churns and my throat goes dry. Or have I heard the name already? *Gygarth*.

I close my eyes, reluctant to recall the horror emerging from that impossibly black abyss, but when I see the flash of teeth and feel the heat of its breath on my skin, I gasp and my eyes open wide, watery with fright. Gygarth. The Father Below. Too terrifying for any tapestry or painting, and too nightmarish for even the Mordorin to idolize. Why does he torment me?

The smallest gap allows me to peek into the room behind the tapestry. There is no one inside the small square space, but there is a door leading to a second room. I slip past the tapestry, again keeping to the sides, my every step light and deft as a feline, even though the weight of my dress makes me feel more like a tiptoeing ox. The door is every so slightly ajar, enough for flickers of candlelight to dapple the floor and the low thrum of voices to drift on the air.

With my back hard against the wall, I notice a mural on the wall across from me. There is not enough light to see things clearly, but I strain my eyes to make out a backdrop of waves and several islands crowned with castles. The island at the center is the largest, with Baev'kalath written in cursive beneath it. The surrounding islands are much smaller, some close, some in the very corners of the mural.

Mor'Thravar. Eyr'Drogul. Thal'Morven. Fyn'Rothar. Gryn'Velcor. Jor'Thalas.

The islands ruled by the thrall houses of the Mordorin, all sworn to King Kaelus.

Mor'Thravar and their Lord Modok, who somehow escaped the banquet with his head still on his shoulders, are the most remote island, and much larger than the other thrall houses.

This must be why he is needed.

I stand as close to the door as I dare and hold my breath.

"What use is an alliance with the humans," Modok snaps. "Do they have an army? Something of worth?"

"No," I hear Kaelus grumble.

"Then what!" Modok roars. "The prince should have been married to one of my sisters. My warriors are second only to the Blades. You know this."

"Unfortunately, your sisters have proven themselves untrustworthy," Kaelus replies curtly.

Modok goes quiet for a moment before muttering. "And she has been dealt with, has she not? I have others."

"Can you remember the last time you saw a Fae baby, Modok?" Lanneth questions tersely. "House Mordorin doesn't just need brides, it needs heirs. A human womb is easier to seed. After all these centuries, I would wager that Fae bastards outnumber we pure Fae."

"So your selfishness would see our glorious Mordorin bloodline tainted with mongrels, then?" Modok snarls.

"Everything I do, I do for House Mordorin," Lanneth replies, her voice a guttural whisper. "You can not dare to perceive the things I have done."

"I don't care," Modok spits. "This marriage is treachery to our kind. As long as she is princess, Mor'Thravar's wings stay sheathed."

"You pledged an oath to serve!" Daedalus booms, his voice sending a shiver through me. "You will fulfil that oath or I will see your house burned to the ground."

"Burn us to ash then," Modok replies with venom. "And see all Mordorin fall to the Legion like the other houses."

Even without seeing his face, I can feel the ire swelling within Daed, his voice a deep, gravely growl. "Or perhaps I cut you down right now? Maybe your sisters will hold true to their oaths when I serve them your head."

"Enough!" Kaelus grunts. "Modok. Your king needs you. What price must be paid?"

"Banish the human, and Mor'Thravar remains yours to command, my king."

Modok speaks so carelessly of me, as if I am property, not a person, and his request is such a simple thing. My heart beats so hard in my chest I fear its thumps will give me away. It feels as if a lifetime passes before anyone speaks again.

"Let us consider your bargain, Modok," Kaelus finally replies in a slow exhale. "We will have an answer for you by morning."

Without warning, the door swings open and Modok strides out. I throw my hand over my mouth, burying myself as deep into a darkened corner as I can. Fortunately, Modok has such fury in his step that he storms through the room, pushing his way past the tapestry without looking back.

I hold the sigh of relief in my chest. I won't let that little breath be my undoing. But now the door is wide open, filling this room with candlelight, allowing no pockets of darkness for me to hide in. Do I sneak out, hoping that Daed and his parents do not walk by the door and see me? If I stay put, I will surely be found when they decide to rejoin the banquet.

I must try to make my escape.

"Your combativeness does nothing to keep the peace between us and Modok," Kaelus says. "You know our position."

"I do not understand why we are even negotiating with him," Daedalus argues. "We are their lords."

"It's not as easy as that. Not now," Kaelus says. "What would you have us do? Destroy them? We might as well destroy ourselves."

I bite my lip, preparing to take a step towards the tapestry, but the next words from Daed's mouth freeze me in place.

"Send her away," he mutters, his voice barely a whisper. "Put her on a ship and send her back to The Grove."

A pang strikes my heart and I'm suddenly cold. He is saying the words I've longed for since I first arrived in Baev'kalath. So why do they hurt like a dull blade through the chest?

"You would send your wife away with such ease, Daedalus?" Lanneth says.

All thoughts of escaping this room vanish as I press my cheek on the stone wall and wait for his answer.

"Yes," he replies. "I do. Let me be rid of her now."

The words pierces through me. His coldness towards me has always been clear, the distance and loathing in his eyes. It wasn't so long ago that I loathed him myself, that his arrogance and cutting words stirred only anger in me. But somewhere in the midst of our clashes, something changed. Words slung in anger would spark and ignite in the air between us. It has been maddening... and intoxicating, but I've grown to crave those moments, those heated exchanges that leave my heart pounding long after he's gone.

I thought—I dared to hope—whatever this is that he felt it too. I was wrong. Even in our most intimate moments, where my body silently but desperately yearned for his touch, it meant nothing to him. I was nothing to him. A burden. A nuisance. How could I have let this happen? I've been falling so fast I can't even remember when I jumped.

"It is not as simple as that," Lanneth says, her voice hollow in my ears. "We need her. *You know this*."

"Then these are your problems to solve," Daedalus replies sharply. "You are the ones who burdened me with this human wife."

"Would you rather it had been a Fae bride?" Lanneth exhales. "Like she was?"

My ears prick and my hand grips the wall, my fingernails digging into the grooves between the stone.

What did she say? Like who was? Am I not the prince's first wife? I recall the portrait over his mantle and the very thought of it fills me with a sadness edged with jealousy.

I am no longer thinking about escaping. I'm not thinking about anything at all. All I want to do is hear more. I take a step forward, closer to the door, but as I move, my foot gets tangled in the beaded hem of my dress. I brace myself on the wall, catching myself before I fall, but all I can do is watch when the string of beads snaps, and dozens of tiny black orbs hit the ground and roll across the stone.

The voices fall silent, and my entire body pulses with every boot step that thunders towards the door.

There is nowhere to run. Nowhere to hide. They will walk in here at any moment, and soon know that I have heard many things. Things I should not have heard. Compared to what I fear they have in store for me, sending me back to The Grove would be a blessing. All I can do is wait.

Suddenly there is a pop in my ears and a burst of smoke fogs my vision. A chain-mail glove covers my mouth, muffling my stunned squeek, and a second later, I am swallowed up into a black void before reappearing in the familiar surroundings of my chambers.

I keel over, stumbling forward and bracing myself on the bed. The nausea is too intense this time, but I'm aware enough to grab a vase hurriedly from the side table to use as a vessel. I drag my sleeve across my mouth when I'm done, my chest heaving with shallow breaths.

"Are you alright, Your Highness?" Arax asks.

With my head still bowed, I return the soiled vase to the table. "No. Not really," I mumble, wrapping my arms around the bedpost to keep steady. I glance around my chambers in a haze. "You can void walk such a great distance?"

"I have been wielding the void long enough to know it better than most. You shouldn't have been in that room," he grumbles, the disappointment evident in his tone.

I give a floppy nod. "I understand that now."

"What did you hear?" he asks.

I turn my head to take in his face, his brow furrowed, his hooded eyes staring at me beneath his bushy gray eyebrows. Even though Arax has shown me some semblance of kindness, I can not let myself believe he is someone to be trusted. Nothing is real in this place.

"I didn't hear anything," I mutter, slowly standing on my own two feet.

His eyes narrow. "I don't believe you."

I shrug, meeting him with an unflinching glare. "So what happens now?"

Arax rolls his broad shoulders and weighs me up in his stern gaze. "Now I return to the banquet to tell the king and queen that the food did not sit well with you, so I escorted you back to your chambers. I'll find Solena to help ready you for bed."

I nod my agreement, but keep my face impassive, my mouth a straight line.

Arax bows, then turns on his heels, closing the doors behind him as he leaves me alone in my chambers. As soon as he's gone, I slump forward, bracing my hands on my knees as I draw in as much air as my lungs can hold. My relief makes me dizzy, but still my nerves and fear knot in my stomach. Arax saved me. He saw I was about to be caught, but rather than raise the alarm or simply watch and do nothing, he aided my escape. Now he goes to lie on my behalf. Those are not the actions of someone who means me harm.

The doors to my chambers swing open, and Solena slips into the room, her expression a mix of concern and curiosity.

"What happened? Where did you go?"

I remind myself to keep my thoughts guarded for my own protection. "I felt unwell," I reply, continuing the lie Arax spun.

"What a shame. I had hoped that now your hand is healed, you might feel better."

130

There's a genuine warmth in her tone that eases some of the tension coiling in my chest.

"Lord Reon was looking for you," Solena says, a teasing lilt to her voice. "He wanted to request a dance."

My brow furrows in confusion. "Really? Why?"

"Because you are beautiful, Your Highness?" she grins, mischief dancing in her eyes.

I frown skeptically. "He did not seem to think that highly of me."

"Your first mistake with the Fae is assuming that if a male seems to dislike you, he doesn't also want you in his bed. The line between disdain and desire is a very fine one."

Her words ring with more truth than she realizes, settling heavily in the air between us.

"Well, I'm glad I wasn't there to accept," I say, trying to brush off the unsettling implications.

"Probably best for both of you. If the prince had seen you, he would have likely served Reon's head for dessert."

"The prince wouldn't care," I mutter, skepticism coloring my voice.

"I doubt that's true," Solena replies, her tone firm. "This may be an arranged marriage, but any Mordorin bride is treated the same by her husband. It's law."

"And what law is that?" I ask, curiosity piqued.

"You are his," she says nonchalantly. "His wife. His confidante. His lover. No man may look at you, touch you, or even think about you. Any who does issues a challenge to the prince."

"Even a lord?"

"Especially a lord," Solena affirms. "I can only imagine what would happen if Prince Daedalus returned to find you in Lord Reon's arms. The prince has a temper."

Images of last night flash through my mind—Daed's eyes completely black, his voice twisted and foreign, as if something dark controlled him.

"Can the moon really make the Mordorin act... differently?" I ask, avoiding her gaze, hoping to conceal the turmoil brewing within me.

Solena eyes me suspiciously. "It can. The Pale Eye has a profound effect on the Mordorin Fae. She brings us into the world and embraces us when we leave. Her phases empower us, stir our memories, and ignite our passions. We like to believe the Mother Above is the reason the Mordorin survived the Betrayers' Battle when all others faded."

"Would she make your eyes turn solid black? Make you act so differently that you become unrecognizable?"

Solena's curiosity deepens, and she furrows her brow. "No. The Mother doesn't cause black eyes. That belongs to something else—something darker."

"The void?" I gulp, the word hanging heavy in the air.

She nods, but her expression remains guarded. "You've heard of the void, then?"

"Arax mentioned it in bits and pieces."

"He seems to have taken a liking to you," Solena remarks, her tone edged with surprise. "Which is rare, especially considering he lost his position because you saved his life."

"That isn't fair, and I'll tell that to the king. Arax shouldn't have to suffer because I didn't want him to die."

"Why *didn't* you want him to die?" Solena asks, her voice sharp, as if this question has been weighing on her mind for a long time.

I sink onto the bed, taking a deep breath to steady myself. "Because death is frightening and final, and I have the power to prevent it. What good is this gift if I don't use it?"

"But why save a Fae?" Solena presses, her intrigue evident.

I ponder her question, feeling the complexities swirl in my mind, making the answer elusive. At last, I reply, "I didn't see him as Fae when I acted. I just knew he was dying, and I could help."

Solena studies me with her thoughtful eyes, assessing. "I think I may have underestimated you, Princess Amara. You're not the simple, treacherous, cowardly human I once thought you were."

I frown, unsure how to take her words. "Thank you?"

She dips her chin slightly, as if to acknowledge my gratitude, but I sense she doesn't realize her compliment isn't as kind as she believes.

"Now, if you are feeling unwell again, would you like me to help you get ready for bed, Your Highness?" she asks, shifting the conversation.

I nod wearily and she hurries to my side and begins undressing me. I'm not concerned anymore with modesty or my dislike of being attended so preciously. I just want this dress off. She pops open each button, easing the dress of my shoulders until it falls under its own weight and it crumples around my knees. Solena tugs at the strings of my corset and when the last one comes undone I can finally hunch forward and breath a little easier.

Solena retrieves a delicate silk nightgown from the wardrobe and slips it over my head, gently tying the ribbon at the bust to cinch the ivory fabric snugly against my chest. She then guides me to the dressing table and sits me down, carefully removing the emerald comb from my hair before brushing it through with soft, methodical strokes.

I lose myself in the glinting prisms of the comb, its smooth surface like a window to another world—still, peaceful, and so safe that I foolishly wish I could shrink and disappear into it to escape everything.

When Solena places the brush on the dressing table, I know she's finished. She strolls to the bed and pulls back the covers.

"Will that be all, Your Highness?"

I rise and drift toward the arch, dodging the falling rain as I gaze out at the rolling ocean. The sounds of festivities float through the air, laughter and music echoing off the stone walls. My mind feels like a prism, fragmented like the emerald in the comb I clutch. Thoughts and feelings swirl within me so intensely that I can't focus on any one thing. Instead, it's a chaotic blend of smoke and ash, moonlight and shadows, desire and despair.

Life was so much simpler before I set foot on that ship—perhaps too simple. Now, I feel utterly unprepared for what I've endured—mentally, physically, emotionally—and even more so for what lies ahead. I know nothing of the politics of the houses or the complexities of Fae law, nor do I understand what is expected of a Fae wife. I don't know how to respond to my husband's touch—whether to refuse him or surrender myself completely.

I am the Jewel of the Tenders, chosen among my people to serve and guide. Yet here in Baev'kalath, I can't shake the fear that I am merely the frail human they perceive me to be.

"Your Highness," Solena calls again, her voice cutting through my thoughts. "Are you alright?"

I offer a smile, but little else. With the weight of the weeks dragging me down, I trudge to bed, shoulders slumped and head low, suddenly too tired to care about anything else but the relief of sinking between the sheets. I lie down, immediately cradled by the plush welcoming mattress, and I pull the covers up to my chin. The doors softly click when Solena leaves and my chest fills with warmth as I stare hazily at the canopy above the bed, my eyes struggling to stay open a second longer. But sleep escapes me. My head falls to the side and I stare at the empty pillow next to me. I imagine Daed there, the silk sheets crumpled at his waist while a tattooed hand rests on his muscled chest, his gray eyes stirring a desire in me I cannot reconcile.

How can I consider myself fiercely strong with sound judgment while I lie in the bed of my enemy, desperately craving the touch of a man who wants nothing to do with me, so much so that he would send me back across the ocean from where I came?

I picture his smile, full soft lips drawing back to reveal sharp canine teeth that scrape against my skin when he kisses my neck. Did he make her feel this way? The Fae woman Lanneth spoke of. I know nothing about her, but just the idea of her fuels me with an anger that has me thrashing my legs restlessly against the silk sheets.

Who was she? A dull ache strikes me through the chest. Did he love her? I am so exhausted, so conflicted, so bitterly lonely, that even a visit from the apparition would be welcomed. Anything to take my mind off the fact that Daed despises me, and the indigestible realization that I do not despise him as I thought I would. But the apparition does not come, and when my eyes finally fall shut, it is Daed's face that follows me to my sleep.

It feels like no time has passed at all when I feel the cold blade against my throat.

"Get up, human," a voice snarls, hard and rough like gravel.

CHAPTER 15

My eyes flash open and I recognize the Fae Lord of Mor'Thravar hovering above me, his teeth grit, his eyes fierce and furious as the moonlight strikes him across the face.

"I said get up. *Now*," Modok growls, pushing the blade deeper against my neck, so deep I'm too afraid to gulp. "And do not waste your energy calling for help." Modok twists his fingers and I notice the air around us shimmer, as if we're surrounded by a transparent wall. "No one can hear you within my boundary."

He rips off the covers, and my hands move to hide the curves of my body, clearly outlined through the thin fabric of my nightdress. Modok's gaze skims over me, and a deviant grin tugs the corner of his mouth. The feeling of his vile eyes upon me makes me want to lash out, ire swelling in my belly. But I am reminded of the knife at my throat, and how easy it would be for him to kill me. Tonight will not be the end of my story.

I slide up from the bed, mindful of the closeness of his blade. It is then I see we are not alone. Four of his men wander the room, rifling through my things. Their filthy hands are in my jewelry box, and flinging dresses from the wardrobe, taking whatever they want and stuffing it into black sacks. Modok notices my grimace as I watch them.

"For our troubles," he sniggers. "Baev'kalath has so much, and we so little. But for their disrespect, we will take all we can from them tonight." My breath hitches when he drags his blade down my neck and rests it just above my breasts. "Starting with their precious human whore."

The sound of his men's laughter fuels my rage. Of all the things I despise, feeling helpless is the one I loathe most, and I will not be some timid lamb waiting to be slaughtered.

"You know what the prince will do to you if you kill me," I say through grit teeth. "He will tear you limb from limb and burn your miserable house to ash."

His eyes narrow with a knowing glare, and I realize Daed had threatened him similarly during the banquet. In a place I should not have been, during a conversation I should not have heard.

"I do not fear Daedalus," Modok mutters, his upper lip twitching.

I grin defiantly. "Yes, you do. That is why you have snuck into his wife's chambers in the dead of night like a coward instead of facing him."

Modok snarls, closing the space between us, his heavy breath beating down on my face. "Maybe I won't kill you," he says, sliding the point of his blade lower down my chest. "Maybe I fly you back to Mor'Thravar and demand a ransom. Let us see how much Kaelus and his pathetic excuse for a Mordorin son will pay for their princess."

Modok jerks his blade, slicing effortlessly through the ribbon of my nightdress. My body stiffens as the flimsy fabric falls open down the middle of my chest, exposing the sides of my breasts. Modok's eyes widen, his teeth scraping against his bottom lip.

"Who knows? It could take weeks, even months, for them to come for you. Mor'Thravar is a remote and formidable fortress." The point of his blade finds the shivering flesh of my breast, toying with the thin layer of fabric that keeps my dignity intact. "We would need to find something to amuse ourselves while we wait."

My face twists with disgust. "Touch me and it will be the last thing you do."

Modok laughs. "Why should the prince have all the fun?"

His men stop ransacking and instead stop depravedly to watch their lord. Modok steps closer, stinking of sweat and wine, and when his body presses to mine, the rough leather of his tunic scraping my skin, my stomach churns. "I've never had a human before," he growls.

The knife does not concern me anymore. Only my wrath for this Fae filth who thinks I will allow him to treat me this way. To scare me. To defile me. To think I will be compliant while he treats me like I'm nothing.

My knee lunges forward, striking him hard in his groin.

Modok's eyes roll in his head as he keels over, grasping his crotch before stumbling backwards.

"And you won't have a human tonight," I spit.

Modok sucks in air as his men stand in silent disbelief. "You'll die for that."

"Are you going to keep threatening me or are you actually going to do something?"

The lightness of the laugh that follows mingled with my condescending grin is motiva-
tion enough for Modok to stand up straight, shrugging away any lingering pain I inflicted.

"You're right," he says. "No more threats."

Modok charges for me, so agile and swift that I can not avoid his lunging hand when
it grabs the back of the neck and throws me across the room. I manage to stay on my feet
before crashing against the dressing table, the hard wooden edge slamming into my lower
back. I grimace, the pain searing through my muscles. Modok twists his dagger in his hand
then charges across the room, this time grabbing me by my hair and pulling so hard I cry
out. But no one can hear me.

Through wincing eyes, I see the shimmering veil of the Mor'Thravar barrier spell
holding strong.

Modok's grip tightens in my hair, yanking my head back so sharply that a gasp escapes
my lips before I can stop it. The pain shoots through my scalp, and I feel the hot sting of
tears welling up, but I refuse to let them fall. My breath catches as he brings the blade to
my throat, the cold steel pressing against my skin. I can feel the point of the dagger, sharp
and unforgiving, as it slides along my neck. The pressure increases, and I know he's not
bluffing.

"Is this better?" he snarls, his stinking, hot breath dampening my cheek. "Is this how
human girls like to be treated?"

My body burns with rage, my eyes glare at him with cold defiance, and I hiss through
my teeth before spitting in Modok's face. The Fae lord flushes with anger as his mouth
curls and when he presses his dagger harder, a thin line of crimson erupts where the blade
breaks my skin, the warm trickle of blood tracing its path.

"No. I don't think I'll take you to Mor'Thravar," Modok says in his gravel tone. "I
think instead I'll leave your bloody body right here for Daedalus to find. But not before I
have ruined it."

I clutch the edge of the dressing table, my fingers trailing over the smooth wood until
they close around the emerald comb. My fist tightens, the sharp edges biting into my palm.
Then, with a swift, decisive motion, I sling my arm and drive the long tines deep into the
side of Modok's neck.

Blood spurts from the wound, splattering across my face, but the claret in my eyes does
not prevent me from watching gleefully as his mouth falls open and his face contorts.
Modok releases my hair and staggers backwards, his blade dangling from his shaking hand

while the emerald comb juts out from his neck. His watery eyes flicker, his earlier malice replaced by shock, and when he almost collapses, his men rush to keep him on his feet.

"Kill her," Modok sputters in shallow rasps. "Now!"

His men reach for the daggers sheathed at their waists as they stalk cautiously towards me. It should be a compliment how weary they are to engage me—a disgusting human—but I'm too concerned about staying alive right now to be flattered. After all, there are four of them and one of me, and I seem to be out of emerald combs.

I take a step back until I'm hard against the dressing table. My heart pounds so hard it feels like it's trying to escape my ribcage while fear coils tight in my stomach. A sense of dread overcomes me as the men come closer. No. This can't be how it ends. If I must die, I want it to be with soil between my toes and sunlight on my face. A quivering breath escapes my throat. And I do not want to be alone.

Without his men keeping him on his feet, Modok stumbles backwards as blood continues to gush from his neck. He grits his teeth and howls as he yanks the comb free and tosses it to the ground, then presses his hand over the wound. Modok's eyes are hazy, the color drained from his skin and I notice as he weakens, so does the barrier surrounding us. The flickers of light begin to dull, and the shimmering wall that was once so clear fades in and out of sight. If there is a moment to save myself, it is now.

"Daedalus!" I scream.

At first the Mor'Thravar are unconcerned, not realizing their lord's power is waning.

But then suddenly at the arch he appears, his black wings spread so wide they block out the moonlight, his chest heaving with ragged breath, the storm of his gray eyes sending tendrils of smoke weaving through the air.

Daed looks at me, his hair wet with rain and clinging to the sharp angles of his face. His gaze settles on the streak of blood across my neck and then the torn remnants of my nightdress.

The room turns ice cold.

His jaw clenches and his upper lip draws back to reveal his canines. Daed extends his hand, and Death Singer materializes in a swirling cloud of black smoke. His chin drops and my breath catches as I watch the rune tattoos that map his body glow and pulsate, and when Daed lifts his head, his eyes are solid black.

He clasps two hands around the silver hilt of Death Singer and it hums with energy, the moonstone at its center gleaming like a shard of some ancient star. Daed slashes at what remains of the barrier, slicing through the veiled curtain of magic until it vanishes completely.

With a deep, all-consuming roar that shakes the very stones beneath us, he charges at the Mor'Thravar brethren, his wings snapping open wider with a thunderous crack. Black sentient smoke surges around him, twisting into tendrils that lash out, grabbing the nearest adversary and yanking him off his feet. Daed's sword is a blur of silver light, slicing through the air with deadly precision. The first of Modok's men barely has time to scream before the blade cleaves him in two, his body crumpling to the ground as smoke pulls him into the abyss.

Before the others can react, Daed vanishes in a swirl of dark smoke, void walking across the room with a speed that leaves them stumbling in confusion. He reappears behind the second foe, the dark mist still clinging to him like a living thing. His sword arcs through the air, a streak of silver that finds its mark in the Mor'Thravar henchman's back. The man falls without a sound, his lifeless body hitting the ground just as the smoke envelops him, swallowing him whole.

The remaining two adversaries turn to face him, terror etched on their faces. They exchange knowing looks before wearily thrusting their hands forward. The charcoal runes tattooed on their palms glow and pulsate, and a wall of shimmering light materializes between them and their Mordorin prince.

Daed lowers his sword and stalks forward. He reaches out, and the rune wall sparks when his fingers graze its surface. I expect him to cut through it, or even void walk and manifest on the other side, but he does neither. I do not know enough about this magic to understand its laws, so I can only assume both are impossible. Instead, he turns to bargaining, and when he speaks, his voice is a rough and ragged growl from deep in his chest.

"Lower your wall and I will let you both live."

Modok's men tremble as they look at each other, neither wanting to be the first to respond.

"This wall will not last long. Surrender now and you keep your heads, but if you do not, and that wall falls, I will send you back to Mor'Thravar in pieces."

Even from across the room, I see a lump lodge in the men's throat as they gulp.

"Do we have your word?" one stutters, his hand wavering.

A low rumble passes through Daed's lips and I hear the contempt in his voice. "Yes."

Again, Modok's men exchange anxious glances, but then they slowly lower their hands, and the barrier protecting them shimmers to nothing. They drop to their knees in unison, and with their heads bowed they do not see Daed vanish in a burst of black smoke, only to reappear behind the leftmost man. He drives Death Singer through his back with such force it bursts through his chest, the silver point glinting as it drips scarlet blood.

The Mor'Thravar on the right yells hysterically, scurrying across the floor, huddled in fear.

"You gave your word, Prince Daedalus!"

Daed withdraws his blade with chilling apathy, and a wave of smoke sweeps the male away before he hits the floor.

"I owe nothing to fucking traitors who dare even *look* at my wife," Daed snarls.

The prince raises his sword once more, but when he drives it towards the surviving henchman, the blade sparks against a rune barrier. The male holds his hands above him, his face burning red and his jaw clenched as he musters enough strength to absorb Daed's blow. He manages to clamber to his feet, maintaining the barrier as he staggers backwards towards the door.

"I was only following orders," he protests. "It is my duty to serve my lord."

Daed takes a feline step towards the male, toying with him, and I almost feel sorry for him.

Almost.

For his sake, I hope Daed's killing blow is swift. Suddenly the doors burst open and with one fluid strike, Arax relieves the Mor'Thravar warrior of his head. It falls to the ground, landing with a squelching thud that makes me clutch my stomach and lurch.

The fury staining Daed's face does not fade with the last warrior dispatched. His upper lip draws back, and he bares his canines at Arax. "Where. Were. You?"

Arax bows his head and drops to a knee. "My Prince. I had retired for the night. I did not..."

"You are supposed to protect her," Daed roars. "Amara could be dead. *Where were you!*"

He thrusts his hand forward, shooting tendrils of smoke at Arax which coil around his throat. Arax gasps, clawing at his neck, but the more he fights, the more the coils tighten. I take slow cautious steps towards Daed. He is a man possessed, and to approach him carelessly, after what I have seen him do, could cost me my life.

"Daedalus," I whisper, my hand inching towards his shoulder.

He does not hear me, or if he does, he does not respond, his outstretched fingers curling into a fist, the noose of smoke squeezing Arax's neck even tighter.

"Daed," I say. My hand rests on his shoulder, his shirt soaked through with rain. "*Husband.*"

Daed's hand wavers and his head jerks as if my voice has broken through the noise. He turns to look at me, and I watch as the black melts away from his eyes, revealing the gray beneath.

"Amara," he mutters. His disoriented gaze soon falls upon the slash across my neck, and his eyes widen as he awakes from his frenzied trance. "Amara," he says again.

Daed releases Arax who falls forward, sucking in all the oxygen his lungs can take while Death Singer turns to smoke in Daed's grasp. He quickly closes his hand around mine, pulling me closer to him while his other hand hovers over my wound, weary of touching it. Then he notices the cut ribbon of my nightgown, his eyes flooding with rage when they fall upon my exposed skin. His teeth grit. "What have they done to you? Did they..." his voice turns ragged before he can finish.

I shake my head. "Nothing happened, and this is just a scratch." I fear Daed will go to that dark place again, that I will lose him to the abyss... to the void. I cup his face in my hands and turn his gaze to meet my eyes. "Daed," I say sternly, calling him back to me. "I am *fine*."

His eyes close, and he leans into my touch as if he's starving for my warmth. "Amara," he mutters.

A sputtering cough followed by a raspy laugh breaks the moment of calm.

"Pathetic," murmurs Modok as he sits slumped against the wall, blood seeping through the fingers pressed to his wound. "You are no prince. You are this human's doting pup."

Daed takes a step away from me and I try to hold him back. Although he loosens my fingers gently from his forearm, I can see his savagery reemerging as he stalks towards Modok. He stands over him, his black boots sinking into the pool of blood surrounding the Lord of Mor'Thravar, who slips in and out of consciousness.

"I can not decide," Daed exhales. "Do I kill you now, or do I pull up a chair and watch the life slowly drain from you?"

Despite his wound and Daed's threats, Modok laughs between bloody gasps. "If you are to defeat the Legion, you need me at your side. You know it. Your father knows it."

Daed shakes his head. "All I need you to do, Modok, is *die*."

Smokes weaves between Daed's curled fingers as his eyes narrow with deadly intent.

"Daedalus!" Kaelus booms from the doorway. "Enough."

The king stands staring in disbelief as he takes in the scene around him, including Arax on his knees and the headless Mor'Thravar warrior at his feet.

"What have you done?" Kaelus growls. "You risk everything, Daedalus."

"Daed did nothing," I cry in his defense. "Modok and his men broke into my chambers and attacked me. I would be dead if the prince had not saved me."

Kaelus barely pays me any attention, far too concerned with the dire political incident taking place.

"Get help now," he snaps at Arax. "Healers. Blades. No one else."

"Yes, Your Highness," Arax coughs as he clambers to his feet and leaves the room to search out aid.

Not that Modok deserves it.

Kaelus pinches the bridge of his nose as he thinks. "You can not stay here tonight, Amara. We must put you somewhere else."

With the floors slick with blood and now decorated with more decapitated heads than I would prefer, remaining in this room is not my preference either. I know there are dozens of rooms on this floor of the castle alone. Any of them will be adequate.

"She will stay with me," Daed interrupts, and I immediately pick up my jaw after it falls open. Daed looks at me. "She is my wife. She should sleep in my... our bed."

"Very well," Kaelus spits bitterly. "Take her now, Daedalus, while I clean up your mess."

Daed leaves me no time to come to terms with the decision. He sweeps me into his arms and carries me to the window, his wings bursting from his back as we take flight into the darkness.

CHAPTER 16

The rain pelts down on us, a torrent of icy needles that washes away the blood staining my skin, as Daed's powerful wings slice through the storm. The sky is a mass of rolling clouds, illuminated by flashes of lightning, casting his face in sharp, angry relief. His jaw is clenched tight, eyes narrowed against the wind, and every muscle in his body is coiled with tension as he keeps me pressed against his chest. I clutch at his soaked tunic, a different kind of rage burning in my stomach.

Baev'kalath was supposed to be my sanctuary—my protection. But it's proven more dangerous than anything I ever faced in The Grove. If the Mordorin can't keep me safe within their own fortress, how could they possibly protect my people from the Legion of Saints across the sea?

We land hard on his balcony, his boots hitting the wet stone with a heavy thud. He steps inside without a word, sparing us from the worst of the downpour as he sets me down. The warmth of the plush rug is a stark contrast to the freezing air, but my toes are already tinged blue and my teeth chatter from the cold. I must look awful—my nightgown clings to my body like a second skin, the soaked fabric tracing every curve, the warm tone of my olive skin peeking through the sheer white.

I catch the way his gaze sweeps over me, lingering a moment too long on the shape of me beneath the wet gown. His throat bobs as he swallows, and then his eyes jerk away.

"I'll light a fire," he mutters, his voice rough, as if forced out against his will. He strides to the massive fireplace where the gargoyles watch us with hideous, bulging eyes, and sets to work stacking the logs.

I watch him in the low light, his broad shoulders hunched, his dark hair plastered to his skull, the ends curling tighter in the dampness.

"What was that back there?" I ask, my voice trembling from more than just the cold. "What happened to you?"

He pauses, half-glancing over his shoulder at me. "What do you mean?"

"Where do you go when you get like that?" I push, taking a step closer.

He turns back to the hearth, jaw tightening. "I don't know what you're talking about."

"It's not the first time I've seen your eyes turn black," I insist, more firmly now. "I thought I imagined it, but I didn't, did I? The same thing took you over last night."

"Enough," he growls, the sound more beast than man. He hurls a log into the fire with a violent snap and rises to his feet, towering as he rounds on me, his face carved in shadow. "What do you want from me, Amara?" His voice is a low, dangerous rumble, but beneath it, there's a thread of something raw. Something vulnerable. "Why do you torment me the way you do?"

I take a step back, confusion and hurt tightening in my chest. "*Torment* you?"

"I didn't *ask* for a wife," he bites out, his tone fierce, but I see the flicker of anguish in his eyes. "My life was simple before you came here. My only thoughts were of the next battle, the next drink. But now—" He stops, chest heaving, and a muscle jumps in his jaw as he forces the words out. "Now I care about The Grove. I care if you're cold, if you're hungry, if you're sad. I care about every damn thing you care about." He shakes his head, his voice breaking on a bitter laugh. "I thought I could ignore it, this thread that binds us. But whenever I try, the ache inside me is unbearable—like a fist strangling my heart, refusing to let it beat for any reason other than to worship you."

This thread that binds us. His words strike something deep within me, resonating in the secret part of myself that feels the same bond. That call in the cosmos that whispers he is mine and I am his. A connection that defies logic and reason, older and deeper than either of us—a bond neither of us can escape, no matter the dangers.

"I feel it too," I murmur, the words cutting through me like a betrayal.

My confession only seems to deepen his torment.

"Then stop feeling it. Be stronger than me," he pleads, his voice rough with desperation. "Because I don't know how much longer I can keep myself from taking what is mine." He takes a shuddering breath, and when his eyes meet mine, they are stripped bare, filled with a raw vulnerability that twists painfully in my chest. "Fated or not, if I am undone by you, Amara, I will lose control completely. And I care for you too much to let my darkness consume you."

The ache in my chest sharpens as his earlier cruelty comes rushing back—the cold detachment in his voice when he ordered them to send me away.

"You don't treat me like someone you care for," I whisper, my words laced with quiet hurt.

"I care so much it feels like daggers in my chest, but I can't—" He cuts off, a tremor running through him as he closes the distance between us. He reaches for me, then stops short, his hand hanging in the space between us, trembling. "Why, Amara?" His voice drops to a broken whisper. "Why have you done this to me?"

The room is silent, save for the relentless pounding of rain against the stone and the wild, unsteady rhythm of my heart. I stare up at him, the air between us thick and suffocating.

"I have done nothing to you," I say, my tone dipping into mockery. "And even if I tried, I doubt I would break the skin."

Daed's exhale is sharp, edged with frustration. "Do not underestimate yourself. If you tried, you could tear me apart."

My gaze locks on his, a tumult of longing and defiance roiling within me. I reach for his face, my fingers aching to trace the hard, smooth planes of his skin, to feel something real between us. But he turns away, and the movement is a brutal severing, as if every stitch his words had woven in my heart tears open again.

"Please," he murmurs, his voice cracking with anguish. "I cannot lose myself in you, Amara. It would only bring you pain—and I'd rather die than be the one to cause it."

His eyes flicker to the cut on my neck, and I see it—the anger flooding back into his gaze. His jaw tightens, and his hand hovers over the mark, fingers trembling.

"Arax should have been there," he growls, low and dangerous. The heat from his body feels close, but his hand remains suspended, just out of reach. "He must suffer for his failure."

"No," I snap, my voice harsher than I meant, the frustration of his constant push and pull finally boiling over. "*You* should have been there. When you choose, your words are passionate, fierce—but when I truly needed you, when it mattered most, you were nowhere to be found."

His expression darkens as he looms over me, rain trailing down his neck, dripping over the runes carved into his chest. His breath is hot against my cheek, and for a moment, it's all I can focus on.

"When you called," he says, voice low, a storm brewing beneath it. "I came."

But his words don't chase away the memory of Modok's filthy hands, the vile things he whispered in my ear—worse than any waking nightmare I've ever had. The feel of his grip on me crawls under my skin, and a cold shudder runs through me. I bite down on the whimper threatening to escape, tears burning at the back of my eyes.

"The things he said..." My voice trembles, but I force myself to stop before the tears fall.

Daed reaches for me again, his hands hovering, so close I can feel the warmth radiating from his skin. His eyes are desperate, full of the same torment I feel, as if he's aching to pull me into his arms. But again, he stops himself, retreating to the place he always does.

"I will kill him for this," he growls, spinning away from me, his back stiff, his fists clenched at his sides. He faces the fireplace and grips the mantle. "And anyone who keeps me from him."

"Your father won't allow it," I say softly, my voice steady even though my tears still threaten to fall.

"And *anyone* who keeps me from him," Daed repeats coldly. He grabs a flint and steel from the mantle, striking them together over the wood in the fireplace until a spark ignites. He crouches down, the glow of the flame illuminating his intense gaze as he nurtures it, feeding it kindling and coaxing it to life.

Silence stretches between us until he finally speaks again, his voice calm but commanding. "You need to get undressed."

The words make my pulse quicken and my stomach tighten.

"You're soaked," Daed says, more softly now, his tone almost concerned. "You already struggle to heal here. I don't want you to get sick." He jerks his chin toward the bed. "One of my shirts is there. Put it on."

My eyes dart to the black silk shirt lying neatly on the edge of the bed. I swallow, my throat dry, every nerve in my body on edge. The rain may have chilled me, but the tremble in my fingers is from something else entirely.

Daed senses my hesitation. He turns fully, his broad back to me, muscles still tense. "Change," he repeats, his voice low. "I won't turn around until you tell me."

I hesitate for a moment, my heart racing before my hands slowly drag the soaked nightgown over my head. The fabric clings to me, making it harder to pull off, and for a brief moment, I'm standing in the pale light of the moon, bare and exposed. My skin prickles, the air cool against me, but Daed doesn't move.

True to his word, he stays perfectly still, his back rigid, as though battling some inner turmoil. I let the nightgown fall to the floor and reach for his shirt, the fabric soft and cool against my skin as I slip my arms through the sleeves and fasten the buttons with trembling fingers.

But as I dress, a part of me wishes he *would* look. Just once. To feel his hungry gaze on my skin, to know that he wants me the way he fears. The same way I want him.

I swallow the thought as I finish buttoning the shirt, the silk clinging to my damp skin. I take a deep breath, trying to stand tall even though the cold still gnaws at me. My hands shake as I push my damp hair away from my face, clearing my throat.

"I'm finished," I say, my voice barely more than a croak.

Daed turns, achingly slow, as though dragging out the moment is a deliberate torment. When his gray eyes finally meet mine, it feels like the world stills. His gaze starts at my bare feet, one stacked over the other to fight the cold, then moves upward, lingering on my knees pressed tightly together, traveling further to where his shirt hangs loosely at mid-thigh. He takes his time, as if every inch of me is his to study, as though it is his right to look as long as he wishes. His eyes trace my body beneath the fabric, and when he finally reaches my face, I hear him exhale, a breath he seems to have been holding for far too long, trying—and failing—to rein in his control. The effort shows in his gaze, which falters just enough to reveal how much I unsettle him.

The fire in the hearth has caught now, flames crackling and casting flickering shadows across the stone walls. The storm rages outside, relentless rain beating against the stone, punctuated by the violent cracks of lightning that tear the night sky apart. Thunder rumbles like a threat, shaking the very bones of the fortress, but the only thing more unsettling is the intensity in Daed's eyes. His face is half-hidden by the shadows, his chin dipped slightly as he watches me from beneath the heavy weight of his brow.

"Get into the bed," he commands.

The way he says it weakens my knees. A warmth spreads through me, unwelcome yet unstoppable, the heat clashing with the remnants of cold still clinging to my skin. My body betrays me, trembling under his command, and pressing my knees together only barely holds back the aching of desire that surges within me.

I glance at the massive bed, its four dark wood posts intricately carved and draped with a midnight blue canopy that shifts gently in the breeze from the balcony. The covers, dark as a starless night, shimmer with silver-threaded swirls, while dozens of silk pillows rest against the ornately carved headboard. I hesitate, uncertainty rooting me in place.

Daed watches me, his impatience palpable when I fail to move. A low growl escapes him, and he steps forward, closing the distance between us in an instant. His hands hover over my shoulders, hesitating and for a moment, I think he'll pull away again—but this time, his fingers grip me. The warmth of his touch seeps through the thin fabric of his shirt, his hands firm and unyielding against my skin.

"You're still freezing," he murmurs, his voice softer now, but no less commanding. "Get into the bed."

When I don't move fast enough, he loses his patience. "Fine. If you won't move, I will."

Without warning, he sweeps me into his arms, and my hands instinctively loop around his neck. His scent—salt and rain—overwhelms my senses, and despite everything, I feel a strange sense of safety, as though I've never been more secure in my life.

He carries me to the bed, and for a brief, stolen moment, our eyes meet. So much remains unspoken between us, truths neither of us fully understands. We are bound by forces we never asked for, yet here and now, all of that fades away. In the privacy of this room, with the storm raging outside, we are simply two people—lost and desperate to be seen.

For once, we are not warriors, not rulers, not weighed down by duties to anyone but ourselves.

We are flesh, blood, and bone—aching to be touched, to be desired, to be loved.

Daed lowers me onto the bed with such care, his fingers lingering on my skin. He pulls his hands away slowly, as though parting from me is a battle in itself. When his final fingertip slips from my arm, I feel the ache of its absence, the silent wish that he would return, that he would stay.

He tugs the covers over me, the touch firm but gentle, drawing them up to my chin before stepping back. My chest tightens as I watch him retreat, settling into a chair in the corner. Shadows consume him, leaving only the sharp outline of his strong form and the gleam of his watchful eyes.

Exhaustion presses down on me, but before sleep takes me, I manage to whisper the words lodged in my throat.

"Thank you," I murmur, barely audible. "For saving me from Modok."

A low growl rumbles from his chest, vibrating through the shadows as he leans back, his face fading into the dark, but his eyes of the storm still glow.

"Whether you wish it or not, you are mine now," he says, his voice a slow burn of possession. "And I will protect you at all costs. I will slaughter anyone who dares treat you as anything less than a Mordorin queen."

Thunder crashes outside, its rumble oddly soothing as it blends with the rhythm of the rain and wind. It calms me in a way I didn't expect, lulling me even as my thoughts remain tangled in the tension between us, growing with every stolen glance and whispered word. The warrior I once doubted is slowly carving out a place where trust might follow, but there's still so much unknown. So much about him I can't yet surrender to, no matter how fiercely my body yearns for him.

My eyes drift toward the fire, flames dancing beneath the portrait above the mantel—a beautiful Fae female, her hands cradling her swollen belly, a serene smile playing on her lips. I must know who she is, the story she holds, but now is not the time. My eyelids grow heavier, and swiftly sleep overtakes me.

The last thing I see are Daed's eyes, still watching me, his gaze never wavering as I slip into dreamless darkness.

CHAPTER 17

When I wake, Daed is gone.

The embers in the fireplace barely flicker, their warmth fading as quickly as the remnants of what could have been. The memory of him still clings to my skin, a cruel reminder of the closeness we shared, and yet I'm left to return to my room alone. Again. When I arrive, Solena is waiting outside, her face plagued with concern.

"Your Highness," she gasps, dipping her head. "I was worried. I heard what happened. Are you alright?"

"No," I reply, in no mood for politeness, even if today I have woken feeling the best I have for some time.

No weakness. No headaches. No nightmares.

I open the door with a mix of hesitation and dread, unsure of what awaits me on the other side. Yet, oddly, I'm not surprised by what I find.

The room has been meticulously restored, every trace of the previous night's horrors erased.

Shattered furniture replaced, bloodstains scrubbed away, and, mercifully, there's not a single decapitated head in sight.

"You look a mess," Solena says, and I respond with a frown.

"In the nicest way," she blurts, "Let me draw you a bath."

I wouldn't mind a soak, my hair matted from the rain and blood caked under my fingernails. Solena runs the bath, helping me undress, and I can feel her eyes lingering on Daed's shirt still on my back. Once I'm finished, she wraps me in a robe and guides me toward the wardrobe when suddenly, the chamber doors swing open.

Frane storms in, her leather cloak snapping behind her. Before she can take another step, Arax is there, his hand clamping down on her wrist.

"Release me, Blade," she hisses, venom dripping from every word.

Arax's grip tightens, his voice a low growl. "Who are you to barge into the princess's chambers unannounced?"

Frane's jaw clenches as they stare each other down, eyes locked in a silent war of rage and bitterness.

"Release me or die, coward."

Arax steps closer, canines lengthening, his fury barely contained.

"Enough!" My voice cuts through the tension, unwilling to let another moment of violence stain these walls. "What is it, Frane?"

Arax lets go reluctantly, his gaze never leaving her as she turns to me, barely managing to hide her scorn.

"A conclave of the houses has been called. Your presence is required by the king and queen."

The words send a chill through me, nerves prickling the back of my neck. "Where is the prince?"

"He is already present," she replies coldly. "You must come now."

"The princess must dress first," Solena interjects swiftly, rescuing me from responding while anxiety coils tighter in my stomach.

Frane's lips curl in distaste, but she bows her head. "Very well. Bring her to the throne room when she is ready." She glares at Arax before spinning on her heel, her cloak whipping the air as she marches out.

Arax's eyes linger on the door long after she's gone, the tension still crackling in the air. He gives me a nod. "I'll be outside," he says, pulling the door gently closed behind him.

Solena wastes no time dressing me for the conclave. I had hoped for something simple, but the weight of the occasion leaves no room for compromise. She selects a black gown—refined, elegant, and thankfully more modest than my usual options.

Even so, it's still a labyrinth of lace and intricate beading, cinched so tightly at the waist that breathing feels like a distant luxury.

She guides me to the dressing table, where she meticulously slicks my hair back, pulling it tight against my scalp. With deft hands, she coils it into a braided bun at my nape, each sharp twist making me wince. Solena slathers on powder, dusting my face with a fine layer, then applies a dark shadow to my eyes, blending it in the way I've come to expect.

When she's done, I may appear poised and regal, ready to face the houses, but inside, I am anything but prepared.

Solena opens the door, revealing Arax waiting for me, his head bowed and a fist pressed against his chest.

"Your Highness. Are you ready?"

The question echoes in my mind, and I silently scream. *No, I am not.*

But what I want holds no weight here. If I deny them, they'll drag me along anyway, and I refuse to give them that satisfaction. So I lift my chin, square my shoulders, and begin to walk. Leaving Solena behind, Arax and I stride forward, taking long, steady steps toward the throne room.

What awaits me there? Am I expected to confront Modok? Will they ask me what happened? Will I be forced to relive that moment, repeat the vile things he whispered in my ear, his hot breath burned into the memory of my skin?

Or is this where I learn my fate—*where I am sent away.*

Daed doesn't know that I heard his wish to be rid of me, even as he comforted me in the dark of his room, making me believe, if only for a moment, that he truly cared. Those are not words spoken about someone you cherish.

Regardless, I feel as lost and hopeless as the day I stepped foot on the ship destined for Baev'kalath. None of this is within the realms of my control. No matter how much I tell myself that I am the master of my fate, deep down, I know the truth. I am a pawn. And these Fae—these monsters—know it too.

We stride through the corridors, and today, the bitter sting of every Mordorin glare feels sharper, cutting deeper. I try to ignore them like I usually do, but this morning their hatred is harder to brush off, forcing me to quicken my steps, drawing closer to Arax.

"Why are they all looking at me like that?" I whisper over his shoulder.

Arax's eyes scan the Blades standing like shadows along the darkened halls, his scowl meeting theirs head-on. "The houses are restless," he says, voice low and edged with caution. "There's discontent among the lords, and their warriors feel it too."

"Because of me?" I ask, though I already know the answer.

Arax grunts in affirmation.

I force myself to keep my head high, but every now and then, my chin wavers, dropping toward my chest. I thought the Mordorin's hatred had already run deep, but clearly, their well of contempt is endless.

We reach the towering doors of the throne room, and Arax presses his weight into the wood, forcing them open. At the far end, Kaelus and Lanneth sit upon their thrones, their hands resting with eerie stillness on the stone arms. Surrounding them in a half-circle stand the Lords of the Untold Sea—the sons and daughters of Mordorin. Some I recognize from the banquet: Reon of Eyr'Drogul, red-eyed Sarberos of Thal'Morven, and the twins, Vashar and Vasheeth of Jor'Thalas.

But today, the room is more crowded. More faces. More Fae. Their disdainful glares piercing straight through me. One stands out among them—a female with dark curls twisted into an elaborate ponytail, her eyes rimmed in black makeup that streaks from the corners of her eyes and drags down to her jaw. I don't know her name, but the jeweled daggers in her belt are unmistakable. The same as Modok's. Relief washes over me when I see that Modok himself is not present.

As we approach every fiber of my being screams that I don't belong here. The urge to turn and flee nearly overwhelms me, but I know that's exactly what they're hoping for.

Frane and a line of Reapers stand just outside the circle. This is where Arax halts, stepping aside and silently urging me forward. I freeze, unwilling to face this alone. The words nearly rise in my throat to ask him to stay, but before I can give them voice, the circle of lords parts.

Daed's hand extends toward me.

He stands tall, draped in a sharply tailored black coat that falls to his knees, its fabric dark as midnight yet it shimmers like moonlight on a calm, obsidian sea. Beneath it, his silk shirt hangs open just enough to reveal the intricate runes etched across his collarbones.

"Wife." His voice cuts through the tension as his fingers curl slightly in a silent invitation, waiting for mine to intertwine.

The burning gazes around us blur into the background, their weight lifting as my focus narrows to Daed. His presence, solid and unwavering, makes those I feared moments ago seem insignificant. I reach for him, and as soon as my fingers slip into his, the warmth of his touch steadies me. He tightens his grip, not forceful but reassuring, guiding me through the circle of lords without a glance at those around us. His indifference to their scrutiny calms me, like nothing can touch me while I'm at his side.

We ascend the dais, and Daed guides me to my throne with a subtle tilt of his head. I nod in acknowledgment, lowering myself onto the stone seat, which feels oddly more comfortable than it did yesterday.

"The princess has arrived," Kaelus announces, his words almost a drawl as he leans into his fist, watching us closely. "Let us begin. This conclave of the Mordorin houses has been called to discuss the events of last night."

"And what, exactly, happened last night?" a female voice questions. The speaker steps forward, golden hair cascading down her back like spun sunlight while her shimmering purple eyes roam over me with great interest.

"Lady Ilyra," Kaelus exhales, a flicker of wariness creeping into his voice. "The life of our dear princess, Amara, was put in jeopardy... by Lord Modok."

Before his words can settle, the female wielding Modok's daggers snarls and lunges toward the dais. Daed moves instantly, stepping in front of me with his canines bared in a feral warning. The female's court reacts just as swiftly, seizing her arms and pulling her back before she can reach the thrones.

"Modok did what you were all too frightened to do," she hisses, her voice a blade. "This marriage is a disgrace, and every one of you knows it."

"Lady Nyraxes," Kaelus' voice hardens. "You've been granted your brother's seat at this conclave. Respect will be shown here. Is that understood?"

Nyraxes' glare is as deadly as her daggers. My chest tightens as the realization dawns—Modok's sister. That's why her hatred sears so deeply.

"I understand," she mutters, retreating stiffly to rejoin her Mor'Thravar kin, though the fire in her gaze doesn't wane.

"We, as a conclave, must decide Modok's fate," Kaelus declares, his voice steady and resolute. "This kind of reckless rebellion cannot be tolerated."

Lord Reon nods, the casualness of his strength not so different from Daed. "Eyr'Drogul stands with Baev'kalath. Modok must be made an example of. He not only threatened the life of the princess, but he laid his hands on another Fae's wife. Both are punishable by death."

"He obviously felt he had no choice, Lord Reon," Sarberos interjects, his voice calm yet simmering. He steeples his fingers beneath his pointed chin, his red eyes smoldering. "Perhaps our noble royal family should have considered calling this conclave *before* deciding to marry our only prince to a human—rather than afterwards."

"Lord Sarberos makes a good point," one of the twins from Jor'Thalas says, though I am still trying to distinguish which is which. Her sister quickly adds to the fray. "Why must we convene to discuss Modok's fate when this situation could have been entirely avoided if you had sought our counsel first?"

Kaelus's jaw tightens, his frustration bubbling to the surface. "Lady Vashar and Lady Vasheeth, you forget—I am king. I am not required to seek your permission. Our announcement at the banquet was a courtesy, not an invitation for your council."

The lords exchange displeased glances, and the tension in the air thickens to the point I can barely breathe.

Kaelus's gaze shifts to the hulking Fae lord standing silently, his hands clasped over the pommel of a great black sword, its tip resting on the stone floor.

"You are unusually quiet today, Lord Horax," Kaelus states. "Tell us. What should be done about Modok?"

Horax looks up from his vacant stare, his lip curling. "You do not want my opinion, Your Highness."

"Of course I do. Speak your mind," Kaelus snaps, his voice edged with impatience.

"Very well." Horax cracks his thick neck, his expression darkening as he glances at me. "I would have done the same thing—only I would have succeeded where Modok failed."

Before Kaelus can intervene, Daed moves, vanishing in a swirl of twisting black smoke and reappearing before Horax in an instant. He clamps his hand around the lord's throat, forcing Horax's sword to clatter to the floor as he struggles against Daed's grip.

Nyraxes throws her head back, her laughter slicing through the chaos. The other lords erupt into a flurry of bickering, their voices rising in a discordant chorus of snarls and taunts.

"Enough!" Kaelus booms, rising to his feet as darkness envelops the room.

The lords freeze, their voices silenced by the encroaching shadows. Only Daed remains unfazed, his grip tightening around Horax's throat, the lord's pale face beginning to tinge with purple.

"Release him, Daedalus," Kaelus commands, his voice thunderous. When Daed hesitates, Kaelus's tone turns fierce. "Now!"

Reluctantly, Daed's hand slips free, and he staggers backward, but the threat in his gaze lingers. Horax rubs at the handprint indented into the flesh of his rasping throat.

"We must put an end to this infighting," Kaelus implores, his tone charged with urgency. "Especially if the rumors hold any truth."

He shifts his gaze toward the Reapers, and Orios steps forward. "My lords," he begins. "Our scouts report the Legion's numbers grow by the day. A small but formidable force is stationed in the valley near the Grove, and if our reconnaissance is correct, they plan to attack within the month. But there are whispers of additional Legion bands scattered across the Sundered Kingdoms, poised to strike at a moment's notice. If we allow this to continue unchecked, it won't be long before they overwhelm us, even with every warrior in the Untold Sea at your command."

My heart races in my chest. No. This cannot be. Please, Souls, do not tell me I have unwittingly married into a deception—that the Mordorin lack the strength to confront the Legion of Saints.

The lords murmur among themselves, the weight of Orios' words settling over the chamber as he steps back into line.

"Now is not the time for reckless decisions," Kaelus presses. "If we are to vanquish the Legion and obliterate their threat once and for all, we must unite against them, not turn on one another. What say you?"

I wait anxiously for their responses, the fate of the Grove teetering precariously in the hands of these bickering Fae.

Reon is the first to speak. "While I draw breath, Eyr'Drogul shall always fight for Prince Daedalus and House Mordorin."

Daed tips his head to Reon, who responds in kind.

"Fyn'Rothar will fight. We are and always will be loyal to the King of the Sundered Kingdoms," Ilyra adds, bowing her golden haired-head respectfully to Kaelus.

Sarberos exhales a measured breath before slowly raising his gaze to the king. "Thal'Morven abstains. We have already endured too much loss to take up arms once more."

Kaelus grimaces, his attention flickering to Horax and the twins. Yet I anticipate their responses even before they articulate them.

"No," the twins declare in unison. "We will not engage unless our demands are met."

Kaelus' features harden. "And what are your demands?"

The twins and Horax exchange a knowing glance, as though they had long agreed upon their terms.

"Banish the princess, and our swords are yours," Horax asserts.

Kaelus' eyes dart nervously to Lanneth. Though he has assumed command of this conclave, he visibly quakes under her seething glare. He turns back, shaken but resolute.

"We cannot acquiesce to such terms," he mutters.

"Then you have no warriors," Nyraxes scoffs.

Kaelus shifts his gaze to her. "Is that Mor'Thravar's stance as well?"

With a playful twist of her curls, Nyraxes' demeanor is unsettling, her charm concealing a predatory edge. "Mor'Thravar is *undecided*, my king."

The houses gasp in disbelief as shock ripples through the room.

I assumed Mor'Thravar would be the first to refuse.

Kaelus chooses his words carefully. "What is it you want?"

Nyraxes narrows her eyes on him. "Release my brother now."

A chill runs down my spine, memories flooding my mind of the monster who dragged me from my bed, whispering horrors that still echo in my ears. Kaelus' hesitation draws a surge of impatience from Daed.

"Father," he growls.

Kaelus raises a hand, silencing him. "If we release Modok, will you fight?"

"Yes," Nyraxes replies with unnerving calm, drawing whispers from the conclave. Her lips curve into a smile. "After he guts your human like a pig."

Daed's rage flares, and he lunges at her, but Reon grabs hold, restraining him as Nyraxes cackles in cruel amusement.

"You're a savage, Nyraxes," Ilyra sneers, disdain dripping from her voice.

Horax steps forward, eyes glinting with challenge. "I didn't realize you had a soft spot for humans, Ilyra."

Ilyra glowers as Sarberos raises his hands. "Please. Kindred. We are all Mordorin Fae here."

The twins confront the red-eyed Lord of Thal'Morven, their voices bitter.

"Is that right? You speak of dwindling numbers," Vashar says, at least I think it is Vashar.

"As if you alone have suffered losses to the humans." Vasheeth growls, "What makes Thal'Morven's lives worth more than any others?"

The sparks of conflict between the houses intensify, all while Daed and Nyraxes remain locked in their standoff.

"Spit your poison again, and I'll cut your tongue from your mouth," Daed warns her.

Nyraxes' smirk sharpens. "Why waste a perfectly good tongue, my prince? One that could pleasure you far better than your human ever could."

Daed's fangs gleam beneath his snarling lip as he melts into smoke in Reon's grasp. Nyraxes raises her daggers just as he reappears before her, blades of his own materializing in his hands. They strike with a sharp clang, and I jump to my feet, heart pounding, as their weapons lock, the raw force between them testing the limits of their strength.

"Why?" Nyraxes demands, her voice strained. "Why fight so fiercely for her?"

"Because she is my wife!" Daed roars. "Mine to keep and mine to protect."

Nyraxes hisses, her face twisted with disgust. "She is human. She deserves nothing."

"No," Daed says, his voice steady, unwavering. "She deserves eternity."

"Enough!" Kaelus commands, his voice booming, the room shaking with the force of his words. "Stop. All of you."

But the floodgates have opened, and anger pours out like a torrent. The houses turn on each other, fists flying as bodies collide. A war rages within these walls, one I never expected, far removed from the one I thought I was supposed to be fighting. Suddenly, blood sprays across the dais as noses break and lips split, and when blades are drawn, I wonder just how far these Fae are willing to go to prove who is right.

"Your Highness!"

I spot Arax pushing his way toward me, and I reach out to him as he arrives at the dais. He takes my hand, lifting me onto his hip, sword drawn, barging his way through the turmoil and shoving aside anyone who gets too close.

Once we break free, Frane is waiting. "I will take the princess to her chambers," she says. "Protect the prince, Arax."

Arax's brow creases with uncertainty. "It's my duty to protect the princess."

"Do as I command, Blade," Frane hisses.

Arax glances at me, but my shock renders me speechless.

He nods to Frane and turns back to the raging tempest before the throne.

Frane grips my wrist tightly. "Come with me, now," she snaps, pulling me away.

We leave the madness behind, charging past the doors. Frane doesn't look back, her fingers biting into my skin as she drags me along and I struggle to keep pace.

"Wait," I say, breathless. "Slow down."

She doesn't respond, quickening her pace until we reach a balcony and when she pulls me outside, the rain hits my face like a thousand tiny daggers.

"What are we doing out here?" I ask, anxiety twisting in my gut.

Frane remains silent, her grip unyielding as she drags me toward the edge of the balcony. I struggle against her hold, planting my feet to resist her pull, but she inches me closer to the precipice.

"Do you know how long I've waited to become a Reaper?" she asks tersely, her gaze fixed ahead as she storms on. "I will not lose it now. I refuse to watch our great houses crumble because of a pathetic human."

When we reach the edge, Frane pulls me close, her fingers digging into the back of my neck like iron shackles. I lash out, throwing my hands at her, but they only thud against the hard steel of her armor as my screams dissolve in the ocean's roar.

"I'll say you ran and slipped," she says, her tone disturbingly calm, as if she's rehearsed this moment a hundred times. "There will be initial unrest, but soon enough, everyone will agree it was for the best."

With a swift motion, she thrusts me forward, and my body tips over the railing. My upper body dangles precariously as I gaze down at the tumultuous waves thrashing against the cliffs, ready to devour me.

"Daed will kill you for this," I snap.

"The prince is clouded by your charms," she hisses, pushing me further over the edge. "Once you're gone, we Mordorin will unite to fight the Legion as one." Her eyes gleam with satisfaction. "At least your end will be quick. That's a mercy."

In that instant, desperation fuels my instincts. As I twist, I grab her wrist, the cold spikes of her vambraces biting into my palm. I pull with all my might, and the world tilts as Frane loses her balance.

We tumble over the railing together.

Time slows as we plummet through the air, the wind howling past us, my heart thundering in my chest like a war drum. Suddenly, the runes etched on Frane's collarbone flare to life, glowing with an otherworldly light as her wings burst from her back. With a powerful flap, she ascends, her laughter echoing in the storm, leaving me to continue my descent alone.

As I brace for impact, I close my eyes, whispering a silent hope that Frane was right about one thing: *that it will be quick.*

But instead of shattering against the jagged rocks below, I come to a jarring halt. My eyes flicker open to find Arax cradling me in his arms, his wings beating against the rain.

"Princess. Are you alright?"

Relief floods over me as I curl against his chest. With powerful strokes, he lifts us back to the balcony and gently sets me down on the stone.

"This human continues to be your downfall, Arax," Frane sneers, hovering above us like a vulture. "I once admired you. Considered you one of the greatest Reapers to ever live. How disappointing you've turned out to be."

Arax wipes the rain from his brow, fury igniting in his gaze as he glances up at Frane. "Enough of this. You will tell the prince what you've done and face his justice."

Frane's smile is menacing as she unsheathes her sword, the blade gleaming with deadly intent. "I think not. Instead, I'll kill you both in his name."

With a roar that shakes the air, they charge at each other, the clash of their weapons ringing out like thunder. My breath catches in my throat as they collide midair, a furious whirlwind of wings and steel.

Frane spins gracefully, fluid and lethal. She strikes first, her blade flashing dangerously close to Arax's throat. He counters with a swift upward arc, his wings propelling him with precision. They whirl through the rain, the sky their battleground.

Their weapons clash again. Frane feints left, then lunges right, her blade finding a gap in Arax's armor, sinking deep beneath his arm. "You think you can protect her?" she shouts, twisting the blade and drawing a pained grunt from him.

Blood mingles with the rain, and my stomach lurches when I see him falter, spiraling downward. He fights against the pull, wings flaring wide as he struggles to regain control. With a heavy thud, he crashes onto the balcony, the impact rattling the stones beneath us.

Frane lands deftly beside him.

"You're nothing but a foolish old Fae," she taunts, kicking Arax's sword away, sending it clattering out of reach. Straddling him, she raises her blade, poised to deliver the final blow. My heart races, panic clawing at my insides as I watch, helpless.

But Arax's eyes blaze with defiance, even as pain darkens his features. He shifts beneath her, summoning his power. His arm dissolves into swirling smoke, passing through Frane as though she were nothing but air.

Her eyes widen, a flicker of confusion breaking through her focus. Before she can react, his arm solidifies within her, and with a swift, ruthless motion, he drives it forward, impaling her.

I gasp, my heart lurching in horror, and instinctively I turn away as a spray of blood arcs through the air, splattering the stone. When I dare to look back, the scene is etched into my mind: Arax's arm, slick and crimson, now free from her lifeless body as Frane lies motionless on the balcony, the relentless rain washing away the remnants of her fury, leaving only silence in its wake.

Arax attempts to rise, but collapses to one knee. I rush to his side, my chest tightening when I see the blood seeping from beneath his arm. His face drains of color, and his eyes begin to glaze over, like fading stars against a darkening sky.

"Princess. Are you safe?" His voice is strained, barely more than a whisper.

I steady his shoulders, holding him upright as his blood mixes with the rain, pooling beneath us. "Yes, Arax, I'm safe. Now let me heal you."

He shakes his head weakly, defiance flickering in his eyes. "I do not deserve a second mercy."

Ignoring his nonsense, I lean closer, my tone resolute. "Arax," I command, locking eyes with him. "As your princess, I order you to sit still and keep quiet while I heal you. Do you understand?"

Rain streams over his brow, and a faint, weary smile breaks through the line of his lips. "Very well, princess."

Sliding my hand beneath his arm, I feel the slick warmth of blood as I locate the wound. He flinches, a sharp breath hissing through his teeth.

"Don't be such a child," I chide gently, forcing a brave smile as the rune around my neck begins to glow, its soft light cutting through the storm.

Chapter 18

The throne room is far quieter today. The lords have been sent home, warned to stay there on pain of treason—punishable by death. And there is one less Reaper in the line.

All because of me.

I might find it flattering to be such a thorn in their side, if only my life wasn't constantly in danger.

I sit silently on my throne, head bowed, hands clasped tightly in my lap, uncertain of what this meeting will bring. Daed is beside me, sprawled across his throne with his legs spread wide, his gaze fixed forward.

I had hoped that after the conclave, things might change—that his declaration would bring clarity, perhaps even solace, to our fated bond. But it has done nothing to close the chasm he insists on keeping between us. The constant whiplash of my husband's emotions feels like it might break me, his relentless push and pull leaving me unable to find solid ground.

Kaelus sits on his throne, a fist pressed to his chin, lost in thought, while Lanneth stands behind him, her nails drumming a restless rhythm against the stone.

"It isn't safe for her here," she says, her voice tinged with an anxious edge. "Now, not only do the thrall houses threaten her, but even our own Reapers cannot be trusted."

"Frane acted alone," Orios says from the line, his voice hard. "Not a brother or sister among us conspired with her."

Daed's head snaps up, his jaw tight. "Maybe you should all share Frane's fate, just to be sure."

"Now is not the time to thin our ranks when warriors are already scarce," Kaelus growls, his face strained with thought. He turns his attention to Lanneth. "What do you suggest, my queen?"

Lanneth's gaze fixes on me. "She should be sent away for a time until the thrall houses are dealt with."

A strange surge of excitement courses through me, swiftly followed by a bitter edge of doubt. The thought of returning to the Grove—my home, the place I've yearned for since setting foot on this miserable rock—should fill me with joy. But things are no longer so simple.

Daed clears his throat. "To the Grove?" he asks, his tone dismissive as he flicks his gaze down to inspect his fingernails.

"No," Lanneth says, and the word doesn't wound me as sharply as I expected. "The Legion awaits her to return to use her against us."

"Then where?" Kaelus rumbles, his brows knitting together.

"Pariseth," Lanneth answers plainly. The word makes both Kaelus and Daed snap toward her.

"Who will take her?" Daed asks, leaning forward now, his casual disinterest gone.

"Isn't it obvious, boy?" Kaelus groans, exasperation creeping into his voice. "You will." Daed stiffens, and I see a lump forming in his throat.

"You may take a maid for Amara, and Orios will serve as your personal guard, but anything more will draw attention. And that is the very thing we are trying to avoid."

Daed rises to his feet, his loose black shirt swaying at his hips. "Would it not be safer to keep her here in Baev'kalath, under the watch of the Ebon Flight with all its might to protect her?"

Lanneth's fingers slither suggestively over Kaelus' shoulder, and he responds by slamming his fist against the arm of his throne, cutting the discussion short. "I have spoken, Daedalus. You leave for Pariseth tonight."

Kaelus steps down from his throne, his boots echoing against the stone as he strides toward the edge of the dais. "Arax," he commands, and from behind the wall of Reapers, Arax steps forward.

He drops to one knee, head bowed. "Yes, my king."

"You have once again shown this great house how much we rely on your strength and wisdom. I hereby relieve you of your post as bodyguard to the princess and reinstate you as a Reaper of House Mordorin. In the prince's absence, you will serve at my side as we deal with these feuding thrall houses."

Arax glances at me briefly, but quickly lowers his gaze. "I am honored, Your Majesty. But I have sworn to protect the princess."

"You still shall."

"But—"

"Arax," Kaelus's tone tightens, leaving no room for further protest. "This is not a request."

Arax bows his head deeper. "Yes, Your Majesty. I live only to serve House Mordorin."

Kaelus waves a hand, dismissing the room. "You may all go."

The throne room empties with the scrape of footsteps and the echo of armor, until only Daed, the king, queen, and I remain. Lanneth steps forward, her long, willowy arms extending toward me, leaving no room to refuse as she takes my hands in hers, her grip tighter than necessary. She pulls me to my feet, her fingers coiling around mine like vines.

"This is for the best, daughter," she says, her voice too smooth, too sincere. "We've failed to protect you twice in as many days, and if anything were to happen to you, this house would be lost."

I force a smile, though the frustration simmers beneath my skin. I can't decide if the queen is my ally or my enemy, and it grates on me more each day. When she thinks I'm not looking, I catch the same disdain in her eyes that the other Fae have for me—like I don't belong here. But then there are moments like this, when she guards my safety so fiercely, I almost believe she truly wants to protect me.

Only Lanneth knows what's going on in her mind, but I wouldn't dare attempt to unravel her motives. That's a web I've no desire to get caught in.

"My place is here, Father," Daed protests, spinning on his heel to face the king, his back now turned to me. "Let Death Singer and I remind the houses of who they are dealing with. I am the Ebon Flight's greatest warrior."

"Which is exactly why you should be the one to protect your wife," Lanneth cuts in smoothly, her voice sharp as glass. "Do you not care for her safety?"

Daed throws a sharp glare over his shoulder, eyes flashing. "Send her to Pariseth. Take every Reaper we have, send Arax himself, if you must. But do not send *me*."

I flinch, the sting of his bitter words settling deep. It's as if the promises he whispers to me in the quiet of night vanish with the morning light. The same man who holds me close in secret, who declares loud and fearless to his brethren that I am his, now wants nothing to do with me.

Kaelus exhales a long, measured breath, his patience wearing thin. "Why must everyone test me today? Am I not king? Is my word not law?"

"Father," Daed grinds out between clenched teeth, "I do not wish to go."

Kaelus' hand grips Daed's shoulder and I see Daed's head drop as he realizes the decision is final. "This bride of yours is the future of our house. There is nothing more important. Do you understand?"

Daed gives only a slight nod, his resistance crumbling as Kaelus strides past him, offering his arm to Lanneth. She takes it with a graceful motion, and together, they turn to me, dipping their heads in a rare gesture of respect.

"Have a safe journey, Amara," Kaelus says. "By the time you return, the houses will be united once more."

The words hang in the air like a promise I no longer trust.

The king and queen leave, and the silence between Daed and me is vast enough to drown in.

"What is Pariseth?" I ask, keeping my tone sharp. I want facts, not excuses.

Daed doesn't turn to face me, still chewing on the nail of his thumb. "It's an island within our territory. It sits in the eye of a storm—deadly to anyone foolish enough to enter."

"And that's where you're sending me for my safety?" I can't help the bite in my voice.

He straightens at that, and I glimpse his gray eyes as he glances over his shoulder. "The island within the storm is beautiful. More beautiful than anything you'll ever lay eyes on in the Untold Seas. Grass and..."

"Grass?" I snap, rising to my feet. "And what else?"

A faint smile tugs at the corner of his lips, cracking through the stony mask he wears. "Flowers. There's a castle there. A sanctuary, used as a safe haven when needed."

"I'll go," I blurt out, with the thought of grass between my toes and the softness of petals against my skin already overtaking my mind. "I'll pack now."

I move to pass him, heading for the stairs, but his hand closes around my wrist—gently, not like I expect. It catches me off guard. His chin dips to his chest, his dark hair veiling his eyes.

"Amara, when I said I didn't want to go, I didn't mean it to sound so...cold." His voice is low, hesitant, as if unsure of his own words.

I pry his fingers from my wrist, forcing him to meet my gaze.

"I don't care," I say sharply, cutting through whatever excuse he's trying to offer. "I'm done with your sweet lies—the ones you whisper when it's just us and the moonlight." I pull my wrist free, straightening my spine. "I'm going to Pariseth to feel the grass beneath my feet, and to hopefully have one day—just one—where Fae aren't trying to kill me."

I stroll across the cold stone of the throne room, and I feel Daed's gave with every step. He doesn't call after me or try to stop me, but even if he did, I wouldn't listen.

Right now, I crave something far more than his lingering glances. If Pariseth has grass, then there is soil. If there are flowers, then there is sun. It may not be the Grove, but it's the closest thing I've had in far too long.

I navigate the halls with ease now, lifting the hem of my dress to quicken my pace. When I reach my chambers, I freeze, no longer greeted by Arax's familiar, stoic form or his ever-watchful gaze. I'm glad he's been reinstated as a Reaper—it's where he belongs, out in the courtyard, sparring, not standing outside my door. Still, his absence stirs a sadness within me, as if Baev'kalath has grown a little lonelier.

Inside my chambers, I pull the bell to summon Solena, who arrives promptly.

"I need help," I say as I rifle through my wardrobe.

Solena's curious gaze follows me across the room. "I do not doubt it. Are you alright?"

"I've never been better," I reply, tossing dresses over my shoulder. "I leave for Pariseth tonight."

"Pariseth!" Solena gasps, her excitement feeding my own.

"Help me pack, please?" I ask. "I suppose I can take a trunk on the ship."

A giggle escapes her, stifled behind her hand. I arch an eyebrow. "Something amusing?"

She shakes her head quickly. "You can't sail to Pariseth, Your Highness. The storm will tear a ship to pieces. You'll have to fly. You'll need to pack light—your Blades can carry a satchel or two on their backs."

"There are no Blades," I correct, turning back to my wardrobe. "It's just Daed, Orios, and myself."

Solena gulps. "Orios? For how long will you be gone?"

"The king didn't say," I reply as I continue sorting.

Solena falls silent, and I realize she is dreading their time apart, even if their love exists only in stolen moments. I pause my frantic searching and turn to face her. "I've been told I need to take a maid. I think it should be you."

Her eyes widen, and a breath catches in her throat. "Me, Your Highness?"

166

I shrug, as if I can't see the happiness simmering beneath her skin. "Yes, you. Who else would it be? But be warned: it'll just be the four of us—alone—on an island that's impossible to reach."

Watching Solena struggle to stifle her blossoming smile amuses me.

"Thank you, Your Highness," she breathes, her voice a mix of disbelief and joy.

"You can thank me by helping me pack," I reply with a smirk.

"Of course!" Solena hurries to my side, burying herself alongside me in the wardrobe. She stretches to reach the very top shelf, pulling down two leather satchels. We both lean in, pinching our chins between our fingers as we survey the layers of lace and silk.

"Not even one of these dresses will fit in that bag," I say. "I can't just take one ball gown."

A thought crosses Solena's mind, and she reaches deep into the back of the wardrobe, emerging with several neatly folded items, along with something wrapped in brown paper.

"What are those?" I ask, curiosity piqued.

"Trouser and tunics," she replies with a smile. "They'll fit and you should wear them for the journey."

I furrow my brow. "Are you telling me these have been here all along while you kept shoving me into those dresses?"

"You couldn't very well wear these to banquets," Solena defends herself. "And if you need something a little more flowy..." She pulls the string on the parcel, and the paper falls away, revealing the dress I wore when I boarded the ship to Baev'kalath.

I trace the delicate gold stitching along the edges, recalling the night my sisters gifted it to me, their voices wishing me well. It feels like a lifetime ago.

"Will these do, Your Highness?" Solena's voice pulls me from my reverie.

I nod with an appreciative smile. "Yes. They'll do just fine."

Solena moves briskly, packing my bags and placing them at the foot of the bed. "You must be excited to spend time alone with the prince, after everything that's happened these past few days."

I swallow hard, my throat tightening. "If only things were that simple between us."

"Perhaps *he's* looking forward to it, then," Solena offers, her tone light.

I shake my head, a bitter scoff escaping. "King Kaelus had to force him to go."

"Nonsense," Solena chuckles. "Why would a husband not want to be alone with his wife in somewhere as romantic as Pariseth? It will be like a second wedding night."

I arch my eyebrows. Is this where I tell Solena I spent that night dazed from blood loss? I decide to spare her the details. "It was not as eventful as you might think."

She purses her lips curiously. "The following night, then. When the maids and I found him in your bed the next morning."

I bite my bottom lip, wondering if she can sense the truth. The way her eyes widen tells me she does.

"Oh," she says, nervously tucking a strand of black hair behind her ear. "Really? You have not... you and the prince..."

I feel my cheeks burn. "After we were wed, Daed made it clear he preferred the company of others. For the longest time, I thought it was you warming his bed at night... or maybe one of the other maids."

Solena takes a deep breath. "You shouldn't put stock in gossip, Your Highness. But I should have silenced those rumors when they first started."

"What rumors?" I ask, my curiosity flaring.

"Prince Daedalus has never shared his bed with a maid here in Baev'kalath, or anywhere else, as far as I know. In fact, he's had no contact with any females... or women."

My head jerks up, disbelief clear on my face. "Then why did the maids say otherwise? Why did Daed himself..." I stop short, unwilling to reveal the humiliation of being told by my own husband that I didn't entice him. "I just assumed," I finish weakly.

"There's no need for assumptions," Solena says, her voice steady. "I can assure you, there is no one else." She leans in, her expression softening with a wry smile. "The help always know, Your Highness. Will that be all?"

"Yes. Thank you, Solena," I manage.

She backs toward the door, head bowed, then quietly closes it behind her. She likely doesn't realize the merciful relief she's given me—relief I wish had come much sooner.

For now, I cannot allow Daed to plague my thoughts, which seems fitting, as he's wasting no time thinking of me. The prospect of touching soil and grass again, feeling the sun on my skin, feels like a sweet escape from the uncertainty he offers. Away from Kaelus and Lanneth and this dreadful place, I might even start to feel like myself again—regain color in my cheeks and not constantly crave sleep.

"You cannot go."

The room grows cold, shadows closing in until I feel their weight surrounding me. In the corner, a dark figure undulates, gliding across the stone like smoke.

"No. Not now," I mutter, pinching the bridge of my nose between my fingers. "No imagining things right now, Amara."

"I am the bones that rattle beneath the stone. I am not here, yet I cannot leave. If you go to Pariseth, your fate will be the same."

"If I go to Pariseth, the king and queen promise I will be safe."

"You are not safe anywhere the prince is. He will be your ruin."

I square my shoulders and stare down the figure, forcing my voice steady. "If you want to help me, why don't you do something other than whisper cryptic messages? How can I trust you are truly on my side?"

"I have never claimed to be your friend Amara. Baev'kalath is a dark place, full of dark things, and I am no better. But only death waits for you here. You must feel it."

The words turn my blood to ice. "Of course I do. But there is no escape."

"Awaken, Amara Tyne. You must awaken."

"I don't know what that means!" I shout.

Suddenly, an image slashes through my mind, bright enough to blind me. I stumble forward, bracing myself against the bed as my eyes squeeze shut. It lasts less than a second, but it's burned into my memory—the portrait of the pregnant Fae hanging above Daed's fireplace. My eyes fly open.

"Wait. Do you know who that female is?"

But when I search the shadows for the apparition, it vanishes, leaving me alone with my unanswered questions. I clench my fists at my sides, fighting against the urge to wish it all away. I cannot let Baev'kalath drive me mad; I refuse to let it claim victory over me. The ghosts that roam these halls must be figments of my imagination. I must keep telling myself that.

I spend the afternoon in my room, clinging to the fragile belief that I'm not unraveling—that once I feel the sun on my skin again, I'll remember who I am. The chair groans as I drag it to the table where my serpentine vine sits, its once-vivid green now dull and lifeless, the few leaves that remain curling at the edges. She withers, and so do I.

The weight of my failure presses into me like iron chains. The Mordorin armies are weaker than we could have possibly known, and the bargain that brought me here is starting to feel more and more like a cruel trick. The Grove took me in when the war left me orphaned. They gave me everything, and I owe them more than I can repay. To fail them is to fail the only family I have left, and that thought alone is a blade to my chest, twisting deeper with every beat of my heart.

But I can't let myself wither like my poor vine, not yet. For the Grove I must keep going. Pariseth. The grass. The sun. It will give me strength. It has to.

I don't notice when the day fades into night until moonlight spills onto my balcony. A cold shiver prickles my skin as a sudden gust of wind sweeps through the room. Rising, I step outside. The sky is pitch-black, rain cascading down in steady sheets.

"Good evening, wife," Daed says, and I turn to see him crouched on the railing, his wings folded neatly behind him, rain glistening on his brow.

"I'd prefer you use the door," I reply, choosing not to look at him.

Instead, I hear the soft thud of his boots as he steps down, striding towards me. He joins me beneath the eaves, and even as I try to ignore it, I feel the magnetic pull of his presence.

"Are you looking forward to our trip?" he asks, his voice smooth and teasing.

"Well I know *you* aren't," I snap, my irritation flaring as he paces behind me. "I'm surprised you haven't disappeared to avoid it altogether."

"I've had time to make peace with being exiled with you," he replies, and I can hear the smirk in his voice.

My face tightens with frustration. "How very gracious of you, husband."

He steps into my chambers and exhales, glancing around. "It looks like the servants did an excellent job scrubbing the Mor'Thravar blood from your floor. Though I see they've replaced the rug."

The rug was the first thing that caught my eye when I returned last night, exhausted and shaken after Frane threw me off a cliff. I finally turn to face him as he paces the room, arms crossed over his chest.

"Yes, you'd never know someone was decapitated in here," I reply with a hint of sarcasm, prompting a throaty laugh from Daed.

"They released Modok, you know," he says abruptly, the laughter fading from his voice. "Nyraxes took him back with her when they returned to Mor'Thravar."

"I'm not surprised," I reply, lingering just outside the archway. "Your father made it clear they need his house."

Daed studies me, curiosity etched on his features. "And what do you think about that, wife?"

"It infuriates me," I snap, my anger bubbling to the surface. "I wish he were dead. I wish you had killed him."

His eyes flash, and he seems to absorb the tension in my voice.

"But I also know that if he aligns with your Ebon Flight, the Grove will be safe—and that is all that matters."

He sighs, feigning boredom. "Do you never grow weary of putting others before yourself, Amara?"

"Do you ever tire of thinking only of yourself?" I retort, raising an eyebrow in mock disbelief.

Daed smiles, his canines glinting in the dim light. "You continue to fascinate me."

"And you continue to exasperate me," I snap. "I won't engage in this with you tonight, Daed," I say firmly. "I'm not a toy for you to play with whenever you're bored and then discard when you lose interest."

"Oh Amara," he laughs, tilting his head slightly. "We haven't even begun to play."

Suddenly, the doors open, and I gasp as the wind rushes in, breaking the spell of Daed's gaze. Orios stands tall, fist pounding against his chest.

"We're ready to leave for Pariseth," he announces.

"Excellent," Daed replies, gesturing toward my bags at the foot of the bed. "Gather the princess's belongings—we take to the skies."

"From here, Your Highness?" Orios asks, motioning toward the balcony.

"My wife prefers I use the door," Daed sighs, his smirk irritating me as I roll my eyes. "We'll depart from the courtyard."

Orios bows. "Yes, Your Highness."

As Daed exits the room, Orios moves to collect my bags, standing by the door, waiting for me to pass.

"Princess Amara," he says, his voice low enough to avoid attracting attention.

I pause and turn to him. "Yes?"

Orios removes his helmet, revealing a hard, rugged jaw and long black hair knotted into a bun at the back of his head. "Thank you for bringing Solena. But know that my duty is to protect you and the prince, and she will not distract me."

"That's a lie," I sigh, watching as his chin drops. "But I won't be watching you, so whatever you and Solena choose to do—or not do—in Pariseth is your business."

Orios lifts his chin, his eyes brightening as a smile blooms on his face. "Yes, Your Highness."

I take another step forward, but Orios coughs, halting me once more.

"Yes?"

His smile fades, replaced by a seriousness. "I also want you to know, Princess, that I meant what I said in the throne room today. I had no knowledge of Frane's intentions. If I had, I would have stopped her myself."

I take a deep breath, a frown creasing my brow. "Another lie?"

"No," he replies sharply, the bite in his tone startling me. "There may be centuries of history between our kinds, but Prince Daedalus has made it clear that you are his wife, and that commands the respect of all Mordorin."

To preserve myself, I cannot afford to show weakness or vulnerability to the Fae—they would exploit it without hesitation. I press my lips into a firm line and give a single, resolute nod.

"Is there anything else, Orios?"

"No, Your Highness," he replies, dragging his helmet back over his head. "Shall we depart?"

I nod and continue down the halls, weaving through flickering torchlight until we arrive at the courtyard. The waves surge below us, crashing against the rocks in their relentless dance of strength. Daed stands at the edge, arms stretched wide as the rain pours down and sea foam splashes against the wall at his feet. He turns to me, a crack of lightning illuminating his figure as his wings burst from his back.

"Wife," Daed calls, extending his arm toward me. I find myself moving to him instinctively, unable to resist the pull he exerts.

His hand envelops mine, lifting me effortlessly to the edge as his wing curves protectively over my head, sheltering me from the rain.

"I will carry you all the way there," he says, his voice a deep, warm sound that caresses my senses. "You will be in my arms as we cross the storm, and you will be in my arms if we fall to it. Do you understand?"

His words reverberate through me, igniting a fluttering warmth in my chest. I look into the depths of the storm swirling in his eyes, my gaze drawn to his mouth as he exhales.

"Yes. I understand," I manage to say.

With that, Daed sweeps me up, and that's when he notices the serpentine vine cradled in my arms.

He cocks an eyebrow. "You're bringing that?"

I shrug. "I can't leave her here alone."

Daed shakes his head, a bemused smile tugging at his lips. "Fascinating."

CHAPTER 19

The night is bleak and endless as we fly over the vast black expanse of the Untold Sea. The rain lashes at us, cold and unforgiving, the wind howling through Daed's wings as he cuts through the storm. Beneath us, the waves churn violently, an endless, merciless dance of fury that makes me feel small and alone out here, far from the shore, far from anything but him. His arms are strong and steady as they hold me close, shielding me from the worst of the storm, and though I should be afraid, I find myself sinking into the warmth of his embrace.

I glance up at Daed's face, watching the way the rain clings to his sharp features, the soft glow of his eyes that never waver, even as the storm batters us from every direction. His gaze shifts to me, and in that moment, the world falls away. My breath catches in my throat as I hold his gaze, my heart pounding against my ribs as though it might break free and reach for him. But I stay silent, torn between the storm outside and the one brewing between us.

As we push further across the endless stretch of black water, the storm intensifies. It's as if the sky itself is unraveling, the clouds thickening into a dark, swirling vortex that looms ahead, waiting to swallow us whole. Jagged forks of lightning crack across the heavens, illuminating the angry sky in bursts of white and purple, their light reflecting off the ocean's roiling surface. The wind howls in wild fury, lashing at us as if trying to force us back, but Daed presses on, his wings straining against the storm's relentless pull.

Ahead, the storm's heart churns in a violent spiral, its clouds twisting into a massive wall of darkness, as if the very ocean has risen to meet the sky. The storm pulses, almost alive, its thunderous roar shaking the air around us, daring us to cross its threshold. And at its core—though I can barely see it—there's a glimpse of something strange and beautiful. An island, shrouded in mist and bathed in an ethereal light, sits quietly within the eye of the storm, as if untouched by the chaos that surrounds it.

But between us and that sanctuary lies a tempest like no other, its winds howling with enough force to tear apart the strongest ships. Waves rise and crash against each other, the sea itself buckling and thrashing beneath the storm's wrath. The clouds above swirl faster, converging into a single, monstrous cyclone that guards the island fiercely, as if no one should reach it without proving their worth. The closer we get, the more the air hums with energy, and I feel the charge of it crawling over my skin.

"We're almost there," Daed says, his voice steady despite the storm raging around us. He grips me tighter, his wings adjusting for the sudden gusts of wind that slam into us like fists.

Out of the corner of my eye, I catch glimpses of Orios and Solena, fighting their own battle against the storm. Orios soars just ahead, his wings thrashing against the gale, his face set in a grim mask of focus. Solena flies beside him, her small frame barely visible in the sheets of rain, but her wings cut through the storm with surprising grace. They, too, are struggling, the wind pushing them off course every now and then, but they never falter. They are just as determined, just as relentless, to reach Pariseth.

A sudden gust of wind hits us, stronger than before, and Daed's body jerks violently. My grip slips, and for one horrifying second, I feel myself sliding out of his arms, the storm ready to claim me. Panic seizes my chest as I gasp, my fingers scrambling for purchase, but Daed's grip tightens instantly, his arms locking around me like iron. His wings beat harder, his face strained with the effort of keeping us in the air.

"I've got you," he mutters, voice rough with effort, and I can feel the truth of it in his hold. Even with the storm raging, even with the odds against us, he won't let me fall.

But it's taking its toll. I can see it in the lines of his face, the tension in his jaw. His wings are trembling now, fighting every inch of the way, and I know we're running out of time. The storm is relentless, but so is Daed—and in the distance, Pariseth gleams brighter, calling to us like a promise, a sanctuary hidden within this nightmare.

Daed grits his teeth, and with one final push against the spiral of rain and wind, we break through the storm wall with a violent thrust, like bursting from the depths of the sea into air. Daed's wings fold tight around us, and we plummet toward the ground. I squeeze my eyes shut, bracing for the impact, and a moment later, we crash into the earth with bone-rattling force. The air is knocked from my lungs as we tumble, Daed still holding me tight against his chest, cushioning the fall.

For a long moment, I don't move. My chest heaves, each breath ragged as I fight to fill my lungs. The roar of the storm still echoes in my ears, but it's distant now, a memory of violence that feels so far away from where we are. Slowly my eyes open to find Daed gazing at me, the two of us cradled within the darkness of his wings.

"Are you alright?" he asks.

I nod. "Did we make it? Are we in Pariseth?"

Daed's wings slowly unfurl, and I roll away, collapsing onto my back beside him. I'm reminded of the serpentine vine in my arms, and my eyes shoot down to check on her. Thank the Souls, she's survived too. My body feels heavy, weighed down by exhaustion and the lingering tension from the flight. My heart still races, my fingers trembling as they splay against the ground, searching for something solid to remind me we made it.

I hear Orios groan somewhere to my left and Solena's soft gasps come from somewhere beyond him, and for a moment, we are all just there—four bodies sprawled in the aftermath of survival, too tired to speak, too grateful for the solid earth beneath us to do anything but breathe.

And then, slowly, I feel it. The warmth. The soft touch of sunlight kissing my skin, gentle and unexpected. I blink against the sudden brightness, raise my head and realize... the early morning sun is shining.

I sit up, disbelief flooding through me as I look around. The storm, that relentless fury we battled moments ago, is still howling beyond the edge of this island, a wall of darkness circling the horizon. But here, inside the eye, everything is calm. The sky is a soft, brilliant blue, with the sun sitting high above us, its rays pouring down over the land like a blessing. It's warm, the kind of warmth I haven't felt in so long.

I'm lying on the softest, most vibrant green grass I've ever seen. It cradles me like a bed, lush and thick beneath my fingers. Flowers, bright and colorful, dot the landscape around us, their petals glistening with dew. The air smells sweet, fresh, and alive, completely different from the salt and damp of the sea.

I push myself to my feet and look up. In the distance, beyond the field of flowers and trees, a castle emerges. It rises from the earth with quiet majesty, its pale stone towers reaching toward the sky, gleaming in the sunlight like a beacon.

A river meanders alongside it, clear and sparkling as it winds through the land. Its gentle murmur fills the air, soft and soothing—a serene melody that's a world away from the violent crash of the waves we left behind.

I glance back at Daed, still lying on the grass, his chest rising and falling as he catches his breath. His eyes are half-closed, but there's a peace in his expression, a rare softness that I rarely see. When his gaze finally meets mine, there's a flicker of surprise there, as if he, too, is stunned by the sudden shift from chaos to serenity.

"We made it," I whisper, more to myself than anyone. The words seem too small to encompass the relief, the awe, of where we are now. But they're all I have.

Daed's lips curve into a tired smile, and he nods, his voice low and rough as he murmurs, "Yes. We did."

I arch a brow as I look at him splayed across the grass. "You look so pale in the sunlight."

Solena releases a giggle, but quickly clamps her hand over her mouth to silence it.

Daed exhales deeply, dragging himself to his feet and shaking off the remnants of damp grass that cling to his soaked trousers. "Sorry to disappoint you, wife," he says, his voice laced with sarcasm. He turns his head toward the castle, his eyes narrowing as he assesses the distance. "Among my shortfalls, I'm also in need of dry clothes."

With a soft grunt, he arches his back, the movement emphasizing the strength that lies beneath his wet clothes. As he rotates his shoulders, his magnificent wings unfurl with a graceful snap, the feathers trembling as they shake loose the excess water. A few droplets glisten in the sunlight, catching the light like tiny jewels as they fall to the ground. The sight is both awe-inspiring and strangely intimate, and I can't help but feel a flutter of warmth at the sheer beauty of him.

"Come," he says, holding his hand out to me. "We will fly to the castle."

I take a step back, and he arches a curious brow at me.

"We must *walk*," I say, as if it's obviously the wisest decision. "I have had nothing but rain and rock for so long. I'm not about to throw away the opportunity to feel the grass beneath my feet."

I balance on one leg, hopping in place as I yank off my waterlogged boot and hurl it across the field. The Fae stare at me, bewildered, as I do the same with the other. The moment my bare toes crunch against the grass, a wave of dizzying bliss washes over me, and I can't help but throw my head back and laugh, earning concerned frowns from my companions.

"Your Highness," Orios coughs, drawing Daed's attention. "We are to... walk?" His voice lingers on the last word, as if it were some strange concept beyond comprehension.

Daed watches me twist into the dirt, giggling as I wriggle my toes into the earth. A grin threatens to pull at the corners of his mouth, even as he tries to suppress it. "Yes. We walk."

Orios rubs at the point of his ear, the very idea seeming so utterly foreign that I can almost hear the wheels turning in his head. To show him, I take my first step, my heart soaring with every movement. I begin to walk, humming a carefree tune with a smile plastered across my face. Each stride through the grass feels like a joyous dance, the blades swishing against my skin, sending shivers of delight up my spine. The sun kisses my cheeks, and the world around me brightens with every step I take.

Eventually, the skeptical Fae follow as we make for the castle in the distance, and I watch Daed closely. His brow is furrowed, lips pressed in a tight line as he looks down at the ground. He's not used to this—walking instead of flying.

"Take off your boots," I say, nudging him with a playful smile.

He raises an eyebrow, clearly unamused, but I can see the curiosity flickering in his eyes. "You cannot be serious."

"I have never been more serious. Walk with me like this. Feel the grass."

He hesitates for a moment, glancing around, as if expecting someone to see this un-princely behavior. But then, with a deep sigh, Daed pulls off his boots, one at a time. The moment his bare feet touch the grass, he freezes. His expression shifts, from wary to surprised, and then something softer. He flexes his toes against the ground, feeling the softness of the earth, the warmth of the sun-soaked grass.

"This is... strange," he mutters.

"It's good, you'll get used to it," I insist, taking his hand in mine and tugging him forward gently. "Just walk."

And so we do, side by side, feeling the grass, the sun on our faces. The storm that rages beyond the island feels like a distant memory now, something left behind in the world we've escaped from. I feel Daed's gaze for a long moment, and even when the hardness returns to his eyes, something in him has shifted.

As we near the castle, its grandeur becomes clearer, and it is unlike anything I've ever seen. Nothing like the dark, imposing Baev'kalath with its endless shadows and gothic spires. This place... it breathes with light. Its stone is bleached pale, almost white, glowing softly in the sunlight that bathes every corner of the island. Tall, open windows stretch along the walls, letting the light pour in from every direction. There are no heavy curtains or iron bars, just vast expanses of glass that reflect the blue sky and the golden fields.

The castle itself feels open, alive in a way that Baev'kalath never could. Where Daed's home is steeped in rain and cold, always surrounded by the howling wind and the weight of a dark history, this place is the opposite.

It feels like it was made to embrace the warmth, the light, the world around it.

Flowers climb along the walls, bright and colorful, weaving between the stones as if they've always belonged here. Sunlight bounces off everything—the white stone, the wide pathways, the golden banners that flap softly in the gentle breeze.

As soon as we enter the castle, my eyes catch the grand staircase that winds its way upward in a graceful spiral, the banister carved from smooth, pale wood, glowing softly in the afternoon sun. Without waiting, I rush toward the staircase, my bare feet barely making a sound on the polished wood. I can't help the laugh that escapes my lips as I take the steps two at a time, the wide spiral carrying me higher, higher, until I reach the landing at the top.

I turn the corner and burst into a bedroom, gasping at the sight. The grand chambers sprawl out before me, bathed in light that pours in through the open balcony. It's massive, with high ceilings and soft, white walls. The bed is enormous, its canopy draped in pale, sheer curtains that flutter in the gentle breeze coming from outside. The linens are the color of cream, soft and inviting, and the whole room smells faintly of fresh flowers.

I find the perfect spot by the window for my vine, then I can't help but run to the balcony, the breeze lifting my hair as I step outside. From here, the view is breathtaking—the island stretching out below us in vibrant greens and golds, the rivers glistening like diamonds, and beyond, I see a small forest that I'm curious to explore. The storm is still a distant threat, but here, within the eye, everything is calm, peaceful.

I close my eyes for a moment, letting the sun warm my face, listening to the grass below swaying gently in the breeze.

Behind me, I hear Daed enter the room, his presence unmistakable. I turn to find him standing in the doorway, watching me with that same intense gaze, his arms crossed over his chest. For a moment, neither of us speaks. The sunlight plays across his face, softening his sharp features.

"You look... comfortable," he says quietly, his voice low.

"And you've already got some color in your cheeks," I reply with a grin.

"It's because you made me walk for hours. In the sun. In wet leather," he says, dipping his head for emphasis.

I roll my eyes. "It wasn't hours." I try not to cast my eyes over the leather clinging to his thighs, but I'm not sure I do well. "Besides. I doubt I could make the Prince of the Sundered Kingdoms do anything he did not want to do."

"I think it would surprise you what you could make the Prince of the Sundered Kingdoms do, wife."

Daed dips his chin and strides towards me, his gaze so intrusive I turn my back to him and stare blankly over the balcony. I hear his steps across the floor and my skin prickles at the thought of what may come next. But I am also finally at peace, and I do not want Daed's fickle interest in me to ruin this meager happiness.

In the distance, I catch a glimpse of Solena and Orios walking together in the gardens below, and it provides a timely distraction. That is until I realize Daed is not aware of their relationship as I am.

When I glance at him over my shoulder, his eyes are narrowed on the pair, watching as their hands brush.

"If we were in Baev'kalath, he would be stripped of his Reaper armor," Daed states, a distaste on his tongue.

I gulp, realizing my promises to Solena mean nothing if Daed punishes Orios here and now.

"It is a ridiculous law," I say tersely. "Allowing your greatest warriors a sliver of happiness does not make them less loyal or ferocious. Even when you took that honor from Arax, which was completely unnecessary, by the way, he still pledged his life to his house. To punish Orios and Solena would be one of the more heartless things you—"

Daed raises a hand, his eyebrow arched. "Take a breath, Amara. I said *if* we were in Baev'kalath, which we clearly are not, because I am not wearing any shoes."

I glimpse his pale bare feet on the marble, and a laugh escapes me. "You could have put them back on."

"I will," Daed says defensively. "In good time." He tips his chin to Orios and Solena. "The same with them. I cannot ignore the oaths he took, but I can overlook them for a moment."

"Is all this sunlight having an effect on you?" I ask with a smile.

Daed says nothing. He would never admit that perhaps he likes it here, this world that is not so jagged and hard. He turns from the balcony, and when I glance over my shoulder

180

at him, I catch the way his eyes trail over the room, taking it all in. Eventually, his gaze lands on the bed—a massive, inviting thing draped in those soft, fluttering curtains.

The bed looms between us, both a symbol of what we are and what we aren't.

"There are other rooms," he says, his voice measured, as if he's carefully choosing each word. "I'll stay in one of them."

I blink, his words crashing into me harder than I expected. For a moment, I don't know how to react. My lips part, but no sound comes out. Instead, I look back at the bed, its empty vastness suddenly mocking me. A part of me that desires him hoped he wouldn't say that—that maybe this place, with its warmth and light, would break through the wall between us.

But here we are, standing apart once again.

I force a smile and nod, hiding the twinge of disappointment that settles in my chest. "Of course," I say lightly, my voice betraying none of the ache inside. "Whatever makes you comfortable."

I turn back to the balcony, biting the inside of my cheek as I look out over the island. The sun is still warm on my skin, but it feels less comforting now, the peace of the moment slipping away. I can't make sense of him. One minute, he's protective, possessive but also tender, and the next, he's pulling away, keeping me at arm's length. Does he care for me at all? Or am I just the wife he was forced to take?

I sigh softly, folding my arms over the balcony railing as the wind tugs at my hair. This place is beautiful—almost perfect. But right now, it feels like even in paradise, Daed and I are standing on opposite shores, an ocean of uncertainty and unspoken words between us.

"So, wife," he exhales, breaking the silence. "Pariseth is at your disposal. What do you want to do first?"

When my stomach grumbles softly, it becomes clear what I need most. "Well," I start, brushing a stray lock of hair from my face, "I'm starving."

Daed tilts his head, a faint smile forming on his lips. "That can be fixed. Though, here in Pariseth, we gather our own food. There are some stores, of course, but for fresh fruit and vegetables, you'll find them in the gardens. Though I imagine they are overgrown, we have not been here for a while. Meat, however." He pauses, his smirk turning into something more deliberate. "We'll have to hunt in the woods."

I cross my arms and shake my head. "No."

His brow lifts. "No?"

"I don't want you hunting while we're here," I say firmly. "If there's fresh fruit and vegetables, that's enough. I won't have us killing anything."

Daed's lips press into a thin line, clearly weighing my demand. "No flying. No shoes and now... no meat?"

For a moment, I half expect him to argue or mock me, as he so often does. But instead, he studies me, his eyes narrowing in thought. Finally, he exhales, rubbing the back of his neck before meeting my gaze again. "Very well," he says, though there's a trace of reluctance in his voice. "No hunting. We'll make do with what the gardens provide."

His agreement takes me slightly off guard, and I find myself staring at him, wondering why he's so willing to give in. I nod slowly, though part of me is waiting for him to pull the rug out from under me.

But he doesn't. Instead, he straightens and gestures toward the door. "Shall we head to the gardens, then? I imagine you'd like to see more of the island before we starve."

There's a trace of amusement in his voice, just enough to stir a smile from me as I step closer. "Yes," I answer. Part of me wonders why things can't always be this easy between us, while another, quieter part dares to imagine what might blossom if we had more time here in Pariseth without the weight of our worlds on our shoulders.

CHAPTER 20

A t first, the garden feels like an impossible task. Tangled vines choke the life out of the space, wild weeds covering what was once a beautiful, orderly sanctuary. I stand still for a moment, overwhelmed by the sight of it. Where do I even start?

But then I drop to my knees and plunge my hands into the dirt. The cool, rich soil between my fingers instantly grounds me, bringing me back to The Grove—to the simplicity and purpose of working with the earth. The feel of it, the smell of it, tugs at memories of home, a bittersweet ache settling in my chest. I close my eyes for a second, allowing the connection to wash over me. I can do this. I've done it before.

Solena is already beside me, her hands deftly pulling herbs from their wild beds, moving with the precision of someone who does not shirk from hard work. Meanwhile, I tackle the job of ripping out the weeds and untangling the vines. It's peaceful at first, the soft rustle of leaves and birdsong in the air. But as the sun climbs higher, the work grows harder, and the heat begins to bear down on us.

It doesn't take long before Orios and Daed reluctantly join us. They stood back at first, clearly unsure of where to even begin, and it amuses me that these fearsome Mordorin warriors are afraid of some weeds and dirt. Orios grumbles as he pulls at a thick root, his movements slow and awkward, while Daed frowns in frustration, ripping at the overgrowth with all the grace of a warrior, not a gardener. Sweat drips down both of their faces as they struggle to keep up with the tasks.

Eventually, even they can't stand the heat. With a grunt, Daed pulls off his shirt, tossing it aside. His chest gleams in the sunlight, muscles rippling as he bends to uproot a stubborn plant. Orios follows, not to be outdone, and soon both of them are working shirtless, dirt clinging to their skin as they toil under the midday sun. The sight of them—normally so poised and composed—now sweaty and dirt-streaked, makes me grin and for a moment Solena loses her focus as her eyes roam every inch of Orios' torso. Their struggle with the menial labor is almost endearing.

By the time we're done, the garden looks immaculate, transformed from a wild mess into a beautiful, orderly space. Rows of vegetables, herbs, and flowers, bloom under the sun, and there's a deep satisfaction in seeing what we've accomplished together.

"Well, that was... an experience," Daed says, wiping his brow with the back of his hand, his usual smugness replaced by exhaustion.

"Didn't expect to be a gardener today," Orios mutters, leaning heavily on his shovel.

I laugh, shaking the dirt from my hands. "The garden wasn't going to fix itself. But I think we did well."

We gather the fresh vegetables—plump tomatoes, fragrant herbs, leafy greens—and with every step, I feel a contentment settle over me.

As we prepare to leave the garden and return to the castle, Orios straightens up, his eyes narrowing toward the distant edge of the field. "Rook," he calls to Daed, his voice low and intrigued, "look."

I follow his gaze, and there, near the tree line, stands a deer. It's a magnificent creature—strong and muscular, with antlers like a crown atop its head. It stands still, unaware of us, grazing peacefully in the golden grass. Orios wipes the dirt from his hands. "Now that's something more substantial," he says with a grin. "We could have a real feast tonight, and it's been so long since I've hunted."

I glance at Daed, feeling a pang of uncertainty tighten in my chest. This is the moment—the test of his promise. The untamed wilderness calls to him, just like it does to Orios. The pull of their instincts, the way their kind thrives on the thrill of the hunt. My eyes flick between the deer and Daed, waiting, wondering if he'll agree and break the peace I hoped we'd find here.

For a moment, Daed stands quietly, his eyes fixed on the deer, his jaw clenched as though he's weighing the choice in his mind. Orios looks at him expectantly, already envisioning the hunt.

But then Daed sighs, turning to Orios with a calm but firm expression. "No," he says, his voice steady and resolute. "There will be no hunting for food or sport while we're here. We'll be eating stew tonight." His lips twist around the words that follow. "Vegetable stew."

Orios blinks in surprise, clearly not expecting such a response. His mouth opens as if to protest, but then he sees the look in Daed's eyes—an unspoken command to let it go. He grumbles under his breath but nods. "As you wish, Your Highness."

I smile with relief, my shoulders relaxing.

"I'll make some bread to go with the stew," Solena adds.

"Wonderful," I say, wiping my hands on my tunic. "Stew and bread it is."

The grand kitchen is a sight to behold, almost too pristine to disturb with the mess of cooking. It's all smooth, pale stone counters and arched windows that let in the golden sunlight of the afternoon. Copper pots hang from hooks above a wide hearth, and shelves made of lightly polished wood hold jars of spices and dried herbs that fill the air with a fragrant, earthy scent.

Solena gives everything a quick dusting. It seems as if no one has used this kitchen for some time. Then I stand at the counter, chopping vegetables for the stew, the rhythmic sound of the knife on the board grounding me in the moment. Across from me, Solena kneads dough, her hands working the flour and water into a soft, pliable mass. She hums under her breath as she prepares the bread, her movements sure and confident. From the store, she's gathered provisions—flour, salt, and fragrant yeast. The dough rises quickly in the warmth of the sunlit room.

Out on the balcony, I can hear Daed and Orios talking in low voices. The murmur of their conversation is punctuated by the occasional laugh from Orios, no doubt still finding amusement in Daed's refusal to hunt the deer earlier. I roll my eyes, wiping my hands on my apron.

The thought of Daed, the Prince of the Mordorin, standing out there idly while I'm working in the kitchen? *Absolutely not.* He may be accustomed to meals served on silver platters in Baev'kalath, but where I come from, everyone pitches in. I narrow my eyes at him through the open doors and call out, "Daedalus!"

He turns at the sound of his name, glancing in through the archway, his brow raised in question.

"Stop standing around out there and make yourself useful," I say, waving him inside.

Daed steps into the kitchen, looking bemused as I hand him a wooden spoon. "You want *me* to help with this?" he asks, his eyes flicking to the bubbling pot of stew over the hearth.

"Yes, *you*," I say, unable to hold back a smile. "Now stir."

He smirks but obeys, giving the pot a slow, deliberate stir. His gray eyes meet mine briefly, a teasing glint in them. "Are you sure this isn't some form of punishment?"

"Absolutely," I laugh. "You're going to stir that stew until it's perfect."

Daed gives a mock glare but continues to stir, the scent of the stew beginning to fill the kitchen with rich, earthy warmth.

When dinner is finally finished, we set the table in the grand dining room. The space is breathtaking—a long table of smooth, pale wood, with chairs draped in light fabric that flutters gently in the breeze. The walls are painted in soft, airy hues of cream and gold, and sunlight pours in through tall arched windows, casting the room in a warm, inviting glow. A delicate chandelier hangs above, its crystals catching the light and sending tiny rainbows dancing across the walls.

We find a few bottles of wine stored in the back of the pantry, rich and red, and we fill our glasses as we sit down to eat. The four of us gather around the table, the stew steaming in bowls before us, the fresh bread warm and fragrant beside it. Solena beams proudly at her handiwork, and Orios is already reaching for a second slice of bread before he's even finished his first.

As we eat, a sense of ease settles over the atmosphere—something light and natural. I glance at Daed, who sits beside me, his shoulders finally relaxed, a faint smile tugging at his lips as he listens to Orios weave a tale. Solena laughs, her face aglow with joy. In this moment, it feels as if the rigid social hierarchies of the outside world fade away. We are no longer a prince or a princess, a reaper or a maid. We are simply people, sharing food and sipping wine, and in that simplicity, everything feels perfect.

I let myself wonder—could this be what normal feels like? What it might be like to live without the constant shadow of Baev'kalath hanging over us? Here, there are no haunted halls, no whispers of the past chasing us at every turn. For the first time in what feels like forever, I'm not thinking about our enemies, about the battles waiting to be fought. I'm just here, in this moment, and I can't help but hope that maybe, just maybe, this is something we could have again.

After our meal, Solena and I clear the table, but we task the Mordorin warriors with the washing up. With the sun still in the sky, I decide on what I want to do next, going to my room before returning to the garden, this time with the serpentine vine in my hands.

I kneel in the dirt, more comfortable than any throne, and run a knuckle along her stem, and for the first time in a long time, I hear her yawn as if she's just waking from a long nap.

"There you are," I smile.

It was a kind gift from the sisters, but I think even they did not realize how she would suffer in Baev'kalath. She needs to be somewhere she can thrive, where her roots can seep deep into the earth and grow strong. I know I must return to the fortress sooner rather than later. I won't expose her to the same fate. Not when I can leave her here in the sun.

I start digging, scooping out soil with my hands before wriggling the vine free from the bowl.

"How did I know I would find you here," Daed says from behind me.

I glance over my shoulder and smile. "Did you enjoy the stew?"

He pats his stomach. "Surprisingly yes. The washing up part, not so much."

"Well, how about you make breakfast tomorrow and I'll do the washing up?"

"You want me to... cook?"

I grin. "I have seen you turn to smoke, vanish into thin air and fly straight into a cyclone, but cooking worries you? I'm sure it's not that bad."

"We can only hope," Daed exhales.

I hold his gaze for a moment longer, then look down at the vine in my hands, its tendrils curling and twisting with life. It feels as if the plant itself is eager to be set into the soil, to root itself here. I smile and glance back at Daed, still watching me with that curious expression, as if he's trying to make sense of the peace I find in this simple act.

"Come here," I say softly, patting the ground beside me. "I want to show you."

He hesitates for a second, but then, as if drawn by something he doesn't quite understand, he crouches down next to me. The closeness of him makes my breath catch, his presence overwhelming in the quiet intimacy of the garden. His shirt is still open from earlier, and his skin glows faintly in the sunlight. I can feel the heat radiating off him as he moves closer, his broad shoulders brushing mine.

"This is how you plant her," I explain, gently placing the vine in the shallow hole I've dug. My fingers move through the dirt, cradling the fragile roots with care. "You have to make sure the soil is soft enough, so she can spread her roots without being suffocated."

Daed watches my hands intently, studying my every movement. I take one of his large hands in mine and guide it to the vine. His fingers brush against mine, rough from battle, but gentle now, as if he's afraid to hurt the delicate plant.

"Like this," I murmur, guiding his hand to cover the roots with earth. His touch is careful, tentative, and it's a strange contrast to the strength I know he wields. I can feel his breath on my skin, warm and steady, and I suddenly realize just how close we are.

"See?" I say, my voice barely above a whisper as I glance up at him. "It's not so hard."

Our faces are inches apart now, the air thick with something that feels deeper than the garden, than the act of planting. His eyes meet mine, and there's something different in them—softer, more vulnerable. I forget about everything else. It's just him and me, here in this garden, our hands in the earth.

"Not so hard," he echoes, but there's a slight rasp in his voice, a tightness in his throat that I can feel mirrored in my own chest.

I release his hand slowly, my fingers lingering on his for a heartbeat longer than necessary. His gaze falls to my lips, then flicks back to my eyes, and I can't tell if it's the magic of the garden or the quiet intimacy between us, but the air seems charged now, humming with something unsaid.

"I think she's going to do well here," I say, breaking the silence, though my voice is a little unsteady. "She's strong. She'll take root and grow."

Daed's hand remains in the soil, his fingers lightly brushing the vine. He turns his head slightly, just enough that his cheek grazes mine, and my breath hitches again. It's a fleeting touch, but it feels like a spark, sending a warmth through me that has nothing to do with the earth beneath my hands.

"I hope so," he says quietly, his voice a low rumble.

His words hang between us, heavy with meaning, and I realize he's not just talking about the vine. There's something deeper in his tone, something that makes me feel as though he's talking about me—about us.

"You seem different here," I say. "Lighter. I've seen you smile at least twice."

"You have a way of making things seem less... difficult," he admits, his voice softer now, his gaze flickering down to where our fingers press into the soil, before meeting mine again.

For a heartbeat, it feels like the world stands still. His fingers tighten around mine, just slightly, and I can't tell if he's holding onto the earth, or if he's holding onto me.

But suddenly Daed pulls away, his fingers slipping from mine as he clears his throat. "I, uh, need to clean up," he says, his voice breaking the moment like a fragile glass. The warmth of his hand is replaced with the cool air, and I watch him step back, the space between us growing wider.

"Of course," I reply, forcing a smile that feels more like a mask than a reflection of my heart. He turns away, and I'm left kneeling in the garden, the serenity of the flowers around me contrasting sharply with the hollow ache that starts to form in my chest.

Once inside the castle, I retreat to my room, a swirl of emotions catching in my throat. I wash my hands of the soil and change into a simple nightgown, the soft fabric feeling delicate against my skin. I sit on the edge of the bed, the plush mattress inviting, but my heart isn't in it.

I keep glancing at the door, hoping to hear his footsteps approach, to feel his presence wash over me again. Before I lie down, I find myself drawn to the balcony, the cool night air brushing against my skin. Stepping outside, I lean against the railing, gazing out over the garden bathed in silver moonlight.

The edges of the moon shimmer like the finest silk, a delicate veil that seems to pulse with life. As it waxes in its fullness, it brings forth an aura of warmth and promise, inviting dreams and stirring desires. The soft glow illuminates the petals of the flowers below, making them appear as if they are sprinkled with silver dust, and the leaves seem to shimmer, dancing in the light breeze.

As my gaze wanders, I catch sight of Orios and Solena nestled beneath the flowering branches, their silhouettes entwined in a tender embrace. Their kisses are soft at first, delicate brushes of lips that speak of their affection. I shouldn't be watching—this moment feels private, sacred—but something holds my gaze. I take in the way Solena tucks her hair behind her ear as Orios cups her face, his touch reverent, the moonlight casting a gentle glow around them.

As their kisses deepen, the atmosphere shifts, a longing radiating between them. Orios pulls Solena closer, and she melts against him, her fingers trailing down his arms, tracing the contours of his sinewy muscles. They breathe each other in, savoring the intimacy of the moment, and I feel the stirrings of envy and admiration mix within me.

But then, as their affection grows more fervent, the warmth turns into a fire, and I realize I should not be watching. I try to look away, but I'm rooted to the spot, lost in the beautiful tableau unfolding before me. It isn't until their hands begin to explore, the kisses becoming more passionate and possessive, that I finally drag my eyes away, feeling a rush of heat and embarrassment, my heart pounding as I retreat inside.

As dawn lightens the sky, I wake alone to the gentle chirping of birds filling the air. I stretch and blink against the brightness streaming through the open balcony doors, feeling the warmth on my skin—a stark contrast to the cold shadows and eternal gray sky of Baev'kalath.

The door creaks open, and Solena steps in, her bright smile illuminating the room even further. "Good morning, Princess!" she chirps, bustling over to my side. "Let's get you ready."

I sit up, pulling the sheets closer around me. "You don't need to do that here, Solena."

She shakes her head, a teasing glint in her eyes. "Nonsense! I get you ready faster and do your hair much better than you do."

With that, she drags me from the bed. Unlike the vast wardrobe of the fortress, I have only what we brought with us.

"Pants and tunic?" she asks.

I shake my head, my gaze landing on the familiar green dress I wore on the ship. "No. I'll wear this today."

"Very well," she says, stripping me out of my nightgown in the blink of an eye.

Usually so stoic and focused, Solena wears an immovable smile this morning. Maybe it's the power of Pariseth that has these typically surly Fae in such good moods, or perhaps it's the lingering blissful glow from what I witnessed in the garden last night.

Once my dress is on, she moves behind me, brushing my hair with soft, gentle tugs that feel oddly comforting.

"You're happy this morning," I remark, glancing at her in the mirror.

Solena's cheeks flush pink. "Yes, I am. Being able to be in the open with Orios is a luxury we are not afforded in Baev'kalath."

"You were certainly in the open with him last night," I say, and my eyes widen as I realize my words have slipped out.

Solena freezes mid-stroke, her cheeks growing even warmer. "Your Highness! You were... watching?"

My cheeks burn too, equally embarrassed. "I couldn't sleep and wandered onto the balcony at the wrong time."

"Well, no harm done," Solena gulps. "Let's just never speak of it again."

I nod, relief flooding me. "Yes. I'd like that very much, thank you."

Solena resumes brushing my hair, letting out a deep breath. "I assure you, we're not usually this adventurous. Must be the Lover's Eye approaching."

I frown, confusion knitting my brows. "What do you mean?"

She laughs softly, a hint of mischief in her tone. "The full moon. It's the Lover's Eye tonight."

My breath catches in my throat. The Lover's Eye. Daed had mentioned it in passing—a night when tradition dictates that the king and queen make love in public under the watchful gaze of the moon, surrounded by their people. A sudden wave of nerves crashes over me, churning my stomach.

"Oh," I manage to say, my voice shaky. "I didn't realize."

Solena leans in, a smile dancing on her lips. "Orios and I have always celebrated it in secret. But not here. This will be your first Lover's Eye with Prince Daedalus. How exciting!"

I force a smile, but it feels brittle as my stomach twists tighter. "Yes. Exciting."

Her gaze flits to the bed—one side rumpled, the other still perfectly made. "He didn't sleep here last night?"

"No," I reply, my heart sinking at the implication.

Solena gives my hair a final stroke before laying the brush down on the dressing table and turning me to face her. I wish she hadn't; the concern in her eyes reveals the anxiety etched across my face.

"You are a good woman, Princess Amara," she says firmly. "And Prince Daedalus is a fine leader, the greatest warrior House Mordorin has ever seen. The Lover's Eye isn't just about physical connections; it's a joining of heart and mind as well. I'm sure the Pale Eye will take care of you both."

I wish I shared Solena's faith—not just in the Mother Above, but in my husband. I nod, though the weight of uncertainty still presses down on me. What if Daed doesn't want me? What if tonight, under the moonlight, we remain as distant as ever? All I can do is wait and see what the night brings.

We leave the bedchamber and stroll down the hall when I spot a room I've never noticed before. Its door is half-open, revealing a clutter of paintings and trunks stacked against the far wall of an otherwise empty space. Curiosity piqued, I pause.

"What's that?" I ask Solena, already stepping inside before she can respond.

She hisses under her breath. "Your Highness, we're not supposed to go in there." Her frown softens slightly. "Though, I suppose you're allowed." Reluctantly, she tiptoes after me.

I make my way to the paintings, flipping through the heavy, dust-covered frames. Faces of unfamiliar Fae stare back—elegant features framed by long, shimmering blond hair and flawless blue eyes. I let the portraits rest back against the wall and turn my attention to a pile of golden fabric on the floor. As I lift it, dust billows around me, and when I shake it out, an embroidered emblem appears: a ship riding the waves, guided by a gust of wind.

"House Ithranor," I breathe, recognizing the symbol of one of the great houses of the Sundered Kingdoms who fled during the Betrayers' Battle. "Why is this here?"

Solena's expression shifts, and it's clear she knows more than she's letting on.

"Solena," I press, my voice firm. "Tell me."

With a reluctant sigh, she explains. "This castle—this entire island—was once part of House Ithranor's territory. When they were aligned with House Mordorin, this served as an outpost for their warriors. But when they fled during the war, House Mordorin... moved in."

I blink, taken aback. "I didn't know that."

"Not many do," she replies tersely. "And I'd prefer to keep it that way. So, if you wouldn't mind leaving this room..."

I frown. "I doubt Daed would care if I knew such a detail. I wondered why this place felt so different from Baev'kalath."

"And now you know," Solena urges, her tone pleading. "Please, Your Highness."

With a dramatic roll of my eyes, I appease her and step back into the hallway. Solena hurriedly closes the door behind us, and I'm about to press her further when a foul stench wafts up the stairs, stopping me in my tracks.

CHAPTER 21

The acrid smell of smoke wafts through the air as Daed wrestles with the cast-iron skillet over the fire. I watch, concern and amusement bubbling within me, as he attempts to fry the eggs. They seem to be fighting against him, sticking stubbornly to the pan while he works hard to coax them into submission. His brow is furrowed in intense concentration, and beads of sweat form on his forehead, the morning light catching his black hair as it falls into his eyes.

"Just a little more heat," he mutters to himself, his determination unwavering despite the ominous sizzle that fills the air.

"Daed," I venture cautiously, "maybe we should just—"

"Sit, wife. I'm almost finished," he grumbles.

I bite my lip, a smile tugging at the corners of my mouth. "If you say so, husband."

As he scrapes the eggs with the wooden spoon, trying desperately to flip them, I can see the frustration etched on his face. He scoops the dubious mixture onto a plate, and I brace myself. I don't want to hurt his feelings; after all, this is his earnest attempt at caring for me, and I appreciate the sentiment.

"Daedalus, are these eggs fried... or... or are they scrambled?" I ask, eyeing his offering that somehow looks burnt and raw at the same time.

Daed looks at me with a vacant expression. "Yes," he replies.

Okay then. Taking a deep breath, I pick up my fork and stab at the gooey yellow mass that sits before me.

The first bite sends my taste buds into chaos—the burnt bits mix with an overwhelming saltiness that nearly makes me gag. I force a smile, chewing slowly as I search for something—anything— positive to say.

"It's, um, definitely...unique!" I exclaim, striving for enthusiasm.

Daed's face drops, his shoulders sagging as he runs a hand through his disheveled hair. "You're lying. It's rubbish." He tosses the frying pan into the sink with a clatter. "Come. Let's get out of here. It smells horrible."

We leave the castle and stroll through the gardens, continuing past the river until we reach an open field. Daed looks remarkably serious for someone whose eyes glint so beautifully in the sunlight.

"Are you still upset about the eggs?" I ask.

He grumbles in response.

"It was nice of you to try," I say, hoping to ease his disappointment.

"You'd think the Commander of the Ebon Flight would know how to handle a chicken ovum," he mutters.

"It was honestly not the worst thing I've ever eaten."

He glances at me from the corner of his eye. "Really?"

"Really." I'm lying, of course. It was dreadful. But there's no point in ruining the day over a bad egg. I haven't seen this side of Daed—relaxed and unguarded—and I don't want to scare it away.

"So, where are we going?" I ask, eager to change the subject.

He tips his head thoughtfully. "There's a small forest beyond the clearing. A stream runs through it—crystal clear. You can see the rocks at the bottom." He pauses, noticing I'm staring at him. "I thought you might like it."

"I'm sure I will," I reply, closing my eyes and turning my face toward the sun, savoring its warmth. "I can't believe this place exists within the Untold Sea. If I were you, I would spend every day here."

Daed glances at me from the corner of his eye. "It's not a place I think of often. There's always somewhere to be, something to take care of. There's never enough time."

"But don't you live forever?" I laugh lightly, but his expression remains stern.

"A longer life simply gives you more things to regret," he murmurs.

"Surely there must be some good?" I ask, refusing to believe that such a gift can be so miserable.

"It never lasts," he replies, his voice low and heavy.

I lean forward to catch his gaze, which lingers on his boots. "Then you're doing it wrong."

He raises an eyebrow, curiosity flickering in his eyes.

"There's far too much beauty in this world to dwell on pain. Pain will always be there; it's a constant. That's why we must find that one thing that turns the night into day. A reason to welcome the sunrise."

"And what is your reason, Amara?" he asks, his tone earnest.

The answer flows from me effortlessly. "Love," I say, and the very sound drains the color from his face.

"Love for my people. Love for the earth. Love for the breeze that knows my name and the taste of fresh honey on my tongue." I turn my face to the sun, letting its warmth envelop me. "Love for the feeling of sunlight on my skin."

Lost in my thoughts, I don't realize Daed is staring at me, his lips parted, his gaze intrusive enough to send a rush of warmth to my cheeks, and I nervously tuck my dark hair behind my ears and turn away.

"Sorry. I..."

"No," he says urgently. "Don't apologize. Everyone should be fortunate enough to see the world through your eyes. To feel as deeply as you do."

I shake my head. "I don't think anyone wants that."

"I do," he says quickly, causing me to jerk my head to meet his gaze. "My world is hard, cruel, and cold, Amara. So cold it feels like my veins are flooded with ice water. But you—your smile, your laughter, and the way you stand tall even in the face of pure malice—make me feel something." He tilts his head slightly toward the sky, his eyes half-closed against the glare of the sun as he exhales. "Warm."

Oh, how I want to touch him. I want to reach out my hand and add the caress of my fingers to the sun on his skin, to have the chance to warm him, too. When he breathes in my ear and speaks of hunger and desire, it ignites every nerve in me, sending surges of warmth to my core. But when he's like this—bare and honest—it awakens something deeper. My heart aches for him.

"That seems like something worth welcoming the sunrise for," I say, my voice soft.

He turns to look at me, the breeze playing with his dark hair, sunlight catching the steel gray of his eyes. In that moment, time feels suspended. "It is not the only thing."

When we reach the edge of the forest, Daed steps forward first, and when I hesitate, he turns, extending his hand toward me.

As I take his hand, our fingers intertwine and the world around me fades into the background. The air is rich with the scent of earth and wildflowers, while sunlight filters through the lush canopy, casting dancing patterns on the soft undergrowth. A sense of peace washes over me, dispelling the weight of my worries. I forget the ship, the Stormwyrm, the haunting shadows of Baev'kalath, and the demons of my past. I forget Modok, Frane, and all those who would rather see me dead than on the throne. In this moment, all that matters is Daed. He is the only memory I want.

Within the forest walls, the trees grow tall and strong, though they lack the grandeur of the Grove. Here, there is no room for the rope bridges that sway between gargantuan trunks or the small houses tucked within their branches. Yet, even without Souls dwelling here, I can feel the forest's pulsating energy beneath my feet. I hear the whispers of the wind and the small conversations of creatures darting through the long grass or hiding inside weathered logs. After so long without hearing it, the symphony is almost overwhelming. I stop to catch my breath, and Daed pauses beside me.

"Are you alright, wife?" he asks.

I nod with a smile on my lips. It's not pain or discomfort, all these feelings, all these voices. It's just a reminder of how much I miss my home.

Daed leads me to a clearing, and the stream he promised is just as he described: crystal clear water so translucent that the stones gleam at the bottom. I crouch by the bank, scooping my hand through the cool water, a delightful tingle racing across my skin. I bring my hand to my mouth, drinking deeply, and the purity of the water carries with it the echoes of the forest's memories.

Daed looms over me, his presence steady and watchful. "I remember that dress," he remarks. "The last time I saw it, it was covered in blood."

I look up, wiping the water from my lips. "And the last time I wore it, you were separating a male from his head."

"I did what I had to," Daed replies, his voice devoid of regret.

"So did I."

He drops into a crouch beside me. "Do you know what I thought when I saw you on the balcony?"

I turn my gaze back to the running water, reluctant to hear what he might say next.

"I thanked the Pale Eye for sending someone strong enough to survive Baev'kalath... someone brave enough to survive me." Suddenly, his hand cups my face. "Someone so beautiful that I have been unable to think of anything else." Daed's thumb brushes away a lingering drop of water from my bottom lip. "It shouldn't have taken me this long to tell you."

I feel as if I am teetering on the edge of a cliff, with nothing to keep me from falling. His words are sweet, but they come and go like the wind. Nothing feels real. Nothing feels true. "Enough," I say bitterly. "I heard you in the room. I heard you tell them to send me away."

A flicker of realization washes over his face, and his jaw tightens. "Did you ever think I was trying to save you?"

"From what?" I challenge. "From Modok? From Frane?"

"From *me*, Amara," Daed admits, his expression wrought with emotion as if these words have been waiting to break free since the moment he first saw me on that balcony. "I was trying to do the one decent thing I could for you—to set you free before I hurt you."

"Did you do the same for her?" I ask, my voice trembling with the weight of the question that has haunted me, pressing against my chest until I struggle for breath.

Daed furrows his brow, confusion shadowing his features. "Who?"

I gather my courage. "The Fae whose portrait hangs in your tower. Was she your wife before me?"

Daed's chin drops, and he rises to stand, but I need to know. I rise with him, grasping his shoulders before he can turn away. There is nowhere to run here—not in this small piece of paradise.

"Was she your wife?" I press again, my heart racing. A lump hardens in my throat. "Did she carry your child?"

His eyes snap back to mine, his chest heaving as he struggles to find his breath. "No, she was not my wife. No, she was not carrying my child. She was my mother, Amara. Her name was Veloria."

I grapple with his words, initially wanting to dismiss them as more lies meant to confuse me. But Daed continues, answering the unvoiced questions swirling in my mind.

"Lanneth is not my real mother," he says, his tone hardening. "She is the female my father married after my mother's death." A shadow passes over his features. "She was an Archdruidess once, but she had higher aspirations. Still, she is the only mother I've ever known."

The relief I expected to feel at discovering the Fae in the portrait is not his wife, is overshadowed by the deep sadness etched into Daed's face, scars hidden beneath his skin.

"It is my fault my mother died. I killed her."

I feel the wind knocked out of me, and I shake my head, refusing to accept such a notion. I have seen his cruelty, witnessed his capacity for violence, but I cannot believe this man is capable of such an atrocity—especially now, as I begin to glimpse the light within him.

"I don't believe you."

"What you choose to believe doesn't change the truth. She died giving birth to me."

"Oh Daed, that isn't your fault. Childbirth is dangerous; it's not something you could control."

"Because I am here, she is not. What other way is there to explain what I did?" His voice trembles, and it's almost too much for me to bear.

Now it is my turn to cup his face, rising on my tiptoes to reach him, but still he tries to turn away, as if too burdened by guilt to meet my gaze. I inhale deeply, trying to match the rise and fall of my chest with his.

"Do you know what I thought when I first saw you from that balcony?"

He doesn't answer, his gaze distant, lost somewhere beyond the trees.

My thumb caresses his sharp jawline, and I sweep his dark hair from his brow, seeking a connection that feels just out of reach. "He is the one who can protect everything I love. I believe that even more now than I did then, Daedalus."

My words draw him back to the present. "Why?"

"Love," I reply, a smile warming my face. "You have loved and lost, prince. Only someone who has had their heart ripped from their chest can possess the strength it takes to protect others from that same agony. How fortunate I am to have the warrior prince as my champion."

His hand moves atop mine, and he closes his eyes, leaning into my palm. "Amara," he whispers, "I want to protect you...but there is so much you do not understand."

"Then tell me," I urge, the heat between our bodies drawing us closer.

"I want to," he mutters, our lips tantalizingly close, the taste of his unspoken words lingering in the air. "But I cannot."

"You must let me in, husband," I plead, nearly begging. "I want to help you. I want to trust you. Please."

He swallows hard, the lump in his throat a reflection of the turmoil between us. His eyes slowly open, revealing a storm of emotions, and he pulls my hand from his face, pressing it against my side as if giving back everything I've poured out to him.

Anger flickers within me, mingling with sadness and that dull ache that fills my chest, leaving me feeling hollow.

"I will protect the Grove. You have my word," he rasps.

Before I came to Baev'kalath, that was all I wanted from him—a protector to shield the Grove from the darkness. But now, I selfishly crave so much more. He has proved his strength, the ferocity needed to stand against the Legion, but also his unwavering loyalty, his devotion. He has left no doubt among his brethren that I am his, and to challenge that claim would mean blood and fury.

But my prince is broken. I see that now, as clearly as the scars he hides. Wounded by his past, haunted by shadows he refuses to let go.

His pain calls to me, as pain in others always does. I want nothing more than to mend him, to piece him back together, to make him whole again. Because beneath his mask, I see who he truly is—the small kindnesses, the tenderness in his touch, the words he swallows down, claiming it is to protect me. But I know the truth: he's protecting himself.

If only he could see that my pain mirrors his. That loss, guilt, and the desperate will to survive are burdens we both carry. Perhaps then, we could shield one another from this world, instead of facing it alone.

CHAPTER 22

We return to the castle, the silence between us stretching like an invisible tether. The day has slipped by swiftly, sunlight giving way to the soft hues of dusk and each step away from the forest is heavy with the echoes of his words, the past he shared, and the truths I left unsaid.

Why didn't I tell him?

Daed mourns a mother, as I do, a father as well. The fire devoured mine the day the war we tried to escape came to our doorstep—flames so fierce that not even ashes remained for me to bury.

I wanted the fire to take me too. But the Grove held me fast, and when, in my despair, I tried to follow my parents years later, I awoke untouched—though I know my blade struck true. I've always believed it was the Souls who saved me that day, whispering that it was not yet my time to die. Since then, it has been my duty to protect life, just as Daed now protects me.

Perhaps, if I told him, we could console each other and find solace in the spaces where we ache most. But the hurt still festers, even after all these years. It has become both my strength—what keeps me fighting—and the shadow that looms, threatening to undo me. The final wound that even the Souls cannot not heal.

I chide myself. Who am I to demand Daed lay his soul bare when I, too, keep my scars hidden?

When we arrive, Solena and Orios are in the garden, their laughter carrying on the twilight breeze. Solena drapes a white cloth over a table, while Orios hangs lanterns from the low branches of the trees.

Of course. The Lover's Eye. What impeccable timing these Fae gods have.

"You've returned, and just in time," Solena calls out, her voice bright. But her smile falters as she notices us, her eyes narrowing. "Though you look far more solemn than when you left." She exhales sharply, refusing to let us sour the mood. "No matter. I've spent the entire day in the kitchen crafting a feast fit for the prince and princess of House Mordorin. However, the moon will not bless us if you're both so gloomy."

Daed's hand finds mine, our fingers lacing together with quiet reassurance. "It sounds nice," he murmurs, his voice meant only for me. "But Solena is right. The Lover's Eye demands our ardent submission."

I furrow my brow, skeptical. "I've heard your tales of the Lover's Eye. Should I be worried?"

A sly grin spreads across his face. "Well, that depends on how much wine and cake you indulge in."

I glare at him, but he chuckles softly.

"I'll be here," he says, his voice lowering. "At your side. There's nothing to fear."

Solena steps away from the table and dips her head toward us, her formality feeling misplaced amidst the informal warmth of Pariseth.

"I've left something for you to wear," she says. "It's on your bed."

I hesitate, briefly allowing myself to hope that Pariseth might have been an escape from the constant dressing for dinner. But apparently, Solena has other plans. She tugs gently at my sleeve.

"Go," Daed encourages, his thumb brushing over the back of my hand. "I'll see you soon."

Reluctantly, I untangle my fingers from his and let Solena lead me inside. Before the castle doors close behind us, I glance over my shoulder to see Daed and Orios deep in conversation. He catches my eye, gifting me one last smile before he disappears from view.

When we arrive in my room, my eyes immediately land on a dress draped at the end of the bed. Unlike the weighty, beaded gowns I endured in Baev'kalath, this one is light and airy, crafted from midnight blue silk that feels like pure bliss beneath my fingertips.

"Where did you find this?" I ask, knowing full well we didn't bring it with us.

"In one of the wardrobes. Left behind by some stunning Ithranor female, no doubt," Solena replies with a grin.

I hold the dress against myself, quickly noticing that there doesn't seem to be enough fabric to stretch across my hips. I frown. "What size exactly are these Ithranor females?"

Solena giggles. "I'm sure it will fit you just fine. Now hurry. My cake is in the oven, and I'd rather it didn't burn."

I've learned it's easiest not to argue with Solena. I undress, and she politely turns her back as I slip into the blue silk. The fabric cascades over my skin like a warm breeze, so light and delicate that I can barely feel it. To my surprise, though it's snug over my hips and backside, the dress fits—its elegant cowl neckline and open back highlighting my frame, while the skirt ripples like waves.

"It's beautiful," I murmur.

When Solena turns to face me, her expression lights up. "I knew it would be." She claps her hands together. "Now. Hair."

I brace myself, expecting to be dragged to the dressing table, then teased and plucked until my scalp burns. Instead, she steps closer, unweaving the simple braid over my shoulder. With only her fingers, she separates the strands, coaxing them into long, full waves that spill down my back.

"Done," she declares, stepping back to admire her work.

I raise an eyebrow. "That's it? No brushing? No pulling? No makeup?"

"No," she says simply. "I believe you're perfect, just as you are."

Then she pauses, her gaze narrowing on a red bump on my chin that I'd miserably noticed this morning. She sighs. "Apart from that. Perhaps some powder wouldn't hurt."

I glare. "I think I smell your cake burning."

"Damn it!" she yelps, spinning so fast she nearly slips as she dashes out of the room.

For a time I pace the floor, nervous excitement coursing through me, my skin alive with a restless, tingling energy. The Lover's Moon hangs heavy in my thoughts. What kind of power could it truly hold over the Fae? And what might that mean for a human like me?

"Stars above and shadows below, Amara. You are... breathtaking."

I turn at the sound of his voice. Daed stands in the doorway, wearing a fresh shirt of a color I've never seen on him before—white. The open collar reveals the runes etched across his chest, and with his sleeves rolled to his elbows, he strides toward me, his hands casually resting in his pockets. There's something in the soft shake of his head, in the disbelief painted across his face.

"I fear the moon is not worthy of you tonight," he murmurs, taking both of my hands in his. His touch is warm, steadying. "I know I'm not."

His words tug a smile from me, and I exhale, feeling their magic wrap around me like a silken thread. "Are you always this charming during the Lover's Eye?"

His chin dips, a faint smile gracing his lips. "Not usually. Are you always this beautiful?"

"Not usually," I reply, smirking.

"Then let's be unusual together," he says, tucking my arm under his and guiding me toward the door.

We descend the grand, sweeping staircase, and even before stepping outside, I catch the enticing aroma of freshly baked bread, sweet confections, and roasted vegetables.

As we pass through the castle doors, the garden comes alive with laughter and the clinking of glasses—a sure sign the wine is already flowing. Overhead, the full moon bathes the black sky in silver light, rendering the storm wall almost translucent. Beyond, the ocean roars, waves crashing rhythmically in the distance.

Orios lights the final lantern, its warm amber glow spilling across the garden, illuminating the feast Solena has laid out. She stands beside him, radiant in a gown of teal silk that flows over her svelte frame like a waterfall.

As soon as he's done, Solena slips beneath his arm with a soft laugh. He gathers her into his embrace, burying his face in her neck, his lips trailing deep, lingering kisses. My cheeks flush hot, and I try not to watch as Daed guides me to a seat at the table.

But my curiosity betrays me, and I steal a glance just as Solena's fingers tangle in Orios' long hair, her giggles echoing softly as his hand slides over her hips.

Is this the sway of the Lover's Eye?

I drag my gaze away, casting my eyes upward to the full moon. No. Surely not. The shape of a moon cannot influence something as primal as desire. Yet, I find myself staring harder, tracing the silvery glow that halos the ivory orb. I don't feel any different. Perhaps, as a human, I'm immune.

But then my skin erupts in a wave of shivers as Daed brushes past, his hand grazing my bare shoulder—a touch so casual, yet achingly intense.

He moves with a quiet command, as though he owns the moonlight, and the stars themselves are no more than his devoted subjects. The pull toward him, that unspoken bond we share, feels stronger than ever. Souls. Perhaps I am not immune after all.

Daed takes a seat across the table, his movements unhurried as he pours himself a goblet of thick red wine. He glances up, lifting the jug.

"A drink, wife?"

I nod, my response a touch too eager, nervous energy coiling in my chest.

Am I sweating? My skin feels so damn hot.

He pours another goblet and slides it across the table. Nearby, Solena's soft gasps reach my ears, but this time I don't dare look.

"Are you alright, wife?" Daed asks, his tattooed fingers curling around his goblet, his voice low.

I force a smile, hoping it passes as normal, and grasp the goblet with both hands, bringing it straight to my lips. The wine is sweet yet tart, smooth on the way down, but it curls my lips with its bite.

I set the empty goblet back on the table with a hollow clink, gesturing for him to pour another.

One of his eyebrows arches in mild amusement. "As you wish."

He fills my goblet again, and I toss the second dose back just as quickly. The warmth I'd hoped to temper only deepens, blooming in my chest and unfurling through my limbs.

Perhaps wine wasn't the best idea.

Over the rim of his goblet, Daed's eyes meet mine. But they do not linger. Instead, they roam—over my hair, my bare shoulders, and lower still, where the thin silk outlines the fullness of my breasts. His gaze stays there as he drinks, slow and deliberate, and the heat in my body ignites into a roaring fire.

The Lover's Eye is said to stir the deepest desires of the Fae, awakening instincts, needs, passions. But as Daed's gaze burns through me, a thought takes root: Is this desire his own? Or is it the moon's doing?

Solena and Orios part long enough for her to slip inside the castle, returning with a cake that glistens under the moonlight. The surface is coated with a delicate sheen of honey, adorned with small, bright red berries. She sets it down at the center of the table, her fingers brushing Orios' as she pulls her hand away and their shared glance does not even attempt to disguise their need for each other.

"This is a Lover's Eye tradition," Solena says, slicing into the cake with a silver knife. "It stirs the heart."

I swallow hard. I don't need any more help with that.

Solena's smile is coy as she places a slice in front of me. Her eyes silently urge me to try it, and when I glance across the table, I catch Daed's grin as he swirls his wine in his goblet.

I pick up my fork, my hand trembling slightly, and cut through the moist corner of the cake. I let out a quiet sigh when I pop it into my mouth. It's soft, warm, and the taste of honey and berries coats my tongue. For a moment, it's all I focus on, but then a strange sensation begins to bloom in my stomach. It's different from the dull warmth of the wine or the prickly tension of Daed's gaze. It's a blend of both, and it's spreading—fast, hot, and my pulse quickens.

Solena feeds Orios a piece of cake, her grin mischievous as he takes a huge bite, right up to her fingers. His eyes roll in bliss as he pulls her closer, his arms snaking around her waist. She giggles against his lips as they kiss—soft at first, then deeper. I can feel the raw, sweltering energy between them, crackling and humming in the air. I drop my fork and turn away.

"Are you alright, wife?" Daed's voice cuts through the haze, and I meet his gaze, praying he can't see the way I'm burning inside. His brow furrows slightly, and for a moment, I'm certain he can.

"I'm fine," I stutter, trying to swallow the lump in my throat. "Just a little... warm."

The heat in my chest spreads lower, pulsing in a rhythm I can't control. When Daed's fingers brush against mine on the table, a jolt runs through me in a place I don't expect. My eyes widen, and my muscles tighten.

Daed's teeth graze his bottom lip. "It's the berries, wife," he murmurs, his gaze narrowing on the cake. "They have... properties."

"What kind of properties?" I ask, my voice strained as the heat grows unbearable, my body shifting restlessly in my seat.

He doesn't answer right away, his jaw tightening. The hunger in his eyes is unmistakable now. "They stir desire. Make everything feel more intense. A touch. A kiss..." He doesn't need to speak the rest. He exhales. "The Fae partake of them on this night."

"You didn't," I say, nodding toward his untouched slice.

His head tilts slightly. "They can dull the senses. I prefer to stay in control. To feel everything."

Heat floods my face, and when I glance at Solena and Orios, they're lost in each other. Their hands roam beneath clothes, their bodies tangled as his hand grips the back of her neck, holding her mouth to his as they devour each other.

Daed watches me, almost curiously, as if studying my reaction to them, to the berries, to this strange and thrilling world opening up around me. He remains calm, still, unshaken.

Does he not feel this too?

Even without eating the berries, the Lover's Eye still shines above. Does it have no effect on him?

My thoughts whirl—what is real and what is nothing more than cake and wine and moonlight?

Orios and Solena rise from their seats, their movements fluid as they step into the moonlit garden. They whisper and laugh, twirling beneath the glow of the Lover's Eye, their bodies moving in perfect rhythm, each touch soft yet charged with tension. Solena tilts her head back, her dark hair cascading as Orios pulls her close, his hands resting low on her hips, guiding her with a confidence that sends a flush of heat through me again. The way they move together is almost mesmerizing—sultry, seductive, as though the night itself is theirs alone.

Daed's presence across from me is heavy, his gaze lingering, the weight of it pressing against my skin. I risk a glance, and the look in his eyes is undeniable—dark, intense, filled with a desire that mirrors the warmth swirling inside me.

"Wife," he says, his voice low, "dance with me."

My heart skips a beat. "I..."

Before I can refuse, his hand closes around mine, firm yet gentle, and in one smooth motion, he pulls me to my feet. His touch sends a shock through me, the heat of his palm igniting a fire that burns deeper than the warmth from the berries. The world spins for a moment as I stumble into him, my body instinctively leaning against the solid strength of his chest.

"I don't know how," I protest weakly, but Daed only smiles, that infuriating half-smirk pulling at the corner of his mouth.

"I'll lead," he murmurs, his voice soft as a caress. Before I can react, he guides me forward, his arm slipping around my waist as he pulls me closer. Our bodies move in sync.

One hand rests at the small of my back, while the other cradles mine. The soft music of the ocean and the moonlit night play around us as our feet fall into a rhythm I didn't even know I could follow. My pulse quickens as we sway beneath the Lover's Eye, the cool breeze mingling with the warmth that radiates from him. The closeness makes it impossible to ignore the magnetic pull between us, the way our souls seem to recognize each other, as though this isn't the first time they've danced.

I glance up at him, my breath catching as our eyes meet and the throb of desire within me grows, fueled by the berries, the moon, and the way his body presses against mine.

"See?" he says, his voice a smooth velvet. "The world did not fall apart."

I open my mouth to respond, but the words catch in my throat, silenced by the way he looks at me—like he could devour me whole. And the worst part is, I want him to. Every last bite.

Daed's hands drift lower, fingers grazing the curve of my hips as we continue to sway, and every nerve in my body lights up in response to his touch. His fingers press gently, exploring the line of my waist, teasing the edge of my dress where it meets the bare skin of my back..

I tilt my head back slightly, the cool night air kissing the exposed flesh of my neck. His lips brush my temple, soft as a whisper, sending a shiver racing down my spine. My body reacts without my consent, leaning into him, a moth helplessly drawn to the flame.

From the garden, Solena's shallow moans drift to us, and I try to block them out, try not to picture what she and Orios are doing beneath the moon. But the berries, the moonlight, and Daed's wandering hands make it impossible to think of anything else.

His breath is warm against my ear, his lips hovering so close that I can feel the ghost of a kiss.

"Amara," he murmurs, his voice dark and thick with intent.

His hand drifts further, fingers firmly sliding over the curve of backside. I close my eyes, a soft gasp escaping as he pulls me tighter, the line of his body pressed flush against mine. Our dance shifts into something else as he releases my hand, his fingers trailing lightly along my arm before brushing up to my shoulder.

My skin hums where he touches, the warmth spreading like wildfire. Every inch of me feels alive, attuned to his every movement, and though my mind tells me to pull away, I lean closer, wanting more. His fingers graze the hollow of my collarbone before tracing the swell of my breast. My breath catches in my throat as he cups me through the fabric, his thumb brushing over my hard nipple in slow circles.

I know I should say something, stop him before it goes too far, but the sensation is too much, too intoxicating. I bite down on my lip, my heart racing as a wave of desire crashes over me, the heat in my body reaching a fever pitch. His hands—strong, sure, possessive—are everywhere, and I find myself arching into his touch, a soft moan falling from my parted lips.

"Do you want me to stop?" he asks, his breath sending a tremor through me.

I can't think. I can't answer.

In the distance, I hear Solena's soft cries, followed by Orios' low, guttural moans, and my mind spins. My body is screaming at me to let go, to give in to the primal pull that's tugging me closer to Daed, but something deeper holds me back.

Is this real? Are these feelings real? If I give myself, all of myself, who am I giving it to?

His fingers press harder, more insistent, and I draw in a shaky breath, my mind battling the sensations that flood my body.

The moon above us seems to pulse, like a heartbeat that beats in time with mine.

Daed's lips graze the shell of my ear, his breath warm and heavy. "I wonder..." he murmurs, his voice a low, seductive growl. "What would you look like wearing only moonlight?"

The words send a shiver through me, but this is different. His question, the one he asked me in Baev'kalath, feels wrong here—under this moon, under its control. My body may be begging for him, but my mind revolts. This isn't real. This isn't us.

I pull away from him, the spell of the moonlight shattering like glass. "No," I whisper, my voice barely audible, but he hears it. "Not like this."

Daed's hand lingers, fingers tracing my arm, his eyes confused and clouded. "Amara..."

"I don't want the moon to decide how we feel about each other," I choke out, my heart pounding as I break free from his hold completely, stumbling back. The ground feels unstable beneath my feet, the effects of the berries making the world tilt.

"What do you mean?" he asks desperately.

"I can't... I won't submit to the moon, to this... this madness." My head spins as I take another step back, and I turn on my heel, running from him before I can think twice.

"Amara, stop!" Daed's voice chases me through the night, but I don't stop. I can't stop. The garden, the moon, his touch—they all blur into one overwhelming force, and I need to escape it all. I need to get away from him before I lose myself to this twisted magic.

I run toward the castle, my bare feet pounding against the stone path. My pulse throbs in my ears, and I can hear Daed's heavy footfalls close behind me, his voice calling my name, but I don't turn back. My only thought is to get away.

I throw myself inside my room, slamming the door behind me with a loud crash. My chest heaves as I fumble for the lock, my hands shaking from the dizzying effect of the berries. I twist it into place just as Daed's hand pounds on the door.

"Amara, let me in," he demands, his voice hard, but I can hear the restraint in it.

"Go away!" I shout, pressing my back against the door as if my body can reinforce the lock.

There's a heavy pause on the other side, his breathing hard against the wood. "Amara..." His voice is softer now, almost pleading, but I'm too dizzy, too lost in the confusion to give in.

I sink to the floor, my head swimming as I clutch the fabric of my dress, the cool stone doing little to ground me.

Daed's shadow looms beneath the door, waiting for an answer I can't give. All I can do is sit in silence, trying to hold on to whatever part of myself hasn't been taken by the moonlight.

CHAPTER 23

I wake where I last remember—curled up on the cold stone floor of my chambers, the remnants of the berries' intoxicating power still lingering in my veins. It's the early hours of the morning, the Lover's Eye still high in the sky, casting its full glow through the windows and across the room. The moon's light feels too bright, too intimate, like it knows all my secrets, like it has been watching me all night.

I sit up, rubbing my eyes, feeling weary and weak. My body aches, but beneath the heaviness, there's something else—a slow, simmering desire that refuses to fade. It stirs in the pit of my stomach, reminding me of the way Daed touched me, how his hands had explored my skin with such hunger, how I had wanted him in a way that scared me.

I crave him still, despite the clarity that has returned to me. I'm not sure if it's the berries, the moon, or simply him, but the need to be desired, to be wanted, pulls at me like a tide I can't resist. My whole life has been spent putting others first, bending to duty and obligation at the expense of my own happiness. But Daed—Daed is the only one who makes me feel something just for myself. And as much as he terrifies me, as much as his power and cruelty frightens me, I cannot deny that I feel more alive when I am with him than I have ever felt before.

I rise to my feet, unsteady but determined. The castle is eerily quiet, only the sound of my bare feet padding softly against the stone as I leave my chambers. The moonlight follows me, pale and soft, casting long shadows across the halls as I move. I don't know exactly where I'm going, but my feet seem to know the way.

I need to see him.

When I reach his room, I pause, gathering myself, trying to calm the whirlwind of emotions swirling inside me. I push open the door quietly, stepping inside. The room is dim, shadows dancing in the corners, but the balcony doors are wide open, and standing there, shirtless and bathed in the moonlight, is Daed. His broad back is turned to me, the black runes etched into his skin catching the moon's glow, making him look like a figure carved from shadow and stone.

My breath catches in my throat, and I stand frozen, watching him. His body is tense, as if even in the stillness of the night, he cannot rest. I see the muscles in his back shift as he moves slightly, his hands gripping the balcony railing as he stares out at the sea, lost in thought.

I take a step forward, my fingers brushing the doorframe for support. He hears me, his head turning just enough for me to catch the edge of his profile, his jaw clenched, his eyes still fixed beyond the storm wall.

"Amara," he says softly, his voice low and rough, like he's been waiting for me.

I swallow, my throat dry. I want to say something, anything, but the words won't come. Instead, I take another step forward, the cool night air from the balcony brushing against my skin as I move closer to him.

He steps away from the balcony, closing the distance between us. The sight of him, shirtless, his pants low on his hips, bathed in the light of the Lover's Eye, takes my breath away. His skin gleams under the moon, every line of his body sharp and powerful, and the black runes scrawled across his chest and shoulders seem to pulse with the magic that lies just beneath his surface.

"Why are you here?" he asks, his voice quiet, his gray eyes searching mine.

"You know why," I say, stopping short of telling him how desperate I am to feel his touch again.

"Do I?" he asks coldly. "The last time I saw you, you were slamming a door in my face and refusing to speak to me."

I swallow again, my throat still raw. "I was scared. I didn't know what I was supposed to do. This is all strange to me. I've never..." I pause, my chin dropping to my chest. "I must know. Was it the moon, Daed? Is that why you wanted me tonight?"

His jaw clenches tight, the muscle in his cheek twitching beneath his skin. His eyes, though, burn with something dangerous, something he's barely holding back.

"I've told you how I feel about you."

A bitter laugh bubbles out of me. "The sweet words you use to draw me in are always followed by cruel ones to keep me away. How can I trust anything that comes from your mouth?"

"Then why are you here?" he asks again, his voice darker now.

"Because I must know once and for all if this is real," I say, the words tumbling out before I can stop them. "That this thing between us is not a figment of my imagination. Another cruel Fae trick. Do you want me, Daed?"

"Amara," he starts, his voice low and gravelly, like he's forcing the words out. "You don't understand—"

I step closer, cutting him off. "I'm done with games. Tell me!"

His chest heaves, and I can see him fighting whatever storm is raging inside. For a moment, I think he'll push me away again, that I'll have to endure the sting of his rejection one more time.

But then the words rip from him like a confession.

"I have never wanted anything more in my life," he says, his voice cracking raw with emotion. "You consume my every thought, Amara. I can't sleep, I can't breathe without thinking of you. You—" His voice falters, and he takes a step toward me, the intensity in his eyes pinning me in place. "You are maddening. The very thought of you drives me to the edge, every damn moment."

The air leaves my lungs as though his words have reached inside me and pulled it out.

I don't just want him. I want him to be mine. I want to claim every dark, hidden part of him, to know him in ways no one else ever has. I want to feel his strength wrapped around me, his whispered promises sinking into my skin, leaving marks only we can see.

And I want to give him everything I am in return. Every fear, every scar, every fragile piece of my soul—I want him to take it all, to make me his as completely as I would make him mine.

Before he can retreat from me again, I ease the thin straps of my dress off my shoulders and it falls to the floor, leaving me standing there bare beneath the Lover's Eye.

"This is what I look like wearing nothing but moonlight," I say, daring him to turn away now.

His eyes darken as he takes me in, the struggle in him clear as day. But this time, it's not enough. He can't resist, not anymore.

And neither can I. I don't want to.

Gently, I reach up, my fingers brushing his cheek. His skin is hot beneath my touch, his breath hitching as I cup his face. He leans into my hand, his eyes squeezing shut like he's holding on to the last shred of his willpower.

"I will ruin you," he mutters.

"Then so be it," I whisper, my thumb stroking along his cheekbone.

His breath comes in shallow, uneven gasps, and I drag my fingers slowly, softly, across his lips. His eyes flutter open, and he exhales into my palm, his breath warm against my skin. For a heartbeat, he doesn't move. But then, so slowly it's agonizing, he kisses my hand.

I let my hand fall to his jaw, guiding him, pulling his face closer, until there's nothing left between us but the space of a breath.

He looks at me, his gaze tortured, his fingers trembling as he lifts his hand to cover mine. "Amara..." His voice is barely a whisper now, full of desperation, full of everything he's held back.

"Shh..." I murmur, my lips hovering just inches from his. "This is where I ask you to take me, husband."

I pull him down to me, our foreheads brushing, and I feel the agony in him, the raw battle waging in his chest as he fights to hold back one last time. But then, like a string pulled too tight, he snaps, and his lips find mine.

At first, it's like the brush of a dream. A hesitant question, as though he's testing whether this is real. But when I kiss him back, answering him with the hunger I've buried for far too long, his sharp inhale is the only warning before his restraint dissolves. His mouth claims me fully, his kiss deepening with a ferocity that sends my head spinning. His tongue sweeps against mine, his hand anchoring me by the waist while the other grips my hair, tilting my head back to take me deeper.

I melt into him, my breasts pressing flush against the solid planes of his chest, the cool breeze from the balcony doing nothing to quell the heat building between us. When I feel the hard length of him press against my stomach, my breath stumbles, and a gasp escapes into his mouth. Any lingering doubts I had about his desire for me are obliterated by the sheer, weight of him. His lips curl into a grin, but he doesn't let up. If anything, his hands tighten, his lips grow hungrier, devouring me like he's starving to death.

I lose myself in him—the roughness of his palms, the friction of his skin, the way he moves as though he's staking a claim on every inch of me. I've never felt this before—never let anyone this close. For so long, I've been hidden, untouched, my heart and body locked behind carefully built walls. But here, with him, those walls crumble like sand, leaving me bare, vulnerable, and entirely his.

Slowly, his hand drifts from my waist, sliding over the curve of my hip and down my thigh. His fingers graze the sensitive skin between my legs, and my breath hitches. I feel the grin against my lips again, wicked and teasing.

"Be sure now, wife." His voice is dark, a low growl that sends shivers rippling through me. "This is your last chance to escape."

Though his warning carries gravity, I cannot deny the aching need coursing through me, the arousal that has my body answering for me. My desire spills from my trembling lips like a plea. "Make me yours," I whisper, the words breaking with the force of my want. "Please."

When his hand cups me, fingers tracing my folds with an almost unbearable precision, my back arches, my body moving of its own accord, chasing his touch. He doesn't push inside—no, he takes his time, letting his thumb glide over my entrance, sending jolts of pleasure through me with every maddening stroke. My breaths come faster, my heart pounding like thunder, and I know this is it. This moment, this touch, this male—it's what I've craved, what I've waited for.

But just as my need threatens to consume me, he pulls back, his lips brushing against mine as he speaks. "No."

For a split second, I want to scream, to demand he doesn't stop, but then he finishes, his voice heavy with promise. "Not here. I want you on the bed where I can see you."

And then, before I can even catch my breath, he sweeps me into his arms, cradling me as though I weigh nothing. His lips don't leave mine, his kiss a tether keeping me grounded as he carries me to the bed.

He lays me down, my body trembling in anticipation, my skin alive with the uncertainty of what comes next. He doesn't rush, doesn't speak at first—he just watches me, his eyes roaming over my naked body as if he's memorizing every inch.

"You're so beautiful, Amara," he says, his voice low. "Even more beautiful than I imagined."

The words send a flush cascading over my skin, but I don't shy away. I want him to see me, to touch me, to crave me as much as I crave him. Daed looms over me, his hand reaching for his belt, and my mouth goes dry. Each notch he loosens is agony, my eyes locked on the thickness beneath his leathers, counting the seconds that stretch into what feels like torturous hours before he finally frees himself, his pants falling to the floor. I don't mean to whimper when I see it, or to stare wide-eyed for so long. But my life has been a sheltered one, and seeing him this long, this thick, this rigid and perfect—it's almost too much. I can barely think straight.

Fortunately, thinking isn't required right now. He moves beside me, settling close but not touching, not yet. When I try to turn toward him, desperate to wrap my hands around him, to feel his lips again, his hand presses gently against my collarbone, holding me on my back.

"Stay just like this," he says, and the heat in his tone makes me shiver.

His finger traces a slow, deliberate path down the curve of my throat, over the swell of my chest, and between my heavy breasts, leaving a trail of fire in its wake. This simple touch alone sends aching tremors through me, but he continues to take his time.

When he reaches my thigh, his fingers draw lazy circles on the sensitive skin. I bite my lip, desperate to stifle the moans threatening to escape, but he seems to sense my struggle. His hand tightens around my soft, dimpled flesh, pulling my leg wide and leaving me open to him, exposed to the cool air that only heightens the ache pooling low in my belly.

"Tell me, wife," he murmurs, his voice a velvet growl that vibrates through me. "Am I right in believing I'm the first man to know your body?"

My eyes fly open, and my cheeks burn and for a moment, I hesitate. Doubts creep in—what if he wants someone experienced, someone who knows how to please him without hesitation or uncertainty? But before I can answer, his lips curl into a soft, knowing smile.

"How fortunate I am," he says. "But it also means I must ensure you're ready. I would never forgive myself if I caused you even a moment of discomfort."

The meaning behind his words clicks into place, but my thoughts scatter the moment his hand finds me again. His palm presses against my heat, the pressure enough to make me gasp. He rubs slowly, my arousal slick, before he eases a single finger between my folds and into me.

The sensation is unlike anything I've ever felt—gentle yet overwhelming, slow and teasing. My back arches, and I gasp when his finger curls inside me.

"Perfect," he whispers, his voice a low, rumbling purr. "So warm. So wet."

He kisses me then, his lips capturing mine in a kiss that's both tender and consuming. When he nips gently at my bottom lip, a sharp thrill races through me, and before I can catch my breath, he slips a second finger inside.

A groan escapes me, unbidden and raw, and my hips begin to move of their own accord, meeting the rhythm of his hand.

He leans over me, his lips trailing a scorching path down my neck, pausing at my collarbone before continuing lower. My head falls back, offering him access, and I gasp when his mouth closes over my breast, his tongue flicking over the hardened peak. The sensation sends heat spiraling through me, pooling deep and low as his fingers coax me further into the haze of pleasure. He moves them faster, deeper, building towards the explosion I can feel coming. When his thumb finds the aching center of my need, my body shatters. A raw, unrestrained cry tumbles from my lips as his mouth tugs at my nipple, the scrape of his teeth sending a lightning jolt through me. The world narrows to the sensation of him—his touch, his mouth, his unwavering focus on my unraveling.

When his fingers slip free, the ache left behind is almost unbearable. I want him back, filling me once more. But before I can protest, he moves between my legs, kneeling, gripping my other thigh and pulling it wide. He gazes at me, his eyes intense, and I catch the flash of his canine's emerging. My gaze drifts over his muscled chest, etched with black ink, down to his tapered waist and the taut ripples of his abdomen, before finally landing on the breathtaking sight of his length once more.

Souls, I want him inside me. Now. He grips my thighs, pulling me higher onto his knees so my hips lift off the bed, my legs wide on either side of him. The blunt tip of him teases against my slickness, each brush making me tremble. One hand finds my waist, while the other rests flat on my stomach. He hovers over me, almost like he's waiting for me to feel him inside me again.

"Look at me, wife," he says, and my eyes flicker to his. "Take a deep breath for me."

I obey, and he pushes forward, his head breaking through my entrance. I gasp at the sharp stab of pain as he begins to fill me. It's overwhelming—a wonderful, burning stretch that makes me wince. But there's something more, something beyond the ache or even the thrill. My gaze lifts to his, but not because he asked—because around him, I see a light pulling at his shadows. A golden thread, glowing and ethereal, winds along his arms, spiraling down to where his skin meets mine before encircling me as well, binding us together.

Daed groans, sinking deeper, and my eyes squeeze shut as I take him in. When I open them, the golden threads have vanished. He feels so good inside me, he has me seeing things. My nails dig into the bed, tension coiling through my body. He stops immediately, his breath uneven as he waits for me to adjust.

"Breathe, wife," he says firmly. "Breathe."

Tears prick my eyes, but I take a shaky breath and nod, urging him to continue. His movements are slow, careful, inch by inch as he pushes deeper. The pain doesn't fully fade, but a new kind of pleasure begins to bloom, warm and pulsing.

He's completely inside me now, the sensation full and foreign, a blend of sting and need that sends sparks of heat through my veins. My body softens beneath him, surrendering as my muscles tighten. I know he feels it—the way I grip him. His jaw clenches, his muscles go taut, and I sense the tremor in his arms as he fights to maintain control. I arch into him, a soft moan escaping my lips, and he begins to move—strong, fluid thrusts that send ripples through me.

"Don't stop," I whisper, twisting the bed sheets in my fingers. "Please."

With a soft growl, both his hands grip my waist, pulling me into him, deeper, harder, his rhythm intensifying with every gorgeous slam, and I cry out, the intensity of the pleasure overwhelming. My body responds to him in ways I never thought possible, waves of heat and ecstasy crashing over me as his pace quickens, driving us both toward release.

"Amara," he groans, his voice rough and breathless as his skin glistens with sweat. "I can't—"

"Don't stop," I gasp, my body trembling. "Never stop."

With a final thrust, Daed's body goes rigid, a broken groan tearing from his throat as he releases inside me, the warmth spreading deep and full. The sensation pushes me over the edge, pleasure crashing through me in waves. I shudder as his fingers dig into my sides, my own release taking hold, and for a fleeting, euphoric moment, we shatter together, lost in the rawness of it all.

He lifts me onto his lap, still inside me, my legs wrapping around him as he grips the back of my neck and drives his lips against mine. I feel his hips move again, still pushing in and out of me like aftershocks, and I whimper into his mouth. When he is spent, Daed buries his face in my neck, our slick bodies entangled.

"You see?" I whisper, my breath ragged. "The world did not fall apart. Nothing is ruined."

Slowly, Daed pulls back, his eyes searching mine. There's something in his gaze that wasn't there before—a vulnerability, raw and unshielded, that makes my chest tighten.

He reaches out, brushing a strand of hair from my face with a gentleness that feels almost reverent and, for the first time, there are no games, no barriers. Just us.

But I know this paradise won't last forever. The sun and soft earth of Pariseth are a fleeting reprieve, and soon we'll have to return to Baev'kalath. To the shadows. To the war that's coming for us all. There will be no more quiet moments like this, no more time to pretend we can escape the weight of our fates.

Even in this bliss, I can't shake the truth of what lies ahead. The danger, the choices we'll have to make, the sacrifices. Daed and I may have found each other in the moonlight tonight, but the shadows are always lurking. And no matter how strong this feels, I know that the storm is far from over.

For now, I let myself breathe him in, let myself believe, if only for a few fleeting hours, that we can survive this—together.

CHAPTER 24

The week in Pariseth passes too quickly. There is no war, no looming threat of Baev'kalath—only the island itself. Soft grass beneath our feet, warm sunlight on our skin, and stolen moments of peace in the garden, balanced by passion at night.

Each day follows a gentle rhythm. We spend mornings in the gardens, where I kneel in the rich soil, my hands buried in its warmth. Sometimes Daed joins me, his movements hesitant but earnest. His skin gains color with each passing day, the darkness of Baev'kalath slowly fading. Here, his sharp edges soften, laughter coming more easily, and he speaks in ways he never did before.

Afternoons take us to hidden coves along the coastline, where waves crash against rocks and the sun casts everything in a golden hue. We swim in the cool water, then lie on the shore, talking of everything and nothing. He feels lighter here, unburdened.

At night, we come together again and again. His touch, familiar yet never losing its power, feels like a discovery each time—a search for pieces of each other we hadn't found before. We make love with the windows open, the cool breeze caressing our skin, moonlight turning everything silver. I lose count of the times I whisper his name into the darkness, his kisses as urgent as my own. The moon seems to watch over us, silent and patient, bearing witness to what we can no longer deny.

The nights leave me breathless, but it's the days I cherish most—seeing light return to his eyes, his body at ease, his laughter unguarded, as if the shadows of our world can't reach him here. This place holds a different kind of magic—a sanctuary where, for a few fleeting days, we are simply Daed and Amara.

But paradise never lasts.

On the seventh morning, as we sit in the courtyard, the island's tranquility is shattered. The sound of wings fills the air, and I turn just as Arax descends, dark armor gleaming in the sun. He's a stark reminder of the world we left behind.

He lands lightly, but his expression is grim. "Your Highness," he says, bowing to Daed. "It's time to return to Baev'kalath."

I feel Daed tense beside me, the color draining from his face. Reality crashes over us. The escape is over. The ghosts are waiting, and the war looms ahead.

I slip into our chambers, the warmth of Pariseth fading as I close the door behind me. The sunlight that bathed the island feels like a distant memory. My scattered belongings barely had time to settle before we're forced to leave again.

A knock at the door pulls me from my thoughts, and Solena enters with a soft, reassuring smile. "Shall we pack?" she asks, moving toward the wardrobe without waiting for an answer.

I nod bitterly. "Yes, let's get it over with."

Solena begins gathering clothes, folding them neatly, while I peel off my dress and change into pants and a tunic. I catch a glimpse of myself in the mirror—there's something different, as if Pariseth had shown me a glimpse of another life, now slipping away.

She approaches with a comb, gesturing for me to sit. "I'll braid your hair for the journey."

I settle onto the chair, and as her fingers begin to weave through my hair, I ask, "You and Orios. You'll have to pretend again, won't you?"

Her hands pause briefly before resuming. "Yes," she admits quietly. "But it doesn't bother me."

I raise an eyebrow, catching her eye in the mirror. "Really? It doesn't?"

She smiles gently, a smile that holds more truth than words. "No. What we had here—these days together—it's more than we ever hoped for. Even if it was brief, it was a gift." She ties off the braid with a practiced flick. "It's something I'll carry with me, no matter what comes next."

A pang of envy hits me, not just for their closeness but for Solena's ability to find peace in something fleeting. I let out a small sigh. "I'm glad you had that."

Solena gives me a knowing look. "We have you to thank for it."

I shake my head. "You don't need to thank me for anything."

She places her hands on my shoulders, her gaze unwavering. "We wouldn't have had this time together without you, Your Highness. That means more than you realize."

I try to smile, but my thoughts drift to Daed. "I'm afraid things will go back to the way they were. That he'll pull away again. Here, it was easy to forget everything. But out there? It's not the same."

Solena's fingers gently smoothing the braid she's finished. "It's different, yes. But what you shared here doesn't just disappear when you leave."

I want to believe her. I want to believe that the connection Daed and I found here will survive beyond Pariseth. But part of me can already feel the shadows of Baev'kalath darkening this beautiful dream.

Solena steps back, gathering my packed belongings and placing them at the foot of the bed. "Whatever happens, Your Highness, you're stronger than you think."

I nod, though the uncertainty still gnaws at me. "Thank you, Solena. But I have one last thing to ask."

"Anything," she says.

"Call me Amara."

A smile tugs at the corner of her mouth, and she bows slightly. "Very well. Amara."

As Solena leaves, I'm left alone with my thoughts. The peace of Pariseth is already slipping away, replaced by the cold reality of what awaits.

I crouch beside the serpentine vine, my fingers tracing the edge of its newest leaf. The green is vibrant against the dark soil, soft and alive, like a whisper of the Grove transplanted here. The vine has been quietly speaking to me since we planted it—small, nonsensical exchanges that somehow bring me closer to home. Even on this unfamiliar island, it thrives, unfurling new life. It's a simple comfort, proof that something good can take root even in strange soil.

"Wife."

Daed's voice breaks through my thoughts, and I look up to see him approaching. He's strong and commanding as always, but his steps are slower, as if he's wary of disturbing this moment. His dark hair is tousled, his gray eyes focused on mine, their softness almost making me forget what we're about to lose.

He crouches beside me, his hand brushing lightly against my knee as he studies the vine. "It's grown already."

I nod, tracing the vine's twisting shape. "It has. It's been talking to me," I say with a small smile, despite the ache building in my chest. "It feels... happy."

A faint smile touches his lips, though a heaviness lingers in his eyes. "I'm sorry we have to leave," he murmurs, regret clear in his voice. "But you understand why."

I do. I wish we could stay here, where everything feels lighter, where the weight of Baev'kalath doesn't press down on us. But I understand the duty that calls us back—the war that looms on the horizon.

"I understand," I say softly, fingers continuing to trace the vine's delicate stem. "We can't hide here forever."

He exhales, broad shoulders shifting as he glances toward the distant sea. "Half the houses have committed their armies, but we still need to negotiate further with the others," he says, his voice tightening. "Modok remains a problem, and Sarberos is... hesitant."

"Modok will always be a problem," I reply, my tone sharp. "He's dangerous. I don't trust him."

Daed's expression hardens. "Neither do I. That's why I need to return—to ensure we have the strength we need when the time comes."

I study him, noting the familiar furrow in his brow. Even here, in this fleeting peace, I can sense the storm brewing within him—the same one we'll soon face outside these walls. I want to offer comfort, to say something that eases the burden on his shoulders, but words feel empty.

So I simply nod, knowing that nothing I say will change what's coming.

I take one last look at the horizon before turning toward the courtyard, where our small group is preparing to leave Pariseth behind. Solena and Orios stand close, their heads bowed together in a quiet exchange of words and soft touches—a final kiss before reality pulls them apart. Their smiles hold a hint of sadness, but also a tender resolve, as if they're trying to imprint the memory of this place on their hearts.

Arax steps forward and bows, his dark eyes steady but softer than usual.

"Your Highness," he asks, "have you enjoyed your time here?"

I nod, feeling the weight of his question. "Yes, I have. More than I expected."

A small, knowing smile touches his lips. "I've never seen the prince so content. It seems you've brought that out in him."

I glance over at Daed, standing at the edge of the courtyard, his gaze lost in the direction of the storm wall we'll soon cross. It's true—he's been different here, lighter, more at ease. A part of me is proud to have been a part of that change, but another part wonders if it will crumble when we return to Baev'kalath.

Solena and Orios begin to pull away from each other, their hands lingering as if reluctant to let go.

Arax watches them too, a faint nod almost to himself. "The Reaper's oath is a hard one to keep," he murmurs, his voice heavy with unspoken meaning. There's an edge of confession in his words, a hint of struggle behind his unwavering loyalty. I don't pry—duty, love, and loyalty often conflict in ways words can't fix.

For a moment, I glimpse the cracks in Arax's facade, the part of him that feels deeply, just like anyone else. It makes me wonder if, like Orios, he too has struggled to keep his oath. And maybe, at times, he hasn't succeeded.

Before I can respond, he straightens, his expression shifting back to one of calm duty.

"We're ready to leave," he announces.

Daed strides over to me, his arms sweeping me into a strong yet hesitant embrace. His lips part, as if he's on the verge of speaking, but the words remain suspended between us—a fragile thread, taut and ready to snap. Instead, there's only the rise and fall of his chest against mine.

Daed's wings burst from his back, black feathers shimmering in the sun, casting long shadows over the grass. We rise into the sky, the beauty of Pariseth shrinking below, warmth and light fading into memory.

Ahead looms the storm wall—a twisting mass of dark clouds and roaring winds, a boundary separating two worlds. The shift is instant and unforgiving as we break through. The sun's warmth is snatched away, replaced by icy rain and howling winds that tear at us, pulling us deeper into the storm's violent grasp. The air grows thick with cold and wet, and I cling to Daed, his wings straining against the turbulent gusts.

Arax flies beside us, Solena and Orios close behind, but the storm's fury tries to rip us apart, relentless in its wrath. Rain lashes against my skin, cold and biting, and I bury my face against Daed's chest, seeking shelter from the wind's sharp edge.

For a heartbeat, I wonder if the storm is a warning—a reminder that Pariseth's warmth was temporary, a brief escape from the darkness that waits beyond. I wonder if, like the sun, Daed's affection will fade as we return to the harsh reality of Baev'kalath.

But then he looks down at me, and in his eyes, I see something new. It's not a promise, but it's real. It's enough to make me believe, even if just for a moment, that maybe he won't let the storm take us.

Baev'kalath soon stretches below, a fortress of stone and shadow, rain pouring in relentless sheets. The warmth of the sun has been replaced by cold gray skies, sending a familiar chill down my spine.

Daed's wings beat harder as we descend into the courtyard, where King Kaelus and Queen Lanneth stand waiting. The moment Daed touches the ground, his arms tighten around me briefly before releasing. His expression is unreadable, jaw set and eyes averted as he steps back, folding his wings and straightening.

Queen Lanneth's face brightens when she sees me. Her cold, elegant features soften, and her hands flutter toward me uncertainly, as if unsure whether to embrace or hold back.

"Amara," she says, her voice filled with a warmth that catches me off guard. "You've returned safely. Are you harmed in any way?"

Her concern always surprises me.

"I'm fine, Your Majesty," I say, dipping my head slightly.

She studies me, her eyes sweeping over me as if to be sure for herself. "Good. But you are soaked to the bone. Let us get you to your chambers and into some dry clothes. I will not allow you to remain in such a state after that journey."

"That's not necessary," I begin, but Lanneth raises a hand, silencing me with a single look.

"It is necessary," she says firmly, her tone leaving no room for argument. "I will not take no for an answer."

I glance toward Daed, hoping for some kind of rescue, but he's already turned his back to me, talking quietly with Kaelus. With a sigh, I follow Lanneth into the castle, my reluctance clear with every step.

When we reach my chambers, Solena tries to follow, but Lanneth is quick to cut her off. "That will be all, girl. Leave us."

Solena hesitates, her gaze flickering to mine, but I nod, letting her know it's alright. She bows and exits, leaving me alone with the queen.

The tension in the room thickens as Lanneth steps closer, her eyes soft but her posture commanding.

"You poor thing," she says, sitting me on the edge of the bed. She collects my robe from the other room, then returns and uses it to squeeze the rain from my hair. "Flying through the storm can be so bothersome, but we'll get you nice and dry."

Once my hair is less drenched, she drapes the robe over my shoulders, a comforting warmth against my skin. Yet all I can think about is how quickly Daed turned his back on me when we returned, as if I hadn't just given him all of myself.

"So, daughter," Lanneth begins, her voice smooth and inviting, and once again I wonder if she has somehow read my mind. "Tell me *everything*."

CHAPTER 25

I recount the storm wall to Lanneth, describing how we broke through the rain's relentless assault. I fill my words with the island's vibrant beauty—the gleaming castle, the replanting of the garden, the warmth of shared dinners. But I make sure to avoid anything from the night of the Lover's Eye.

Yet as I speak, her gaze remains distant, a shadow lingering beneath the surface that my stories can't reach. No matter how vividly I paint the scene, she stays unmoved.

"Amara," she says, her voice tinged with a soft edge, "I believe there should be no secrets between us. We are bound now—by family, by blood. There's no need for walls."

Her words are deliberate, calculated.

Family. The term feels foreign, even wrong, coming from her.

"I agree," I reply, keeping my tone steady. "Secrets only breed mistrust."

"Then you understand why I must ask," she continues. "How did Daed behave in Pariseth? Especially under the Lover's Eye. I'd expect him to act as any male would, but I need to hear it from you."

"Daed behaved... as Daed always does," I answer curtly, the memory of those nights stirring emotions I have no intention of sharing with her.

"You're being evasive, Amara," she presses, her smile polite but her eyes sharp. "There's no need to hide from me. I only want what's best for you—and for him."

"It's not something I wish to discuss," I say firmly, though tension coils inside me.

Her smile doesn't falter, but a flicker of anger crosses her gaze. "I understand. But as his mother, I hope you can trust me. After all, I raised Daed, nurtured him. He is who he is today because of me."

The words hang between us, and before I can stop myself, I blurt out, "He told me you're not his real mother."

226

Lanneth's expression freezes, genuine surprise flashing across her face. She quickly recovers, clasping her hands over her lap.

"I see Daedalus has spoken out of turn," her voice trembling slightly. "It's true—I didn't give birth to him. His real mother died when he was just a baby. But I have been the only mother he's ever known. I raised him, cared for him through every trial, every wound, every mistake. I am his mother in every way that matters."

Lanneth stands, regaining her composure. "Remember, Amara. You and I share more than just Daed—we share the responsibility of this kingdom. I have given everything to protect it, and I hope you will do the same." Her eyes sweep over me, and even fully clothed, I feel exposed under her scrutiny, as if she sees more than my skin—more than I even understand of myself. "You look better. Pariseth clearly agrees with you. Let's hope Baev'kalath does not drain this renewed light. We need you strong." Her smile stretches, thin and strained, before she bows. "I'll leave you to settle in. I'm sure we'll see each other tonight, when Kaelus and Daedalus depart."

The mention of Daed leaving twists the knot in my chest tighter. If Lanneth's presence hadn't already unsettled me, her reminder of the departure I've been trying not to think about only deepens the ache. She turns, her gown sweeping behind her as she exits the room. The doors close with a soft thud, but the tension lingers, heavy in the air.

I fall back onto the bed and wish I could sink—deep enough to escape, deep enough to disappear, deep enough to reach the bottom of the world.

I can't bring myself to face the doors. If I step through them, if I watch him leave, the last week will dissolve into a distant memory. I need it to be real. If it isn't—if this feeling between us is just a fleeting illusion—then I don't want anything at all.

I sit stiffly in the chair by the fire, staring at the flames as they dance, the heat creeping across my skin until it stings. But I welcome it. The burn is easier to bear than the fear curling inside me—the fear of losing Daed.

The familiar sound of wings stirs the air behind me, followed by the heavy thud of boots on stone.

"I told you," I mutter, not turning to look. "I prefer when you use the door."

"So domineering, wife. Are we still in Pariseth?" he teases, the smirk evident in his voice. "Should I take off my boots? Dig in the dirt with you?" His hands slide over my shoulders, and despite myself, I melt into his touch, my eyes closing as warmth spreads through me. His voice drops lower, closer. "Can I make requests, too? I prefer you wearing only moonlight."

His fingers trail down my arms, gliding toward my breasts, and I lose myself in the warmth of him, laying my hand on top of his and holding it still, because if he moves an inch I'll fall apart.

"Daed. Stop," I mutter somberly, clutching his hand tighter than I mean to.

The room falls into an uncomfortable silence. I can't look at him. My gaze stays fixed on the fire, each flicker of flame reflecting the frustration twisting inside me.

After a long pause, his voice breaks the quiet. "Have I done something to upset you?" His tone is softer now, unsure. "Or... do you really just want me to use the door?"

I exhale slowly, struggling against the pull of his playfulness, the pull of him. But I can't let myself surrender to it. Not when it will only lead to more pain—the kind he promised me from the start.

"I don't want you to go." The words slip out bluntly. There is nothing else to say, no point in disguising. We are plain before each other now. He has seen me, all of me, in the day and beneath the moon, at his side and in his bed. There is no more to hold back.

His hands find my shoulders again, but this time I don't push him away. Instead, I hold on, curling my fingers around his rough skin, leaning into him as if this is the last time I'll feel his touch. It's ridiculous, I know—he's only going to Mor'Thravar. But there's a heaviness in the air between us, something inevitable that I can't explain or understand.

"Wife," he whispers, then softer, "Amara."

He moves around to face me, and when the firelight catches the angles of his face, casting flickering shadows over his skin, I can barely bring myself to look at him. His beauty feels like something too far away to hold onto, too otherworldly to keep. Daed drops to his knees in front of me, his grip firm on the chair legs as he pulls me closer with a sharp scrape of wood. He slides one hand between my knees, parting them just enough for him to settle in between, his hands trailing up my thighs before gripping my waist.

My heart flutters under the weight of his gaze, the gray in his eyes deepening, locking onto mine with an intensity that makes my chest ache.

"I don't go because I want to," he says, voice low, rough around the edges. "I go because I must. If it were my choice, I would stay by your side always, and nothing—" his gaze darkens as his grip tightens on me, "—*nothing* could drag me away from you."

His words sink into me, each one sending a wave of warmth through my body. My heart swells, but I still feel the ache of what's coming, of him leaving. I exhale a deep, weary breath. "I'm being selfish, aren't I?"

He grins, a soft, crooked smile that makes my heart skip. "I don't think you're capable of such a thing. But if you are, then I'm flattered to be the cause of it."

Despite everything, a smile tugs at my lips, softened by the way his hands grip me, how his touch is both tender and possessive. "How long will you be gone?"

"For a Fae, it's less than a blink," he teases, mischief dancing in his eyes. "Human years, on the other hand…"

I clench my jaw, narrowing my eyes. "Husband!"

He laughs, pulling me deeper into his arms, his warmth spreading over me as his embrace tightens around my waist. "Two days. Maybe three. As soon as I settle things, I'll return to you. I swear it."

I don't respond. I know he's telling the truth, but that doesn't make it any easier to accept. Daed watches me carefully, his brow furrowing, and then he tilts his head slightly, studying my expression. "Perhaps you need something to keep you company. Something to be here while I cannot."

I raise a curious eyebrow, trying to understand his intent. "What do you mean?"

Daed extends his hand, and I watch as spirals of smoke rise from his skin. The wisps are dark and ethereal, twisting and curling in hypnotic patterns. I can't help but be mesmerized by the way it moves, its magic undeniable. Then, with a soft breath, Daed blows the smoke into the air. It floats, curling and shifting until it descends, pooling into a cloud at his feet. I stare, wide-eyed, as the smoke solidifies, taking on the form of a sleek charcoal kitten made entirely of swirling shadows.

The tiny creature meows, and I gasp at the sound—a soft, echoed cry—and watch in awe as it slinks toward Daed, brushing itself lazily against the heel of his boot.

"Is it real?" I ask, barely believing what I'm seeing, unable to tear my gaze from the kitten's every movement.

"As real as I am," Daed replies, "but infinitely better."

He bends down and scoops the kitten up, his fingers sinking into the smoky form as it drifts around his hand. The kitten has no distinct features, only its glowing white eyes stand out from its shadowy body, like stars in a sea of darkness. For a moment, I feel unsettled by it, despite the soft cries it makes and the way its little legs kick helplessly in the air.

"Don't hold him like that," I chide, reaching out instinctively. "He doesn't like it."

Daed raises an amused eyebrow. "Oh? My apologies... and what should we call him?"

I gingerly take the smoke kitten from his hands, half-expecting it to dissolve right through my fingers. But it doesn't. There's weight to it, a form that feels solid, yet at the same time, wisps of smoke drift lazily from its body. The sensation is strange—a tingling that lingers against my skin, but oddly comforting.

Black as the ash in the hearth, the little creature nestles against me as if it's always belonged there. I scratch under its chin with a knuckle, and its eyes flutter closed as it purrs—a low, rumbling sound that vibrates through its shadowy form.

"Ashen," I say, the name slipping from my lips as if meant for him. "His name is Ashen."

Daed rises to his feet with a groan, brushing off his knees. "Ashen it is. I leave you in his capable... paws."

I laugh softly, glancing down at the kitten. It's impossible to imagine how this tiny wisp of smoke could protect me in Daed's absence. But as Daed mutters something under his breath in Fae tongue, a string of words I don't understand, Ashen lets out a low growl—so deep it makes me pause. For a brief moment, the kitten's form flickers, its features sharpening into something far more dangerous, more ancient. But the shift happens so quickly, it's gone in the blink of an eye, leaving me to wonder if I imagined it at all.

I'm so lost in Ashen, his tiny paws kneading against my chest, his smoky form curling into my hair, that I don't notice Daed watching me. His gaze lingers, intense and quiet, and when I meet his eyes, a flush creeps up my neck. The warmth of his attention should soothe me, but instead, it feels heavy, like he's memorizing every detail before it all fades away. I smile, trying to ease the tension, but it only seems to deepen the sadness etched in his face.

He swallows hard, his voice soft but weighted. "I have to go."

The ache in my chest tightens as I run my fingers through Ashen's smoke-like fur for comfort. "I know."

Reluctantly, I stand, letting Ashen slip down to the floor where he curls at my feet, a loyal shadow. My hands find Daed's waist, steadying both him and myself as his palms cradle my face. When he kisses me, it's tender but filled with a passion that threatens to undo me. In that kiss, we say all the words we cannot speak aloud, a silent plea for time to stop, for everything to stay as it is. But when we pull apart, the absence of his touch leaves me hollow, like a part of me has been left behind.

Later, as I join him in the courtyard, I'm greeted by the familiar gloom of Baev'kalath. The moonlight is dim, hidden behind the ever-present clouds, casting the world in muted shades of gray. Daed stands there, dressed in his formal attire, the dark fabric gleaming under the rain that always seems to accompany this place. His hair falls messily over his brow, and though he tries to hide it, the tension in his body is palpable. His eyes lock onto mine, and I can see it—the burden of what's to come, the heaviness of his departure. Behind him, Arax, Orios, and the other Reapers stand like shadows, ready to follow him into whatever fight awaits them.

The warmth of Pariseth, the soft grass, and the peace we found there feels distant, almost like it never existed. Now, there's only the rain, the darkness, and the overwhelming dread of what might happen while Daed is away. He senses my hesitation, my heart faltering under the weight of it all, and his hand tightens around mine.

"I'll be back before you know it," he murmurs, his voice rough but filled with sincerity. He leans forward, pressing his forehead to mine, our breaths mingling and in that simple gesture, I feel everything. It's a promise, a farewell, and an unspoken fear all wrapped into one.

I close my eyes, trying to memorize the feel of him, the warmth of his presence, but there's a knot of foreboding twisting in my chest. I want to cling to him, to keep him here, but I know I can't. There's too much at stake.

"Amara," Daed whispers, pulling back just enough to look at me.

Words sit on his lips, close to spilling, but I can't let him say them. I can't hear those words, not now. If he says what I think he's about to, I'll never be able to let him go.

"You should go," I say, harsher than planned. I step back, creating space between us, desperate to keep my emotions from consuming me entirely.

His jaw tightens, and I catch the brief flicker of hurt that crosses his face, but he doesn't argue. He takes a deep breath, letting his hand fall from my cheek. It's strange—we've spent so much time pulling away from each other, yet tonight, the thought of it tears at him as much as it does me.

"It's time," King Kaelus announces from the edge of the courtyard, his voice slicing through the heavy tension. The Reapers are already gathering, their figures as dark and looming as the shadows of Baev'kalath.

Lanneth steps forward, her grip firm as she pulls me close, her presence as cold and oppressive as ever. I don't move, my eyes still locked on Daed, who staggers backward, hesitant. With a sharp nod, he turns, his wings unfurling from his back in one swift motion. The powerful gust of air from his wings sends a shiver through me, but I remain still, rooted to the spot as I watch him join his father. Together, they take to the skies, disappearing into the inky darkness. The familiar ache settles deep in my chest, an ache that only grows the farther he flies from me.

"Do not fear, daughter," Lanneth murmurs, her voice like a snake's hiss as she leans in, her cold breath curling around my ear. "At last, you and I will be able to spend some much-needed time together."

Her words coil around me, suffocating, but even she can't stifle the sharp pang of regret that cuts through me.

I should have said it. *I should have told him.*

The words on the tip of my tongue, words that feel too dangerous to say out loud but are too powerful to ignore. I wish I had screamed them into the night, sent them chasing after him.

My eyes burn, tears welling up behind them, not from the rain or the cold, but from the fear that I may never get the chance to speak them to his face. The fear that I may never hear him say them back.

CHAPTER 26

The first night was terrible.

In Pariseth, I'd slept so peacefully in Daed's arms, waking only when the sun warmed my face. But here, in Baev'kalath, the sorrow of this place is a noose, tightening with every breath, draining the life from me. By morning, I've barely slept at all. My head throbs, exhaustion clawing deep into my bones. A glance in the mirror confirms the worst—the healthy color Pariseth had restored is already fading, leaving my skin pale and ghostly in this cursed fortress. I hate this place. All it does is take.

Breakfast with Lanneth is no better. Her questions are always sharp, prying. She insists I eat the meat, pushing the platter toward me as though her will alone might make me give in. I refuse again, and her smile tightens with disappointment. I excuse myself as politely as I can and spend the rest of the day avoiding her, wandering aimlessly through the cold halls, staring out at the sky as it shifts from dull gray to black.

It's unnervingly quiet without Daed, the king, or the Reapers. The absence of Arax's ever-present shadow feels disorienting, and I catch myself yearning to glance over my shoulder, hoping to see that familiar frown I've grown so used to.

I find my way to the throne room, leaning against the heavy wooden door. It groans open, revealing the vast, empty space beyond, where each step I take echoes like distant thunder.

I ascend the dais, my fingers grazing the cold stone of Daed's throne, wishing it were his warm skin beneath my touch. I wander to the stained glass window, where the waning moon rises like an ominous herald, casting slants of ivory light through the intricate designs. Prisms of colored light dance across the floor, illuminating the shadows with fleeting beauty.

In that moment, I imagine Daed as the warrior immortalized in stained glass, his powerful wings unfurled, his imposing form towering over me. Pressing down on me. Touching me. My skin goose-pimples and a welcome heat throbs between my legs. I close my eyes, letting my mind drift deeper into the desire that coils within me.

"It's the Reflective Eye," Solena says, startling me as she appears at my side. I jump, and she laughs, the sound light and warm. In my solitude, it's comforting to know I have her at least.

"I didn't mean to scare you," she adds, her eyes twinkling.

"No. I'm glad you're here," I say, releasing a long breath. "I could use the distraction. So, the Reflective Eye. Tell me more."

Solena shifts, drawing closer. "It's a time for storytelling," she explains. "A time to share knowledge, to speak of the past. After the indulgence of the Lover's Eye, the Reflective Eye is a reminder of our history, of lessons learned."

Heat creeps up my neck as memories of Daed's hands on my bare skin flash through my mind, and I pray Solena doesn't notice my blush.

"Share some knowledge with me, then," I say, clearing my throat in an effort to change the subject.

Solena dips her chin in acknowledgment. "As you wish." Her gaze sweeps the throne room before landing on the large tapestry draped over the doorway—the same one I remember from that night of the banquet. She motions for me to follow her, and when we stop before the dark fabric, she points to the image embroidered on it. "This is the Pale Eye," she begins, indicating the pure white eye that stands out against a dark, starry sky. "She is the Mother Above—protector, seducer. As the moon shifts, so does her influence. The Mordorin believe she watches over us, guiding us through life's cycles, testing us with temptation and indulgence."

"A test I've seen you fail more than once," I say.

Solena grins, playful and unashamed. "Perhaps. But aren't we Fae supposed to be creatures of indulgence?"

Her words are light, but something in me stirs, and suddenly I'm reminded of my nightmares. That vision of smoke and ash, eyes burning into me, the words echoing in my mind like a curse. I don't realize I've spoken aloud until Solena's expression changes.

"Father Below."

Her eyes widen, and her voice tightens. "What did you say?"

I blink, snapping back to the present, shrugging it off with more casualness than I feel. "Nothing. Just something I think I heard once."

Solena steps closer, her playful demeanor gone, replaced by something colder, more serious. "Where did you hear about the Father Below?"

I'm still certain it was just a dream. A nightmare spun from the shadows of Baev'kalath, but I tell Solena everything. Every detail. The room, the altar, the monster of smoke and darkness forcing me to choke on its essence. And how I fought back—how I never dreamt of it again.

"That's how your hand healed?" she asks, eyes wide with disbelief.

I nod, flexing my fingers at the memory. "I still don't understand it. I don't know how I absorbed the pain or where it went. It was just a dream."

Solena exhales sharply, her expression tight with unease. "You don't just dream about the Father Below, Amara. If you've seen him... it's because he sought you out. And if he seeks you... it's for a reason." A chill runs down my spine as she continues. "A terrifying reason."

"You believe me?" I ask, the words catching in my throat.

She nods, her gaze firm, unwavering. "Yes."

"And you're saying it was... real?"

Solena scans the throne room, checking for any prying eyes even though we are utterly alone, as if she worries the shadows are watching us. Her hand shoots out, gripping my arm as she pulls me closer. "Baev'kalath is cursed—there's blood in these stones, stains from tragedies that even the rain cannot wash away. While the Pale Eye is worshipped openly, there are those who wear the inverted crescent. In secret, they praise the demon of the void. His name is Gygarth."

The image of the beast surges behind my eyes, sharp and searing like broken glass. I wince, clutching my head, desperate to block it out.

"Princess!" Solena gasps, holding me steady. "Are you alright?"

I shake my head, feeling the throbbing intensity growing. "I think I need to lie down."

"Of course," she says, quickly guiding me from the room. She's urgent now, almost frantic, as she hurries me back to my chambers.

Once there, she helps me out of my dress and into a nightgown, her fingers trembling as she dims every candle to ease the strain on my eyes.

"Do not tell Lanneth," I whisper, my voice barely audible. "I don't need her hovering over me."

Solena nods gravely. "I'll check on you during the night."

As the doors close behind her, I am left alone. But the solitude is fleeting. As I lie in bed, cradling my aching head, smoke begins to form at the foot of my bed. That familiar wraith— *the ghost of Baev'kalath*—has returned to torment me.

"Not you. Not now," I moan, turning over and pulling the covers over my head.

"Where is the prince?" the ghost asks, its voice hollow and distant. *"I... I cannot feel him."*

"He's gone," I groan. "And if I wish hard enough, maybe you'll be gone too."

"You were both gone for a time," the ghost continues, its smoky tendrils creeping across the room toward Ashen, who sleeps soundly by the fire. *"What did you do?"*

"You ask more questions than Lanneth," I mutter, each word another stab of pain behind my eyes.

"Lanneth?" The smoke shifts, hovering over Ashen, a tendril brushing over him almost like a caress.

"The queen," I mumble, barely coherent.

"Lanneth is not *the queen,"* the ghost says, its voice firm and unnerving in its certainty. *"Veloria is queen."*

I drift between sleep and consciousness, the ghost's words echoing faintly in my ears, hollow and distant. "No... Veloria passed after Daed was born," I murmur, slipping closer to sleep's edge. "Lanneth is queen now."

"What..."

The room shifts, the temperature plummeting so fast my breath turns to mist, hanging in the freezing air. I shiver violently, clutching the covers tighter against me, my skin prickling from the sudden cold. My eyelids flutter, teeth chattering, as I watch the ghost by the fire stretch and expand—a wall of dark smoke that looms ever larger. Ashen hisses, leaping from the chair, scurrying across the room as the ghost's presence swells, its smoke extinguishing the fire in a smothering wave of darkness.

"She is not dead. She cannot be dead. You lie."

I bolt upright, fully awake now, my body trembling beneath the suffocating cold. The ghost grows, its smoky tendrils snaking across the bed, sweeping over the covers until I feel its weight pressing me back against the headboard. I gasp as its icy touch sears into my skin, the cold burning like fire.

"Who told you this lie?" the ghost demands, its voice a growl of rage.

"Daedalus," I rasp, my voice barely a whisper as I struggle against the pain throbbing in my head.

For a moment, the ghost is silent, its presence vibrating in the air, the only sound a low, hollow hum that fills the room.

"Yes," it finally gasps. *"I remember now. I remember the day she died. I remember the day Daedalus killed her."*

I shake my head, remembering our time in the forest and the tragedy he shared with me, one that has haunted him his entire life. "He didn't. That is not what happened."

"You speak as if you were there, that you saw it, that you watched her die."

"A mother dying in childbirth is not the fault of the child," I say sternly, defending Daed's suffering.

"Is that what he told you?" There is a cruel mocking tone to the ghost's hollow voice that knots my stomach. *"He is lying."*

"You are lying," I snap. "That can't be true."

"I linger. I forget. But I do not lie. I was there."

The smoke travels over my body, sliding like cold silk across my shoulders, down my chest, until it pins me flat against the bed, its weight crushing down on me. My lungs scream for air as it presses into me harder, colder, until I can barely breathe. Then it reaches my belly, and without warning, it releases me. The smoke whips away, spiraling into a furious, howling wind, retreating to the far corner of the room.

"What have you done?" the ghost wails, its voice a desperate cry that reverberates through the room. *"You have doomed us all."*

I don't answer. I'm too busy gasping for air, my chest heaving, my skin branded with cold, red marks that sear with the memory of its touch.

"I told you to run," the ghost laments, its voice cracking like distant thunder. *"Why did you not run? Now it's too late. You will die, just as she did."* The smoke dissipates, unraveling into wispy strands as it fades from view. Its last words hang in the air, chilling me deeper than the cold ever could.

"Daedalus will kill you, too."

I'm not sure when I fell asleep again, but the next thing I know, morning light is filtering through the windows. My head throbs worse than ever, a dull, insistent ache that makes me wince as I sit up. Solena waits by the doors, concern etched across her face.

"You slept through the night," she says softly, coming to my side. "I checked on you like I promised. Not even the storm that hit before dawn woke you."

I blink in confusion, trying to recall anything from the night—any memory of the thunderstorm. But it's like a thick fog has settled over my mind, and I can't remember a thing. Still, despite my exhaustion and the ghost's lingering presence, one small comfort lifts my spirits.

Daed returns tomorrow.

I just have to make it through today. I won't let the ghost's words take root in my mind. It's a creature of mischief, sent to torment me, nothing more. Daedalus might not be innocent, but killing his own mother? No. He couldn't. I refuse to believe it. I couldn't possibly care for a monster like that.

But as much as I try to push the ghost's warning away, it lingers in the back of my mind, gnawing at my thoughts. I can't avoid Lanneth either when I'm summoned to breakfast, and no matter how much bread I eat, nothing satisfies the gnawing hunger inside me, the constant drain of energy.

"The meat would make you feel better," Lanneth sighs, feasting on her portion, delicate yet unbothered.

The shimmer that surrounds her is unnaturally bright today, so much so that I can't meet her gaze without the light stinging my eyes.

"No, thank you," I reply again, reaching for more bread. Anything to keep her at a distance.

Lanneth exhales, the sound thick with frustration, just as I knock over a glass vase. It crashes to the floor, shattering into jagged pieces.

"Damn it," I mutter, instinctively reaching down to collect the shards.

Lanneth snaps her fingers toward the servant standing nearby. "Leave it, Amara. They can clean it up."

But I ignore her, whether out of stubbornness or a need to focus on something other than this gnawing hunger. I continue picking up the shards, my movements clumsy and unfocused. It's only a matter of time before a sharp piece slices into my palm. Blood wells up immediately, hot and painful, dripping onto the table as the broken glass slips from my fingers and shatters further.

"You silly girl," Lanneth scolds, her voice cold with irritation. "Look at what you've done."

I glare at her, prepared to snap back, but my anger dissolves into pure horror. Her shimmer is gone. In its place, her face... it's not hers. Not anymore.

The skin hanging from her skeletal frame is sagging and grotesque, stretched like thin leather over sharp bones. Her mouth is a gaping hole of crooked, broken teeth, her eyes are nothing but empty, black voids. And there, in the center of her forehead, is the mark—an inverted crescent, dark and deep, just like the one I saw on the Archdruid at our wedding when he cut my palm. I stumble back, my heart racing as I knock over the chair behind me. A silent scream catches in my throat as I backpedal, desperate to put distance between myself and the monster she's become.

Lanneth rises from her chair, reaching out toward me with gnarled hands. "Amara," she growls, "what is wrong with you? Look at me."

I can't. I squeeze my eyes shut, trembling, my back pressed against the cold stone wall, but I can still feel her presence, looming, suffocating.

"Do as I say, girl!" she snaps, her voice filled with impatient command.

Slowly, fearfully, I force my eyes open, just a sliver. But the monster is gone. Lanneth stands before me, appearing as she always has, poised and immaculate, her face elegant and refined, the shimmer back in place.

Everything I just saw... vanished as though it never existed.

"Forgive me," I stammer, stumbling toward the doors of the dining room. "I have to go."

Lanneth's voice follows me, but I don't look back. I clutch the hem of my dress and run—away from her, away from the horrors my eyes can no longer seem to avoid. My heart pounds in time with my footsteps, the weight of her gaze clinging to my back. Only when I reach the sanctuary of my chambers do I let my body give in, collapsing onto the bed, my breath ragged, my mind a mess of tangled thoughts.

I press my face into the pillow, desperate to hold back the tears threatening to spill. My fingernails dig into the fabric, clutching at it like it might somehow anchor me, keep me from spiraling further into the darkness. What is wrong with me? Why do I keep seeing these horrors? Ghosts, demons, monsters—it's as though they've been waiting, creeping at the edges of my vision, only to pounce now that we've returned from Pariseth.

A sob hitches in my throat, but before it can escape, I feel the soft, comforting brush of fur against my legs. Ashen. He rubs his smoky back against me, his rhythmic purring like a balm against my fraying nerves. It's a small comfort, but in this moment, it's everything.

I tap the bed beside me, inviting him up. He bounds onto the covers with graceful ease, curling into a small ball at my side, his belly exposed in a rare show of vulnerability. I can't help but smile, my fingers running through the smoky tendrils that drift from his body, scratching him where he likes it most. His purring grows louder, filling the quiet with a sound that soothes the despair inside me. How did Daed know Ashen would wrap himself around my heart in a way that makes everything feel a little less unbearable?

But that calm shatters when Solena bursts through the doors.

"Amara," she gasps, her eyes wide with worry. "I heard you were hurt?"

Her gaze drops to my hand, and I follow her eyes to the blood trailing down my arm, staining the bed covers. I had completely forgotten.

She hurries to my side, her hands deft as they clamp around my wrist to inspect the wound. I wince as she applies pressure, the sharp sting dragging me back to the present.

"Again?" she mutters, incredulous. "How does this keep happening?"

I don't answer. My focus drifts to Ashen's purrs, still steady beneath my touch, as if nothing in the world could disturb him. Solena works quickly, wrapping my hand in fresh bandages, though each movement sends a jolt of pain up my arm, awakening me from the haze of last night.

"Pain," I murmur, the word slipping from my lips, unbidden. "*Awaken.*"

Solena pauses, her brow furrowing. "What was that?"

"Only pain can awaken me," I repeat, stroking Ashen with a stillness that feels at odds with the frenzy inside me.

Solena mutters something under her breath, likely cursing my rambling nonsense, but I'm not paying attention. Instead, I sit up, watching as Ashen leaps from the bed, his smoky form disappearing into the room's shadows. My thoughts shift, focusing on something she mentioned at the banquet.

"You spoke of those Fae at the banquet," I say, my voice distant as I recall the details. "You said they use magic to change their appearance."

Solena hesitates, still working on my hand, but now more attentive. "Yes. Some High Fae have the power to glamor."

"And what would something glamored look like to someone on the outside?"

She exhales, clearly exasperated. "It would look completely normal, Amara. That's the point of a glamor. It's meant to disguise. What good would it do if you could tell it was glamored?"

"But," I press, my voice low, "what if someone *could* see through it?"

Her hands still, her expression shifting from mild irritation to something more serious, more guarded. "If you could see through a glamor," she says slowly, almost as if testing the thought, "that would mean you are awakened." There's a long pause before she adds, her voice just above a whisper, "But awakened beings are very...rare."

We lock eyes, the weight of my words hanging between us like a fragile thread. I gulp, feeling the tension coil tighter. "There's a shimmer," I begin, my voice barely above a whisper. "It surrounds them, like a veil. I've seen it almost every day since coming to Baev'kalath—on people, and on things."

"Things?" Solena echoes, her voice hesitant, almost fearful of where this conversation is headed.

I nod, leaning closer to her, my heart pounding in my chest as though the very walls could be listening. "Stairs that don't belong. That lead to rooms that shouldn't exist."

"What else?" Solena's voice drops lower, barely audible now, a whisper carried on the air.

"Lanneth," I murmur, my breath catching in my throat. "The Archdruid... and when I saw the Father Below—" I correct myself quickly, my voice faltering, "Gygarth... it was after the wedding, when my hand was cut." My eyes drop to my hand, now bandaged and bound. "When it healed, the shimmer was gone. But I think... I think the wounds open my eyes to it. Is that even possible?"

Solena's expression softens, a deep sadness crossing her features. She reaches out, her fingers gently curling over mine, offering comfort I wasn't expecting. "I don't know," she whispers, her voice heavy with empathy. "But what a terrible burden for you to bear."

"There's something happening to me," I say, my voice trembling as the fear tightens in my chest. The words feel too big, too real now that they're out. "I'm afraid... everything I've tried to convince myself was just in my mind might actually be real. I need to speak with Daed."

Solena's expression softens, her understanding immediate and wordless. "Do you know when he'll return?" she asks gently.

"He said two days," I whisper, my mind spinning. "He should be back tonight."

Solena offers a small, reassuring smile. "In the meantime, you need rest. Let me make you some tea."

I nod, but only because I don't know what else to do. My thoughts are such a tangled mess that I can't separate one fear from another, each one screaming for attention in the chaos of my mind. Maybe if I lie down, I'll find some clarity, or at least a moment of peace.

When Solena returns with the tea, I take a tentative sip. Its warmth seeps through me, but it barely scratches the surface of the conflict raging inside. My body, worn down by exhaustion and confusion, gives in, sinking into the bed. Solena's gentle hand strokes my hair, each pass like a lullaby. My eyes close, though sleep doesn't claim me. My mind is too frantic, tangled in fears and unanswered questions. But for a brief moment, the tension eases, the relentless worry softening as her touch grounds me, and the shadows seem a little less sharp.

That is, until night falls and the unmistakable sound of wings slicing through the air jolts me from my rest. My heart quickens, every nerve alive, pulling me toward the window before I even realize I'm moving.

CHAPTER 27

I rush to the balcony, my heart racing, and when I see black wings blotting out the moon, hope blooms in my chest. For once, I'm relieved that Daed didn't bother with the door. I step into the rain, lifting my hand to shield my eyes from the blinding moonlight. But as the boots touch down on the stone and the glow fades, disappointment hits me hard. The familiar ivory hair, streaked with gray, and the rough-hewn face that's seen too many battles come into focus.

"Arax," I murmur, unable to hide the sinking feeling. My gaze shifts past him, searching the night sky for another set of wings. But the sky remains empty.

"Where is the prince?" I ask, my voice tight.

"He is delayed," Arax replies solemnly, as if he knows how much I didn't want to hear those words.

I bite back my frustration, but it churns inside me, twisting into something raw. "Why?"

"Negotiations go poorly, Your Highness. Modok..." he begins, his tone cautious.

"Of course, Modok," I snap, turning sharply on my heel and storming into my chambers, the rain still clinging to my skin.

Solena stands in the archway, draping a robe over my shoulders, the soft fabric absorbing the wetness from my skin. The gesture is comforting, but it does nothing to ease the ache settling in my chest.

"How long until he returns to Baev'kalath?" I demand.

Arax hesitates, and the silence only stirs my anger. I whirl on him, my frustration visible in the hard line of my jaw.

"Your Highness," Arax starts carefully, wringing the rain from his beard before stepping fully inside. "If we are to defend the Sundered Kingdoms from the Legion, we need the full strength of the houses. Without their swords, the Grove will never be safe."

"You think I don't know that?" I snap, my voice sharp and brittle. "Everything I do, *everything*, is for the Grove. I gave myself to the Fae, not caring what it cost me. But this..." My voice wavers, the strength in it cracking as exhaustion takes hold. "I just need this one thing for myself. *I need my husband.*"

Arax's expression shifts, guilt and sorrow softening his usually stoic face. He looks down, unable to meet my eyes, ashamed of how deeply my words affect him. "I know I am an unworthy substitute, Princess. But the prince believed hearing this from me would soften the blow."

I cradle my face in my hands, feeling the sting of unshed tears. "I'm sorry, Arax. I'm just so... tired."

Arax casts a concerned glance at Solena, worry flickering in his gaze. "The princess is unwell?" he asks quietly.

Solena nods, her voice gentle. "Much has happened since the prince left. We must protect her until he returns."

Arax's face hardens, his loyalty like iron. He pounds his chest with a clenched fist. "Always." He strides to the door, drawing his sword in one swift motion, the blade gleaming even in the dim light. "I will cut down anyone who dares to pass through these doors until the prince can stand guard himself."

With a firm thud, the doors shut behind him, leaving me with the knowledge that I am about to spend another night without my prince. Daed knew what he was doing when he sent Arax. The bond between us grew when I felt adrift, long before my connection with Daed became something real to cling to. While I'd give anything for my husband to be here with me now, Arax was mistaken—he's far from a poor substitute.

He's the only other Fae I'd trust with my life.

Solena tucks me in, pulling the covers up to my chin, leaving a soft smile with me, but for the first time, she doesn't leave. Instead, she settles into the high-backed chair near the fire, her gaze lost in the flicker of flames as exhaustion pulls at me.

I feel a gentle patter across the covers and soon Ashen is by my side. He circles a few times, finding just the right spot before curling into a ball, his smoky whiskers brushing against my nose. Somehow, in this moment, things don't seem quite as hopeless as they once did.

When I first arrived at Baev'kalath, I was convinced it would be my undoing. I still can't say for certain that won't be true. Despite my best efforts, this place claws at me, trying to unravel me at every turn. But never did I imagine I would find friendship here, among the Fae who despise my kind. Arax's unwavering loyalty and Solena's quiet strength are what keep me anchored, sacred threads holding me together in a world intent on pulling me apart. Without them, I know I would not survive this alone.

And then there's Daed. My dark prince. My husband. I refuse to believe the ghost's venomous lies. I have seen the good man beneath the warrior's fierce exterior, felt it in every tender touch, in the way he looks at me when no one else is watching.

I will endure. I will continue to resist the forces that seek to unravel us, to break me. I just need rest. My heavy gaze falls on my bandaged hand, the dull ache there a reminder. But even as I try to will myself to sleep, the ghost's words slip through the cracks of my thoughts, lingering in the darkness.

Pain is your awakening.

And then I drift away.

I know I cannot dream, yet I'm caught in some twisted reality between sleep and waking and the floor beneath me is cold and unforgiving.

I cannot move. My arms, my legs—they feel like lead, pinned to the ground by forces unseen. Around me, runes pulse—shapes etched into the stone, their glow throbbing in time with my racing heart. They snake out in every direction, forming a perfect circle that cages me in.

The air hums with whispers, faint tendrils at first, then swelling into a chorus that presses in from every direction. My eyelids flicker open, vision blurred, and through the veil of confusion, I make them out—figures cloaked in black, their faces shrouded by deep hoods. The chanting begins, a low, guttural rhythm of words I cannot grasp. They stand motionless, their voices weaving a suffocating fog that coils around me.

I try to scream, but no sound escapes. My eyes strain upward, and that's when I see it—the void. It tears through the ceiling above me, not like a window, but a wound in the world, leading to a darkness so vast it seems to stretch forever. It pulses, slow and menacing, as if alive, the very air trembling and with each pulse, the robed figures' chanting grows louder, more frantic, pulling me closer to the gaping abyss that threatens to devour me whole.

The void pulses again, and within it, something stirs—something ancient, a presence that fills me with a dread so deep, I can feel it down to my bones. My heart pounds in my chest, the rhythm echoing in my ears as the air around me thickens with smoke. The chanting intensifies, rising to a fevered pitch, a cacophony of voices that makes my skin crawl. The robed figures shift, their heads tilting toward the void as if in worship, and my stomach turns with a sense of impending doom.

I see him then, within the dark maw of the void—a shadow, larger than anything I can comprehend, creeping closer. A beast born of nightmare and smoke, Gygarth, the demon of the void, takes form. His body is a mass of swirling darkness, tentacled arms extending outward in all directions, writhing and twisting like serpents made of smoke. His face is featureless, save for a gaping, jagged mouth that seems to consume the very essence of the void around him. And there, at the center of the beast's face, are two startling white eyes—blinding in their intensity, empty, and cold.

The chanting grows louder, the robed figures swaying as if possessed by the ritual, their hands outstretched toward the creature, their fingers charred black as it looms above me. I want to move, to scream, but I'm trapped, frozen by terror as Gygarth hovers just inches from my face.

Then, slowly, agonizingly, the demon's mouth opens, a swirling black maw that seems to suck the very light from the air. Thick tendrils of smoke begin to drift from his mouth, curling and twisting toward me. I thrash against my invisible bonds, panic flooding every inch of me, but it's no use. The smoke snakes its way toward me, and though I fight it with everything I have, I can't stop it.

The first tendril of smoke slips between my lips, cold and bitter, filling my lungs with a suffocating darkness. I choke, gasping for air, but more smoke pours from Gygarth's maw, winding its way into me, filling me with his essence. It tastes of death and decay, of something ancient and malevolent, and as it enters me, I feel a searing pain, as though the very fabric of my soul is being torn apart.

I can't breathe. I can't think. All I know is the smoke, the darkness, and the demon's cold, empty eyes staring down at me as he claims me for the void. The chanting rises to a deafening crescendo, the robed figures swaying wildly, their voices echoing in my head as the smoke invades every part of me, dragging me deeper into the abyss.

Panic grips me like a vice, squeezing the breath from my lungs as the smoke fills every corner of my body. I feel helpless, utterly alone. No one is coming to save me—not Daed, not Arax. No one.

My mind races, but it's too slow, too heavy, weighed down by the smoke, by the pull of Gygarth's power. The chanting grows louder, the haunting words wrapping around me like chains, and I feel myself slipping, sinking into the dark. But then, through the haze of fear, a memory flickers—blurry at first, but gaining clarity with every heartbeat.

The last time I faced the demon. The moment I escaped. The pain... the pain in my hand. I remember the light, the green light that surged from within me, blasting him away, giving me the smallest window of freedom. My hands clench involuntarily, and I feel it again, the sharp sting of my wound. The bandage tightens around my palm, the familiar throb cutting through the thick fog of dread.

Suddenly, the ghost's words echo in my mind, clearer now than ever before. *Pain is your awakening.*

This isn't the second time I've been here. This isn't a nightmare that I've escaped only once.

No. This is where I am brought every night.

When I wake in the morning, weak, my head throbbing, my mind slowly slipping away, it is because I have been here in this room with him. This is where Gygarth feeds me shadows, where he pours the void into my veins. But I never remember. Until now. Until the pain cuts through the veil that clouds my mind, showing me the truth.

This is real.

A surge of clarity hits me like a tidal wave, and my pulse quickens with the realization. I can feel the cool sweat on my skin, the way my lungs burn as they fight for air, the icy press of Gygarth's tendrils tightening around me. The circle is real. The robed figures are real. And Gygarth, hovering above me, his smoke pouring into my soul, is real.

My eyes snap open and I force myself to move. My hand shakes, but I unravel the bandage, my fingers trembling as the cloth slips away. The wound is raw beneath, the skin torn and red, but it's enough. The blood flows, and with it, so does my awareness. The veil lifts entirely, and I see everything as it truly is—the dark room, the symbols pulsing around me, the void above, and Gygarth.

I grit my teeth, every nerve alive with the agony in my hand, but I use it. I need it.

Pain is my awakening, and I am finally awake.

The green light comes from deep inside me, a flicker at first, then a burning flame. It surges through me like wildfire, traveling down my arm, and before I know it, my hand glows with a fluorescent brilliance, vibrant and blinding. The robed figures stumble back, their chants faltering as they shield their eyes, and Gygarth—he pauses, his swirling mass of darkness pulling back as if sensing the power I'm about to unleash.

I thrust my hand forward, and the green light explodes from my palm, a beam of energy so bright it illuminates the void itself. The force of it sends Gygarth spiraling back, his tentacled arms flailing as the light tears through him, unraveling the shadows that bind him. His guttural roar fills the space, shaking the very ground beneath me, but I don't stop. I pour every ounce of strength, of will, into the light, watching as it pushes Gygarth deeper into the void, further from me, until he is nothing more than a distant speck swallowed by the dark.

The robed figures scream, their voices shrill as they retreat into the shadows, their ritual shattered, their control broken. The circle around me flickers and dies, the runes fading as the void above collapses in on itself, leaving nothing but silence. I fall back onto the cold floor, my hand trembling as the green light dims. My body is spent, my mind teetering on the edge of exhaustion, but I'm alive.

I'm awake.

Then I bolt upright and I am in my in bed, a scream ripping from my throat before I can stop it. My chest heaves, my hands gripping the sheets as if they'll keep me tethered to reality. Solena jerks awake in the chair by the fireplace, her eyes wide with alarm. In an instant, the door bursts open, and Arax storms in, his sword already drawn. Ashen arches his back on the bed, hissing, his smoky body shifting with agitation.

"Amara, what is it?" Solena asks, rushing to my side, her hands gripping my shoulders. "Are you hurt?"

I shake my head, gasping for breath. "It wasn't a dream," I choke out, my voice trembling. "It was real. I was... I was there again. The altar. The chanting. Gygarth. It's not just in my mind—*I was there.*"

Arax takes a step closer, his brow furrowed, while Solena's grip on me tightens. "Start from the beginning," she urges. "Tell us everything."

I squeeze my eyes shut, trying to calm my racing heart, but the images of the void, of Gygarth's monstrous form, flood back into my mind. "There were runes... on the floor, surrounding me. Chanting voices, people in robes. I couldn't move. Then a demon came, this beast of smoke, with tentacles and these horrible white eyes. He—he was feeding me shadows, filling me with the void." I shudder, my skin crawling at the memory. "I fought him off... with the light, the green light. I used my wound, and I forced him back, but it was real. *It was real.*"

Solena and Arax exchange a look, their expressions tight with concern, as if they know more than they're saying. Solena stands abruptly, her gaze sweeping over the bed, something sharp in her eyes. She circles, her fingers skimming over the sheets, then kneels down, tugging at the edge of the rug that lies beneath.

"Amara," she says, her voice tense. "Get out of the bed."

My heart pounds in my ears, but I do as she asks, swinging my legs over the side and stepping onto the cold floor. Solena motions for Arax. "Move the bed."

Arax steps forward without hesitation, his face grim. Using the smoke that trails from his fingertips, he summons a tendril, coiling it beneath the heavy frame of the bed. With a grunt, he pulls the bed and the rug aside, sliding them across the room as if they weigh nothing.

And then I see it.

My breath catches in my throat.

The runes—those same pulsing, ancient symbols that surrounded me in the void—are painted on the floor beneath my bed, beneath the rug, an inverted crescent moon at the circle's center. They glow faintly in the dim light, twisting and spiraling into patterns I now recognize from my visions. I stumble back, my mind reeling.

"Void runes," Arax mutters, his hand tightening on the hilt of his sword.

"Every time you've slept here," Solena says softly, her gaze fixed on the runes with a look of horror, "your soul has been sent somewhere else—somewhere between reality and the void."

My stomach twists. "How... how long has this been happening?" I whisper, my voice barely audible.

Inside, I already know. The void has been siphoning its essence into me since the first night I arrived, and the only times I have felt well have been when I spent the night somewhere else.

249

It's not just a nightmare. It's a trap.

Suddenly, the sound of heavy boots echoes through the hallways, the pounding growing louder as they approach. My heart leaps into my throat just as the door to my chambers flies open. A fleet of Blades storm inside, their faces hidden behind their shadowy helms, their weapons gleaming in the torchlight. Arax steps in front of me, his sword already drawn, its black edge catching the dim light from the runes on the floor.

"Stand down!" Arax barks, his voice filled with authority. His sword gleams, poised to strike. "You have no place here."

But the Blades don't falter. The captain among them steps forward, his voice cold and unyielding. "We answer only to the queen."

My blood runs cold.

As if summoned by his words, the Blades part, and Lanneth stumbles into the room. She looks nothing like the regal queen I've come to know—her face drained, drawn, her usually poised figure hunched with exhaustion. And when I look at her, something far more sinister unfolds before my eyes.

Her glamor wavers.

In the low light, her beautiful face shifts and flickers like a candle about to go out. The Lanneth I've known ripples away, leaving behind the monster who first showed itself to me across the table. Her fingers... they're blackened, charred like the hands of the robed figures from my dreams. And on her forehead, faint but unmistakable, is the same inverted crescent moon rune from the circle beneath my bed.

A guttural rage rises within me. My vision narrows as the pieces snap together, the truth hitting me like a blow to the chest. "It's you," I say, my voice trembling with fury. "You are behind all of this. You..." My voice breaks as anger surges through me. "When Daed returns—"

Lanneth laughs, a chilling, hollow sound that sends a shiver down my spine. Her face continues to flicker, her true self—twisted and cruel—peeking through the glamor she wears. Her smile stretches unnaturally wide, and her eyes, dark and empty, lock onto mine with a wicked glee.

"Daed?" she sneers, her voice dripping with contempt. "When Daed returns? Oh, you stupid, naive human." She steps closer, her voice lowering to a hiss. "When Daedalus returns, he will hold you down until we can finish what we started. Do you understand nothing?"

The flickering of her glamor ceases, her face fully morphing into that of the priestess of the void. I can see it now—her true self, the evil that lurks beneath the queenly facade. Her blackened fingers flex, crackling with dark power as the air around her shrouds with darkness.

My heart races, but her next words rip the ground out from under me.

"Daedalus knows," she says, her eyes narrowing. "He has *always* known. He is the Prince of the Void."

The world tilts.

"No..." I whisper, shaking my head in denial, my voice weak, fragile. "No, that can't be true."

Lanneth's lips twist into a cruel smile, her eyes gleaming with a cold certainty. "It can and it is. This bargain was not just for a bride, Amara Tyne of the Grove. It was for a womb, for an heir, for a sacrifice. Gygarth fuels the Mordorin—he grants us aspects of the void. That is why our house rules over all others. But he must be fed. This is the cost for such glorious power."

She straightens, her composure rigid and terrifyingly calm. "Now, not all is lost. Had you simply played your part, you could have lived for a time in our world, blissfully ignorant of your fate. You would've tasted a life no other human could dream of. But you've ruined that for yourself, Amara. Now things will be much harder for you. There is no avoiding that." She pauses, her eyes narrowing as if piecing together something that unsettles her. "But I must know..."

Her voice lowers, and I feel a tremor of dread as her face flickers, shifting between the queen and the priestess of the void. "How did you see through the glamors? There is only one way..." She speaks with disbelief, as though she already knows the answer but refuses to acknowledge it. "You cannot be awakened."

"I don't know what I am," I snap, the bitterness coating my words. "All I know is that I see you for what you truly are—hideous, treacherous, and evil. And when Daed—"

"Are you deaf or simple, girl?" Lanneth's laughter slices through me, her voice dark and sharp. "How can I make this any plainer? The prince knows. Where do you think his power comes from? Why do you think he's stronger, faster, more than any of us could ever be? The Father Below blessed him when he came into this world, and the price for that blessing was the life of Queen Veloria."

My breath falters. I stagger, the truth unraveling like a noose around my neck. But I am not the only one shaken. Arax, standing guard, looks as though the ground beneath him has crumbled. Solena's hand flies to her mouth, stifling her gasp of horror.

"I served my god," Lanneth says, her voice dripping with righteousness. Her gaze slides to my stomach, and her words slither through me like poison. "And you... you shall offer the same gift to his heir. The Father must be fed, Amara, and you were chosen long before you knew it. His essence is already inside you, seeping into your very being, filling you with the void's dark power. One day, it will infuse the Fae child you will carry. It is your purpose—to be the vessel that will feed the Father."

I stare at her, my heart pounding against my ribs. Every word she speaks burrows into my mind like nails. "There's no going back now," she continues, her voice a mockery of pity. "The dark bargain was struck long ago, and bargains... can never be broken."

I can't breathe. My chest feels tight, like it's caving in. The room spins as the full weight of her words settle inside me. This fate, this horror—it was sealed long before I even knew Daed. I was never a bride. I was always a vessel.

"Now, we are wasting time. Arax, bring her. Kill the maid."

The air in the room freezes, heavy with shock. I take a step back, my heart thundering in my chest, and instinctively reach out for Solena. Her fingers lace with mine, trembling as we stand in silence, eyes locked on Arax. He stands still as stone, his face unreadable, his hand hovering over the pommel of his blade.

"Arax!" Lanneth shrieks. "You are a Reaper of the Ebon Flight. You have served this house for centuries, fought for your prince since the day he was born. *Obey me!*"

Arax bows his head, his hand lingering near his sword. My breath catches, dread pooling in my stomach. I know his loyalty, his sense of duty, and honor. It is that very loyalty that makes me certain he will carry out her orders. I can't blame him for that. I can't fault him for what he must do.

"Princess," his voice is low, almost a whisper.

I swallow, squaring my shoulders, forcing my voice to remain steady. "Yes, Arax."

"Move."

A rope of smoke lashes from his hand, wrapping around the high-back chair, and before I can react, Solena and I drop to our knees as he flings it over us, sending it crashing into the Blades. Half of them tumble to the floor, while the others draw their swords with a sharp ring of steel.

252

They charge, but Arax doesn't flinch. His sword remains untouched at his side as his hands move in fluid, mystical patterns, weaving threads of smoke that grow in size and intensity. The black tendrils lash out like whips, ensnaring the remaining Blades, hurling them against the walls with a sickening thud. They struggle, limbs kicking, but they are no match for the smoke that pins them, suffocating their efforts.

"Go!" Arax yells.

But Lanneth is already shedding her black robe, revealing her body covered in the cursed runes of Gygarth. Smoke coils around her fingers like living creatures, and she raises her hands, eyes blazing. Arax sends another tendril toward her, but she merely flicks her wrist, turning it to ash before it crumbles to the floor.

Solena grabs my arm, yanking me toward the wall where a Blade writhes against the shackles of smoke. She taps the hidden panel, and with a soft click, the secret door swings open.

"Hurry!" she urges, pulling me inside.

I glance over my shoulder just in time to see Lanneth's smoke wrapping around Arax, twisting his body in mid-air. His eyes lock onto mine, his jaw tight, pain etched across his face.

"Go, Princess!" he roars.

Solena yanks me into the tunnel, slamming the door shut behind us. The sound of footsteps echoes from the other side.

"It won't hold them," I murmur, fear creeping into my voice.

Solena's eyes dart around the tunnel, panic seeping into her movements as she searches frantically for something.

"What? What are you looking for?"

Suddenly, she notices the layer of dust on the door. Without a word, she draws a rune into the dust with her finger. As the final stroke is completed, the rune pulses, glowing faintly, and I feel the magic ripple through the air around us.

"I am not a great runeweaver, but that should hold them," she says, breathless. "But not for long."

CHAPTER 28

We stumble through the winding tunnel, the air damp and suffocating as we run, our feet slapping against the stone floor in a frantic rhythm. My breath comes in short gasps, my legs burning with every step. Solena is just as panicked, her usually nimble form stumbling as exhaustion grips her. Despite moving as fast as we can, we're gaining not nearly enough ground.

Lanneth's voice echoes through the fortress, growing louder with every passing second, her cruel laughter bouncing off the walls. "You cannot run, Amara! You cannot hide!"

There is no way out. I know this in my heart. Baev'kalath is a prison with no escape.

Solena cannot fly us away from here—she doesn't have the strength. And even if she could, where would we go? We would never make it across the Untold Sea, just the two of us.

Lanneth will catch us eventually, and when she does...

Solena stumbles beside me, her breath ragged. "Amara," she gasps, grabbing my arm to steady herself. "I can't—"

"We have to keep moving!" I shout, fear twisting through me.

But as we round the next corner, we come to a sudden stop. There, standing in the middle of the tunnel, blocking our path like the worst possible omen, is the ghost of Baev'kalath.

It's the last thing I want to see right now, and the shock on Solena's face suggests she can't decide what's worse—that the ghost is real, or that I'm not afraid of it.

"Amara," Solena whispers, fear seeping into her voice. "Do you know what that is?"

"Unfortunately," I reply.

"You have finally awakened," the ghost says, its voice a low, hollow echo.

"Yes," I exhale. "I understand now."

"Are you ready to run?"

I blink, the weight of the ghost's words sinking in. My heart hammers in my chest as I realize what it means.

"Yes," I say, my voice trembling. "Yes, I'm ready."

A door, hidden in the stone, creaks open beside us.

"Climb the stairs that do not exist," the ghost intones, *"to the room of nothing."*

Solena glances at me, confusion clouding her face, but I tug her forward. We don't have a choice.

I drag her through the door, then we sprint down the dimly lit halls, every turn a fevered guess, my senses straining for the sound of Blades in pursuit, or worse—Lanneth's maddened voice. Solena stumbles behind me, her questions barely registering as I fixate on what I must find. *The stairs that do not exist.* But the endless, identical corridors make everything blur together, and doubt creeps in with every step.

Suddenly, I skid to a halt, Solena crashing into my back.

Ahead, a shimmer flickers between the two branching corridors—just like the ghost had said. The stairs are there, though I can't see them. Only the faint glimmer gives them away. My pulse quickens as I glance down at my hand. It's healed. Too healed. I can see the shimmer, can feel the veil of magic between realities, but it's hazy. Incomplete.

I know what this means. The only way to tear down the veil is through pain.

I have no blade, no way to hurt myself in this barren hallway.

I take a deep breath and turn to Solena, my heart hammering. "Break my finger."

Her eyes widen in disbelief. "Pardon?"

"There's no time to explain," I say with urgency, thrusting my hand toward her.

"Yes, well, perhaps you better," she says firmly, shaking her head. "I will not."

The sounds of approaching Blades—footsteps, metal clanging—fill the hall. Lanneth's screeches echo down the stone passage, closer now.

"You heard her. I refuse to be trapped here. Baev'kalath cannot be my end." I swallow the fear crawling up my throat. "Please, Solena."

Solena glances over her shoulder, the voices growing louder. Her hesitation is agony, and I nearly take matters into my own hands when she finally grabs my wrist. With a sickening snap, she breaks my finger.

The pain shoots up my arm, blinding and hot, but I bite down hard, swallowing the scream that burns in my throat. Tears sting my eyes as I turn back to the shimmer, watching as the stairs slowly materialize, step by step. But they're still not fully solid.

"Another," I grit through clenched teeth, the dizziness threatening to drag me under.

Solena hesitates for only a second before taking another finger and snapping it cleanly. The pain is so intense I nearly double over, muffling my scream in my sleeve. The world tilts, and for a moment, everything spins, but then—the stairs are there. Fully formed. Solid.

"Go," I manage, dragging Solena forward as we climb the ethereal steps. My hand dangles uselessly at my side, the throb of pain a constant reminder that we are teetering between life and death.

"Come on," I urge, tugging Solena as the steps flicker in and out of existence, and she falters, her eyes wide with fear. But I tighten my grip on her, pushing us forward.

Ahead, the door looms, the ghost's words lingering in my mind. *The room of nothing.*

We halt before the door, memories of the last time flooding back—just emptiness beyond it. I cling to the hope that the pain surging through me will show me what I need this time. My hand trembles as I push the door open.

What greets me is no longer a barren room. A cage dominates the space. Inside, there's a lavish bed draped in silk covers, a velvet chair beside a pile of worn books, and a table laid out with silver platters of food and jugs of water and wine. It's a beautifully curated prison, designed for comfort and elegance—but a cage, nonetheless.

And then she appears. She glides past the bars, her fingers trailing along the cold metal. Her blue-black hair frames her sharp, delicate face, and her gray eyes glint like polished slate. A mischievous smile curls on her lips, and when she giggles, the sound is haunting, almost hypnotic.

"Are you ready to run, Amara?" Her voice is light, playful, as if we're sharing a secret.

"It's you," I gasp. "The ghost."

Her fingers tighten around the bars, pressing her face so close it's almost as if she's trying to break through. "No, not a ghost. Ghosts are dead. And I am very much alive—despite their best efforts." She tips her head toward the lock. "Now, be a dear and let me out, won't you?"

I take a hesitant step forward, but Solena's hand shoots out, gripping my arm tightly. Her touch grounds me, making me question myself.

"How can I trust you?" I ask, my voice shaky.

The female tilts her head, her smile never faltering. "Trust? There's nothing I could say now—or before Lanneth finds you, drags you down those stairs, and locks you in a cage like mine—that would convince you of my character. Instead, I'll ask you one thing—do you want to die?"

My throat tightens. I shake my head.

"Then. Open. The. Cage."

"Amara," Solena hisses, her warning clear as my hand moves toward the handle.

But I can't stop. We need to escape Baev'kalath, and I'll just have to take my chances with this specter. My fingers wrap around the handle, and I pull. To my surprise, it opens effortlessly, the door creaking as it swings wide.

The female steps out, her entire form cloaked in black leather fitted to her like armor. Tall and statuesque, she exudes a presence that's both intimidating and captivating. She's the most beautiful Fae I've ever seen, dangerous and untouchable.

"Why didn't you just open it yourself?" I ask, still shocked. "It wasn't locked."

Her smirk deepens at the corner of her mouth. "It was enchanted. Only I couldn't open it."

She steps across the threshold as if testing the ground beneath her, her excitement barely contained. Her foot lifts, then a pulse of power ripples through the room, strong enough to send Solena and me stumbling backward. The walls crack, splintering apart like shattered glass. The illusion is breaking, crumbling away, and for the first time, I see the truth of this room—the mirror-like glamor dissolving into nothingness.

"Time to go," the female says with a thrill of finality. She grabs my hand, her fingers curling around my broken ones, and I bite back a whimper of pain.

"She must come too," I say quickly, nodding toward Solena, my voice tight with desperation.

The female's eyes flick toward Solena with clear disdain. "Fae cannot be trusted."

"You're Fae!" I yell, my voice filled with pain and frustration.

"Exactly," she sighs, exasperated, but relents. "Fine. She comes."

She takes Solena's hand too, and in a swirl of smoke and shadow, we're pulled into the void, slipping through the cold nothingness. Moments later, we land with a hard thud in the courtyard, the rough stone beneath our feet grounding us back to reality.

For a fleeting moment, hope blooms in my chest—I convince myself I've made the right choice. This stranger, this female who walks with the void, must possess the power and will to free us from Baev'kalath. But that hope shatters the instant I realize we are surrounded by Blades.

From the balcony above, Lanneth emerges. Arax dangles from a tendril of smoke, his face bruised and bloodied, his arms bound. The queen is calm as ever—until her gaze locks onto the female who stands beside me.

So this is what Lanneth looks like when she's afraid?

"What have you done?" Lanneth screams, her voice cracking with fury. "Kill them! Destroy them! But spare the human!"

The Blades draw their swords and close in. Solena and I instinctively backpedal, but there's nowhere to go, only the jagged rocks and crashing ocean below. The courtyard is yet another cage. My heart races, panic rising like bile in my throat. But the female... she's still smiling, as if this is all part of her plan.

Her eyes flick toward the docks, where the Mordorin ship bobs at the far end of the wharf, repaired and good as new since the Stormwyrm's attack. She glances at Solena.

"Are your little wings strong enough to fly you both to that ship?" she asks, her voice dripping with mockery.

Solena bristles, insult flashing in her eyes. "Yes. I can get us there."

"Then go," the female groans. "Must I spell it out for you?"

Solena clenches her jaw, clearly biting back a tirade, but then shifts her focus. Her wings unfurl and she hooks her arms under mine, lifting me off the ground. We soar into the air, the ship in sight as we rush toward it.

But before we can breathe a sigh of relief, several Blades summon their own wings, launching into the sky to pursue us. Panic grips my chest again, the sound of their wings beating like thunder behind us.

We'll never outrun them.

Suddenly, a wall of smoke erupts from the ground, surging upward like a black tidal wave, towering so high it vanishes into the clouds. The Blades falter, gasping in shock, while the female's laughter echoes through the courtyard.

"Surprise," she giggles, flicking her wrists with a devilish grin. "I. Am. Free."

The Blades reel back, their flight cut short as the smoke consumes them. Solena flies harder, her wings straining with the effort as we near the ship, leaving the chaos behind.

The Blades recover from their shock; they waste no time setting upon the mysterious female, swords raised, their wings slicing through the air with deadly precision. But she doesn't flinch. With a flick of her wrist, tendrils of smoke burst from the ground like serpents, wrapping around the legs of the nearest Blade and yanking him down with a bone-crunching thud.

Another Blade dives at her from above, but she vanishes into the void just before his sword cleaves the space where she stood. He stumbles, caught off-guard, and before he can recover, she reappears behind him, a cruel smile playing at her lips. A whip of smoke cracks through the air and lashes at him, sending him careening into the stone wall.

More Blades surround her, their swords gleaming in the moonlight. But instead of fleeing, she stands her ground, her body flickering between solid form and smoke. Each step they take is met with black wisps that bind their limbs, slowing their advance. Shadows dance around her like loyal soldiers, her power swelling with each passing moment. She's toying with them, and I see it now—this is no ordinary Fae.

"Is this truly all you've got?" she sneers, her voice thick with mockery. "I expected more from the Blades of Baev'kalath."

Despite her strength, the odds are stacked against her. More Blades swoop in, closing off every path of escape. Their swords cut through the swirling smoke, dispersing it but never quite reaching her. One Blade finally lands a hit, grazing her arm. She hisses in pain, eyes blazing with fury—then vanishes into the void. Just as suddenly, she reappears by the docks, her back to the water, a smirk curling her lips.

The Blades surge toward her again, but it's too late. In a swirl of shadow and smoke, she leaps from the dock, landing gracefully aboard the ship, her feet barely making a sound on the wooden deck. She turns to face the Blades one last time, and with a wave of her hand, the air between them fills with a thick, impenetrable fog.

"Come along, darlings," she calls, her voice ringing through the mist. "Our time here is done."

Solena and I land on the ship just as the gangplank rises, the vessel beginning to pull away from the dock. I glance back through the fog, watching the Blades flounder, their wings flapping uselessly as they try to clear the smoke. Lanneth seethes on the balcony, her fury palpable, while Arax suffers beside her, bound and silent.

My heart lurches in my chest, panic flooding my veins.

"We can't leave him!" I cry, desperation tightening my throat.

The female sidles up beside me, her brow furrowed in confusion as she absorbs my frantic gaze. "Really? Him too?" she muses, her voice laced with a mix of amusement and irritation. "Why does a human have so many Fae in need of saving?"

I grip her arm with my good hand, desperation spilling over. "Please," I beg, my voice cracking. "I freed you. Do this one thing for me."

She gestures around us, to the ship engulfed in shadows and the swirling fog. "I believe I've already done plenty for you."

"Please!" I plead.

She heaves a dramatic sigh, rolling her eyes. "Fine."

With a loud pop, she vanishes into the void, and I barely have time to react before I see her reappear on the balcony beside Lanneth. My breath catches in my throat. I know what I asked for, but I never expected her to confront Lanneth directly. Even from here, I can see the way Lanneth shrinks before her, the queen's haughty demeanor faltering. Their lips move in a silent exchange, and I would give anything to know what they're saying. It doesn't last long—just enough to unsettle the powerful queen.

The female takes hold of Arax, and in another blink, they reappear on the deck beside me. She casts him to the ground with a careless flick, his body battered and broken, but alive.

"Happy now?" she groans, and she almost sounds bored. "Can we go?"

I nod, dropping to my knees beside Arax, cradling his head as his pained eyes flutter open.

"Let's hope you're as good at sailing as you are at playing with smoke," Solena mutters.

The mysterious female chuckles, the glint of amusement returning to her eyes as she brushes past us. "Sailing?" she muses, her voice filled with mischief. "Who said anything about sailing?"

And just like that, the ship lurches forward, not propelled by wind or water, but by the shadows themselves. The sea bends to her will, the ship gliding as if carried by invisible hands. I watch in awe as Baev'kalath drifts further into the fog, its dark spires disappearing into the night.

Just as I'm certain we're safe, a blur catches my eye. A single Blade, emerging from the fog, hurls his sword toward the ship. It spins through the air, a silver arc of death aimed straight for the female. I try to call out, but it happens too fast. The blade lodges itself in her back with a sickening thud.

She wavers in place, her body stiffening as the shock settles in. A thin stream of blood trickles from the corner of her mouth, and she raises a hand to wipe it away, staring at the crimson smear on her fingers with confusion.

Her teeth grit, her expression darkening as her gaze locks onto the lone Blade. She raises her hand, extends her fingers, and with a slow, deliberate clench of her fist, the Blade screams, his body disintegrating into ash that down into the sea.

Then, without another word, she collapses onto the deck.

Arax stirs, reaching out to me. "You must help her," he says, his voice hoarse but urgent. "She is our only hope of surviving any of this."

I trust Arax's words without explanation. My fingers wrap around my rune necklace, the decision clear in my mind. But before I heal her, I must know one thing.

"Who is she?" I ask, my voice low, almost afraid of the answer.

Arax hesitates for a moment, his eyes distant as if dredging up memories from long ago.

"She is the bones that rattle beneath the rock," he mutters darkly. "Her name is Zyphoro."

CHAPTER 29

I never believed this day would come. That I would be on a ship, sailing toward a home I thought I'd never see again. Yet, as I sit here, my joy is tainted.

Daed. My dark prince. My husband. *My betrayer.*

I don't want to believe anything Lanneth said, but her words cling to me, haunting the corners of my mind. He wasn't there when I needed him. And though I try to deny it, there are questions swirling in my head, questions I can't answer, no matter how hard I try.

But still, despite everything, my heart aches for him. Souls, how it aches. Not only has Daed betrayed me—he has betrayed my heart. The heart that foolishly made me care for him. The betrayal cuts deeper than I ever imagined.

I wince as I sit in the chair, my back throbbing from absorbing Zyphoro's wound. She lies asleep on the cot, her breathing shallow, while Solena carefully sets my broken fingers. I glance at my hand, recalling how I healed myself against Gygarth, how the green light had surged through me. I still don't understand it. Until I do, I'll have to heal the old-fashioned way. Now that I'm free from Baev'kalath and the rituals of the demon's worshipers, I should recover. Although the weight of Ashen weaved through my hair is putting a crick in my neck. It appears to be his new favorite place to hide and sleep.

"Do you know who she is?" I ask, gritting my teeth as Solena sets the second finger.

"No," Solena replies, her voice low, cautious. "But Arax has seen many more dawns and dusks than I have."

"He won't say," I mutter, frustration creeping into my tone. "Claims it's not his place."

"Then you'll have to wait for her to tell you," Solena says, which only deepens my irritation. "But she's powerful—no question about that. I've only ever seen one other with abilities like hers."

I nod, the name heavy on my lips. "Daedalus."

Solena's hands still for a moment, but then she resumes her work. "Yes."

"Does that mean she's infused with the void as well?" I ask.

Solena sighs, a shrug barely visible as she finishes with my fingers. "I do not dare to presume the workings of the void. But to my eyes, that is how it seems."

I watch her tidy up the bandages and splints, her head hanging low. There's a quiet sadness in the air around her, one I can't ignore.

"You're unhappy to be here?" I ask softly.

Solena looks up, a half-smile tugging at her lips, but her eyes betray her. "I fear I will never see Orios again."

Her pain weighs on me like a burden I can't lift. Guilt gnaws at me, the realization sinking in deeper than before. "I'm sorry, Solena. I should never have dragged you into this."

She shakes her head as she heads for the cabin door. "No, don't be sorry. I came of my own accord. And though I may not be awakened like you, for the first time, I feel alive. I'm glad to be here with you..." She pauses, her smile blooming like the first warm light after a storm. "With my friend."

Her words are a balm I hadn't realized I needed, a warmth that reaches deep into the cold places inside me. Solena will never know just how much I treasure them.

"I'll leave you to rest," she says softly. "The ship seems to know its course, and the weather is stable. We should reach land soon."

"Thank you, Solena," I murmur as she closes the door behind her.

I force myself to my feet, every muscle protesting as I make my way toward the cot across from Zyphoro. She sleeps soundly, her chest rising and falling with each steady breath. Her body heals while mine aches with the strain of mending her wound. I know I must sleep to recover, but something catches my eye—something glimmering beneath the deep neckline of her vest.

My heart stutters in my chest. I would know that glow anywhere.

I carefully reach down, not wanting to disturb her, holding my breath as I pinch the leather cord around her neck. Slowly, I lift it, and the luminous stone slips from beneath her leathers, cool and smooth against my fingertips.

A moonstone, hewn in half.

The sight of it sends a harsh pang through my chest, and a gasp escapes my lips. The soft sound is enough to make Zyphoro stir, and I quickly stumble backward, collapsing onto my cot as she rolls to her side, the necklace now hanging in plain view.

I know who wears the other half of that moonstone, though I wish I didn't. I don't want to admit what it could mean. That stone is precious to him, and whoever wears the other half... they must be just as cherished.

Sleep. I tell myself. *Just sleep.*

But even as exhaustion pulls me under, the moonstone takes up all the space in my head. I knew this female was no ordinary Fae, but she may be even more than I bargained for. Either my salvation, or another of my prince's betrayals.

The cot across from me is empty when I awaken.

I prop myself on my elbows, grateful to find the pain of Zyphoro's wound has vanished. My fingers, though, will take more time, and I grimace when I accidentally put too much weight on them when I swing my legs over the side of the cot.

The moonstone.

It's haunted me since I closed my eyes, and if I dreamed, I'm sure it would have followed me there too.

I climb to my feet and make for the cabin door, and when I open it and warm sunlight spills in, I can't help but feel that we have made it. That we have truly escaped. I walk onto the deck and see Solena leaning on the railing, lost in her thoughts as she gazes at the clear sky. At the opposite end of the ship, Arax and Zyphoro stand huddled in discussion, and whatever they are talking about, I very much want to be a part of. I stride across the deck, feeling Solena's eyes on me as I approach the two whispering Fae, and I have only one question on my lips.

"Who are you?" I demand.

She half turns, her fingers steepled. "I am Zyphoro."

"That much I know," I bite, aware that she is toying with me. "But who are you, *truly*? Why were you in that glamored prison? Why does Lanneth fear you?" Then there is the question that burns at the forefront of of my mind. "Who gave you that moonstone?"

"Ah," she says with a grin. "That is what you *really* want to know, isn't it?"

I don't reply, fighting to keep my control even though I am desperate for her answer.

"This belonged to someone very special to me," Zyphoro replies, her fingers gripping the stone. "A long time ago."

My eyes find Arax as I try to put the pieces together, and he bows his head, almost separating himself, leaving me to figure this out alone.

"I... I have seen another stone, just like it. In fact, I believe it to be its other half." A lump burns in my throat, and though my feelings about Daed are still uncertain, I must know. "Did Daedalus give you that stone?"

Her chin dips, and she looks at me from beneath her brow. "Yes."

An ache grips my heart and chokes it. "Are you... are you and he..."

Zyphoro's brow furrows, and she takes a moment to understand my meaning, and when she throws her head back and laughs. I can't help but feel that she is mocking me.

"Do not laugh at me!" I snap tersely. "Tell me. Are you his lover?"

My anger silences her laughter, and for the first time there is some seriousness on her face.

"No. Daedalus is not my lover. *He is my brother.*"

"Twin brother," Arax exhales.

Zyphoro looks down at the stone clenched between her fingers. "When this was whole, it belonged to our mother, the Queen Veloria. After she was murdered, our father had it cleaved and gave us each a piece."

"Brother..." The idea did not even cross my mind, but now I see it so clearly. The dark curls, the sea storm eyes, a charisma and confidence both infuriating and alluring. They are cut from the same cloth. "I didn't know. Daed never told me."

"There is much Daedalus has not told you, and only half of that is his fault. Our family history is a long, dark tale that frightens even me." She smiles. "And I do not scare easily."

"You seem awfully cheery for someone who has been locked in a cage and haunting Baev'kalath for hundreds of years," I say, not realizing my tone is a little rude until after I've said the words.

Zyphoro simply sighs. "The first fifty years were unpleasant, but after that, I developed a sense of humor about it. The rest of the time flew by."

Arax lets out a low chuckle, the sound deep and knowing, and when Zyphoro catches his amusement, she laughs too—a soft, melodic sound that's oddly comforting. I stand there, watching them share this moment, and suddenly I feel entirely out of my depth. These two Fae have seen centuries pass, have witnessed wars, kingdoms rise and fall, the birth of stars, and the crumbling of empires.

What must it be like to measure time not in years or decades, but in lifetimes?

To have watched mortals love and die, generation after generation, while you remained untouched by it all? They have witnessed more than I could ever imagine—an endless horizon of time that stretches behind them like a shadow I'll never reach.

I fall silent, my gaze drifting as I process everything I've just heard. Zyphoro notices, her eyes sharpening as they take me in, her arms folding casually across her chest, but there's a subtle intensity in her posture.

"You have questions," she says, smirking, though her tone is softer now. "I'll answer them as best I can, but I warn you—some answers may not sit well with you."

I draw in a steady breath, straightening my back as I meet her gaze. I nod. Those are acceptable terms.

Zyphoro and I settle ourselves on the deck, the afternoon sun pouring down over us. Unlike Daed when we were in Pariseth, Zyphoro seems to bask in the warmth just as much as I do. But then again, she's been locked away in that cursed room for over a century. I imagine even the smallest pleasures feel like a luxury to her now.

"I'll start with what I know," she begins, her voice losing its playful edge. "The Mordorin are the only Fae who harness the void. It's what grants us the ability to void walk. Older Fae, like Arax, can manipulate smoke, bend it to their will. Then there are Fae like Daedalus and me—so deeply attuned to the void that it's become part of us. We wield powers beyond what most Fae could even dream of. But the price is steep. The Father Below demands a sacrifice for such gifts."

"Queen Veloria. How did she die?" I mutter under my breath, and I instantly regret it.

Zyphoro's eyes darken, a flash of something bitter crossing her face. "Yes. Queen Veloria. What I know for certain is as Daedalus came into this world, our mother was taken from it, and in return, he was infused with the void. But then there was me."

She leans back with a mischievous grin, a sharp edge of satisfaction in her voice. "I was the surprise. They never expected me to follow Daedalus, let alone consider that I, too, would be touched by the void. And while Daedalus is seamless with it, the perfect weapon molded by Gygarth, I... well... Let's just say that I'm a little more *unpredictable*."

The grin lingers on her lips, but there's a darkness beneath her words.

"Daedalus' bond with the void is both his greatest strength and his undoing," Zyphoro says. "When he's in control, he can resist it. But the moment he's vulnerable—whether through fear, doubt, or weakness—Gygarth and Lanneth can bend him to their will. They can make him do things he'd never choose for himself. When they realized I couldn't be controlled the same way, I was tricked, imprisoned in that dungeon, and glamored out of memory. But it seems the spell is breaking. Still, some might say I was the lucky one."

My chest tightens. Could this be the reason behind Daed's betrayal? Could Gygarth and Lanneth have controlled and manipulated him? A fragile spark of hope flickers within me, but it's quickly snuffed out as Zyphoro leans closer, her piercing gaze locking onto mine.

"I couldn't leave my cage," she continues, her voice barely more than a whisper. "But I could split a part of myself away—only for brief moments. It tore at my very soul, hurt worse than anything I've ever known. But it was the only way I could reach you. You see, I saw you when you first arrived in Baev'kalath, through the window in my little cell, though it appeared empty to the rest of the world. And I knew immediately what they planned for you."

Zyphoro flicks her wrist, conjuring a wisp of smoke that dances between her fingers like a flame, casting eerie shadows across her face. "What if I told you that what I've done so far is just a fraction of what I'm capable of? That at full strength, I don't just control smoke and ash—I control the void itself. If I wanted to, I could tear open the very fabric of this world and swallow it whole. And after what I've suffered, I'd say it would only be fair."

A shiver runs down my spine. "Is that... something you want to do?" I ask, my voice barely steady.

Zyphoro tilts her head, pondering for a moment before giving a half-hearted shrug. "Not today. But even if I did feel like annihilation, I couldn't. My power is fading. It's subtle, but I can feel it, which means Daedalus feels it too. Gygarth is hungry again.

Apparently, a few hundred years without consuming a pregnant woman gets under his skin."

Her casual tone makes my stomach churn. I try to hide my horror, but Zyphoro's sharp eyes catch everything.

"I'm sorry if my manner offends you," she says, her smirk barely there. "But Fae and humans are different. Death is not so... shocking to us. The point is, when I saw you, I knew you were to be the next feast for the beast. My dear brother was to plant a Fae child in your human body, and when it was ripe, they'd crack you open like a melon and toss the scraps to the void. To Gygarth."

I flinch, turning my head away from her, trying to block out the image. I can't be as calm as she is, not when she's speaking so coldly about my life, about Daed's role in my death. "And if I were to die," I say, my voice trembling, "your power would grow stronger,?"

"Oh, yes."

I stare at her, the pieces falling into place. "Then why did you warn me? Why save me if it means you've lost your chance?"

Zyphoro's expression softens, but only slightly. "Power was never something I asked for. It was a curse—paid for with the blood of the mother I never knew. I'd rather have nothing than live with the weight of what I am. So, I told you to run. It took you longer than I expected. Humans can be a little slower on the uptake... but... here we are." She stretches her arms to the sky. "In the sun."

There's a stillness between us, a heavy silence as Zyphoro's revelations settle in. Shadows no longer lurk in corners—they're laid bare before me, leaving nowhere to hide. But none of it... not one word she's spoken... redeems Daed. Only damns him further.

There's no comfort in her truths, only more pain.

"Lanneth says Daedalus knew what would happen to me," I say, my voice trembling. It's almost too much to ask, too terrifying to speak the words aloud. "Is that true? Did he know I would be sacrificed?"

Zyphoro's gaze sharpens, her head tilting with a faint smirk. "What would you like me to say?" she asks, as if testing me, her curiosity cold and detached.

"No," I answer without hesitation, clinging to the hope that the truth is less terrible than I fear.

I want to hear that this was all some twisted misunderstanding, that Daed was a pawn. *Just as I was.*

"Then no," she says, and her eyes bore into mine, watching me too closely, like she's dissecting my emotions, learning something foreign through the agony that twists my face.

I wish I could leave it there—accept the lie, bury the truth deep inside and never unearth it.

It would be easier, wouldn't it? To pretend that Daed didn't know. That deception did not taint the nights we spent in each other's arms. But the truth gnaws at me, a relentless force, and I can't stop myself.

"*Is* that the truth?" My voice cracks, betraying the anguish inside me.

Zyphoro's lips curl slowly, a knowing smile that feels like a blade to my heart. "No. It is not the truth." Her eyes are merciless as they hold mine. "Daedalus knew. He knew all along, Amara."

Her admission shatters something deep inside me, and for a moment, I can't breathe. My chest tightens, my world narrowing into a suffocating tunnel as the weight of her words crashes down like a tidal wave.

Betrayal.

The word pulses through me, leaving cracks in my very soul. I cared for him. I trusted him, let him into my heart, my body. I had given him everything—pieces of myself I didn't know I had to give.

And all the while, he knew.

He knew I was to be a sacrifice, that I would be handed over to the void like an offering, my life nothing more than a pawn in their dark game. I squeeze my eyes shut, my hands curling into fists as the flood of emotions crashes over me. I hold back the tears that blur my vision. I hate myself for them. I feel like I've been ripped open and left exposed.

I feel like a fool!

Zyphoro watches me, silent, perhaps even pitying me in her own cold way, but I don't need her pity. All I need now is my rage.

"Princess," Arax calls from the bow of the ship, his voice cutting through the wind. "You should see this."

I stand, feeling Zyphoro's gaze heavy on my back, but I don't acknowledge her. Not now. Not after everything. Instead, I move toward Arax, joining him at the edge of the ship. When I follow his gaze, my breath catches in my throat, and for the first time since we left Baev'kalath, the weight of my anger lifts, even if just for a moment.

Land.

A sliver of green on the horizon, vibrant and alive, shimmering under the sun's rays like a beacon. My heart lurches in my chest, and it takes a second for the joy to settle in, the disbelief warring with the reality before me. The Grove. My home.

The coastline comes into sharper focus, a blend of lush forests and rolling hills that stretch endlessly, their emerald hues reaching out toward the sky. Even from this distance, I can see the towering trees that define the Grove, their canopies thick with life, leaves glistening as if they are welcoming me back. The winding rivers that snake through the land gleam like silver threads, their waters flowing toward the heart of the forest—the place I thought I might never see again.

My throat tightens as familiar landmarks take shape—the gentle rise of the mountains in the far distance, the cascading waterfalls. I know this place like I know my own heartbeat, and now, standing at the bow of this ship, I feel the pull of it, the overwhelming desire to set foot on that soil, to feel the embrace of the trees and the whispers of the wind.

"We will drop anchor when we get close enough," Arax says, his voice steady despite the visible toll Lanneth's fury has taken on him.

I study his face, noting the bruises, the cuts—marks of a battle fought not just with weapons but with will. Gently, I cup his jaw, my thumb brushing over the worst of the scrapes. "Look at what she's done to you," I murmur, guilt twisting in my chest.

His hand closes over mine, firm but tender. "No," he says, his tone firm. "If you try to heal me again, I'll toss that damned rune somewhere you'll never find it." His lips curve slightly, softening his words. "Besides, I look good with scars."

A grin tugs at the corners of my mouth, and for a brief moment, everything lifts. "Yes," I say, our hands lingering together. "I suppose you do."

I leave Arax at the helm and find Solena on the deck. She stands nearby, casting wary glances at Zyphoro, who lounges beneath the sun, basking as if she hasn't just shattered my world with her truths.

"I don't like her," Solena mutters under her breath.

"You don't like anyone when you first meet them," I remind her, my tone light despite the storm churning in my mind. "Remember?"

Solena's glare could burn through stone. "I know for certain I permanently dislike *her*."

I place a hand on her shoulder, grounding both of us. "We'll drop anchor soon and fly ashore. Then we'll head straight to the Grove. I need to tell Keeper Tovar everything. There's no time to waste."

With reluctance, I approach Zyphoro once more.

She tilts her head, amusement flickering in her eyes. "Back already? I thought I'd scared you off."

"We'll drop anchor soon," I reply, turning my back, eager to put distance between us. "Wait."

The word is a command, and despite myself, I stop. Her footsteps are soft behind me, and then she's at my side, too close, her presence unsettling.

"I know I've said things you didn't want to hear, and perhaps my delivery lacks... tact," she says, her voice surprisingly gentle. "But believe me when I say all I ever wanted was to protect you. To spare you the fate my mother suffered. That's all."

I search her face for signs of deception, but all I find is the raw truth. "I believe you," I admit, my voice quieter now. "You helped me escape Baev'kalath. For that, I am grateful."

She steps closer, so close I can feel the heat of her body. Her hand rests lightly on my belly, the touch both intimate and invasive. "But I couldn't save you from everything. You brought something back with you from Pariseth."

Her fingers tighten slightly, and my breath catches. I stare down at her hand, heart pounding. "That's not possible."

Zyphoro's smirk deepens. "Oh, Amara. You're not that innocent. You know it is."

I swallow hard, my mind spinning. "Even if I am... how could *you* possibly know?"

"I'm attuned to the void," she replies, her voice low and certain. "And the life growing inside you—it's a part of the void."

A tremor runs through me, and I don't know whether to laugh or collapse under the weight of it all. Zyphoro's hand drifts away, her face distant, as though lost in some private thought. "Daedalus will come for you," she continues, her voice heavy with meaning. "That much is certain. But for what purpose, I cannot say. All I know is, I will do what I can to keep you safe. For the sake of my cursed bloodline, and yours."

Her words linger in the air long after she leaves me standing there, alone with the enormity of what I now carry. Slowly, hesitantly, my hands sweep across my stomach, cradling it as if I might feel something—anything. But I don't. I'm not attuned to the void. Yet in the quiet recesses of my heart, I know Zyphoro speaks the truth.

Daedalus and I have created something... something born of both smoke and vine. Beautiful and terrifying in equal measure. There's no escaping it now—this bond between us—this force that ties us together.

Forever.

CHAPTER 30

Valorne is just as breathtaking as I remember, a tapestry of rolling hills and lush forests that seem to stretch endlessly. The sky above is a vibrant blue, unmarred and pure, with fluffy white clouds lazily drifting across its expanse. And the sun—there's no warmth like it anywhere in the Sundered Kingdoms, not even in Pariseth. It bathes the landscape in a golden glow, making everything feel alive and vibrant.

In the distance, the town of Kale Harbour comes into view, but we won't dock the Mordorin ship there; it would draw far too much attention. Instead, Arax deftly guides us into a sheltered cove, releasing the anchor with a splash that echoes against the tranquil water. His gaze sharpens as he scans the horizon, assessing the distance to the shore.

"Shall I carry you to land, Princess?" he asks, extending his hand to me.

Before I can respond, Zyphoro steps forward, her lips curling into a grin. "Family should have that honor," she says. Her wings, dark and sleek, burst from her back with a snap, the black feathers unfurling like shadows stretching against the sky.

"Very well," I say, but just before she lifts me into her arms, I catch her gaze. "Do not tell them."

My voice is low and steady, though my heart is anything but. If I am carrying Daed's child, I'm not ready for anyone else to know. Not until I've had time to make peace with it myself.

Zyphoro tilts her head, amusement flickering across her face. "I wouldn't dream of it," she replies softly. "Such bonny news should come from your lips only."

With ease, she lifts me into her arms. Her strength is both surprising and effortless. Her wings beat once, twice, and we rise into the sky. Below, Arax and Solena follow, flying low as we leave the ship behind and head inland.

As we near The Grove, nestled in the heart of Valorne, it unfurls before us, cradled in a deep valley and framed by mountains that stretch toward the clouds. Once, it was even larger—an endless expanse, until the Maledannan Fae burned half of it to ash and another third fell during the Betrayers' Battle. Yet, the forest endures, resilient in its beauty, and in time, the trees will reclaim their former glory. They tried to destroy it for good, but the roots of the Grove run deep.

At the mouth of the forest lies an open field, where long grasses sway and wildflowers bloom in vibrant colors. To an outsider, it might seem a serene and pretty spot, but for me, it is forever stained by memory. It was here that the Mordorin made their final stand on the last day of the war. They emerged victorious, but at a tremendous cost, and the Grove bore the brunt of that battle.

That day still haunts me—the flames licking the sky, the echoes of screams, the acrid smoke that filled the air, suffocating me, burning my eyes and stealing my breath. It was the last day I saw my parents. So now, as I glimpse smoke rising from the mountains, my stomach tightens with dread.

"What is that?" I murmur, my voice barely audible against the wind. "It is not coming from the Grove."

Zyphoro's gaze follows mine, her expression unbothered, a stark contrast to the chill that runs through me. "No. It is just beyond the mountains. An army camp."

"The Legion of Saints," I say, more to myself than to her.

A wicked grin curls her lips. "A pleasure I missed out on from my cage. Perhaps if I had been free, we would have won that war."

I frown, my thoughts turning. "You *did* win that war."

She laughs, the sound grating against the reality that weighs on me. "Did we? Half the great houses destroyed, and barely enough Mordorin left to hold another uprising at bay. Sounds more like a delay than a victory. Who leads this pitiful army?"

"They call him the Golden Son," I say. "As a boy, he was scarred by fire when his village was razed to the ground. Now he wears a mask of gold."

Zyphoro chuckles, her grin widening. "How dramatic. I can't wait to rip off that pretty mask and gouge his eyes out."

The viciousness of her words sends a shiver through me, but I welcome her fury. We will need that fire if we are to defeat the Legion. After witnessing Zyphoro's prowess in Baev'kalath, I know she will be a formidable weapon.

As we soar above the Grove, the canopy below is thick, with ancient branches entwined and cloaked in dense leaves, allowing only thin slivers of sunlight to break through. We touch down at the mouth of the forest flanked by two massive boulders dressed with moss, and are immediately confronted by half of the Blades dispatched from Baev'kalath.

They came as part of the bargain, sworn to their oaths and blissfully ignorant of the chaos that has unfurled across the Untold Sea. The fragile alliances fracturing the Fae. The bitter negotiations. The blood that has already been spilled. They do not know that I, a princess bound by a promise, have just clawed my way from the dark clutches of their queen—saved not by armies, but by a maid, a scarred warrior, and a void-wielding princess long forgotten.

As soon as they see Arax among us, their rigid stance softens, but only slightly. The captain of the Blades steps forward, his face like stone. "Reaper Arax," he says, voice taut with formality. "Do you bring word from Baev'kalath?"

I swallow, a heavy dread settling deep in my bones. This isn't the return to the Grove I imagined—not with the weight of the secrets I now carry.

"Your orders remain unchanged," Arax replies, his voice steady. "You will defend the Grove from any threat, even if that threat comes from our own."

The Blades exchange wary glances, suspicion clouding their eyes.

"Under whose authority?" the Blade asks, his jaw clenched tight.

"Mine," Arax says, his tone brooking no argument.

But the Blade doesn't back down. "A Reaper's word isn't enough to make us fight our kin. Where is Commander Rook?"

Arax's resolve never wavers, though the truth he holds back teeters on the edge of spilling. His silence is a shield, protecting us from losing the allegiance of these elite warriors.

"He is indisposed. I assume command in his absence."

The Blade's loyalty to their prince is absolute, and his brow furrows in distrust. "These orders are unacceptable. We will return to Baev'kalath for clarification."

"No," a voice cuts through the tension, sharp and smooth. Zyphoro steps forward, her expression lazy, as if the conversation bores her. "If you require the word of Mordorin nobility, then you may take mine."

The Blade's eyes narrow. "We don't know you."

A slow, dangerous smile spreads across her lips. "Then your existence until now has been tragically meaningless." She lifts her arms, her fingers curling like talons. "Allow me to enlighten you."

Without warning, tendrils of smoke burst from her hands, dark and sinewy, snaking through the air before latching onto each Blade's throat. They choke and gasp, but Zyphoro's gaze remains as cold and detached as ever, her eyes flashing like a storm brewing on the horizon. Despite the violence, there's a cruel playfulness in the way she toys with them, her lips twitching with amusement.

"I am Princess Zyphoro Phaedren," she purrs, tightening her grip on their windpipes. "And you will serve me—or I will snap each of your necks until the sound becomes tiresome." Her smile widens, a wicked gleam in her eyes. "And it *never* becomes tiresome."

The Blades struggle, their faces growing pale as Zyphoro casually dangles their lives in the balance. She holds them there, savoring their helplessness like a predator toying with its prey.

One of the Blades struggles to speak, his hands clawing desperately at the tendrils coiled around his throat. His face turns crimson, veins bulging at his temples as he gasps for breath.

"What's that?" Zyphoro tilts her head, her expression mocking, leaning in as if she might actually care to hear his reply. She flicks her wrist, and the smoke retracts, the tendril dissolving into the air. The Blade crumples to the ground, gulping in sharp breaths, his body trembling from the shock.

Zyphoro hovers over him, her eerie calmness more unsettling than her violence. "Who do you serve, Blade?" Her voice is soft, almost purr.

Through grit teeth, the Blade coughs, his voice a raw rasp. "You, Princess Zyphoro."

Her smile is slow, deliberate, as if she hadn't just dangled the lives of his comrades in front of him like puppets on strings. She releases the tendrils with a wave of her hand, and the rest of the Blades collapse to the ground, wheezing and choking, their strength sapped.

"Excellent." She steps back with casual grace, not a hint of remorse on her face. "Now, show us to your lovely home, Amara."

I nod, stepping around the fallen warriors who are still recovering, and with every step into the forest, a familiar warmth spreads through me. The moment my feet touch the soil, it's as if the world shifts, as if I've passed from darkness into light. The earth beneath me thrums with life, and I am filled with a bliss that transcends words, that no tongue, either human nor Fae could ever fully describe. It's more than just contentment; it's a deep, undeniable sense of steadiness, of belonging.

It is home.

The scent of the trees, the feel of the soil, the distant hum of the forest's heartbeat—it embraces me, wraps around me like an old friend. Here, the weight of Baev'kalath and all its horrors slip away. For the first time in what feels like forever, I feel safe. Safe and grounded. And if there is one thing in this world I can trust, it is the Grove.

"I will stay here and gather a report from these Blades," Arax mutters, glancing down at them with a trace of disdain. Despite knowing the power that subdued them, he seems almost disappointed by how easily they had fallen, as if they had forgotten the elite warriors they were.

I nod then turn to Zyphoro and Solena, who fall in beside me. The Grove is unlike anywhere else—alive in a way that must be felt, not explained. The ancient trees tower above, making us seem no bigger than ants, their thick trunks humming with age-old secrets. Vines twist upward, a chaotic tapestry of green and gold. Rivers thread through the landscape, their waters glinting under the dappled sunlight that filters through the branches above, the sound of their gentle flow soothing, as if the very air hums with peace.

The woodland creatures—rabbits, foxes, even the elusive hart—move freely, their paws and hooves barely making a sound as they dart between the trees. They move as though they are unbothered by the presence of Fae or human, as if they know they are the true masters of this place. Overhead, birds flit through the canopy, their songs spilling into the air, weaving a harmony that floods my senses like the richest wine.

The entire forest is thick with life, vibrating with magic, a pulse that comes from the earth itself. Every step I take, I feel it beneath my feet—a heartbeat, steady and strong, as if the Grove itself recognizes me.

Zyphoro remains silent at my side, her eyes sweeping across the lush landscape with quiet curiosity, while Solena seems more at ease, her steps lighter as we continue through the overgrowth. But my heart beats a little faster with every step, a tension tightening in my chest. Despite the beauty and serenity of the Grove, there is no ignoring the darkness that still follows us, a shadow that clings to the edges of this peaceful place, waiting for the right moment to strike.

Then suddenly, I hear them—the voices I've longed for, the ones I've missed more than anything in this world. Their absence has been a hollow ache, a bottomless pit that has widened with every passing day since the last time I heard them.

Amara. Jewel. You have returned.

I freeze, my breath catching in my throat, my heart swelling until it feels like it might burst. Tears well at the corners of my eyes, unstoppable. I press my hand against a tree, the rough bark warm and alive beneath my palm, and I feel them—the Souls of the Forest—coursing through the earth, through the air, through me. Every nerve in my body sparks to life, ignited by their presence.

Yes, I answer. *You cannot know how much I have missed you.*

Amara. You feel so sad.

That simple statement undoes me. The dam breaks, and the tears spill over. I crumble against the tree, my knees giving way as the weight of it all, the burden I've carried, comes crashing down. For the first time in what feels like an eternity, I let myself feel the fear, the despair, the brokenness that I have hidden away.

I have been so terrified—terrified to leave the Grove, terrified of what awaited me across the Untold Sea, terrified of Baev'kalath and the husband who waited for me there. But I buried that fear, locked it away beneath the façade of duty, telling myself that I had to be strong, that I had no other choice.

Admitting my fear would have meant admitting that I wasn't as strong as I pretended to be. And that was the only thing that got me through any of it—the belief that I was capable of facing everything alone. But now, here, in my forest, within the embrace of the Souls, I feel stripped bare. Exposed.

When I remember that Solena and Zyphoro stand behind me, I fight to compose myself, wiping my cheeks with my sleeve and sniffling back the last of my tears. They look at each other. Anywhere but at me.

"We're almost there," I say, forcing my voice to steady despite the ragged breaks. I pull my hand away from the tree and continue forward, guiding them through the forest.

As we venture deeper, the air around us shifts, becoming thick with the scent of damp earth and lush foliage. Stone archways, etched with runes and draped in vibrant moss, emerge from the overgrowth, carving a winding path through the verdant wilderness. Then the sound of water reaches my ears—a gentle roar that grows louder as we approach. A waterfall tumbles gracefully over the edge of a moss-covered bank, cascading into a crystal-clear stream below. The water sparkles in the sunlight, a lively ribbon weaving through the underbrush, guiding us toward the heart of the forest.

We follow the stream to the vine wall, a massive curtain of living, writhing vines that serve as the Grove's strongest and final defense. Wings snap the air, and I look up to see the remaining Blades walking the wall.

"Open," I call. "I am Amara Tyne. Jewel of the Tenders. I have returned."

I hear my name whispered on the breeze, spreading from one mouth to the next until the entire forest seems to herald my return. The gates of the vine wall part, the thick greenery unfurling to reveal the Grove. We step through, and immediately, I feel I am home.

Wooden steps wind around thick trunks to reach the dwellings nestled in their branches high above, where soft lamp light casts a warm amber glow through the windows. Rope bridges of vines crisscross between the treetops, swaying gently with the breeze while below, on the forest floor, smaller cottages sit cradled within between giant roots, their walls covered in moss, blending so perfectly into the landscape that you might miss them at first glance.

A deer passes by, moving lazily between the homes, and a pair of rabbits scurry underfoot. No one pays them any mind—this is their home too. The people of the Grove move in harmony with the animals, weaving between the creatures as naturally as they do each other. The scent of fresh earth and wild herbs fills my lungs as I take it all in. The sounds of daily life hum in the background: children laughing, tools working against wood, quiet conversations flowing as easily as the streams that run alongside the homes.

I pass a group of villagers sitting beneath an ancient oak, sewing and chatting softly, their clothes simple, woven from linen and dyed with the colors of the forest. One of the women looks up as I pass, her face lighting with recognition. "Amara," she says, her voice filled with warmth, and the others soon follow suit, murmuring my name like it's a song they've missed.

We approach the great tree where the council reside. The vines that cover the doorway slowly untangle, parting with a whispering rustle as Keeper Tovar steps forward. He is as much a part of the forest as the ancient trees that shelter the Grove, his tall, lean frame draped in a cloak woven from moss and ivy. A braid of deep brown threaded with silver sits over his shoulder, and his tawny skin bears the lines of age and wisdom, each wrinkle telling stories only the forest itself might remember.

In his hand, he holds a staff of gnarled wood, twisted and knotted like the roots of the oldest trees. The wood is engraved with faintly glowing runes—symbols of protection and wisdom—that pulse gently with an emerald light. His oak-brown eyes widen in surprise as they settle on me.

"Amara," Tovar breathes, and I notice his throat bob.

"Keeper Tovar," I murmur, bowing my head slightly.

His eyes search mine, as if to confirm that I am truly here, his hand rising to touch the vines around the doorway for stability. "You've... returned," he says. "I feared... I feared we might never see you again." His arms unfurl. "Come to me, child."

I waste no time running up the stairs and throwing my arms around his waist, burying the side of my face in his chest. He wraps one arm around my shoulder, while his hand gently strokes my hair, his head resting gently above mine.

This man is not just our Keeper, he is our guardian, our guide, and the closest thing I had to a parent after mine perished in the Betrayers' Battle. In fact, the entire Tenders Council became my family, but it was always Tovar I idolized the most.

Wise. Kind. Fair. Loyal. *All the things I wanted to be.*

Slowly we part and Tovar's expression softens with relief, but it doesn't take long before his gaze shifts toward the strangers at my back. His brow furrows slightly as he takes them in, his voice dropping lower.

"You carry more with you than when you left."

"They are friends," I say.

"Friends?" Tovar repeats, his tone laced with disbelief, startling me. He quickly softens, his usual composure returning. "Friends are always welcome, as long as they assure us no harm will come to the Grove or its people."

Zyphoro shrugs, a lazy smirk playing on her lips. "Don't mind me. I'm just along for the ride."

Solena rolls her eyes, clearly annoyed by Zyphoro's flippant attitude. Every word from her seems to grate on Solena's nerves.

"This is Solena," I begin, gesturing to her. "And this is Princess Zyphoro Phaedren."

Tovar's eyes widen in surprise. "Phaedren... you are the prince's...?"

"Sister," Zyphoro cuts in smoothly. "And Zyphoro is fine."

"I did not know he had a sister," Tovar says, his voice betraying a flicker of unease.

Zyphoro sighs dramatically. "You're not alone. But don't worry. I'll fix that."

Tovar forces a tight, polite smile, but his weariness is clear.

The Grove's Keeper, always composed, is unsettled by Zyphoro's presence.

"Amara, your friends are welcome to enjoy the hospitality of the Grove," he says. "Our home is your home. Make yourselves comfortable." He steps aside, motioning toward the entrance of the hall, his staff tipping slightly. The runes etched into the wood catch the light, glowing faintly. "Come, Amara. There is much we need to discuss."

I glance back at Solena and Zyphoro. "I won't be long. You're safe here."

Both of them look around, clearly skeptical. The serene surroundings, the towering trees, sunlight shimmering through the leaves, and rabbits bounding freely through the village—all of it seems to baffle them. I'm not sure whether they're more perplexed by the idyllic scenery or the warm smiles from everyone who passes by.

Leaving them behind, I follow Tovar through the vine curtain and up the wooden stairs that spiral around the great tree at the heart of the village. His familiar scent, earthy and comforting, and the reassuring hand he places on my shoulder as we ascend, threatens to bring tears to my eyes again.

"You look different," he says softly, studying my face with concern, as if trying to read the changes etched into my features.

"I feel different," I admit, my voice quiet, burdened with the weight of everything I've endured.

Tovar nods knowingly, his sharp eyes never leaving mine. "The price we paid was great. But if the Fae sent you back, what does this mean for the Grove?"

"I wasn't sent back," I correct him, a flicker of nervousness in my voice. "I left. Ran away, actually."

Tovar's brow furrows deeply. "What? And those Fae helped you?"

I nod. "And one other, Arax. He's with the Blades guarding the entrance."

Tovar's calm demeanor slips. His movements grow swift as he ushers me through the arch and into the hall, another vine curtain closing behind us with a soft rustle.

The hall is carved into the great tree, its walls intertwined with thick, twisting roots and blanketed in soft moss. A large, round window on the far wall offers a breathtaking view of the Grove. Tovar's staff taps lightly on the floor as he leads me deeper inside, his expression tight with the questions that now hang heavily in the air.

Gathered around a recessed table are eight men and women, all draped in cloaks similar to Tovar's, though less intricate. When they see me, they rise in unison, my name whispered like a prayer on their lips. Keeper Erania rushes to me, taking me into her arms, her hand smoothing over my hair as if she needs to confirm that I am real.

"Jewel," she gasps, holding me so tightly I can hardly breathe. "You've come back to us."

"She ran away," Tovar cuts in, his voice sharp and disapproving. His demeanor, which was once warm and reassuring, has grown colder, harder and it startles me.

Erania stiffens, glancing at him with a raised brow. "If she did, it must have been for good reason."

"It was," I say quickly, desperate to defend myself. "Keeper, the things they had planned for me... You wouldn't believe me if I told you. I can barely believe it myself."

Tovar shakes his head, his expression distant, as though my words aren't even reaching him. "I must speak with King Kaelus. We must put things right."

"Tovar," Erania snaps, pulling me closer as if to shield me from his harshness. "Our Jewel has returned. We should be welcoming her, not scolding her."

"It's not that I'm unhappy to see you, precious child," Tovar says, brushing his hand lightly over mine, though now his touch feels colder, more distant than ever before. "But you know the bargain to protect the Grove rests on you being in Baev'kalath, with your husband, the prince. No matter what drove you to leave, there will be repercussions—repercussions we are not prepared for. Even the twenty Blades at our gates, sent to protect us, could destroy the Grove if they so wished. Let alone the army that camps just beyond the hills."

I swallow hard. "I saw them."

"Then you understand. The Legion of Saints waits. If they learn you've returned, it could give them the reason they need to attack. You are the wife of their enemy. You being here without the prince puts us all in danger," he says, and the weight of his words makes my heart sink. He pauses, realizing the gravity of what he's just said, and his face softens, his hand pinching the bridge of his nose. "I don't mean to sound so callous."

"Then you are failing, miserably," Erania snaps. "Come, Amara. There are those here who have prayed to the Souls every day for your return, who will celebrate that you are finally home."

Erania guides me toward the council, her arm still wrapped around me protectively. She is right—their faces are filled with warmth and relief, not a hint of disappointment. They cup my face, press gentle kisses to my brow, murmuring words of love and welcome. But in the corner of my eye, I see Tovar, the man I would pretend was my father as a child, standing apart. His jaw clenched, his mind clearly spiraling with thoughts he hasn't voiced. His silence, his distance, weighs on me, and suddenly, this homecoming feels like a wish gone wrong, far from the reunion I had hoped for.

CHAPTER 31

Night descends upon the Grove, blanketing the forest in a peaceful stillness.

I spent the day among my people, sharing stories of my journey across the Untold Sea. All of it lies, of course. I could never tell them the truth—what had been done to me or what they planned to do. The things I saw that haunt me every time I close my eyes.

The prince who betrayed me.

But the tales I spun filled their eyes with wonder and amazement, stories of faraway lands they would never know. I envy them for that ignorance and the illusion of safety it provides.

Zyphoro, unperturbed by any of it, fell asleep as soon as she was shown to her room in a small cottage amongst the branches, drifting off without the slightest resistance. Meanwhile, Solena and I sit around a small fire on the forest floor, the crackling flames casting a warm glow over her face. Ashen, now confident in his new surroundings, weaves in and out between my legs. His soft purrs rising with the night's quiet hum before he finally collapses into sleep, exhausted after becoming the main attraction amongst the children of the forest.

"So this is the Grove," Solena murmurs, her eyes taking in the forest surrounding. "It's very... green."

"Not to your liking?" I ask, a hint of a smirk on my lips, though my heart feels heavy.

"No. I like it," she admits, her usual sternness softening just enough. "I like it so much, I'm worried what will happen when the king and prince discover we're gone."

I bow my head, feeling the weight of her words settle over me. I reach down, running my knuckle along Ashen's fur, grounding myself in the simple comfort of his presence. "You'd get along with Keeper Tovar," I say quietly. "He fears I've doomed us all too."

"You did what you had to," Solena says, her tone resolute. "We all did. And not for a second do I regret leaving Baev'kalath with you. But we can't hide here forever. They *will* come."

"I know," I whisper, my voice trailing off as I meet her gaze. "And we must be ready when they do."

"You cannot defeat the Mordorin," she says softly, a warning laced in her voice.

"No," I reply, holding her gaze steady. Solena flinches slightly at the intensity of my stare. "I cannot defeat the Legion either. But I can fight them. With everything I am, everything I have left, I will fight them until my last breath."

I stand, brushing off the dirt from my clothes. Ashen stirs from his slumber, stretching lazily before pattering after me as I move away from the fire.

"Where are you going?" Solena calls.

"To see my sisters," I say over my shoulder, glimpsing her confusion before I disappear into the vines, leaving the warmth of the fire and the quiet of the night behind me.

Beyond the heart of the forest lies a clearing that, at first glance, seems perfectly ordinary. Tall trees circle the space, their shadows stretching over soft grass blanketed with delicate purple flowers. I sit cross-legged at its center, gazing at the stars peeking through the gaps in the canopy. The familiar moon, once a guiding light, now feels like an enemy. The wind rustles the grass, brushing against me as Ashen curls up by my side, his smoky form becoming a constant comfort.

The rune around my neck pulses softly, casting brief flashes of green into the darkness. With each heartbeat, it grows brighter until, with a sudden surge, a blinding light sweeps through the clearing, and I find myself somewhere else—though I haven't moved an inch.

Here, the woods are darker, denser. The trees stand like ancient sentinels, their gnarled, twisted branches draped with thick moss, casting eerie shadows. Their bark pulses with green threads, glowing faintly as if veins of light run through their core. The air hums with energy, thick and heavy, as though the very magic of the forest has come alive. The power here is more than just a sound or sight—it thrums beneath my skin, a force I cannot ignore.

And there, before me, stands the shrine. A massive tree whose ancient branches have woven themselves into a perfect circle. Suspended within the circle is a shimmering web, delicate yet strong, its strands aglow with fluorescent green light while runes etched across the web pulse with a mysterious energy, their power undeniable.

Huddled around the base of the shrine are my sisters—Lira, Mirael, and Saren—standing hand in hand. They turn toward me, sensing my presence even before I make a sound.

"Amara," Lira greets me with a warm smile, her rosy cheeks a sight I had almost forgotten.

Their arms reach for me, and I stumble to my feet, falling into their embrace as if I've leapt off a cliff. We stand together in silence, holding each other close for what feels like an eternity. No words pass between us because none are needed. The bond we share speaks louder than any language could.

"The Souls told us you were here," Mirael says softly when we finally part, her voice carrying the gentle hum of the forest.

"We thought you'd visit us sooner," Saren adds, a hint of playfulness in her tone.

"Keeper Tovar and the council kept me longer than expected," I explain, my voice tight with the weight of it all. "He is displeased with me. I fled Baev'kalath, and now he fears the Mordorin will bring their wrath upon the Grove."

They exchange knowing glances, concern etching their faces, but they remain silent. Instead, they take my hands and lead me to the shrine. We sit in our familiar circle, and as the rune tree pulses brighter, I close my eyes and share everything with them—Baev'kalath, the dark, looming presence of Kaelus and Lanneth, Gygarth, the demon of the void, and the relentless threats to my life since I entered that cursed place. Despite my attempts to hide it, they see Daedalus and I entwined under the moonlight in Pariseth, our bodies bare and tangled in passion.

When the vision fades, we face each other, but we are no longer alone. The Souls of the Forest have joined us, their voices whispering constantly in my mind, a symphony of unseen presences.

"They called me awakened," I say, my voice trembling. "I can see through their glamors."

Then you are a threat, the Souls whisper, their voices threading through my thoughts like vines. *Anything that wields power outside their control is always a threat.*

"I didn't know," I whisper.

You wouldn't. The gift would not reveal itself until needed. Glamor magic does not exist within the Grove, but you have not yet touched the deeper mysteries of the Fae.

I glance down at my hand, where the wound is healed, not even a scar remaining. "I healed myself," I murmur, almost ashamed. "I didn't mean to, but... how could I have possibly done it? I thought the gift was to heal others. Not myself."

There is a long pause before the Souls answer.

You take on another's pain when you heal them. But to heal yourself, that pain must be transferred. When you faced the demon of the void, the pain you carried turned into raw energy. You wielded that energy against him—and in the process, healed yourself.

I swallow, dread tightening in my chest. "So... to heal myself, I have to give my pain to someone else?"

Yes, they reply, their tone steady and unwavering.

"How bad is it?" I ask.

You have been trained to absorb the pain through meditation and deep sleep. They have not. It would be excruciating for them. Perhaps even deadly.

The thought is as fascinating as it is horrifying, that I could be something monstrous—leeching life from others to preserve my own. Yet, in that moment, facing Gygarth, I was grateful. Without that power, I would not have survived. My fingers curl around the rune at my neck, feeling its pulse beneath my skin, and I notice my sisters do the same.

My lungs tighten as if my chest is caving in as I look at them—Lira, Mirael, and Saren—knowing that I am not telling them everything. My eyes glance at my belly. Is Zyphoro right? Do I carry the heir of House Mordorin? But I cannot tell them of the possibility. I'm ashamed of giving myself to the prince completely only to be deceived, and scared of how my sisters and the Souls will react.

I must carry this secret with me longer.

There is only one thing I am certain of, and I feel the truth settle in my bones. I may keep my secret for now, but I cannot run from what is coming.

"I must fight them now," I say, my voice steady despite the whirlwind inside me. "All of them. The Mordorin. The Legion. I failed the Grove once by leaving, but I won't fail it again."

The words hang in the air, more final than anything I've said before. My heart pounds, a steady reminder of the price I've already paid, the sacrifices I've made—and those that are yet to come. But my resolve is clear. I cannot stand idle, not when I carry both the power to heal and the potential to destroy.

I am both a shield and a weapon.

Lira steps closer, her brows knitting together in concern. "Amara, you didn't fail the Grove. You did what you had to do to survive."

I shake my head, the guilt too heavy to dismiss so easily. "Surviving isn't enough, not anymore. I need to protect this place—our home."

Mirael touches my arm, her grip gentle but firm. "The Grove has always protected us, sheltered us. But if we're truly under threat from both the Mordorin and the Legion... this fight won't be like any we've faced before."

I meet her gaze. "Which is why I can't do it alone."

Saren's eyes, always the quietest but most perceptive, search mine. "You won't be alone," she says. "We stand with you, Amara. We always have. But this path you're choosing... it's dangerous. What you can do with that power—it changes things."

There's a flicker of fear in her eyes, the same fear that I feel deep within myself. The fear that I may fight the enemy but become something unrecognizable in the process.

Something monstrous.

I swallow hard, unsure if it's my power that scares me more—or the part of me that's willing to use it.

"We can't hide from what's coming," I reply, though my voice cracks. "I'll use whatever I have to. We'll use whatever we must. The Grove can't fall, and neither will we."

There's a silence that stretches between us, and I can feel the shift, the acceptance settling in. My sisters don't challenge me, though their eyes reflect the magnitude of my decision.

Lira speaks first, her voice soft but resolute. "Then we will fight alongside you, Amara."

Mirael nods, her expression solemn. "Together."

Saren hesitates for a moment, then steps forward, her hands wrapping around mine. "No matter what this power does to you, we won't leave your side."

I blink back the tears that threaten to spill. They don't understand the full extent of what they're promising, but they don't have to. I have enough doubt for all of us.

As we stand there, the pulse of the rune grows stronger, thrumming with a strange, dangerous energy that now feels both familiar and foreign to me. It courses through my veins, a reminder that I have power. That I am more than just a scared girl trying to survive.

I'm ready to become something more. To fight for them—for the Grove—and to face whatever comes.

For better or for worse, I know now that this is who I am.

And I'm ready.

I close my eyes and when I open them again, I'm back in the peaceful clearing. The familiar scent of earth and flowers greets me, but a startled rabbit bolts through the underbrush, spooked by my sudden appearance. Ashen meows, padding toward me, his smoky form brushing against my leg, but Arax is the one who stands frozen, his mouth agape as if he's seen a ghost.

"Am I mad, or did you just appear from nowhere?" he asks, his voice low, disbelief lacing each word.

"You're possibly mad," I say, groaning as I drag myself to my feet, muscles aching from the journey. "But yes, I did appear from nowhere."

Arax shakes his head. "This place is strange."

"I could say the same for your home," I reply, walking toward him. He sits back down on the large rock he'd been resting on, looking worn from not only the last few days but a lifetime of service.

"Home," he mutters, a small chuckle escaping him, though it's tinged with exhaustion. "In all my years, I don't think I've ever called it that. But I have served regardless, fiercely and loyally. I've served my king. I've served my prince."

"And your queen?" I ask, finding a spot beside him. I hold his gaze, forcing him to meet my eyes. "Arax, you've seen more than most. Did you know what happened to Queen Veloria?"

He exhales slowly, his broad shoulders dropping as if under the weight of centuries. "I was deceived, as we all were. We believed what we were told—that the good queen died giving birth to Prince Daedalus. The truth about Princess Zyphoro... was hidden from me. It was as if she disappeared, not just from sight but from memory."

"Glamored by Lanneth," I whisper, a chill creeping up my spine. "How can such a thing even be possible? What kind of power would that take?"

"Lanneth is more powerful than any of us ever realized," he says, his voice heavy with the admission.

"But that power is tethered to Daedalus," I murmur, and just the sound of his name tightens something inside me, something that threatens to break.

"I know we Mordorin walk with the void," Arax says softly. "But I never imagined the lengths Lanneth would go to, to keep us strong. And I swear to you, Amara, I didn't know what they had planned for you. I would never have let you step foot on that ship if I did. I am Mordorin, but I am not a monster that murders innocent girls."

"I've learned there's a monster in all of us," I say, as the evening wind tangles in my hair. "But sometimes, monsters can be used for good. The best way to fight one is with another."

From within his sleeve, I notice a flash of red as Arax twists that ribbon around his finger, a movement so small, but it draws my attention like a flame in the dark. I remember the ribbon from the ship. He held it tight then too, when he was moments away from death.

"Who was she?" I ask at last, the question that's lingered on my mind since then. "A wife?"

Arax shakes his head, the hint of a sad smile playing on his lips. "A daughter. A warrior. A Blade. She fought by my side in that valley," he says, gesturing to the stretch of land we flew over earlier, beyond the borders of the Grove.

"But I thought..."

"That Reapers aren't allowed families?" he finishes for me, and I nod. "She wasn't of my blood, but she was just as precious. I found her in Valorne, left to rot in a gutter—battered, bruised, defiled by Fae who thought they could take whatever they wanted. She was from a low caste, treated as less than dirt."

"Like humans," I say quietly, the vileness of the words settling between us.

"Yes," he agrees with reluctance. "Like humans. I took pity on her. Fed her and nursed her back to health. She asked me to teach her how to fight so she'd never feel helpless again, and I did. Then she never left. It's surprising how quickly you can get attached to someone over a century." His voice softens, the hint of a smile tugging at his lips. "When I was recalled to Baev'kalath, I took her with me, and she trained as a Blade."

"You can do that?" I ask, raising an eyebrow. "Become a Blade even if you're from a lower caste?"

"Yes," Arax replies. "The only skill needed to be a Blade is to kill better than you die, and she mastered warfare like she was born to it."

"She sounds like a good student," I say, trying to imagine the warrior she must've been.

"She was more than that," Arax says quickly, his voice dropping to a hushed reverence. "She was brave and vicious, but also kind and curious, and she made me laugh. No one makes me laugh."

"I've managed to pull a few out of you," I tease. "When you're not too busy practicing the world's greatest scowl."

He glances at me, a smile softening his worn face. "Yes. You have, haven't you?"

The moment feels too personal, too raw, and I glance down at my feet, chuckling lightly to diffuse the intensity. "Where is she now? I'm almost offended I haven't met this amazing warrior."

Arax's smile fades, his fingers twisting the red ribbon tighter around his hand. "She died on the battlefield, on the last day of the Betrayers' Battle," he says, his voice hollow. "I couldn't bring her body back. We won, but we were few. No ships, no way back across the Untold Sea except by flight. Half of those who survived the battle fell from the sky—wounded, exhausted, or both—drowning before they could reach Baev'kalath." His chin drops, and his voice grows quieter. "I should've carried her. I should've tried."

I can hear the tremor in his voice as he continues, the pain of his loss as sharp now as it must have been on that day. "I heard they burned all the bodies. I just pray it was at night, so the Pale Mother could lift her into her arms."

Tears prick at the corners of my eyes, and I feel a lump rise in my throat.

Arax's fingers twist the ribbon again, and only now do I see the stains.

Not dirt, not time—blood. *Her blood.*

"It's why I hated you," Arax says, his voice raw. "Why I hated your kind. You killed her. She was good, and brave, and beautiful, and your kind killed her." His jaw tightens, the words heavy with old anger. "But I've realized it wasn't humans, not really. It was this world that took her from me. This cursed world, where we're born, we fight, we die—over and over. And somewhere in between, if we are lucky, we are gifted small glimpses of happiness."

He breathes deeply, his eyes unfocused as he speaks, as if lost in those fleeting moments. "Those are what I hold on to. Not the hatred, but the love I had for her. For Estra." His eyes meet mine, softer now. "That's why I hold no ill will toward you, Amara Tyne. For healing me on that ship. That's not where I wanted to meet my end. I'll die on the battlefield, or not at all. In her honor."

His last words hang in the air, a vow as unbreakable as the love he still carries for Estra. And as I sit beside him, I realize that even in all this darkness, Arax's heart clings to love and loyalty, just as mine clings to the pieces of a life shattered by betrayal. Despite everything, neither of us has let the cruelty of this world strip away what we hold dear. We may be scarred, but we are not broken.

Not yet.

CHAPTER 32

The next morning, the village awakens to the rhythmic thud of Blades marching through the village, their boots pressing into the soft soil, sending children scattering like startled birds into the safety of the trees. Once, I might have been frozen with fear, but after all I've seen, their presence no longer holds the same sway over me.

"What is the meaning of this?" Keeper Tovar's voice booms as he descends from the council hall, his robes trailing behind him like the forest itself made flesh. His gaze sharpens on the gathering of Blades, irritation flickering across his features.

Arax steps forward, his posture one of quiet command as he faces the warriors. "Why are you here? What is happening?"

The Blade captain steps forward, his face tense. "We scouted the valley before dawn," he begins, each word measured, heavy. "There was no smoke from the Legion's camp. The first time in weeks." He hesitates before continuing. "We investigated. The camp was empty. They're on the march, Reaper Arax. They'll be here within days."

Tovar's face pales, his disbelief tangible. "No," he whispers, the word almost lost in the morning air. "Not now. Not when they're at full strength..." He lifts his head, his panic palpable. "They'll tear through our defenses like we're nothing, burn us to the ground for not siding with them." His eyes lock onto mine, wild with accusation. "We should have bent the knee. We made a bargain with the wrong enemy."

The words lash through me like a whip, but before I can speak, Tovar turns, his cloak swirling as he rushes back up the stairs, his retreat betraying the fear curling inside him.

I follow, my heart pounding as Solena and Arax fall into step beside me. Zyphoro trails behind, a silent specter in her own right. When we pass through the vine curtain into the hall, Tovar spins to confront us, his face twisted in outrage.

"How dare you bring their kind into this sacred place?" His voice cracks like thunder, and the tension in the room swells, suffocating.

Erania rises from her place at the table, her brow furrowed. "Tovar, what's happening? Explain yourself."

"We are doomed," Tovar snaps, pacing like a caged animal. "The Legion of Saints marches toward us as we speak, and now, because of Amara's selfish choices, we stand defenseless. The Mordorin will not protect us."

I stiffen, the accusation hitting harder than any physical blow. "You're fortunate to even have the Blades," I bite back, my voice steady, though inside I feel myself unraveling. "The Mordorin forces are thin, stretched to their limit. Before I left, my husband—" my voice falters on the word "—Prince Daedalus, was forced into negotiations to rally enough warriors to stand against even half the Legion."

Tovar's eyes narrow, and I can see the disappointment etched deep in his expression. "I have raised you as my own, Amara. You were taught to understand duty. You knew what it meant to be the Jewel of the Tenders. Yours was a life of *sacrifice*, and yet when we need you most, *you betray us.*"

The air feels too thick, like his words might suffocate me.

"*Sacrifice?*" I repeat, my voice laced with a bitterness I can no longer hide. "*Betrayal?* You dare speak of these things as if you know their true meaning?" My hands clench at my sides, nails digging into my palms. "I gave everything, Tovar. Everything. And still it wasn't enough for you. What more could you have wanted from me?" My voice cracks as the pain slips through. "My life?"

His face darkens. "That was the bargain, Amara," he thunders, slamming his staff into the floor.

The gnarled wood, etched with ancient runes, rings out with a sharp crack that reverberates through the hall. But it's the crack inside me that shatters the most. A hollow, unbearable pain that seizes my chest, twisting and pulling until I can barely breathe.

For a moment, I can't speak, can't think.

I feel something break, something deep and vital.

"You... *you knew?*" My voice trembles, barely a whisper.

Tovar's gaze falters, and the room falls into a heavy silence, all eyes turning toward him, waiting for an answer he can no longer hide.

Tovar's words hang in the air, empty and hollow. "I knew only what I was told," he says, his eyes flickering, unable to meet mine. "That you may not return, but that your sacrifice would guarantee our protection."

My sacrifice.

The bitter laugh escapes before I can stop it, sharp and biting.

"Sacrifice?" I repeat, the word tasting like ash on my tongue. "You throw that word around as if it means nothing. But I know its meaning, Keeper." My hand moves to my chest, clutching the weight of everything I've lost—my freedom, my trust, my innocence. "Far better than you ever will."

"Tovar," Erania says, her voice low, her disappointment heavy. "This is unacceptable. If you willingly sent Amara to her death, there must be consequences."

"I will show him the consequences," Arax says, calm as ever, yet the sound of his sword sliding free from its sheath cuts through the tension like steel on bone.

Tovar staggers back, his face paling, his back pressed against the wall as we close in. "I did what I had to," he pleads, his voice cracking. "As Keeper, it is my duty to protect the Tenders. To protect the Souls. To protect the Grove. Why do *none* of you understand? I was willing to give them our Jewel, our Amara, who I love as my own daughter."

"You are not worthy to call her that," Arax growls, his sword raised, ready to deliver justice.

The Keeper flinches, cowering in the shadow of the blade.

And then, silently, I reach out and place my hand on Arax's arm. His eyes meet mine, and for a moment, I see the tide of rage he's holding back, barely restrained. Slowly, his arm lowers, and with reluctance, the sword slides back into its sheath.

"Look at what I've done for you, Amara," Tovar insists, his voice dripping with arrogance as he clings to his delusions. "I gave you power. You have Fae who serve you now, because I made you their queen. Use this power, and save us!"

His words sting. His betrayal stings deeper.

"I am not their queen," I say, my voice steady, though my heart is anything but. "They are not here because of you. They are here because they are my friends. They have fought for me in ways you never did, even when you claimed to be my father. You signed away my life as if it meant nothing."

Erania stands beside me, her eyes dark with fury. "It was you who was wronged, Jewel. You should decide Tovar's punishment."

"I am Keeper Tovar!" he yells, his entire body trembling with rage and fear. "You cannot strip me of my title."

"That title is the first thing you've lost," Erania says coldly, her words sharp and final. "Our Jewel will decide what's next."

From the corner of the room, Zyphoro smirks, leaning lazily against the wall as she inspects her nails. "Kill him," she says, her tone as casual as if she were discussing the weather. "It seems the quickest solution."

"I actually agree with her," Solena chimes in, her jaw tight, her voice laced with disgust.

It would be so easy. So simple to end him. After everything he's done, everything he's taken from me—the trust I once had in him as a father, the belief that he truly cared for me—ending him would feel like justice. He betrayed not just the Tenders as their guide, but me, as the girl who believed he loved her. The part of me that has been hurt and hardened screams for blood. *For revenge.*

But something stops me. The anger coursing through me, the sharp sting of betrayal, it burns deep—but this isn't who I am. I glance at Arax, at Solena, at Zyphoro, and I think about the choices they've made, the loyalties they've shown, the battles they've fought beside me. I think about Arax, holding on to love and hope, despite everything that has been taken from him. I am not the monster Tovar has become, or the one Lanneth has always been. I am better than that. I have to be.

"I could end this," I say, my voice quieter now. "I could kill you, and it would be justified. But I won't." My words hang heavy in the air, thick with emotion. "Not because you deserve mercy, Tovar, but because I won't let you turn me into someone who revels in that kind of power."

Tovar's eyes widen in disbelief as I step away, and the room seems to breathe again, the tension loosening.

"Your punishment," I say, my voice steady now, "is to live knowing that you betrayed the very people you swore to protect. And that you will never hold power here again. You are banished from the Grove."

Tovar stands frozen, his eyes wide with disbelief. His lips curl into a sneer, but there's something else behind it—fear. "You cannot banish me," he spits, though his voice trembles with uncertainty. "The Grove is all I've ever known."

"As it was for me," I snap, my voice cutting through the air like a blade. "Yet you sent me to the wolves without a second thought. Now leave your staff and your cloak, and get out before these Fae dish out their own justice. Because if they choose to, I won't be able to stop them."

Arax's hand hovers over his sword, a silent threat, while Zyphoro lets smoke swirl in her palm, the crackling tension ready to explode at any moment.

Tovar's face tightens in defiance, but his hands betray him as they slowly reach up to untie the robe from his neck. The once-proud symbol of his authority slips from his shoulders and crumples to the floor. The staff follows, its gnarled wood hitting the ground with a thud that reverberates through the hall, a final punctuation to his downfall.

His shoulders sag, and for the first time, he looks small—like a man unmoored from the only thing that gave his life meaning. He stands there, trembling, his gaze darting to the faces around him. He searches for mercy, but there is none.

With slow, reluctant steps, he turns and walks toward the door. His feet drag across the floor as if every step costs him something, and the weight of his banishment presses down on him, visible in the stoop of his back. As he reaches the threshold, he hesitates, his hand hovering over the vine-covered doorway as if he might say something, might plead for forgiveness. But there are no words left for him here.

He pushes through the vines, and the door closes behind him, sealing him away from the only home he's ever known.

The silence that follows is heavy, but I feel no triumph in it—only the bittersweet sting of loss, for what he once was and what we've both become.

"What now, Jewel?" Erania asks, her voice trembling with uncertainty, and the entire council turns toward me, waiting for my next word. Their eyes are on me—expectant, hopeful, desperate.

I walk over to the discarded symbols of power that once belonged to Tovar, the Keeper's robe and the elder staff, lying on the ground. My fingers close around them, and the weight is heavier than it should be. As I turn to Erania, I hand them both to her. She fumbles with them, her eyes wide with disbelief.

"Jewel. I cannot take on the role of Keeper. The council must—"

"You are now Keeper," I interrupt, my voice steady though my heart pounds in my chest. "We do not have time for meetings and politics when the Legion threatens everything we hold dear. We need a leader now."

Erania gulps, the responsibility sinking into her bones. "Then you should be that leader, Jewel." When I hesitate, she steps closer, pleading. "I will take on the mantle of Keeper, but you've seen the outside world, you know what we face. If the Grove has any chance of surviving this, it must be with you leading us."

"She's right," Solena says softly from beside me, her hand warm on my shoulder. "You are no mere human, Amara. You've faced the Father Below and lived."

I turn back to Enaria, finding an uncomfortable logic in her words. "I will see us through this," I finally say, forcing strength into my voice. "Whatever happens, we will not go quietly."

Erania nods, determination flickering in her eyes. "We will not."

But even as I say the words, a wave of uncertainty crashes over me. Suddenly, Arax is at my side, vying for my attention, while Solena whispers something else in my ear. The council descends upon me with more questions, all of them leaning in as if I hold every answer. Zyphoro arches a questioning brow, her gaze sharp, waiting for instructions. The room is closing in. The weight of their expectations presses down on my chest, and the edges of my vision blur.

"I'll be back," I mutter, my voice tight, trying not to let my panic show. I slip from the hall, trying not to run but desperately needing to escape.

I find a quiet place away from them all, away from the eyes that look to me for salvation, and the moment I'm alone, my knees give out beneath me. I crouch low, leaning forward with my hands braced on my thighs, gasping for air. I'm suffocating beneath it all—the pressure, the duty, the fear.

They expect me to lead. To save the Grove. To be strong, but I feel anything but strong.

I close my eyes, willing the tears to stay hidden, but my thoughts betray me. They drift to Daedalus. Even after everything that has happened, after the betrayal, after the lies, I still yearn for him. The memory of his touch lingers on my skin, his kiss, his hands in my hair. A part of me misses him so fiercely it feels like another betrayal—this time, of myself.

I swallow hard, forcing the thoughts away, but the ache remains. He wasn't there when I needed him most, and yet... I can't stop wanting him.

I shake my head, burying the thought, because even now, in the midst of all this, I can't afford to let myself feel this way. Not when there's so much at stake.

Some time later, I find them all gathered around a fire, sharing food beneath the stars. The warm glow of the flames casts long shadows over the group as they sit on the ground, passing bowls of stew made from the vegetables we've grown in the soil of the Grove. It's quiet, almost peaceful, though I catch Arax hungrily eying up any rabbit that bounces by. Solena smirks but says nothing, merely stirring the stew with an amused flick of her wrist.

"We'll need more than vegetables to survive a war," Zyphoro murmurs, though her tone is more teasing than serious as she leans back on her elbows, eyeing the fire with disinterest. Her appetite seems as distant as her thoughts.

"Tomorrow," Arax begins, his voice cutting through the calm, "we'll need to assess our situation. We've counted our numbers, and they're... not promising." His eyes meet mine, the flickering firelight dancing in them, but even the warmth of the flames doesn't soften his expression.

"How many?" Solena asks, her tone as sharp as ever, but there's a quiet determination in her posture.

"The twenty Blades will fight," Arax says, "but they're not enough. And while they serve you for now, I do not trust them without Commander Rook. They follow Zyphoro because they must, but their loyalty wavers. Without their true leader, they're unpredictable." He pauses, running a hand over the pommel of his sword. "If the Legion reaches us at full strength, our numbers will be like dust in the wind."

Zyphoro snorts, her smirk widening. "Twenty Blades and a handful of Tenders against the Legion of Saints? This should be interesting." Her voice drips with dark humor, but beneath the surface, there's a seriousness that lingers. She knows what we're up against.

"We'll need to get creative," Solena adds, her brow furrowing. "Anything that can give us an advantage in the forest. The Grove is our best defense—it will fight for us. But we should think of the children and the elders. They will need somewhere safe to hide if the worst happens."

I nod slowly, their words settling on my shoulders. "I know this land better than they do. That's our advantage. Every inch, every shadow, every tree can be used against them." My voice is steady, though beneath it all, my heart pounds with the uncertainty of what lies ahead. "In the days of old, the Sisters of the Vine were said to summon the very power of the forest, and even the animals rose to fight alongside them."

The three Fae exchange skeptical glances, their disbelief evident.

"Pardon, Your Highness," Arax says, his brow furrowing. "Animals?"

I give a small, secretive smile, stirring my bowl of stew before blowing on the steam lazily. "You'll just have to wait and see, won't you?"

CHAPTER 33

In the days that follow, there just don't seem to be enough hours, each one slipping away faster than the last as the Grove transforms from a peaceful sanctuary into a place bracing for war. Knowing that we will receive no aid from Baev'kalath, Arax and Zyphoro take charge of training every able man and woman, their approach to teaching wildly different but equally effective.

Arax, with his calm and methodical precision, focuses on the basics—how to hold a sword, how to block, how to strike without wasting energy. His patience is endless, though the frustration is palpable in the set of his jaw whenever a trainee fumbles or hesitates.

"You're holding that blade like a broomstick," Arax growls at a young man, stepping behind him to adjust his grip. "If you swing like that, you'll cut your own head off before you even reach the enemy."

Beside him, Zyphoro grins wickedly as she demonstrates far more... unorthodox techniques. Her voice is smooth, almost teasing, as she whirls through the air with her daggers, her agility and precision something so instinctively naturally that it's entrancing to watch. "Forget blocking," she tells a group of wide-eyed recruits, most of whom are still struggling to keep their balance. "Your enemies will be faster, stronger, and crueler than you. So instead, be unpredictable. Be crueler. No one ever won a battle by fighting fair."

She spins around one of the more timid trainees, whispering as she slashes her blade through the air mere inches from his ear. "See? Terrifying, isn't it?" She laughs as the man stumbles back, pale-faced, while Arax rolls his eyes.

"Maybe try not to kill them before the battle," he mutters under his breath. When he sees the concern plaguing my face, he straightens his broad shoulders, solid as a mighty rock, shattering anything that dares break upon it. "They will be ready, Princess."

It's a fragile reassurance, and we both know it, but it's enough to keep us moving forward.

Meanwhile, Solena has taken on a different task, one suited to her more practical mindset. She spends her days fortifying an underground shelter hidden deep within the forest, gathering whoever isn't training to help her shore up the walls with thick wooden beams and stone reinforcements. Her work is meticulous, ensuring that if the worst happens, there will be a place for the children and the elders to hide.

"I didn't think it would come to this." I mutter to her as the Tenders carry water, dried fruits, nuts and seeds into the sanctuary. "Maybe I should have stayed in that castle."

"Don't do that to yourself, Amara," Solena says. "You would have died in Baev'kalath."

"But the Grove would have been safe," I reply quickly, a breath hitching in my throat.

"But for how long? You have seen how the houses quarrel. The Fae are holding on by the thinnest of threads. There is nothing to say your sacrifice would have saved the Grove. It is better off with you here, alive, to fight alongside them."

"And if I fail?" I ask. An impossible question to put on Solena's shoulders.

She answers it with the spirit I've come to expect from her. Strong and resilient. "Then we fail together, and I will consider that an honor if it is by your side."

I reach out and grip her hand and when she squeezes back, it is all the reassurance I need. But there is one last thing I can try before I meet the Legion on the battlefield. One last attempt to spare innocent Tender lives.

"I must speak to the Golden Son," I say, and Solena's hand loosens.

"Don't be ridiculous, Amara. He will kill you on the spot."

"He met with me once to discuss the terms of the Grove's surrender. Perhaps he will meet again."

"So now we are surrendering?" Solena says with mocking disbelief. She gestures to the sanctuary. "Do not tell me I have been digging in the dirt for nothing."

"We are not surrendering," I say firmly, "and that is an oath I take with every measure of my being. Instead, I will ask him to spare us from his war on the Fae. I have returned alone. I am no longer a part of their conflict."

"You have returned with three Fae, including a princess and a lieutenant of the Ebon Flight, and still have a small company of Blades serving you," she frowns. "I do not know this Golden Son, but if he leads an army as large and well organized as the Legion, I assume he has some common sense."

I furrow my brow. "You are supposed to be on my side."

Solena shrugs. "A true friend would tell you when you're teetering on the edge of madness."

My hand slips free from Solena's and she releases a heavy breath. "I'm going, Solena."

"Then I am going with you."

"No," I protest. "I need you here to take care of these people if things do not go as planned..."

"Which they won't," she mutters under her breath.

I pretend I didn't hear. "I will take Arax."

"And leave me with Princess Zyphoro?" Solena rolls her eyes. "If you want us all dead, I'd prefer you get it over with now and spare me being alone with her."

"I'm trying to save lives," I say, working to soothe Solena's ire. "Before it's too late."

"I know," she grumbles. "But if you don't survive this, I'll kill you."

I nod. "I wouldn't expect anything less."

I turn my back, heading towards the council hall, already planning what I will tell them.

"Amara," Solena calls to me, and I look over my shoulder at her. "If the opportunity presents itself. Kill him."

Her words slam into me, leaving me disorientated. But when my mind slips back into focus, I realize she is right. Without the Golden Son, the ranks of the Legion would fall into disarray, and the Grove would be safe, if even for a short while. Long enough for us to prepare for the next onslaught. I nod and Solena returns to her work while I tramp through the dirt to the council hall.

"You're sure?" Erania asks, her dark eyes wracked with uncertainty.

The council all have their chins against their chests, muttering amongst each other.

"I'm sure. If I am to lead the Tenders, then I must lead in a way fitting of our people. War is not our philosophy. We must strive to make peace first, avoid bloodshed at all costs."

"That is what Keeper Tovar attempted to do, and look what came of it," Erania growls angrily.

Tovar's actions still strike a pain in my chest. My outrage mingled with a lifetime's worth of favored memories. I briefly wonder where in Valorne he is right now. If in his exile, he is lost or scared with no voices to comfort him in his darkest moments.

"We are outnumbered and barely have enough swords to put in hands. Even we sisters are not the warriors we once were. We are for mending and guiding now, not battle, and we have the aid of a handful of Fae, but they are no match for the share size of the Legion army." I knew all this before I came to the council hall, but saying it out loud allows it to truly sink in, leaving my chest hollow and my blood cold. "I must try, Keeper Enaria."

She nods. "Very well. We will continue preparations and if you return unsuccessful, Jewel, we will be ready to fight." A half smile trembles on her mouth. "Just return, alright?"

As I leave the hall and walk through the Grove, watching the training sessions, the fortifications, the preparations that hum beneath every conversation, it's a strange feeling—being surrounded by so much activity, so much focus—while knowing the storm that looms on the horizon.

I find Arax on the training field, and we go back and forth on my decision for far too long. He growls and scorns me like a child, but then immediately apologizes after each scathing remark.

"Are you coming with me or not?" I ask him with finality.

"Of course I bloody am," he groans, as if my asking only infuriates him more. "I'm your bodyguard."

"Have you forgotten? King Kaelus released you from that duty." I say it almost jokingly, but the severity of his face hints he does not feel the same way.

"No one, not even a king, will keep me from protecting you, Es..." His voice cuts off, his breaths ragged with his realization and I feel it too, the pain and regret that scars him. "Princess," he finishes.

I take a step towards him, reaching out and clasping my hand over his and when his weathered eyes meet mine, the understanding between us is more than words can convey.

"Let's leave now," I say.

He nods. "As you wish."

I choose not to fly to the Legion camp.

I want to arrive on my own two feet, not in the arms of the Fae whom this rebel army despises. However, they are still two days' ride from the Grove. Arax's solution is simple in theory but complicated in execution. We will void walk there, but the distance is too great to cover in one jump. Instead, as he describes it, we will "leapfrog" through the void, jumping from portal to portal until we reach the Legion camp. He warns me that it will hurt and that even the oldest Mordorin Fae struggle not to get lost in the void. I tell him I trust him.

Arax's hands tighten over the reins as he leads the stag through the overgrowth. The creature is powerful beneath me, towering over Arax with its eight feet of earth-brown fur, patched with green and gold. Its antlers branch out before me, twisted like tree roots and adorned with glowing moss and vibrant flowers that bloom in a riot of color.

My green robes trail behind me, the gold stitching glinting in the afternoon sun as we emerge from the Grove and step onto a field of wildflowers—such beauty sewn with the blood of a battle long ago. A battle that not only took from me but from Arax as well. I can see it in the way he surveys the long grass swaying in the breeze, recalling bodies falling as steel clashed and screams echoed through the air.

I touch his hand on the reins, stirring him from his memories, but he does not dwell on them. He is a being of action, and there are things to be done.

"Are you ready, Princess?"

When I nod, Arax shrugs off his cloak. The runes on his back pulse just before his black wings, streaked with gray, burst forth with a sudden snap. He narrows his eyes on the horizon, where the approaching Legion sets up camp, then thrusts his hand forward. Ribbons of smoke soar through the air before stopping abruptly to form a swirling circle. Slowly, the smoke gives way to a vast emptiness—a black, endless maw that I have seen in my waking nightmares. The void. A place of untold power and endless despair.

With a beat of his wings, Arax rises into the air, hovering beside me, waiting for me to make the first move. I take a deep breath, exhaling any doubt or fear. There is no room for that here. I place my hand flat against the stag's muscular neck, feeling the warmth of its body beneath my palm. *Run*, my mind whispers.

The stag's powerful legs spring into action, its hooves pounding against the ground with a sound like war drums echoing through the air. Arax pins back his wings, flying alongside me as we charge toward the portal. I grip the reins tightly, my heartbeat syncing with the stag's, our minds merging as we near the encroaching darkness. I feel both of us hold our breaths as we leap blindly into the void.

It's like plunging underwater—eerily silent and all-encompassing, with no way to breathe. The emptiness wraps around us, an eternal abyss, but I refuse to surrender to its calm. I know what lurks here. This is the domain of The Father Below, and he always hungers.

Before the darkness can settle into my bones, we emerge on the other side, transported miles from where we entered, The Grove now a distant memory. Arax releases another series of smoke arrows, and a new portal bends into existence before us. We charge into that one as well, emerging further away, the Legion camp growing closer with each leap.

Arax clenches his jaw, the strain evident on his face as we void walk yet again. Despite his warnings, I find I've managed to remain composed, enduring only a few sharp jolts of pain that force me to grit my teeth and tighten my grip on the reins until my knuckles turn white and my nails dig into my palms.

Though I'm relieved not to be sick, a nagging worry lingers. Is my resistance to the void a sign of the part of it that grows within me?

With one final jump we appear at the foot of the Legion Camp, and the wall of guards release a collective gasp, the ring of their swords almost deafening.

I quickly raise my hand as I gasp for breath, my stomach churning. "Wait," I say with urgency before they attack. "I am Amara Tyne. Jewel of the Tenders. Guardian of the Grove. I wish to parlay with the Golden Son."

The soldiers, clad in gilded armor and heavy red cloaks, exchange glances through the narrow visors of their helms, each crowned with a sharp steel crest. Their chestplates bear the emblem of crossed swords framed by praying hands—a motif repeated on their scaled pauldrons and gauntlets.

Their ranks part, allowing me a pathway into their camp, and with a thought, the stag takes a step forward. But when Arax tries to walk alongside us, the soldiers fall back into line.

"Not the Fae. He stays here."

Arax snarls, his canines emerging, his hand hovering over his sword. "Not on your life, boy."

The Legion reach for their own swords, and I throw my arms up in protest. I will not have a war break out here and now.

"Fine. I accept your terms," I say, and I feel Arax's eyes burning through me.

I look down at him, offering a smile I know gives him very little comfort. "Please, Arax. Wait here."

"But, Princess,' he pleads.

I shake my head lightly. "If I do not return, then you must protect the Grove. Do you promise me that?"

Arax exhales, then nods slow and reluctant. "Yes, Princess."

The Legion soldiers part once more and the stag strides between them, and I feel Arax's gaze with every thundering step. The makeshift encampment sprawls before me, an arrangement of tents and flickering campfires. Soldiers huddle together, their faces drawn and weary, exchanging glances filled with disdain as they watch us approach. The scent of smoke hangs heavy in the air, mingling with unease.

But the stag and I remain steady as we weave through the throng of soldiers and when I look into the distance and see how far this army stretches, dread sears beneath my skin. If it comes to war, the Grove can not possibly survive. Finally, we come to a stop outside a large tent, its fabric slightly tattered, marked by the swords and praying hands.

I dismount from the stag, its powerful form shifting beneath me, and it takes a moment before my feet touch the ground. A soldier at the door glares at me through his visor, then pulls back the curtain of the tent. The interior is dimly lit, and anticipation coils within me as I take a deep breath and step inside.

A single lantern casts a warm, flickering glow, illuminating a modest wooden table scattered with maps and scrolls. In the opposite corner, a simple bed is made up with a raggedy blanket.

When my eyes finally find him, I take a sharp breath.

I have seen him before, but each encounter jolts me, though I can't explain why. He sits casually on a makeshift stool, his presence both commanding and relaxed. One hand props up his sword, the point embedded in the dirt as if it were an extension of himself, while the other drapes lazily over his knee. The flickering light from the nearby lantern casts shadows across his figure, highlighting the crimson of his tunic, which sharply contrasts with the darkness of his black trousers and the striking yellow-blond of his hair.

But it is his mask that captures my attention—a stunning creation of gold, its crafts-manship resembling flames caught in mid-surge. The design is both beautiful and fearsome, the golden hues shifting with the light, creating the illusion of flickering fire. Encased within are the bluest eyes I have ever seen.

"Jewel of the Tenders—or is it Princess Amara of the Mordorin?" he greets me, his voice steady and unhurried, carrying an air of calculated calm. "To what do I owe the esteemed pleasure of your visit?"

"It is just Amara, and I've come to speak with you about the Legion and the conflict brewing on our borders," I reply, forcing my voice to remain steady despite the unease churning in my stomach.

He leans back slightly, studying me with an intensity that feels palpable, even through his mask. "And what exactly do you wish to discuss? The Legion has taken root, and soon it will be too late for negotiations."

I stand tall, my resolve hardening. "I believe there's still a chance for peace, but it requires understanding from both sides. The Grove cannot afford another war."

The Golden Son nods slowly, but his expression is a mystery behind the mask. "No, it cannot. But you knew that months ago when I came to you in peace and offered you a solution. Not only did you refuse my generous offer to be your master, you attacked my men."

"They attacked first. We were defending ourselves—"

"And to further insult me, you marry the Fae responsible for the deaths of *thousands* of human lives." His hand grips his knee, the roped muscles of his forearms tightening, the only sign of his anger.

As his words hang in the air, I realize that this conversation will not be easy.

"I'm asking you to consider a different path," I say, my voice steady despite the tension coiling in my chest. "A path that could spare countless lives, including those of your own men."

"Where is your prince?" he asks, disregarding my plea. "My scouts say he was not amongst the Fae you arrived with."

"That is not your concern," I reply curtly, my heart thumping hard in my chest. "All I care about is—"

"Yes, yes. *Your people.*" He rises from his chair, and with a fluid flick of his wrist, he returns his sword to the sheath at his waist. He steps toward me, closing the distance between us. "You ask me for mercy, but what do I get in return?"

I hear his breaths beneath the mask as he looms over me, his gaze so intense that I struggle to meet his eyes. "What is it you want?"

A rumble escapes his throat. "I want to crush every Fae into dust beneath my boot. I want to feel the snap when I rip their wings from their backs with my bare hands. I want to burn their houses to the ground and then piss on their ashes with my human cock. Can you give me any of that... Amara?"

I gulp, his words leaving me speechless, and I fight to keep from trembling before him. I shake my head.

His eyes roam over me, lingering longer than they should.

"Then you have nothing I want," he mutters bitterly. "Get out."

He turns his back on me, and my ire flares. "No. You cannot do this. My people—"

"*You are the reason this is happening to your people!*" he bellows, snapping back to me. "You refused to bend the knee, insisting on your precious neutrality. But there are no innocents in this war. Whether human or Fae, this is the way the world is. This is how we made it. It is them or us. There can be no in-between. Yet, despite your piousness, you sold yourself to those winged bastards instead of fighting alongside your people. Us. The Legion. *Humans.* Instead, you chose the Fae." His fist clenches. "And what was the price paid, Amara, Jewel of the Tenders? How much gold and jewels were bartered for your... charms?"

My teeth grit, anger surging in my belly, rage clawing at my neck like a rabid beast. "How dare you? You know *nothing* of which you speak."

"Fine. Let me tell you what I do know, *Princess* Amara. I know that the Legion marches for the Grove at dawn, and I know the next time we meet, I will not be so gracious." He leans in, his eyes narrowing. "Now leave while I still allow it."

I don't waste time arguing. I throw back the curtain of his tent and storm out into the makeshift stronghold. The stag drops onto its knees so I can mount its back, and once I grip the reins, it rises to its hooves. With a whisper from my mind, it breaks into a gallop, soldiers scrambling out of its path or risking being trampled.

At the perimeter, Arax waits for me, relief flooding his face when he sees me coming. His wings burst from his back, and he takes to the air to keep pace with me as I flee.

"Princess," he asks, the wind whipping against us. "What happened?"

I hiss through gritted teeth as I urge the stag to run faster. "We go to war."

Here in the moonlight, I've never felt like such a fool. My attempts to stop this conflict only led to the Golden Son spitting vile threats and reducing me to a stuttering girl pretending to be a leader. I'm not sure which is worse: returning with my tail between my legs or informing my friends, my people, the council, that I have failed and the Legion marches at dawn.

Solena paces the room we share, assuring me I did all I could, but her words offer little comfort when I know there was one more thing I could have done—followed her advice and killed the arrogant bastard when I had the chance.

I can't stay here, consumed by these thoughts.

If war is coming, I must be as strong as I can be for the last stand.

I push myself off the bed, craving the cool air to clear my mind and pull myself out of this haze. My feet carry me through the village and into the woods, toward the clearing. The night is crisp, the breeze a welcome reprieve from the heat of anger and disappointment. When I reach the clearing, I sit in the soft grass, closing my eyes and allowing the world around me to fade away.

When I open them again, I am no longer in the clearing. The shrine of the Sisters of the Vine rises before me, its glowing runes casting an ethereal light across the ancient tree and its web of power. My sisters—Lira, Mirael, and Saren—are already gathered there, kneeling in silent prayer, their eyes closed as they commune with the Souls.

"We need the power," I say urgently as I approach them.

My sisters look at me with arched brows.

"If we are to defend the Grove, our people will need more than just our healing," I continue, slipping into the circle. "They will need the power of the sisters who came before us."

I add my hands to the chain, and energy surges through us unbroken.

"That magic is dangerous," Lira warns. "It will drain you dry, and no amount of sleep will restore what you've lost."

"That is why the sisters before us let it go," Mirael adds. "Focusing only on healing and growth."

I shake my head. "That will not save us, sister."

Saren smiles. "Our Jewel is right. We have been passive long enough. If we truly love the Grove, then we should do whatever it takes, no matter the price. Shouldn't we?"

I look at Lira and Mirael, eager to see if Saren's words have swayed them to our cause.

Mirael speaks first. "When I was chosen as a Sister of the Vine, I was told it was my duty to protect the Grove. How can we hold true to those oaths if we are not willing to risk ourselves? I say we fight."

The three of us turn to Lira, who holds her ground for a moment before finally relenting, her shoulders slumping.

"Very well," she exhales. "We fight."

Soon, the Souls fills my mind, their voices soft yet powerful.

Amara, they greet me, their voices wrapping around me like the whisper of leaves in the wind. *You ask for the power of the forest itself. It is not given lightly, but we will grant it to you. The Sisters of the Vine shall be amplified, their strength entwined with the ancient magic that flows through the trees, the rivers, the earth beneath your feet. You will have dominion over the forest, but the price remains: pain for pain.*

I glance at my sisters, seeing their resolve harden. This is the burden we must carry if we are to protect the Grove. The Souls offer power beyond measure, but nothing comes free in this world. I already understand the weight of such a price—how the energy to heal or to harm must come from somewhere.

"We understand," I say, my voice low but firm. "We accept the price."

The others nod solemnly in agreement, and we drop to our knees, our hands pressing into the earth.

Then it begins.

The forest stirs around us, the trees groaning as if waking from a deep slumber. The glow of the runes in the shrine brightens, their fluorescent green light spilling over the branches and casting an eerie glow through the twisted limbs. Slowly, the light spreads—into the ground, through the roots, up into the trees. It moves like a pulse, the ancient magic of the forest coming alive with a power that thrums beneath our skin.

The glow intensifies, and as it reaches us, I feel it. The energy of the forest surges into me, filling each of us with the strength of the land itself. My body hums with it, the power thrumming through my veins, connecting me to the roots beneath my feet, to the leaves above, to every living thing within the forest.

The Souls of the Forest have infused us with their power, and I feel it in every breath, every heartbeat. We are not alone. The forest will fight with us, its strength ours to wield, but the reminder of the price lingers at the edges of my mind. *Pain for pain.*

I leave my sisters at the shrine and transport myself back to the clearing where Ashen waits for me, chasing moonbeams that shift between the rustling leaves. We return to the village, and as I walk through the darkness of the forest, the silence presses in on me, thick and stifling. The path back is familiar, one I've walked countless times, but tonight it feels different.

Everything feels different.

My mind is tangled in the weight of what's happened—the power that thrummed through me in the den of the Sisters, the energy I absorbed, the warnings of pain for pain. I reach for the rune around my neck, my fingers tracing its worn edges, feeling the subtle charge that hums beneath my skin.

Ashen pads silently at my side, his small form blending into the shadows. And then I hear it—a sound behind me, a faint rustling, barely perceptible but unmistakable. I stop, my heart thudding in my ears, and listen.

Silence.

I take a few steps forward, but the noise comes again, closer this time. A shiver runs down my spine. Slowly, I turn, scanning the darkness behind me.

Nothing.

"Ashen," I whisper, hoping for some comfort. He stays close, ears twitching, but even he seems tense.

Another sound—soft, deliberate, a warning. Someone's there. I can feel it, the hairs on the back of my neck standing on end. My mouth goes dry. "Who's there? Show yourself."

From the shadows, a figure steps forward, just beyond the reach of the moonlight.

My heart nearly stops when I see him. Tall, broad-shouldered, cloaked in darkness, but I know that form. I know that presence, the aura that surrounds him like a storm.

"No," I breathe, shaking my head as if denying it will make it go away. "You're not real."

The figure steps closer, his face emerging from the shadows, and my breath catches in my throat.

It's my prince.

My husband.

My betrayer.

Every inch of him is just as I remember—the fierce gaze that once unraveled me, the sharp, commanding lines of his face, and the cold, enigmatic intensity in his eyes. For a brief, aching moment, I can almost feel the pull of him, the bond that ties us together. My heart clenches, betraying me with its yearning, even as my mind screams in disbelief.

"Amara," he says, his voice low, filled with everything I don't want to hear, everything I've been trying to forget.

I take a step back, my hands shaking, my heart pounding against my ribs. How is he here?

"Amara," he calls again, his voice soft but commanding, and in that moment, something in Ashen shifts.

The air around him ripples, and before I can comprehend what's happening, his slight form grows, expanding in a swirl of smoke and shadow. His fur darkens, lengthening, as his body morphs into something enormous—something fierce. He roars, a deep, earth-shaking sound that sends a chill down my spine. His eyes blaze with an eerie, spectral light, his body now massive, powerful, like a creature from a nightmare.

"Ashen?" I gasp, my voice barely audible as I stumble backward.

Ashen, now a towering lion of smoke and shadow, charges forward, his growl vibrating through the trees as he leaps toward Daedalus with claws outstretched and a mass of writhing tentacles twisting from his back. The force of his transformation is violent. The ground trembles beneath my feet, the air crackling with energy.

Panic grips me, and without a second thought, I turn and run, my legs burning as I race through the forest, branches tearing at my skin. Behind me, the sounds of a battle I don't dare to witness rages on—Ashen's monstrous roars, the clash of shadow and darkness.

I run faster, the terror gripping me like a vise, because I can't look back. If I do, I might find that Daedalus isn't real—or worse—*that he is.*

CHAPTER 34

I run for the village, the vine wall parting just long enough to let me slip through before it closes behind me. The ancient vines are strong, but I know they won't keep him out.

Nothing will.

The village is eerily silent as I dash through the paths, the only sounds the dying crackle of embers and the wind rattling chimes that hang from the eaves of the tree houses. My heart hammers in my chest as I reach the spiral stairs that lead up to the canopy. I spin on my heel, searching the shadows for any sign of him, my skin prickling with dread.

Then I hear it—that sound. The soft pop of him stepping through the void. My breath catches as I turn to see Daedalus across the courtyard, his long black coat swirling around his legs, his high collar framing his sharp features. His dark hair falls to one side, and his pointed ears peek through, but he's not flawless tonight. A deep scratch mars the pale skin of his cheek, and his shimmering cloak is torn at the shoulder.

"Amara," his voice is calm, almost pleading. "Stop this now."

For a heartbeat, I want to.

I feel that same pull, that magnetic force between us, tempting me to believe in him again. But then I remember. I remember the lies that slipped too easily from his lips, the betrayal hidden behind every promise. This man would have *sacrificed* me for power.

He's a deceiver. A trickster. And I won't fall for it again.

I back up the stairs, my legs trembling as Daedalus moves toward me, each step deliberate and unyielding.

"I just want to talk," he says, his voice smooth, but his eyes flicker with something darker.

Before I can respond, another pop shatters the night, and in a blur of smoke and fury, Ashen leaps at the prince, roaring like a creature pulled from a nightmare. His glowing eyes burn with rage as his claws flash in the moonlight.

"Ashen. No!" Daed growls, but Ashen is relentless.

The two collide, a snarl ripping from Daed's throat as they roll to the ground, a feral tangle of limbs and teeth. For a moment, it's impossible to tell who is the beast as Daedalus bares his canines, his growl deep and primal, matching Ashen's every move. Then, with another deafening pop, they both disappear into smoke.

I don't wait to see where they reappear. I scramble up the stairs, my foot slipping on the wood as I push myself faster. I stumble across the bridge, the boards clattering beneath my weight, until I finally burst into my room, slamming the door behind me. Solena bolts upright from her bed, eyes wide with alarm.

"Amara? What's wrong? Is the Legion here?"

I press my hands against the door, panting, my chest heaving as if I can somehow hold it shut, as if I can keep him out.

"Worse," I gasp, my voice tight with fear. "The prince is here."

Suddenly, a thunderous bang reverberates through the door, and I stumble back while Solena leaps out of bed.

"Is that him?" she whispers urgently, her gaze darting to me. "Amara?"

"Princess!" Arax's voice booms from the other side of the door. "Are you alright?"

I lunge forward, just enough to reach the knob and pull it open. "Close it," I say quickly as Arax steps inside.

He swings the door shut and immediately draws his sword, his eyes scanning the room. "Where is the danger?"

"Everywhere," a cold voice cuts through the silence from behind us.

We all turn sharply to see Daedalus lounging in a chair like it's his throne, bathed in a streak of moonlight that slices across his face. His skin is scratched and bruised, a trickle of blood running down his lip, but his eyes glint with that same dangerous calm that I've come to fear... and desire.

Solena gasps, stumbling backward to hide behind Arax, and even he takes a beat to catch his breath at the sight of the prince.

Daedalus taps the arm of the chair lazily with his fingers. "This was not the welcome I expected."

"It's the welcome you deserve," I snarl, my voice low and bitter.

Suddenly, that pop rings out again. Ashen reappears mid-air, a blur of spectral smoke, his jaws wide as he lunges for Daedalus, but the prince doesn't flinch. He only groans, raising his hand with a flick of irritation.

Ashen freezes in mid-leap, suspended in the air. His powerful legs thrash, claws outstretched, tentacles whipping, trying desperately to reach Daedalus, but he's held just beyond the edge of striking. And then, with a slow, deliberate curl of his hand into a fist, Ashen dissolves. His smoke spirals into the air before sweeping back toward Daedalus, absorbed into his skin like a whisper.

"No!" I scream, my heart shattering. "You made him for *me!*"

"And I have *un*made him," Daedalus snaps cruelly. His eyes lock onto mine, burning with an intensity that turns my blood cold. "And I will unmake everything in existence if that's what it takes to get close to you. Is that what you want?"

How could I have forgotten this arrogance?

The audacity that runs through him, unyielding and insufferable.

"You would threaten the entire world for something as insignificant as a *word* from me?"

His eyes burn into mine, unblinking. "Can you imagine what I would do for a touch?"

The room crackles with tension, heavy and suffocating, until the sharp ring of metal fills the air. "You are not welcome here, my prince," Arax declares, his voice solemn yet firm. "Leave now, or face me."

Daedalus rises, unhurried and baleful, his presence so calm it sends a pulse of terror through us all. His eyes stay locked on mine, as if this entire moment is a game only he knows how to win. The power in his restraint is terrifying. His fearlessness, the lethal grace in how he holds himself, could tear down armies long before a sword is even drawn.

"Stand down, Arax." A command, not a plea.

Arax's face twists, torn between duty and the bond he holds with his prince. It's written across every line in his face—the pain, the struggle. But still, he raises his sword, defying everything he's ever known. "I will not ask again," he grits out, the finality in his voice like a warning.

Daedalus' calm, his unrelenting control—it's a weapon in of itself, and I hate that I'm drawn to it. It's as if the more dangerous he becomes, the deeper my desire roots itself inside me. I despise this part of myself. And yet, I can't turn away.

Without warning, Arax brings down his sword, and I cry out, my heart leaping into my throat. But Daedalus moves in a blur of darkness, Death Singer materializing in a swirl of black smoke just as the blades collide. The clash sends sparks flying, the sound of metal on metal resounding through the room, drowning out everything but the wild, chaotic rhythm of my heart.

Neither gives an inch, muscles wound tight as they push against each other, testing who will bend first. Arax grits his teeth, smoke rising from the corners of his eyes, refusing to yield. His blade trembles with the effort, but the prince remains composed, his movements calculated, as if he's always a step ahead.

"Put your sword down, Arax."

"I cannot, my prince," Arax groans back. "I am sorry."

With a sudden surge of power, Daedalus moves faster than I can see, breaking the deadlock and twisting his body with such force that Arax stumbles. Daedalus spins, his blade catching the light for a split second before it finds its mark, disarming Arax and sending him crashing to one knee.

"No!" I scream, lunging forward, but the prince has already pressed the edge of his sword to Arax's throat, smoke rising from where the blade connects. Arax doesn't flinch, even with his life hanging on the edge of Daedalus' blade. His chest rises and falls heavily, and I can see the endless fight in his eyes. He knows he's beaten, and yet he would die here if it meant protecting me.

"I do not want to do this, old one," Daedalus breathes. His eyes soften, just a flicker of emotion on the hard set of his face. "But if you *fucking dare* to keep me from my wife, I will cut you down."

His threat hangs in the air, the fierceness of it sinking deep into my bones.

Wife.

The word hits me like a punch to the chest, forcing me to confront what I've been trying to deny since the moment I saw him again. We are bound—whether I like it or not—by the vow we made, by the threads that tie us together, and by the inescapable fate we share, even if everything between us has become twisted and shadowed.

Arax looks up at me, his jaw clenched, waiting for my command. My heart hammers in my chest, my pulse roaring in my ears. I do not doubt Daedalus would kill Arax if he had to.

"Arax," I whisper, my voice breaking. "Please... stand down."

316

His gaze flickers, and slowly, agonizingly, he lowers his head. "As you wish, Princess."

Daedalus' eyes remain on mine as he releases Arax, stepping back as his sword dissolves into smoke.

"Leave us," I say, my head bowed.

"Amara," Solena says with worry. "Are you sure? I can get..."

"No," I say, stopping Solena from finishing. "I need to talk to him."

She nods as Arax climbs to his feet, gathering his sword from the floor. He looks at me, as if to say sorry, but it is a wasted effort. I couldn't be more proud to have him as my protector.

When the door closes, the room turns cold, and for what seems like an age, Daed and I stand in silence, locked in a gaze consumed with every fear and doubt. I wonder if either of us will ever speak—as if whoever speaks first is the first to surrender. It feels like a game, one where we're both showing our control by not falling apart, by pretending we don't care.

But I can feel it in me. I can feel the break, the rip, the tear. I can feel my heart bleeding, and the tears behind my eyes threatening to break their dams. *This silence is unbearable.*

"You deceived me," I whisper, and it's like tearing open a wound. The words taste bitter on my tongue, and my voice trembles with the rage boiling beneath the surface.

Daed's face remains unreadable, but his eyes flicker. "I did."

His calm admission sparks something wild inside me. I can't breathe, I can't stop.

"You lied about everything! About the bargain—about my life!" My fists hit his chest with a force I didn't know I had.

"I know," he says, his voice steady, unflinching, even as I strike him again.

"You—" My voice breaks, my fists pounding harder. "You would've let them kill me! You stood by and let them plan my death!"

"I did." His voice is like a whisper in a storm, and his eyes are locked on mine, unwavering. He doesn't even flinch as my hands slam into his chest again, harder this time, the anger and pain flooding through me.

"You made me care for you!" My hands hit him again, and again, the pain too much to keep inside. "You made me *believe*—"

"I know," Daed murmurs, his tone still calm, still aching with that damnable regret.

I can't stop. I don't want to stop. The fury is spilling out of me now, uncontrollable, the dam at last breaking, sundered by everything he's done. My fists keep hitting him, weaker now, but still desperate. "You broke me! You broke me, and you don't even care."

"I do," he says, quietly, letting me strike him again. "I care."

My hands falter, the strength leaving me all at once, and I crumple against him, my fists falling limp against his chest. The tears stream down my face, unchecked, and I hate that I'm crying in front of him. I hate that he's seeing me like this—*broken, shattered, ruined.*

Daedalus takes my wrists, holding them gently, as if he knows I'm too weak to fight anymore. I struggle in his grasp, but I can't break free. I'm too tired. Too tired of all of it.

He lifts my chin, forcing me to meet his eyes.

"I love you," he says, the words raw, cutting so deep I fear I'll bleed to death.

I hate him for saying it, hate him for making me feel anything after everything he's done.

"I love you," he says again, and the weight of it pulls me under.

I want to scream, to fight, to run, but all I can do is stand there, my hands still in his, trembling as I try to hold myself together.

Daed's eyes glass over, a beautiful storm held within the swirl of gray. The tension between us is unbearable, so thick I can hardly breathe. He's holding me so gently by the wrists, as if he's afraid I'll shatter if he lets go. His chest rises and falls with each labored breath, and I know he's holding back—holding back everything he feels, everything he wants.

I don't know who moves first. Maybe it's him, or maybe it's me, but the next moment, he releases my wrists, and his hands slide up to cradle my face. His touch is like fire, igniting something deep within me I've been trying so hard to bury. My heart pounds so violently it echoes in my ears, and the tears in my eyes blur everything but him.

"Amara...my princess," he whispers, his voice breaking. His forehead leans against mine, and I close my eyes, overwhelmed by the closeness, by the heat of his skin, by the undeniable pull between us.

I breathe him in—his scent, his presence, everything I've missed and fought against. His thumb brushes away a tear from my cheek, and the gentleness of that single act undoes me. Slowly, his lips hover just above mine, and time seems to stop. The world outside fades, and in this moment, it's only us—caught in the web of everything that's broken between us and everything that remains.

And then, finally, he kisses me.

It's not soft. It's not tentative. It's a kiss that shatters the fragile space between us, a collision of all the hurt and love and passion we've been holding back. His mouth moves against mine like a man starving, desperate, tasting the tears on my lips, drinking the pain he's caused. There's an edge to it that speaks of everything we've been through, but despite that, it's tender in a way that only he can be.

I kiss him back, my hands gripping his coat and pulling him closer, but even pressed hard against me, he still feels too far away. I hate how much I need this—how much I need *him*.

Daed's hands glide down my back, his lips breaking from mine to trail relentless, burning kisses along my jawline and down my neck. My head tilts back, a gasp escaping my lips as I struggle for breath.

"Amara," he murmurs against my skin, his voice rough. "My wife. My love."

His words are raw, a confession steeped in longing so profound it aches. I feel it in every touch, in every kiss. But I don't respond—I can't. My heart is a mess of broken shards, yet his hands on my skin and his lips on mine make me forget. Forget everything but this moment. This feeling. I pull his mouth back to mine, silencing his beautiful lies.

We stumble backward, his hands never leaving me, until the wall presses firm against my back and he leans into me, his body flush with mine.

"I've missed you so fucking much," he breathes between kisses, his words tumbling into the space where our lips meet. "I need you, Amara. Please."

His voice fills my head and my heart shatters all over again. I want to tell him I need him too, that I love him, but the words lodge in my throat. Instead, I kiss him harder, my fingers tangling in his hair and pulling him closer. I pour every unspoken word, every fractured piece of myself, into this one kiss.

Daed's jacket falls to the floor, and I waste no time tugging at the buttons of his shirt, my fingers frantic as I pull it open, desperate to feel him. My hands slide across the hard planes of his chest, tracing the outline of his runes, lingering over his taut muscles as his lips devour me with a hunger that mirrors my own.

His fingers trail down my body, slipping under the hem of my dress, his touch burning through the fabric as he grips my thigh and lifts my leg to his hip, grinding himself against me. I gasp at the feel of his body molding to mine and I whimper when I feel the hard length of him, desperate to have him fill the ache he's caused. His hand slides between us, finding me already wet and wanting, and I moan into his kiss as his fingers explore me, stroking, teasing, knowing exactly where I like to be touched.

"I have dreamt of how warm and tight you feel wrapped around me," he growls against my lips. I can feel him harden, pulsing through the fabric of his pants. "You call me cruel, but it is you, wife, who has left me in torment. Knowing how perfect you feel—how our bodies are made for each other. That no one else could ever make us feel the way we do. You are all my body craves, and taking that away from me? That is the real betrayal."

My jaw tightens, anger blazing through my chest, nearly indistinguishable from the heat pooling low as his fingers maintain their slow, maddening rhythm. *Bastard. How dare he.* But still my body trembles, and the moan he pulls from me is a mix of bitterness and need, desperate for him not to stop as his thumb circles my core, sending relentless waves of pleasure coursing through me.

Daed trails kisses down my throat, and I flinch at the scrape of his canines against my skin.

"I need you," he rasps, his voice ragged. "I need what's mine."

His fingers press deeper, and I gasp, shuddering under his touch. "Please, Amara," he murmurs, his breath hot against my skin. "Let me have you. Now."

I can barely form words, the ache inside me too intense, my body demanding more. Instead, I let my actions speak for me. I reach for his belt, fumbling with the buckle, my hands shaking as I undo it and let it fall. It is all the invitation he needs. He pulls the front of his trousers down, just enough to free himself. I take in the sight of him—hard and powerful, every inch of him ready for me.

He presses against me, his body fitting perfectly against mine, just as he said, as he lifts me higher, pinning me between him and the wall. I gasp at the feel of him, the heat of him pressing against me, teasing me. His lips claim mine again, and I wrap my legs around his waist, pulling him closer, needing him closer.

"I can't wait. It's been so long, my love."

With one slow movement, he slides inside me, filling me inch by inch. The sensation is exquisite, the stretch of him both aching and perfect. I throw my head back, a soft cry escaping me as he begins to move, his rhythm agonizingly precise, each thrust sending a ripple of pleasure through my body.

His hands grip my hips, his fingers bite, holding me steady as he drives into me, his pace quickening as we both give in to the heat between us. My nails dig into his back, clinging to him as he takes me higher, our bodies moving in desperate harmony. I can feel every inch of him, every hard stroke, every brush of his skin against mine, and it drives me wild with need.

"Amara," he groans into my open mouth, his voice thick with desire. The sound of my name on his lips sends a shiver through me, my body tightening around him in response.

His lips capture mine in a fierce, claiming kiss, and I lose myself in him—in the way he moves, the way he makes me feel like I'm the only thing that matters. Every thrust, every touch, every breath is a fire that consumes us both, and I know in this moment that there is no going back.

Not from this. Not from us.

The intensity of his storm-cloud eyes becomes too much for me. I bury my face in his neck, hiding from him as I bite the soft skin of his earlobe. "Harder, Daed."

A rumble sounds from his chest, and he complies with my demand.

He pushes me closer to the edge, his hand slips between us, finding the spot where I need him most. His fingers work in time with his thrusts, and the pleasure builds inside me, too intense, too powerful to resist. My body tightens, and with a final, desperate cry, I fall over the edge, shattering around him as pleasure washes over me in waves.

He follows me soon after, his body stiffening as he drives into me one last time, his release crashing through him with a raw, broken groan. He holds me close, his breath ragged in my ear, and for a moment, the world feels still, like nothing else exists except for the two of us.

We linger in that moment, tangled together, our bodies still pressed close as we descend from the high of one another. His chest heaves, slick with sweat, and he pulls me tightly against him, inhaling the scent of my skin. He clenches my bottom lip between his teeth, his breath heavy and warm against my mouth.

When he finally releases me, he opens his eyes, gazing at me through a dreamy haze that softens the world around us. "I love you, Amara."

The sigh that leaves my body is heavy with sadness and regret.

I meet his gaze, gently sweeping his dark hair away from his brow. "I love you too, husband."

"I'm supposed to bring you back to Baev'kalath," Daed admits quietly in the darkness, his voice carrying the weight of the impossible task. "I flew through the storm, across the sea, to drag you back—kicking and screaming—to live out your days as a prisoner."

A bitter laugh escapes me as I rest my head on his chest, listening to the steady beat of his heart. "Is that right? Sorry to disappoint you," I murmur, "but I won't be going with you."

"I expected as much," he sighs, his fingers tracing lazy patterns along my shoulder.

A warm silence settles between us. Through the open window, the wind whispers through the trees, their leaves rustling like secrets shared in the night. For a moment, it feels as if time itself has paused, and everything is just as it was in Pariseth, where the world outside mattered little in our small piece of paradise.

But, like all good things, this too cannot last. Not when I am the Jewel of the Tenders and my husband is the Prince of the Mordorin Fae. I gaze into Daed's eyes, wishing it could be different—that it could be as simple as two people who love each other. Yet it isn't, and it can't be. Not as long as we are who we are, with his lies and deceptions dividing us like a chasm that even my love for him cannot bridge.

"I can't trust you, can I?" I whisper into his skin.

"No," he breathes, the weight of his words hanging heavy between us. "The void and I are one, and the hold the Father has on me... it's beyond my control, no matter how much I fight him." His voice grows bitter. "I'm a puppet, Amara, and the queen and Gygarth pull my strings when they please."

I close my eyes, the ache in my chest growing. "Why didn't you tell me all this in Pariseth?"

He lets out a soft, regretful sigh. "And ruin the best days of my life? I wasn't brave enough. Besides, you would have left me sooner. And I... I was selfish. Once I had you, once you were mine, I couldn't let you go. Not even to protect you."

His words are beautiful, but I'm not so lost in him they can erase the hurt. Silence stretches between us, leaving me to wonder how much more there is I do not know. His fingers run through in my hair and he exhales.

"You don't know if you can be with me, do you?"

My breath catches, his question cutting too close to the truth. I sit up slightly, looking into his stormy gray eyes. "You said it yourself. Lanneth and Gygarth have control over you. How can I believe anything you say, or trust that you won't betray me again... even if it's against your will?"

He turns his gaze away, jaw clenched. "So, this was what? Pity?" His voice is sharp, but there's a vulnerability there too, buried beneath the bitterness. "One last beautiful taste before you send me away?"

My heart twists. "It wasn't meant to be this way."

Daed chuckles darkly. "Amara Tyne, Jewel of the Tenders... did you just use a Mordorin prince as a plaything?" There's a teasing lilt to his voice, but the ache beneath is unmistakable.

I let out a small laugh, tracing the hard lines of his muscles. But the moment softens, my smile fading. "Why can't it be simple?"

"Because we are not simple creatures," he says, his voice low, fierce. "Simple is easy. Simple is safe. Neither of us has ever been granted that luxury. We live with fury, with passion, with every breath balanced between life and death. Simple creatures die quietly in their beds, surrounded by loved ones singing sweet songs. You and I... we will meet our end in blood and fire, in smoke and ash. And if I'm fortunate, I'll burn with you in my arms."

I lift my head, resting my chin on his chest, and meet his gaze. His gray eyes churn like a storm, wild and beautiful. "I would see my end the same way. I love you, Daedalus Phaedren. More than I ever thought I could love someone. More than I should love someone who's wronged me, as you have. But if I can't trust you... I *can't* stay with you."

His chest rises beneath me, the truth sinking in. "So, what do we do now?"

"The Legion is marching on the Grove, and I doubt Baev'kalath will send more Blades now that I know the truth."

He shakes his head. "I came alone."

"You're enough. Fight this battle with me. And if we survive... I'll decide."

He nods, his eyes softening. "Very well."

Then, in a smooth motion, he pulls me on top of him, my legs straddling his hips, his length hardening beneath me as his hands skim the bare skin of my back. His fingers tangle in my hair as he gazes up at me, his voice a husky whisper. "If this is to be our last night, wife... then please, show me your sweet pity once more."

CHAPTER 35

When Daed and I emerge at dawn, Zyphoro waits for us on the rope bridge.

Or, more accurately, she waits for Daedalus.

I feel like an ant amongst giants as their gazes lock, sizing each other up with an intensity so thick you could choke on it. The air hums with tension, the weight of so many secrets and lies and heartbreaks bearing down on their shoulders.

"Sister," Daed says, smoke curling ominously between his fingers. "It has been a long time."

Zyphoro's lips twist into a smirk, and with a flick of her wrist, a dagger shrouded in shadow manifests in her hand. She points it straight at him, her eyes gleaming. "Longer for me, brother."

They stalk towards each other, these sleek predators, almost identical, even their halved moonstones seeming to sway in time around their necks. As Zyphoro conjures a second dagger, the smoke swirling around it like tendrils of darkness, Daed extends his hand, summoning Death Singer from the void, the gem in its hilt glinting, its silver blade shimmering in the morning light.

I don't know what to do. I'm frozen, useless—what can an ant possibly hope to stop between these two forces of nature? My heart pounds in my chest, expecting the inevitable screech of their weapons colliding, bracing for the violence that is sure to follow.

But when they meet in the center of the bridge, instead of the clash of steel, they collapse into each other. Their weapons vanish as they grab with a fierceness that feels like both an embrace and a battle, gripping as if to hold on to something they've both lost.

"Zyphoro," Daed murmurs, his voice breaking. "I'm sorry."

Zyphoro's face remains hard for a beat longer, but then the sharp edge of her fury dulls when she buries her face in her brother's shoulder. "You should be," she mutters.

"But you're here now." She pulls back slightly, her expression shifting into something more playful. "With the two of us, these humans might just win this war... against other humans." Her brow furrows, confusion slipping into her voice. "Have I been absent so long that Fae fight human wars now?"

Daed shakes his head, his voice resigned. "No. This is recent."

It's impossible to look at them without seeing the startling similarities—not just in the way their dark hair falls in the same way or how their eyes churn with the same storm, but in the power they carry, the way they command those around them. Their very presence is overwhelming. I wonder, fleetingly, what a battle between them would look like—whether it would end in an instant with both of them destroyed or rage on for a hundred years.

Zyphoro's gaze shifts to me over Daed's shoulder. "I've met your wife," she says. "It seems... complicated."

"You have no idea," he replies, a small smirk tugging at his lips, but it fades quickly when Zyphoro's expression turns cold again.

"You must control yourself, brother," she warns, her voice dropping low. "If you are to survive this."

He looks at her, his brow furrowed. "I don't understand..."

"Gygarth sits within you, Daedalus, like a man sits in a chair. I see him in your eyes, staring back at me." Her voice tightens. "He hungers. He *always* hungers. But now that I am free, I will make him starve." She steps closer, her presence looming like a dark shadow over him. "Your complicated human wife is the one who freed me. Not a Fae, not a Mordorin, not you. Her. And because of that, I will not allow her to become meat for the beast, like our mother."

For the first time, I see the cracks in Daed's armor, his walls faltering under the weight of her words.

"If I sense, for even a moment, that you've lost control," Zyphoro continues, her voice sharp, "I will free you from your curse. Permanently. Do you understand me now?"

Daed doesn't flinch. His reply is steady, without fear or resistance, only calm acceptance. "Yes, Zyphoro. I understand."

The village stirs, the cold air biting at our skin as we brace for what's to come. The soft shuffle of feet and hushed whispers fills the morning, no one daring to speak above a whisper. An unsettling tension hangs in the air, pressing down on my chest and making it hard to breathe.

Elders and children are hidden away, their faces pale and eyes wide with fear as they are led into the underground shelter. They're instructed to remain silent, no matter what sounds echo from above, no matter the chaos unfolding outside. It feels cruel, forcing them into silence while the world collapses around them. But it's necessary. The den will protect them, and we will safeguard the den.

As I secure the entrance, I glance at the warriors preparing. Their faces are grim but determined. I spot Arax off to the side, his hands steady as he adjusts Solena's grip on her sword, showing her how to hold it properly, his voice low and instructive.

Zyphoro, perched silently on a tree branch above them, watches with sharp eyes. Her dagger spins in her hand, waiting for the hunt to begin, her focus unshakable.

Then I feel Daed's presence long before I see him, like a cool shadow falling over me, consuming and inescapable. He crosses the distance between us in his leathers, embodying the dark with every movement, every look, every breath. When he reaches me he takes my hand, curling his around it, the runes tattooed on his knuckles pulsing.

"The Blades here are few, but they are loyal to me," he says. "Arax and Zyphoro's skill will be in our favor on the battlefield, and the warriors of the Grove are strong enough to hold the line."

I force a smile, anything to distract me from my racing heart. "You speak as if we could win this."

"We do not need to win," Daed says, his voice the strength I need to keep my focus. "We just cannot let *him* win." He pulls me closer. "I do not want you out there today."

I shake my head. "I will not be herded into the shelter with the children, if that's what you're asking."

"I wouldn't dream of it, wife," he says wryly. "I am simply stating the idea of you in danger fills me with irrationally violent thoughts."

"Good," I say, a grin tugging at the corner of my mouth. "Express those violent thoughts on the Legion."

He grins, his eyes a paler gray than usual. "I have something that belongs to you."

I raise a curious brow, watching as he summons plumes of smoke and tosses them in the air before they fall upon the ground with a splash of wafting mist.

My heart swells when the smoke takes form, and Ashen hisses angrily at Daed, his ears flat against his head, his teeth bared, as if he is still the massive lion he was the last time I saw him, not the little kitten before me now. Ashen swipes at Daed, sharp claws cutting through the air, but Daed doesn't flinch. He only watches with calm annoyance.

Ashen slinks away, his body low to the ground, before he curls himself around my legs. I pick him up, rubbing my nose to his, then he leaps lightly onto my shoulder, his weight familiar and comforting as he settles into my hair.

"Thank you," I say as Ashen's soothing purr rumbles at my ear.

"I fear that creature will replace me," he sighs.

I exhale. "Well, that all depends on how well he can fry an egg."

Daed laughs, and the sound seems to startle him. "I will take you back to Pariseth after this is done."

My chest heaves, my head dropping to look at my feet. I can't think about this now, not with a million terrors screaming for attention. "Daed... please... I..."

"Forgive me," he says. "If not for everything I've done, then just for that. We will talk after the battle, when we both survive, and you decide to let me love you for the rest of your life."

A laugh escapes my chest, and I need it. I need to feel something other than fear right now. "Alright then."

Before either of us can say more, the sound of horns cuts through the air.

The Legion is here.

We move silently through the forest, the leaves brushing against us as we pass. I can hear the whispers of the trees, the low hum of the Souls weaving through the earth beneath my feet. The forest feels alive, almost thrumming with the same tension that coils inside me.

We reach the edge of the Grove, where the dense trees thin out into the open plains, and there, on the horizon, the Legion of Saints wait. My stomach knots as I see them—an army in the hundreds, their gilded armor gleaming. The sun reflects off the polished steel, casting a blinding light that only makes their numbers seem greater.

"We are vulnerable in the open," Daed says as we linger near the entrance to the forest. "If we confine the fight here, they will not be able to overwhelm us."

"But then we risk them reaching the Grove," I protest.

Daed nods his understanding. "Very well. The field it is."

Our meager army of mismatched warriors passes the giant boulders, striding onto the grass with unbroken strides just as a rider breaks away from the Legion's line, his horse snorting and stamping as he approaches us. The rider's red cloak trails behind him like a banner, his face hard and unforgiving. He pulls his horse to a rough halt in front of me, his eyes filled with contempt.

"Turn back now," I demand, my voice steady, though my heart races. "The Grove want no part of your war. Leave, and we'll let you go in peace."

The rider sneers, leaning forward in his saddle, his lips curling in disdain. "The Golden Son has already given you his answer. The negotiations are over. You can no longer claim neutrality."

I swallow hard, anger flaring in my chest. "We have children in this forest."

He chuckles darkly, straightening in his saddle. "Turn over your weapons and bend the knee, then perhaps The Golden Son will show mercy upon the children. But your head, Jewel of the Tenders..." His eyes flash with a cruel smile. "Your head will serve as a warning to any who dare defy the Legion."

Before I can respond, before the fury bubbling in my throat can find words, Daed steps forward, his hand outstretched. A dark, smoky mist swirls around his fingers, and in a single, fluid motion, his sword manifests in his grip—Death Singer, gleaming and hungry for blood.

The rider stiffens, eyes widening as Daed's presence swells, his power rolling off him like a storm ready to break. He stands tall beside me, his cold gaze locked on the man before us.

"You would dare threaten her?" Daed's voice is low, dangerous, the sound of it reverberating through the air. "You come into her land, seek to slaughter her people, and you think you will leave here alive?"

The rider shifts in his saddle, clearly unnerved, but he doesn't back down. "Your Fae tricks don't scare me," he snarls, his hand gripping the hilt of his sword. "We will crush you just as we've crushed all who stood in our way."

"Boring," Zyphoro yawns, emerging from our numbers. "Kill him already, brother."

Daed smiles, the smoke around him thickening, swirling like a living thing as his power surges. The rider's mouth opens, but before he can speak, Daed lifts his sword, hovering the sharp point over the rider's trembling throat.

Then, a new sound emerges from the ranks of the Legion—a steady rhythm of hooves. The soldiers part like a wave as a figure appears from their midst, and the sun catches him in such a way that at first, he is nothing but a blinding light in the distance. My eyes squint against the glare, heart thrumming in my chest as the new rider draws nearer.

The brightness lessens as he approaches, and I make out the details—long, flowing red cloak billowing behind him, shimmering golden armor that seems almost too pristine, marked with a pair of crossed swords, framed by praying hands. But all that pales compared to his golden mask.

The Golden Son tilts his head ever so slightly, his gaze landing on Daedalus first. His blue eyes burning with a quiet fury, cold and calculating.

"Prince Daedalus," he says, his voice like silk stretched over steel. "I was not expecting to see you here."

Daed stiffens beside me, his sword still poised, smoke curling from the blade as his power thrums in the air. "You threaten the sacred home of my wife. Where else would I be?" he bites back, his voice dripping with venom.

"Wife." He looks at me and scoffs, his gaze intrusive, as if he can see my heart beating through my robes. "*Traitor,*" he hisses. "You have already wasted so much of my precious time. Perhaps I should have killed you when I had you all to myself the other day and saved my horse's legs."

Daed's eyes snap to me, his brow furrowed. "You were *alone* with him? When?"

"I tried to negotiate," I say bitterly, my eyes narrowing on The Golden Son. "But he refused."

Daed continues to seethe even after my explanation, and I cannot reason why he would allow such a thing to bother him when nothing else seems to.

The Golden Son's chestnut mare stamps her hooves, growing more irritable with each passing second. "You look upset, Prince Daedalus," he says, and I can hear the smirk on his lips. "Perhaps you worry it is not only your head I will take from you."

"You have lived too long, Golden Son," Daed snarls, his anger building like a storm rolling over the sea. "You should have died in that pathetic hovel of piss and shit you called a village with the rest of your family when we burnt it to the ground."

I freeze, words lost to me as if I can no longer recall the way my mouth should move or how they sound on my tongue. The only ones who do not look in shock are the Fae, and I realize this is no secret to them.

But rather than retaliate with rage, The Golden Son only laughs.

"It is you who has lived too long. *All of you.* The time of the Fae is finished. Humans will take back the Sundered Kingdoms and our lands will be washed clean of your filth."

Smoke swirls around Daed, wrapping him in a cloak of darkness. As it dissipates, he stands clad in sleek black armor, a shrouded helm concealing his face. The scaled plates glisten with a menacing sheen, while razor-sharp spikes line every hard edge of the steel. He grips Death Singer with two hands and raises it over his shoulder.

"Then let us begin."

And with those words, the battle erupts.

The Golden Son's horse rears into the air, then stamps its feet as it turns to rejoin the ranks. But the first rider does not escape so easily. As he turns, Daed releases a smoke tendril that lashes out and grabs the rider around his waist, dragging him from his horse and tossing him on the ground. The rider scrambles for his sword, but it is a wasted effort. Daed plunges his sword through the rider's chest and as he sputters blood from his mouth, smoke envelops him, dragging him to the void.

The Legion surges forward like a wave, the ground trembling beneath the weight of their numbers, their swords raised, their shields gleaming in the dawn light. The air comes alive with the sound of clashing metal and the roars of men with more fight in them than sense.

I stand at the edge, watching as Daed rushes into the fray, his sword slicing through the first line of enemies like a reaper harvesting souls. Smoke curls from his blade, wrapping around the Legion soldiers, choking their screams from their lungs. Zyphoro follows close behind, her movements fluid and precise as her daggers flash. She conjures tendrils of smoke from the void, weaving them into deadly weapons that strike down men before they can reach her.

Arax is a wrecking ball of destruction, his sword heavy and relentless as he cuts through the Legion's ranks. There's no grace in his movements—just raw, brutal force. He swings his blade with such power that it shatters shields, crushes armor, and leaves bodies crumpled in his wake. He roars with each swing, the sound primal, full of rage and grief that fuels him.

But the Legion is vast. Endless. For every man we cut down, three more take his place. They press in closer, relentless, and the battlefield becomes a sea of chaos—blood, steel, and screams.

Daed and Zyphoro are shadows in the mayhem, void-walking in and out of the battle like death itself. One moment, Daed is beside me, his sword cleaving through the neck of a Legion soldier, smoke curling from his blade as it absorbs the man's last breath. The next, he's gone, disappearing into the void, only to reappear behind a line of archers, slaughtering them before they can even register his presence. Zyphoro moves like a wraith, her daggers dripping with blood as she carves through the Legion's ranks. Her face is a mask of calm, her eyes alight with the same storm as Daed. Every flick of her wrist sends another man to the ground, gasping for his last breath.

The warriors of the Grove, brave and determined, fall faster than the Sisters and I can heal them. I press my hands to a man's chest, feeling the rush of warmth as the Souls of the Forest flow through me, knitting his torn flesh back together. But even as he gasps back to life, more fall behind him, their blood soaking into the earth.

Overhead, the twenty Blades from Baev'kalath take to the skies, their wings stretching wide as they rain down strikes from above. But they, too, are falling. Legion archers aim their arrows high, and one by one, the Blades are shot from the sky, their bodies crumpling to the ground in twisted heaps.

I glimpse Arax as he collects Legion lives, his sword swinging in wide arcs, cutting down anyone in his path, his battle cry a guttural roar that sends chills down my spine. He fights with the rage of a man with nothing left to lose and yet, even he is beginning to tire. I see him stagger, just for a moment, as another wave of Legion soldiers presses forward, and my stomach lurches with fear.

Zyphoro vanishes into the void once again, appearing in the midst of a group of Legion commanders, her smoke tendrils wrapping around their throats before she drags them to their knees. But even she cannot stop the endless tide of men. Her lips curl into a snarl as she slashes at them, her face splattered with blood, and still they keep coming.

I rush to another fallen warrior, my hands trembling as I press them to his wound, desperate to keep him alive. But I'm too late. His eyes, once filled with the spark of life, now stare blankly at the sky. I choke back a sob, pulling away as another soldier falls beside me, blood pouring from his mouth. I try to heal him, but the sheer number of the dying and wounded is too much.

"They're too many," I gasp, my voice cracking.

Suddenly an explosion of arrows rains down from above, and I scream as one grazes my arm, the sharp pain tearing through me. The world spins, but I fight to stay standing, to keep moving. Blood drips from the wound, warm and thick, but something else stirs inside me. I grip my rune necklace, feeling it pulse beneath my fingertips.

It's as if the very earth hums in response to my pain. My veins throb with new life, a rush of energy coursing through me, stronger than before. I can almost taste it, the bitterness of the arrow's cut transforming into power. A power I can use.

I look out onto the battlefield, the chaos consuming everything around me.

So much cruelty. So much death.

A warrior of the Grove stumbles, barely able to hold his sword, his face pale, his movements labored. A Legion soldier raises his blade to strike him down, but before I can think, before I can even cry out, the energy inside me snaps free.

A bolt of green lightning surges from my hand. It hits the soldier square in the chest, sending him flying back into a mass of his brethren, their armor clattering in the wake of the blast.

I press my hand to the wound on my arm, the blood flowing faster now, and I feel it—the power building, gathering, waiting for release. With a growl, I use it, my body trembling as another arrow strikes me in the leg. Instead of buckling, I channel it, using the searing pain as fuel. My vision blurs, but through it, I see everything with a clarity that terrifies me. The earth hums beneath me, alive, begging to be unleashed.

My veins pulse, the green light threading through my skin, snaking up my arms, my legs, my throat. I feel my hair lift, weightless in the air, carried by the surge of power that grows with every heartbeat. I stumble for a moment, my body fighting to contain the raw energy surging through me, but I give in, letting it take over.

I drive my fingers into the soil. The earth responds in kind, trembling beneath me as the green veins in my skin expand, my eyes glowing brighter, burning with the same furious energy. My breath comes in ragged bursts, each one carrying more power, more fury. I can feel the forest answering my call.

An army of creatures—wild, frenzied, their eyes glowing with the same green fire that burns within me. Wolves, bears, boars, stags. They charge forward, their roars deafening, and the Legion falters for a moment, confusion and fear rippling through their ranks.

The animals descend upon them, tearing through armor, trampling soldiers beneath their paws and hooves. The chaos intensifies, the battlefield erupting into a storm of violence as the creatures of the forest unleash their fury. I push my hands deeper into the soil, finding more beneath the surface, sleeping giants waiting to wake. With a loud crack, the boulders at the mouth of the forest transform, the stone creaking and groaning until they become massive rock golems dotted with moss, and when they join the battle, picking up men and crushing them to a bloody pulp, the Legion start to flee.

I scream again, but this time it's not from pain. It's from the sheer power that rips through me. My hands press deeper into the ground, and the earth obeys my command. Vines twist from beneath the soil, snaring Legion soldiers by their legs, dragging them down, crushing them in their grip. I can hear their screams, but the sound barely registers over the wild beating of my heart.

The power is consuming me, threading deeper into my skin, into my bones. My entire body pulses with the green glow, my vision blurring as the energy inside me grows, relentless and uncontrollable. I should be afraid, but I'm not.

I bury my hands deeper into the earth, the power overtaking every rational thought. The forest is alive with the spirits of the Souls, and I'm their vessel, their weapon.

The creatures fight with a madness I've never seen, tearing through the Legion's forces as if driven by the same unrelenting force that consumes me. Blood splatters the ground, the air thick with the scent of iron and death. And still, I push the power further, deeper, my hands trembling as I channel it all.

But the more I give, the more it takes.

A sharp pain lances through me, but I don't stop. I can't. The forest, the Grove, all of it—depends on *me*.

The green light pulses around me, wrapping me in its grip, pulling me deeper into the earth's fury. But even as I fight, even as I hold the Legion at bay with everything I have, I know I'm losing myself. The pain I've drawn on burns through me, a fire I can't control.

I am the forest. I am the fury of the earth. And I will not stop until the Legion is buried beneath my feet.

The Grove has the advantage, the tide of the battle shifting as Legion soldiers falter. They retreat, stumbling back from the onslaught of the forest's creatures and the relentless force of the Fae and Grove warriors. The air is thick with the smell of blood, sweat, and dirt. Victory feels so close, I can taste it—within reach, a breath away.

But then, like a beam of righteous light tearing through the darkness, he appears.

The Golden Son charges toward me, a blur of gilded fury. Before I can react, his boot slams into my face, sending me sprawling backward. The sudden shock breaks my concentration, the power I've been channeling from the earth flickering and sputtering as I hit the ground hard. My vision blurs, stars exploding in the corners of my eyes as pain radiates from my skull.

He dismounts and looms over me, his golden mask glinting in the sunlight, the brilliance of his eyes cold and piercing beneath it. I try to reach for my power again, but I'm too weak, my connection to the earth severed by his brutal strike.

"You fight well, for a traitor," he sneers, his voice low and venomous, dripping with contempt. His blade gleams as he presses it against my throat, the sharp edge biting into my skin just enough to draw blood. "But this is where your story ends, Amara of the Grove."

My limbs feel heavy, useless as I struggle to lift my hands, to fight him off, but my strength is draining fast. I grit my teeth, the fury burning in my chest, but I can't move, pinned beneath the weight of his blade, the taste of dirt and blood on my tongue.

Just as I'm about to give in to the darkness creeping in at the edges of my vision, a shout pierces through the haze.

"Get away from her!" Arax's voice thunders, and in the blink of an eye, he is there.

Arax's sword swings in a vicious arc, forcing the Golden Son back, his blade barely deflecting the strike in time. They clash with a resounding crash, steel meeting steel as sparks fly. I scramble to my feet, gasping for air as I watch them, my heart pounding in my ears.

Arax fights like a demon, his every strike powerful and precise, his body a blur of motion. But the Golden Son is just as fast, just as ruthless, and they collide with such intensity that it shakes the very ground beneath them.

For a moment, I think Arax might win, his sword cutting through the air with deadly precision. But then, The Golden Son feints, a quick flick of his wrist, and before I can even shout a warning, his blade finds its mark.

"No!" My scream tears from my throat as Arax stumbles, his sword slipping from his grasp as he falls to the ground, blood pouring from the wound in his abdomen. The sight of him crumpling, his strength fading, rips through me like a jagged knife.

The Golden Son stands over him, victorious, his blade slick with Arax's blood. He turns his gaze to me and stalks forward, but my eyes are mesmerized by the sight of my friend's life force staining the grass, turning the flowers red.

"Such a waste," he mutters as he looms above me and raises his sword over his head.

Then suddenly Ashen leaps from within my tangled hair, transforming from a little bundle of paws to the giant, feral lion I know he can be. Tentacles shoot out from his back, ensnaring The Golden Son and tackling him to the ground.

The Golden Son calls out, slashing and stabbing at Ashen, but his blade simply glides through the smoky form of my protector.

I claw my way across the field, falling to my knees beside Arax, my hands trembling as I cradle his head in my lap. His face is pale, blood soaking through his tunic as his breathing comes in ragged gasps. "Arax, stay with me," I whisper, my voice shaking. "Stay with me."

His eyes flutter open, just barely, and he looks at me, the pain etched in every line of his face. "I'm sorry... Princess..."

"No," I choke, tears spilling down my cheeks. "I can save you."

I press my hand to his wound, and the rune around my neck gives a faint glow.

He reaches up, his bloodstained fingers brushing against my cheek, his grip weak but steady. "Amara. Stop. I'm ready."

"No," I weep, "I will not lose you."

Arax's hand trails down my cheek, his knuckle wiping a tear from my jawline, and I'm so focused on his wound, I don't notice when he grips my rune in his hand and it vanishes in a wisp of black smoke.

My eyes widen. "No! No! What have you done?" I grasp around my neck, but it's gone. "Where is it! I can't save you without the rune. Where is it!"

I plunge a hand into the soil, praying that the Souls will grant me the power to save him. But I have drained the earth completely. There is nothing left. I panic and suddenly I'm shaking Arax, my tears flowing without limits, my voice screaming into the air, unbridled and unchained and bursting with pain.

"Arax! Bring it back! Please bring it back!" Without my power, all I can do is push hard against his wound, trying to stop the blood. But there's too much. There's just too much. "You can't leave me, not like this. You promised."

He smiles as blood trickles from his mouth, his gray hair soaked through, the glint of his eyes fading. "Estra," he murmurs.

My heart shatters as his smile fades, his eyes distant, focused on something beyond me, on someone I cannot see, and when his eyes close, the blood-soaked red ribbon slips from his sleeve as his hand falls limp on the grass.

"No... no, please." My voice breaks, sobs wracking my body as I hold him close. "Don't leave me."

The battle rages on around us, the screams of dying men and the clash of steel a distant hum in my ears. The Golden Son frees himself from Ashen's jaws and mounts his horse, and I glimpse his golden armor retreating into the distance. But here, in this moment, everything else fades away. The Grove, the Legion, the Fae.

Arax of House Mordorin, Reaper of the Ebon Flight, the man who stood by my side, who protected me when I couldn't protect myself—who I brought back to life twice—now lies dead in my arms.

In the place he chose. With the name of the daughter he lost on his lips.

CHAPTER 36

The Grove is victorious.

The Legion of Saints has retreated, their ranks shattered and scattered to the wind, but as I recall the carnage, the victory feels hollow. Bodies strewn across the battlefield—warriors who fought to protect this sacred place, who gave their lives for something far greater than themselves. But they are gone now, their blood soaking into the earth they swore to defend.

Morning sun streams through the window, and I stare blankly at the shimmering slants of golden light from my bed. My face is somehow numb yet aching at the same time, my left eye swollen and sealed shut, the last thing it saw being The Golden Son's boot. The rest of my face is in no better shape, marred by cuts and bruises, leaving my skin more blue and purple than brown.

Solena sits beside the bed, cleaning the arrow wound in my thigh and applying a fresh bandage. The other arrow wound in my arm healed when I used Fae magic fighting the Legion. These last scrapes came after, but even if I could heal them, I would not want to. It would be an insult to the memory of those who died if I used magic to cure my inconvenient scratches when I still draw breath.

"An arrow wound is very impressive," Solena says as she finishes up. "And it will leave a scar that you can show off at taverns."

I know what she's doing—trying to joke, keeping her voice light, which is unlike her. She's attempting to help me forget about Arax. But how does one forget a heart that is breaking? How do you reconcile the realization that you will never see someone again, never hear their voice, never feel their touch? How do you return to normalcy when the world is darker than it was the day before because someone you cared for is gone?

No. Not gone. Taken, with no regard for the agony their absence leaves behind?

The Golden Son took Arax from me, and today I am a hollow shell.

There's a knock at the door, and it creaks open. Keeper Enaria peers in, hesitant to enter.

"Jewel, the returning starts soon. But if you are too unwell…"

"She is weak and exhausted," Solena replies bluntly.

I shake my head and push up on my elbows. "No. I'm fine. I will come."

Solena looks at me, concern etched on her face. "Amara, you can barely walk."

I fix my one functioning eye on her. "They are Tenders of the Grove," I say, my voice ragged. "I must be there to send them home."

She bows her head, lightly nodding, and I understand she doesn't know our ways. But I *will* be at the returning, even if I have to crawl there. I drag myself out of bed, stumbling when I finally get to my feet, unaware of just how damaged my leg is. I grit my teeth, fighting through the pain.

Solena frowns as she watches me stagger, banging into the walls as I try to pull on my green robe. She rises and snatches the garment from my hands, tugging it over my arms and shoulders.

"Thank you," I mutter past my swollen lip.

Next, she tames my hair, stiff and dry from dirt and smoke, twisting it into a braid that trails down my back.

"There," she says. "Now you don't look as horrifying."

I nod my thanks and take a step toward the door where Enaria waits, only to feel my knee buckle beneath me. Solena's groan is immediate, and before I can protest, she throws my arm over her shoulder and hooks me around the waist to prop me up.

"I can do it myself," I grumble.

"Be quiet, Amara," she snaps, startling me. "I'm going to help you, and that's the last I want to hear about it."

We fall silent for a moment, and I grip her shoulder, dropping my weight slightly to let her support me. My thigh appreciates the reprieve. But just before we take our first step toward the door, Solena mutters softly, "I miss him too."

We leave the room, and it's more difficult traversing the rope bridges and stairs with an aching leg than I expected. Solena farewells me at the bottom step. I'm sure she would come if I asked, but I don't. I would rather spare her from the pain.

"I will see you later," she says, and I nod in silent reply.

A stag waits to carry me from the village to the clearing, saving me from dragging my miserable, sore body through the forest.

A procession of survivors stands ready to join me—warriors who fought bravely, along with the elders and children who hid in the sanctuary. As I look down at them, I know each soul missing from our family, their faces etched into my memory forever. We are even fewer now, and I add that pain to the ever-mounting despair in my chest.

The vine wall opens before us, and we pass through. The hums begin—low and melodious—as we, the Tenders, with our heads bowed, move slowly through the brush, every cracking twig and rustling leaf echoing through the trees. As we approach the clearing, my heart tightens when I see them lying in the long grass, their bodies draped in moss and bright purple flowers. Rows upon rows of Tenders, their eyes closed forever.

My Sisters wait for me, their faces obscured behind thin green veils. The stag bows, allowing me to dismount and when I touch the ground, Lira places a veil over my face. I take a step and wince; her gaze flickers down to my injured leg.

"You need to be healed," she says, concern lacing her voice.

I shake my head. "I need nothing. Please, I want to begin."

We Sisters take our places before the still bodies, the soft breeze fluttering through their hair, sunlight dappling their pale skin, which was warm and brown just yesterday. We join hands, our power surging through us. The Souls of the Forest hum in the trees, their presence a faint comfort against the suffocating silence, but it isn't enough to ease the ache threatening to consume me.

The Tenders drop to their knees, their gentle sobs lost to the wind as a green light pulses beneath the fallen. We Sisters chant, our words barely audible—echoing loss, love, hope, and the return of our people to the earth. The earth shudders in reply. Slowly their bodies sink into the soil, welcomed home as we continue our song. After a time, the bodies vanish beneath the ground and the glow subsides, the veins of light dimming to nothing until the earth is still and the soft grass sways silently in the breeze.

One by one, the villagers rise and somberly return to the Grove. We Sisters finish our song and embrace, sharing our pain. Even so, the ache inside me does not subside.

"Your rune," Mirael says. "Where is it?"

"Lost," I murmur, my veil brushing against my lips as I speak.

"We will have to make you a new one," Saren replies. "It will take time. We need to find the right tree and have it blessed by the Souls."

I nod, understanding the process of creating our runes of power.

"But you are home now," Lira adds, her hand gently gripping my shoulder. "So it doesn't matter how long it takes."

I can barely form a smile, barely make a sound. My mind drifts elsewhere, scattered and unfocused, knowing and dreading that while this is painful, there are worse things yet to come.

"You should rest, Amara," Mirael says gently. "The battle has taken much from you."

"There is no time for rest," I mutter, pulling my voice from the depths of my sorrow. "The Golden Son cannot go unpunished. He must pay for what he has done."

I can sense my Sisters' disapproval.

"No, Amara. We are done with this war. He tried to crush the Grove and failed. We have won," Lira insists.

"No, we have not," I protest, recalling Daed's words. "We have only kept *him* from winning. That does not mean he won't return, and now we are even weaker than before."

"Listen to Mirael," Saren interjects, her tone low and firm. "Go and rest. When you're better, we can discuss this further."

I feel their gazes piercing through their veils, their judgment hanging heavy in the air around me. I do not want to rest. I do not want to discuss. All we Tenders do is sit, talk, and wait while terrible people commit terrible crimes against the innocent, and no one takes action to stop them.

Our people are dead. Arax is dead. Someone must suffer as they suffered.

Pain for pain. More meat for the beast.

"Amara," Mirael says, her voice sounding distant, as if a million miles separate us. "Are you alright?"

My head snaps up, the wind catching my veil. "I'm fine," I reply blankly. I cannot share my thoughts with them. They could never understand. "You're right. I will go and rest."

Without uttering a word, the stag approaches, bowing so I can grip its soft ruff and pull myself onto its back. It leads me away, but I can still feel the weight of my Sisters' gaze on me. For the first time in my life, I feel the links of our bond straining. We have always agreed on what is best for the Grove, but not today.

Not about this. I wish I could articulate it, explain it to them in a way they might accept, but those words elude me.

When we arrive at the village, I pause long enough to remove my veil and glance at the vine wall before whispering my thoughts to the stag who carries on through the forest. We pass by the stream and the place where the roots are large enough to walk under until the trees thin and the field beyond the borders of the forest comes into view. The massive boulders still flank either side of the forest entrance. Though they are slightly askew now, the golems not returning to exactly the same spot when they sat down.

The wind howls softly, still carrying the smell of blood and smoke, and I wrap my arms around myself, shivering despite the lingering warmth of the fading sun. The sleeve of my robe catches in the breeze, revealing the red ribbon tied around my wrist. I stare at it for a moment, memories of Arax flooding my mind, so vivid I can reach and touch him. But a bird calling out as it soars through the air snaps me back to my hard reality. Arax isn't here anymore. I pull my sleeve down, swallowing the lump in my throat.

In the center of the field, I catch sight of Daed and Zyphoro. They have constructed a wooden pyre and the few Blades that remain swoop in from the sky, their arms bundled with branches which they stack beneath the structure.

Daed turns as if he can sense me. He steps into the void then suddenly appears beside me, his arms outstretched to lift me down from the stag. His dirty, calloused hands grip my waist and I slip down into his embrace. He holds me to him, long and silent with a firm tenderness that helps calm the anger and sadness raging within me.

When we part, I find his face marred by battle, but he is far more concerned with my face.

"Wife," he mutters, his voice a low growl, his hand hovering above my swollen eye. "I will kill him for this."

"It doesn't hurt," I say as his hand cups the side of my neck, his thumb tracing the line of my jaw.

"It hurts *me*," he replies. "But then again, you are stronger than I ever could be."

My gaze drifts past him to the pyre, where a row of silhouettes shrouded in black Mordorin cloaks lie still. Though I know what lies beneath those cloaks, I can't bring myself to voice the truth. To do so would shatter me completely. I turn my attention to the horizon, where the sun sinks low, the sky awash in hues of red and orange, as if the world itself is bleeding alongside my heart.

"What moon is it tonight?" I ask.

Daed exhales, his face hard, his lips a straight line. "The Mourner's Eye."

342

A sad laugh escapes me, and I know how strange and inappropriate the sound is, but I can't help it. "Really?" I ask in disbelief. "So the Warrior's Eye is for battle. The Lover's Eye is for passion. The Reflective Eye for learning. Does The Mourner's Eye mean death?"

Daed shakes his head, his expression steadfast. Like Solena, he wears a mask of lightness, a façade meant to comfort me, but it doesn't help. Nothing helps.

"It doesn't mean death. But it does mean it's a good day to die."

Tears well in my eyes, and his stoicism ignites my fury. "How can you say that? How can there ever be a good day to die?" My heart pounds painfully against my chest, stealing my breath and tightening my throat. "Arax should be here with us, not alone in the darkness." I claw at my neck, desperate for release. "Why are you just standing there, staring at me? Do you feel nothing?"

"Amara," Daed says softly, his brow furrowing as he reaches for me.

"No," I snap, yanking my hands from his grasp. "You Fae are horrid, heartless creatures. You ruin lives and shatter hearts without a second thought, dancing and drinking while the world crumbles around you." My voice quivers as I watch him remain silent. "Will you not say anything?"

Daed's broad shoulders rise and fall with a heavy exhale. "Hold me, wife. I am cold."

I look at him for a moment, calm and collected despite my assault. When my anger surges, it clouds my vision, building until it erupts in a spray of words I don't mean. But Daed doesn't deny me that release; he accepts it as part of who I am, and he loves me still. I step closer, looping my arms around his neck while he encircles my waist, his fingers tracing gentle lines on my back.

We stand like that for a while in the field while Zyphoro and the Blades complete the pyre and the moon rises behind us. When Valorne is blanketed in darkness, with only a scattering of stars and a half moon to light the way, Daed strikes a flint and lights a torch before pacing toward the pyre. He lowers it to the branches, and the flame catches the dry kindling, its first flickers barely visible against the encroaching darkness. Slowly, the flame catches hold, a timid glow that begins to dance. With a soft crackle, it spreads, consuming the kindling with greedy tongues of fire that leap higher and flicker orange and gold.

The heat radiates outward, casting shadows that flicker across Daed's face as he takes a step back. The flames grow bolder as they consume the offerings laid atop the pyre, transforming the wood into a radiant blaze. As the fire roars to life, it sends up spirals of smoke that twist into the night sky, soaring so high it's as if the moon is breathing it in.

I recall Arax's words, how he hoped they had burned Estra at night, and this is what he meant. Just as the Tenders are returned to the earth, the Mordorin are heralded home in smoke and moonlight. A weight lifts from my chest, allowing me to breathe more easily. This is what Arax wanted—to die here, in this field, and to be consumed by the flames beneath the Pale Eye. Free from his pain and reunited with Estra. I glance over at Daed, and our eyes connect through the flickering fire. In that moment, I finally understand.

For Arax, it *was* a good day to die.

Zyphoro appears at my side, arms crossed over her chest. "You look dreadful," she remarks, amusement lacing her tone even while Arax burns only a few feet away. But I wouldn't expect anything less from her.

I grimace, doing my best to manage a frown with half my face swollen. "I'm aware."

"But you fought like a beast," she adds, her grin widening. "Couldn't be prouder, and it's good for the little one to experience battle early on."

I gulp, glancing around to ensure no one can hear her. "Be quiet," I hiss. "I haven't told anyone yet."

"I know," Zyphoro replies, delighting in my frustration. "And I wouldn't dare ruin this beautiful family moment. But do try to break the news to him before the little demon pops out. Daedalus hates surprises."

My eyes widen. "...Demon?"

Zyphoro throws her head back and laughs, placing a hand on her chest. "Did I say demon? I meant baby."

"Well, you said demon," I reply through clenched teeth.

She shrugs nonchalantly. "Well, when the little bundle of joy is gnawing on your nipple as though it were dried beef, I'm sure you'll feel the same way."

With that, Zyphoro slithers away into the night. Despite the new dread twisting in my stomach, she has managed to distract me, if only for a moment.

I stand in silence, watching as the flames ferociously engulf the pyre. With a loud crack, the structure begins to collapse, the logs surrendering to the fire's hunger. Red hot sparks spiral into the air, swirling like lost souls escaping into the night and as time stretches and the moon climbs higher as the flames begin to dwindle. The once brilliant fire fades to glowing embers and what's left of the pyre collapses in on itself.

He's gone. Nothing but ash and smoke. I couldn't save him.

I am the forest, I remind myself. I am the fury of the earth. But without that piece of wood on a leather string, I am practically useless. As my Sisters said, we will have to create a new rune. Find the right tree, seek the blessing of the Souls. My first rune wasn't finished for months. What do I do until then? How do I make sure I never lose someone again?

Daed returns to my side, intertwining his fingers with mine before lifting my hand to lay a soft kiss on my knuckles. As he does, I can't help but notice the intricate black runes etched into his skin. The power to void walk. The power to soar through the skies. The power to unleash fury. All at his command, a silent testament to his strength.

My eyes widen, caught between the brilliance and absurdity of my thoughts. "I want my rune of healing on my skin," I declare boldly, though the look in his eyes leans toward the absurd.

"No," he replies bluntly, yet he doesn't release my hand; instead, he grips it tighter.

"Why not?"

"Because you are human. Humans do not wear runes on their skin."

"But I am the wife of a Fae. Doesn't that make a difference?"

"Maybe to some, but not to me," he growls, his voice low and unyielding.

"Arax took my rune. It vanished into smoke. I don't even know where it is."

"Consider it lost forever," Daed replies with finality. "You can craft another."

"Husband!" I say firmly, forcing him to meet my eyes, which he does reluctantly. "I never understood the consequences of losing my rune until it was gone, and I don't want to feel that way ever again. Please."

Daed studies me, his eyes narrowing, his lip twitching in contemplation. "Even if I said yes, we don't have a runeweaver."

Determination flaring within me, I loop the red ribbon around my finger, its presence strengthening my resolve.

"Yes, we do."

"I won't do it," Solena states firmly, pacing the room.

"I need this, Solena," I plead. "It will take me months to craft a new rune. I cannot afford to be without power for that long, not with everything feeling so ominous."

"It's forbidden," she protests.

"And who will dispense justice? Lanneth? She wants us dead for reasons beyond this," I argue.

Solena turns to Daed, who stands silently in the corner, his back against the wall, his chin pinched between his fingers. "Have you told her this is madness?" she asks.

Daed shrugs, his features obscured by shadows. "Of course I have. But you can imagine how well that went."

Solena groans. "No. I will not do this. Not only is it against every rule of the runeweavers, but I'm not skilled enough. My hand could slip, or I could mix the ink wrong."

I square my shoulders and lift my chin. "As Princess of the Mordorin, I command you."

Solena crosses her arms over her chest, raising an eyebrow. Even Daed lets out a quiet chuckle at how foolish I sound. I exhale, abandoning the idea of forcing Solena to do it, as if I ever could. But my sadness creeps deeper under my skin. "I could have saved him if I had my rune."

"Did you think for a minute that he didn't *want* to be saved?" Solena counters. "That his death wasn't *your* fault?"

"No. It wasn't," I retort, my jaw clenching. "It was The Golden Son's fault, and he will never take from me again." I pull back my sleeve, exposing my wrist looped with the red ribbon. "Now, please, Solena. Do it."

Solena takes a deep breath, her foot tapping anxiously on the floor. She glances at Daed as if seeking permission, and I let out a relieved sigh when he nods reluctantly.

"Very well," Solena says, her voice weary. "I will need a needle and some blood." She looks back at Daed. "Yours as well. If this is to work on a human, I need blood from a High Fae, and fortunately, we have a prince." Her eyes scan my wrist. "And it won't be going there. As you said, you're a Princess of the Mordorin, so your rune should be placed somewhere that signifies your status."

I narrow my eyes at her, curiosity piqued as I lower my sleeve. "Where?"

Solena grins wryly. "Have I ever mentioned you have a lovely neck?"

Under the amber glow of lantern light, Solena prepares. On the table beside her is a small bowl of thick, dark liquid. My blood and Daed's blood mixed with coal. She sits behind me on the bed, brushing my hair aside as she prepares herself.

"Take a deep breath," she says.

The first prick pierces through me, sharp and bracing, and I gasp, but I do not pull away. Instead, I focus on the lantern, on the flames dancing within, and I remind myself of my purpose. I will not be weak. I will embrace this pain as a testament to my strength.

Daed's hand rests on mine, steady and reassuring, grounding me as Solena works, the pain ebbing and flowing, each line a reminder of my commitment to myself and to those I love. The rune takes shape. Hard, thick lines that feel alive beneath my skin. With every stroke, I feel something surging within me, something even stronger than my necklace.

Time blurs, the world outside fading away, leaving only the rhythmic punctuations of the needle and the warmth of Daed's presence beside me. I breathe through the pain, letting it fuel my resolve.

Finally Solena steps back, her fingers black with the ink. "It's done," she announces, but there is no pride or joy in her voice, and for a brief second I wonder if I should have asked this favor of her.

But when my fingers nervously reach for my neck, hovering just above the ink speckled with blood, I feel the pulse of life and the gift of the Fae that has flowed through us for generations. Now it marks my skin, and no one will take from me ever again.

I am the forest. I am the fury of the earth.

CHAPTER 37

The next days are the hardest of my life. No one, not even Daed, can offer me comfort. I feel lost. Adrift. The anger that burns white hot in the pit of my stomach won't give me a moment's respite.

Though I know their worries differ from mine, my Fae companions are just as restless. The Grove may be my home, but it is not theirs. It is too quiet. Too peaceful. They take no joy in listening to the forest or digging in the soil. They are beings of passion, fire, and smoke, and this place drains them just as Baev'kalath drained me.

The Fae cannot stay here. Daed cannot stay here. The Grove will wither them to nothing.

Daed has slept by my side every night, but I have not felt the heat of him inside me since the night before the battle, even though I know he longs for me. I can feel it in his touch and see it in the way his eyes roam over every curve of my body with silent need. But my heart still aches for my people, for Arax, and my body craves nothing. Not food. Not sleep. Not Daed.

Then there is the question that lingers on his lips. I can sense it, even if he doesn't speak it.

Have you decided?

I have not. Do I love him? Yes, despite myself, despite being a person of sense and reason, I love him with a fierceness that could see me undone. But there cannot be love without trust. Surely that must be true, and where once I would have defended my dark prince fiercely, now I wonder if the man I lie next to would slit my throat in the night if Gygarth so willed it.

So no, I have not decided. To do so, I must choose what I value more: my life or my love.

I've struggled to leave my bed, burdened not just by the physical wounds but by the deeper scars that keep my sadness lingering. Yet this morning, I sit up as sunlight streams through the window, filling the room with warmth while the soft murmur of the village rises in the air.

Daedalus and Zyphoro spend most of their time in the forest, forbidden to hunt the animals, so instead, they chase each other through the trees. It's a dangerous game of hide and seek that often ends with one of them needing healing from my Sisters. As of now, I believe the score is tied.

The sun blinds me as I open the door to seek them out, and I raise my hand to shield my eyes from its brightness. The birds sing sweetly in the air, and the distant sound of the waterfall creates a perfect harmony I will never tire of. But I find myself missing a different melody. The sound of rain on stone and thunder rolling over the ocean.

I grip the rope bridge as I cross, limping awkwardly down the stairs until I reach the forest floor. My name is on everyone's lips, accompanied by bright smiles and well wishes. I smile back, waving and ensuring I greet each of them by name, letting them know how much I respect and care for each soul.

But inside, I feel hollow. There's an emptiness within me that no amount of love or adoration can fill. Even I don't know what could ease that ache. *All of my aches.*

I pass the vine wall and wander deeper into the forest, the soil beneath my feet and the sun warming my skin, slowly untangling the knots in my stomach. But that fleeting moment of peace shatters when a plume of smoke erupts before me, and Ashen leaps from the void. He roars, landing on me with a thud, his massive front paws pinning my shoulders hard against the ground. The impact knocks the wind out of me, leaving me gasping for air.

It wouldn't hurt so much if he were still in his kitten form, but instead, he's a massive lion again with tentacles flailing from his back. He snarls inches from my face, hot breath washing over me, and I'm shocked to discover that smoke cats drool.

"Ashen!" I growl, wiping the thick, dark mucus from my eyes. "What are you doing?"

His roar cuts off abruptly as his head cocks back, his wild, full mane framing his startled face. He whimpers, immediately withdrawing and backpedaling a couple of steps before sitting on his hind legs, looking thoroughly chastened.

Pushing myself up on my elbows, I flick the saliva into the brush and meet his bright white eyes with an irritated glare. "Why are you so glum? I'm the one who got mauled and slobbered on!"

Suddenly, two more pops punctuate the air, and Daed and Zyphoro land almost silently beside me.

"Amara," Daed says, concern etched across his face as he crouches down. "What happened?"

"What happened?" I grumble, lazily pointing in Ashen's direction, who continues to whimper, his eyes drooping and a trembling pout forming on his face. "He just appeared out of nowhere and tackled me to the ground!"

Zyphoro and Daed exchange knowing looks, both struggling to stifle their laughter.

"Apologies, Amara," Zyphoro says, failing to hide her grin. "Daed and I were tiring of hunting each other, so we invited the kitty to join. He must have mistaken you for one of us."

Ashen shrinks to his kitten form, his tentacles retreating into his fur. Daed helps me to my feet, a grin still lingering on his face as he dusts me off.

"I suppose that means he loses," Daed says, glancing at me with a teasing smirk. "Isn't that right, sister?"

Zyphoro nods playfully. "Only seems fair, brother. That leaves you and me tied at twenty-five while the fluffball languishes at zero."

Ashen arches his back and hisses, grumpily padding away.

"Twenty-five? How many times have you played?" I ask, raising an eyebrow.

Daed exhales, tilting his head in thought. "In truth, I've lost count. But that doesn't matter. It's good to see you up. How are you feeling? Do you need anything?" He brushes his fingers against my cheek, now only mildly swollen, and I place my hand over his, smiling at the warmth of his touch.

Zyphoro rolls her eyes. "I'm going to find some wine."

I furrow my brow. "It's the morning."

"And yet here we are," Zyphoro sighs, stretching her arms toward the sky as she backpedals away from us.

Daed pulls me close by the waist, his hips pressing against mine, and I can already sense the hunger radiating from him. "Do not mind her."

"She hates it here," I mutter. "She grows wearier each day."

"It doesn't matter how she feels. If she doesn't like it, she is welcome to leave. She is not a prisoner here."

"What about you?" I ask bluntly, my expression turning serious.

He hesitates for a moment. "What about me?"

"Are you a prisoner here?"

"No."

"But yet you stay."

"Yes, because you are here, so there is nowhere else I want to be."

His answer comes so quickly that it's hard to doubt him. Yet I must confront the truth he's evading.

"We cannot stay in the Grove, Daedalus."

He tilts his head, studying me with a furrowed brow. "And why is that, wife?"

"You and Zyphoro don't belong here. You are beings of ash and smoke. Those things do not exist in this place."

"I belong where you belong," he replies, leaning in to brush his nose against mine. A familiar shiver travels down my spine, one I thought had been lost.

"There is nothing for you here," I murmur as his mouth trails along my jaw toward my ear. "Nothing you want."

His lips graze my earlobe, and soon I feel the heat of his tongue tracing the pulsing vein in my neck.

"I want what you want," he whispers, his hand inching down my thigh, sweeping over the warmth between my legs.

"No, you don't," I whimper, my back arching as his hand explores, finding the opening of my robe.

He kisses my neck hard, his lips stinging where they meet the raw, healing skin of my rune tattoo.

I hiss, caught between pain and pleasure as his canines scrape against my sensitive flesh.

"I do," he growls into my skin, his fingers finding their way to my core. "Name it and I will make it yours."

I don't know what I want. Or at least I can't remember. With his hands on me, needing me, desiring me, all I can think of is him pushing my back against the tree and sliding between my legs, the hard length of him thrusting deep inside me.

But I'm reminded of the relentless thud knocking at the back of my mind, driving me mad with its persistence. I first heard it when I lost Arax, and since then, it has drowned out everything else. That constant thumping is a reminder of something I can't articulate.

As Daed eases his fingers inside me, I gasp, clenching his shoulders as his tongue traces my collarbone before his lips find my chest.

What do I want?

I want Lanneth to *suffer.*

I want Modok to *suffer.*

I want Gygarth to *suffer.*

I want The Golden Son to *suffer.*

I crave pain for pain, and at last the word I've been searching for surges to the surface of my mind, bursting forth as if from the depths of the Untold Sea.

"I want revenge," I gasp.

Daed freezes, his head lifting from between my breasts, his hand withdrawing from my robes. "What did you say?"

"I want revenge," I repeat, feeling the word gain strength with each utterance. "I refuse to hide here in the Grove, living out my days oblivious to the horrors beyond these trees. They must pay, Daed. *All of them.*"

"Death?" he asks, tilting his head slightly.

I shiver at the thought. "If that's what it takes."

"The Golden Son will not be easy to face, wife. We encountered only a small sample of his army. Rumor has it he has gathered thousands in Rethmar, waiting for the right moment to attack Baev'kalath. For now, however, his ships are limited. When House Ithranor fled during the Betrayers' Battle, they took most of their vessels with them."

"Then we'll need a larger army," I reply, my determination unyielding. Although he has stopped exploring inside me, the heat between my legs remains.

"There is only one larger army," he counters. As I watch his lips move, I ache to crash my mouth against his. "The houses of Mordorin, but the thrall houses only serve the king."

I exhale, realizing that my lust intensifies with every mention of war and revenge.

"Then we make you king," I mutter breathlessly.

Daed cups the back of my neck, the smile dancing on his lips enough to send me spiraling toward climax before he even enters me. "How fortunate I am to have such a wise wife at my side."

He pulls me closer, our lips colliding in gasps. His canines graze my bottom lip as he fists my robe, the hem inching higher toward my hips. But when his hand hovers over my stomach, he stops cold. I continue kissing him, tangling my fingers in his hair, pulling him back to me. But he doesn't respond.

"Husband," I whisper, my lips still brushing against his. "What's wrong?"

His hand flattens on my stomach, and my eyes widen.

"What is this, Amara?"

I gulp, scrambling for words. "I don't know what you—"

"Don't," he snaps, his voice slicing through the air and sending birds fleeing from the trees. "Don't lie to me. Not about this."

"I don't know for sure," I say quickly. "Zyphoro says—"

"Zyphoro? She knows? Since when?"

I gulp again. "Since we arrived in Valorne."

"And you didn't tell me?"

"You were not here!" I protest, anger rising in my voice. "And if you recall, we were not doing well. Or had you forgotten that I found out you knew Lanneth was poisoning me with the void?"

He says nothing, his jaw clenched and eyes narrowed coldly at me, the earlier desire replaced with an emotion I can't quite place—anger, disappointment...no, *fear*. At first, I think this is part of our game, the passion between us fueled by our disagreements. But then he steps away, and the chill in his gaze seeps into my bones, leaving me shivering.

"Besides," I gulp. "I thought you would have noticed sooner. Zyphoro sensed it immediately. She claims she's attuned to the void and could feel it within me."

"I didn't," Daed replies, his face etched in thought as he stares off into the distance. "Something didn't want me to know." He glances back at me from the corner of his eye. "Because it knew what I would do."

"Something?" I question, though I already know the answer. "Gygarth? But he's in Baev'kalath, and you are here."

Daed closes his eyes, shaking his head slowly. "Gygarth is wherever the void is, and the void is everywhere, Amara." He clutches his chest. "It's in me, and now it's in you."

Turning to face me fully, he takes a step forward, crunching the undergrowth beneath his feet. Instinctively, my hands move to my stomach, and I take a step back.

"I told you what happened to my mother. I can't let the same thing happen to you. I love you too much to watch you be destroyed."

He takes another step, and another. My heart pounds in my chest, loud enough to drown out everything else.

"You're scaring me, Daed," I say, glancing behind me with each wary backward step.

"You don't know what fear is," he replies, his voice low. Suddenly, his eyes roll over to pitch black. "But you will."

Without thinking, I turn and run, but I barely get a few strides before colliding with Zyphoro. I want to scream, but the sound catches in my throat. She looms over me, a dark grin playing on her lips, pinning me between two Mordorin Fae with blood tainted by the void.

"Amara," she says, her tone unnaturally light. "Did you tell him the good news?"

I can't answer, my voice trapped somewhere deep inside. When I open my mouth, only stutters and murmurs escape.

"Looks like he didn't take it well." Zyphoro leans closer, urgency lacing her words. "Get behind me, dear."

"Step away from my wife," Daed growls, his voice low and menacing as he stalks toward us, smoke weaving ominously between his fingers. I brace myself, knowing what comes next.

I do as Zyphoro says, standing behind her as she clasps her hands behind her back, striding toward Daed with an air of nonchalance that belies the crackling tension in the air. "Now, brother, I warned you what would happen if you lost control. Didn't I?"

Inch by inch, Death Singer materializes in Daed's outstretched hand, its sharp point dragging through the earth with a chilling scrape.

Zyphoro halts, a sigh escaping her lips. "Very well. If that's how it must be." She reveals her hands from behind her back, brandishing daggers wreathed in swirling black smoke. "Tag. You're it."

The forest transforms into a blur of motion as Daed and Zyphoro clash. Daed lunges, swinging Death Singer with lethal intent, but Zyphoro dances aside, her movements fluid and precise. She counters with a swift punch that snaps against his jaw, sending him reeling back. He shakes it off, his black eyes narrowing.

Zyphoro seizes the opening, her blades flashing as they slice through the air. Daed deflects her first strike, but the second dagger grazes his arm, a thin line of crimson marking its path. He hisses in pain, retaliating with a brutal kick that sends her crashing into a nearby tree, the trunk cracking under the impact.

But Zyphoro is quick to recover, rolling to her feet and launching back into the fray. She ducks under his outstretched arm, landing a punch to his side that makes him wince. She strikes again and again, relentlessly hammering at his ribs until he keels over. Just when I think she has him, Daed void walks, leaving her fist to collide with the tree trunk, which splinters around her hand.

She spins on her heels, scanning the forest for where he might reappear.

"Zyphoro! Behind you!" I scream as Daed emerges from a plume of smoke, driving his boot hard into her back. She's flung through the air, crashing into a fallen log, her back bending painfully around the wood.

Zyphoro winces, clutching the arch of her back as blood trickles from her mouth, but she manages a defiant smile.

I reach down to help her up as Daed stalks toward us, but she suddenly clamps her hand around my wrist and flips me over her head, dragging me to the ground and wrapping her legs around me.

I struggle against her grip, watching helplessly as Daed closes the distance.

"What are you doing?" I yell furiously, but no matter how hard I thrash, I can't break free.

"Stay still," she growls, and out of the corner of my eye, I see her dagger move toward my throat. "I promise it won't hurt. Then this will all be over."

Lying Fae! I manage to wrench an arm free, plunging my hand into the soil, hoping the Souls will hear my plea. Before I can utter a word, Zyphoro slices her blade along my skin—not my throat, but my chest—just deep enough to draw blood that cascades down in a thin curtain.

"Time to test out that rune," she says, pointing her blood-tipped blade at Daed.

Realization sweeps over me, and I can't help but smile. *Tricky Fae.*

I extend my hand, palm facing Daed, as the power builds within me. My veins glow green, my skin darkens, and the hum of energy fills my head, infusing every nerve in my body. A surge of green light beams from my hand, so bright it's almost blinding, and slams hard into Daed's chest, catapulting him backward until his back impacts against a tree. The ancient trunk sways, its very foundations rocked, but it stands firm while Daed slowly slides down its bark, crumpling to the ground.

His eyes close, and he doesn't move. Panic grips me for a moment, but Zyphoro pats my back as her blades vanish into smoke. "Don't worry. He's alive. Just going to have a colossal headache when he wakes up."

I stare at Zyphoro, bemused. When she doesn't react immediately, I gesture to her legs, still wrapped around me. "Do you mind?"

She laughs and unhooks herself. "Right. Sorry about that. But I didn't have time to explain."

I glance down at my chest. Wiping away the blood reveals the cut completely healed.

"Looks like the rune works, then."

I nod in quiet appreciation. "Looks like."

Zyphoro groans to her feet, brushing dirt from her leather trousers. "I guess he's not thrilled about becoming a daddy?"

I shake my head, my gaze drifting into the distance. "No. It doesn't seem that way. But what do I do now?"

"About the baby?" Zyphoro asks.

"About everything. Before he turned, I told him I wanted to return to Baev'kalath. I wanted him to be king so we could use the Mordorin armies to destroy The Golden Son once and for all."

Zyphoro nods, pursing her lips. "That's a sound plan, and we have a ship. So what's changed?"

I gesture to my husband, crumpled unconscious at the foot of a tree. "How can I trust anything about him, knowing he could fall under the control of the void at any moment?"

Zyphoro grins. "Do you know the difference between Daed and I? Aside from the fact that I'm prettier?"

I'm weary of getting tangled in Zyphoro's web, but I proceed nonetheless. "What?"

"The void holds no sway over me, and it's not just a Mordorin king who can command our armies. A Fae queen will do just as well."

"You?" I ask, and Zyphoro drops into a mock bow.

"I would look wonderful in a crown," she says. "When do we leave?"

CHAPTER 38

When I tell Keeper Erania I am leaving, she threatens to lock me in the very shelter we built to protect our people. Even as I explain my reasoning—that the Grove will never truly be safe until The Golden Son is destroyed—she begs me not to return to Baev'kalath. But there is no other choice. All Fae have fled, only the Mordorin remains, and the humans of the Sundered Kingdoms either join the ranks of the Legion or die at the edge of their swords. I could never muster a human army strong enough to challenge him.

This is the only path forward, but it is fraught with challenges.

To take control of the houses, Kaelus and Lanneth must be dethroned, and an heir must ascend. I had hoped it would be Daedalus, but once again, I find myself torn between my love for him and the knowledge that he is a volatile weapon, one that could turn on me at any moment. But the thought of Zyphoro as queen gives me pause.

Convincing Solena is nearly as difficult as persuading Keeper Enaria.

"I thought you would want to return to see Orios," I say, sitting across from her in my room while Ashen weaves between her legs.

"I do," she replies quickly, as if uttering anything else would be blasphemous. "But I'm scared, Amara. What if it doesn't go as planned? What if Lanneth captures us?" Her voice trembles. "I do not want to die."

Her words strike me hard, pure and heavy, making me question whether I'm doing the right thing. Solena told me that Fae are not immortal. That they die quite well, and I have seen that. Souls have I seen that, and so has she. That is when I truly understand the difference, that immortality and invincibility are two different things.

"Do you want to stay here? In the Grove?" I ask. "You're welcome to. The Tenders will gladly take you in."

She shakes her head abruptly. "No. I can't stay. I don't belong here. I'm just afraid."

I reach out and grip her hand. "So am I. But I can't let that stop me. If anything is going to change in this world, I need to be the one to change it."

Solena exhales wearily. "How can you be so brave?"

I shrug and offer her a comforting smile, hoping to ease her worries. "I never had a choice when I was named Jewel of the Tenders, or when I became a Sister of the Vine, or when Keeper Tovar sent me away to marry a Fae prince. Even now, I still don't have a choice. I have to be brave. Otherwise, all is lost."

"Aren't you tired, though?" Solena asks. "Tired of having to be?"

My smile falters, but I force it to remain. "I'm exhausted. But I can rest when it's over."

Slowly, her expression softens. "*We* can rest when it's over."

I nod. "*We*."

As I leave the room, I find Daedalus standing on the rope bridge, nursing his swollen jaw. His eyes, now clear swirls of gray, draw me in.

"I'm sorry," he says, his voice muffled by the swelling.

"I know you are," I reply, leaning against the doorframe. "But how many more times do we pretend this is normal?"

He dips his chin, a grin tugging at the corners of his mouth. "Every time, if possible."

When I do not soften to him, Daed releases a heavy breath, his tattooed fist gripping the railing of the rope bridge.

"I promise I will do better, Amara. For you *and* our baby."

His gaze drifts to my belly, and I instinctively shield it with my hands.

"It's still early," I say. "Anything can happen. I don't even know for sure. Zyphoro could be wrong."

"She's not," Daed says confidently, sending a shiver down my spine. "You carry an heir of the Mordorin with you. But I can't tell yet if it's a prince, a princess, or both. Twins run in my family."

"Are you trying to scare me?" My eyes widen with worry at the idea, my face tightening.

A light laugh escapes Daed's lips, and he bows his head. "No. Never." He looks up from beneath his brow. "Never again."

I exhale, shaking my head. "Never for now is all you can promise me."

A lump forms in his throat, and he fights to swallow it. "Never for now, then."

I should force him to his knees. Make him beg. Make him crawl. And maybe I will—soon. But if I am to claim the revenge I crave, I need Daed by my side. He is the

358

most formidable warrior to ever step onto a battlefield, a powerful ally for my cause. I will see him crowned king of the Sundered Kingdoms. I will wield the Mordorin's darkest weapon. I will use them as they intended to use me.

"Shall we go claim a crown?" I ask him.

Daed's fingers lace behind his neck. "My father won't abdicate easily, and you know what Lanneth is capable of."

"You're the commander of the Ebon Flight. Will the Reapers and Blades take your side?"

Daed's brow furrows as he considers. "Perhaps. But I can't be sure. We may need reinforcements."

"Who?" I ask. "From where?"

"Leave that to me," Daed replies. "The remaining Blades and I will prepare the ship. The sooner we return to Baev'kalath, the better, before the king and queen receive too much information about what has happened here."

"Yes. Let me say my goodbyes, and I'll be ready to leave."

Daed turns to go, but in an instant, he spins around, closing the distance between us in three strides. He cups my face in his hands, drawing me to his lips. He kisses me deep and long, stealing my breath and leaving my knees wobbling. What power does this man wield that I can shift from despising him to desiring him in the blink of an eye?

"I love you," he whispers, and all sense slips away from me like dust in the wind.

"I love you, too," I say.

Daed steps back with a parting smile, and in an instant, his wings unfurl with a sharp, resonant snap. He launches into the air, ascending swiftly and when he breaks through the canopy, a shower of leaves rains down around me.

I cross the swaying bridge and descend the winding stairs, making my way through the village and past the vine wall, until I reach the clearing. Settling into the soft, pillowy grass, I close my eyes. In an instant, I'm transported to the shrine, where my sisters are already waiting for me.

"You're leaving," Saren says, her voice a mixture of disappointment and concern. "Again."

"I must," I reply, desperation creeping into my tone. "I wish you could understand."

Lira shakes her head in disbelief. "You have everything here, Amara. You are the Jewel. There is no greater honor among the Tenders."

"There will be no Tenders if I do not go," I assert firmly.

Mirael's expression hardens with anger. "Then we forbid it. You cannot leave."

"I'm not asking for your permission," I counter, determination steeling my voice. "I came to bid you farewell and feel the warmth of our circle one last time."

Mirael turns her back on me, a clear sign of her refusal, while Saren and Lira begin to relent.

"Will you return?" Saren asks, her voice softening.

"If everything goes well, then yes," I reply with a light laugh, trying to bring some cheer to the moment.

Lira reaches for me, and I rush into her arms without hesitation.

"We love you, Amara," she says, glancing over my shoulder at Mirael. "Especially Mirael."

Reluctantly, Mirael turns and links hands with Saren, joining the circle. Our arms wrap around each other, our heads resting on one another's shoulders. Energy surges through us, and once again I feel the power of our unbroken bond.

Mirael jerks back, startled. "Your power, Amara, it's greater than I've ever felt."

Lira frowns. "It's that rune on her neck. Perhaps we should get one too."

"It only works if you use High Fae blood in the ink," I explain.

Saren grins. "Maybe we should get ourselves one of those as well."

"I wouldn't recommend it," I laugh. "They're very troublesome."

"You love him, though?" Lira asks quickly.

I nod. "I do."

"Then it's worth all the trouble in the world," Mirael says.

We hug once more, and as I step away, another ache settles into my heart, adding to my growing collection. When I return to the Grove, Zyphoro and Solena wait for me, and a sorrow falls over the Tenders as I farewell them a second time. I can barely meet their eyes, reminding myself that what I do is for their safety, no matter how much it pains me to leave.

Zyphoro grows impatient, tapping her heavy boot on the ground, and I wonder if she's more eager for this fight than I am.

Bending down, I lift Ashen into my arms. He lets out a small cry, as if he too feels the weight of our departure. He crawls onto my shoulder, sinking into my hair, his little purrs tickling my ears.

"Ready?" Zyphoro asks, and when I nod, she sweeps me into her arms, her wings unfurling majestically behind her.

With a powerful push off the ground, we rise, watching as my people below shrink into tiny specks. We break through the canopy, emerging into the brilliant blue sky. The sun blazes down on me, and I close my eyes, allowing its warmth to seep into my bones. I will hold onto it, knowing that in Baev'kalath, the sun seldom shines to light the dark places.

The ship remains anchored where Arax dropped us, and it takes everything in me not to fall apart at the thought of him standing at the bow. I feel the ribbon tied around my wrist—a touchstone, a reminder of him during these hardest moments. I wonder if he knows that even now, he is protecting me.

Daed and the seven remaining Blades wait for us, and with the combined power of the siblings, the ship surges forward at twice the speed, waves of smoke racing alongside us across the still harbor toward the perilous Untold Sea.

As night falls, I lean against the railing, staring toward the approaching storm. The rain begins to fall lightly, but I know soon it will pour. Part of me feels a thrill at the thought of its icy sting against my skin once more.

Daed joins me, his arms snaking around my waist from behind, pulling me against his chest. He buries his face in my neck, his lips brushing softly toward my ear, until a screeching hiss sends him stumbling back.

Ashen leaps from my hair, landing deftly on the deck, his back arched, smoky fur bristling.

"How long has he been doing that?" Daed asks, clutching his chest.

"It's his favorite spot," I laugh as Ashen scuttles away in search of a more peaceful place to sleep. "When you made him for me, I assumed he was just a kitten, not a giant beast with tentacles."

"He is neither," Daed replies, cautiously wrapping his arms around me again, wary of any other surprises lurking in my hair.

"What do you mean?" I ask.

"He isn't a kitten. He isn't a lion. He's something else entirely. A creature of the void. But he's loyal to you, at least. I didn't expect him to attack when I arrived in the Grove that night, but I *did* tell him to protect you when I made him, so perhaps that's my fault."

"He didn't protect me from Lanneth," I say, my voice tinged with frustration.

"Sometimes it takes longer for them to understand their form. He'll grow stronger and shift forms more often now that he knows how."

As we speak, the rain falls heavier, and the boat begins to rock, the waves pounding harder against the bow. Daed closes his eyes as the rain drips from his forehead down the bridge of his nose, and when it trickles onto his lips, he licks it away.

"It's been some time since I've felt the rain." He opens his eyes, looking down at me. "Are you sure you want to do this?"

I nod without hesitation.

He smiles. "Very well, wife. I will see you soon."

With that, Daed's wings erupt from his back, and in an instant, he soars into the air, disappearing into the silvery-gray clouds.

Time passes slowly in his absence, but when an eternal night falls over the ship and thunder cracks overhead, splitting the sky with flashes of lightning, I know we have arrived.

The rain beats down relentlessly now as the fortress of Baev'kalath looms on the horizon, a jagged silhouette waiting to swallow me whole. My heart thrums in my chest, a wild drumbeat of anticipation and dread. Death could very well await me within those stone walls, yet I can't let fear take hold. No, I won't allow it. I have come too far and lost too much to turn back now.

The cold wind whips through my hair, but the chill I feel is not from the elements. I remember Arax, and the pain of his loss aches in my chest. I can't let his sacrifice be in vain. The thought of revenge fuels me, igniting a fire in my belly. I want to make The Golden Son pay for the destruction he's wrought. I want justice for my people, for Arax, and for myself. The Mordorin have the power I need, and there is no other option but to take it from them.

With each passing wave, my resolve strengthens. I will not back down. I will not falter. I will claim my destiny. I am ready.

I cast my eyes to the stormy sky, anxiety coiling in my stomach as I wait for Daed's return. His absence gnaws at me, and the worst fears creep in—what if something has happened? But I refuse to believe that any force in this world could take him down or keep him from me. My doubts about his loyalty may linger, but not his love. That Fae's heart belongs to me, fractured as it is.

Zyphoro slinks across the deck, smoke enveloping her with each step, transforming her leathers into black-scaled armor adorned with jagged pauldrons and vambraces, a flowing cloak of midnight billowing behind her. Her moonstone necklace glimmers against the dark steel, and for the first time, her hair isn't a mass of ebony curls but tightly braided against her scalp.

She stands beside me, her gray eyes fixed on Baev'kalath, before shifting to the seven Blades at the bow, their gaze darting back and forth between us as they whisper.

"They mean to betray us," Zyphoro says, a grin curling her lips. "As soon as we dock, they'll flee to the fortress."

"They've sworn loyalty to Daed," I argue, but Zyphoro's conviction doesn't waver.

"They're still the king's Fae. As long as my father wears the crown, he commands the Ebon Flight."

"But they fight alongside Daed in battle. Does that count for nothing?"

"The Blades are the finest warriors in the Sundered Kingdoms. Their strength is forged in loyalty. They couldn't fight like they do without being devoted to their cause. They followed Daed in Valorne because he was sovereign there. But until he takes the crown from our father, Kaelus' power is absolute in Baev'kalath."

As the Blades turn their backs on us to take in the fortress, doubt settles in my gut. If the Ebon Flight doesn't rally to their prince's side, it leaves just the four of us—Daed, Zyphoro, Solena, and me—to face the might of House Mordorin. How can we possibly succeed?

Another crack of lightning splits the sky, illuminating the night like day, and a wall of Blades lines the courtyard, their faces obscured in the flickering dark, rain spraying against their armor. Solena emerges from below deck, her eyes wide as she surveys the formidable presence of Baev'kalath's army.

"They knew we were coming," I murmur.

"They knew," Zyphoro replies. "And they feared it enough to be ready." She glances up at the sky. "If my brother is waiting for a dramatic entrance, now would be the time."

"He will come," I assert, my voice ringing clear against the thunder. "All I need to do is call."

Zyphoro exhales mockingly. "Then be quick about it, or we'll be slaughtered before we even set foot off this damned boat."

The ship rolls into port, and the smoke that guided us evaporates into nothingness.

"What should I do?" Solena asks, her usually steady tone trembling.

Zyphoro rolls her eyes. "Nothing. Stay below deck and pray that we survive."

Solena shakes her head, determination burning in her gaze. "I want to fight."

"You're a low-caste maid. Unless you plan to hurl your feather duster at them, I'm not sure what you can offer."

"Zyphoro," I scold, narrowing my eyes. "If she wants to fight, then she will fight. Give her a weapon."

Zyphoro glares at me before reluctantly extending her hand toward Solena. A slender black blade with a silver hilt materializes in her grip. "A weapon from the void," she says, a hint of mockery in her voice. "May it serve you well."

I refuse to let Zyphoro diminish Solena's already dwindling resolve, especially since it was Solena who helped me escape Lanneth with nothing but her wits and bravery. Solena takes the sword, and as she holds it, I'm reminded of Arax and his words about Estra—not a noble or a High Fae, but low-caste, like Solena. Estra rose to become a Blade, and if Solena wishes it, she can do the same.

"We will win this battle together," I say, gripping her forearm.

"Or I will die by your side," she replies solemnly. "Unafraid."

I nod, a smile breaking through the dread tightening around my heart. "Unafraid."

"Amara. Jewel of the Tenders," a voice booms through the darkness. "Welcome home."

I turn to see Kaelus standing on the balcony, lightning splitting the sky behind him. He looks taller, broader, and more menacing than I have ever known him to be. For the first time, I understand the warnings Daedalus gave me. This is not just a Fae king—this is a ruler with a legacy written in blood.

"This is not my home," I yell.

"Then why have you returned?" Kaelus taunts.

I muster my courage, feeling my resolve strengthen with the weight of everything that has brought me to this moment.

"For your crown," I call back, venom lacing my words.

Kaelus laughs, but I refuse to be underestimated.

"Then I'm afraid this will not end well for you, my dear. But you still have worth. The bargain still holds, and you remain a desperately treasured princess of the Mordorin. Put aside this futile squabbling, and we will receive you with open arms."

"You plan to kill me to further your own power!" I scream.

Kaelus pauses, lightning illuminating his face in a fleeting flash. "In this life, sacrifices must be made for the greater good. You know this better than most, Amara. But I promise, it will be without pain."

"There is always pain," I yell through gritted teeth. "But I have learned to embrace it, and I will gladly share it with you."

Suddenly, my boldness falters as another lightning strike bathes Lanneth in an otherworldly, spectral glow, revealing her silhouette behind Kaelus.

"Daughter," she hisses, her elegant face shimmering, her glamor intact. "Igniting this conflict is dangerous, and we cannot risk losing you—not with the precious cargo you carry." Her hand stretches out, and even from this distance, I feel her malice reach for my stomach, chilling me to the core.

"How does she know?" I mutter.

"The void knows," Zyphoro replies.

Solena furrows her brow. "Knows what?"

"Zyphoro. Daughter," Kaelus calls, his voice steady amidst the rain.

Zyphoro turns her head toward him, droplets cascading down his face.

"You are welcome here, too. Join me, and the Mordorin will be the strongest house in all Fae history. Forget this foolishness and rule by my side."

Silence hangs in the air, and I suddenly fear Zyphoro is wavering. She glances at Solena and I, doubt etched on her face.

"I still love you, daughter. Return to me, and be greater than your traitorous brother ever dreamed."

Slowly, her gaze returns to Kaelus, and I hold my breath, waiting for her response.

"Why rule beside you when I can just take the whole fucking thing?"

With a swift motion, Zyphoro extends her hand, and an arrow of smoke streaks through the air, aimed straight for Kaelus. He barely has time to react as the sharp tip pierces the side of his neck, blood erupting from the wound and spraying Lanneth's face, soaking her ivory gown.

"Damn it. Missed," Zyphoro hisses.

Kaelus drops to one knee, clamping a hand over his neck as Lanneth screams, her voice a high-pitched wail that echoes like a chorus of tortured souls, hollow and endless, as if drawn from the void itself.

"Bring her to me!"

A wave of black wings erupts into the air, the thunderous snap drowning out the storm as the Blades take flight.

"This is it," I murmur, swallowing the last vestiges of doubt that threaten to choke me. There's no time for hesitation now.

The Blades on the bow turn toward me, and I brace myself for their treachery. But instead, they draw their swords, the metallic ring resonating in unison.

"For Princess Amara!" the boom as they unleash their wings, soaring to meet their brothers and sisters in battle.

Zyphoro's lips curve into a smirk. "Guess I was wrong. Excellent." Her eyes widen at the flood of Blades pouring from the fortress, surging toward the ship. "But now would be a good time to call for Daedalus."

To delay the attack, Zyphoro conjures a wall of smoke that erupts between the advancing Blades and the ship, soaring skyward and halting them in their tracks. But I know it won't last.

I look to the stormy sky, rain pelting my face and wind whipping through my hair. With every ounce of my heart—my fear, my passion, my strength—I call into the night, "Daed!"

The sudden sound of wings cutting through the wind drowns out everything else. When I turn east, I see them—a wave of warriors descending upon Baev'kalath, with Daed leading the charge and a Fae lord with striking copper hair at his side. Lord Reon and the warriors of Eyr'Drogul have joined the battle. As they collide with the Ebon Flight, their fury ignites the night, shaking the storm itself into submission.

CHAPTER 39

The ring of steel echoes like thunder as I descend the ramp, my heart lodged in my throat. I gaze up at the tumultuous sky, where the battle unfolds—so far out of my reach. The Blades clash with the warriors of Eyr'Drogul, swords sparking violently as they meet in midair.

Their cries form a haunting cacophony, thick with rage, striking each other down with brutal force. Bodies plummet from the sky, crashing into the courtyard below with sickening thuds.

I lock my eyes on Daed, fierce and unwavering as he navigates the chaos like a tempest, his wings slicing through the rain-soaked air. Each powerful strike sends foes sprawling, infused with the raw strength of the void. Beside him, Zyphoro moves with fluid grace, her smoke blades flickering like black flames in the night.

Yet above it all, Lanneth looms on the balcony, her gaze sharp and calculating. My jaw clenches, and my hands curl into tight fists at my sides. I wasn't always this way—bent on vengeance and tainted by hate. The Fae have shaped me, I am certain of that. The darkness growing within me is a seed they planted, flourishing in Baev'kalath, as if returning here has made its roots stronger.

I hate her. I hate her for everything she's put me through, for what she's turned me into, and for the power she exerts over Daed, a power that threatens to tear us apart. He will never be truly mine as long as she controls him. *As long as she lives.*

Solena's wings burst from her back, the sword gripped tightly in her hand. "Come, Amara. I'll carry you," she offers.

I shake my head, my gaze fixed on Lanneth, nails digging into my palm until I draw blood. "I will get there myself."

Solena scans our surroundings, confusion flickering in her eyes, but she doesn't need to understand.

"Come, Ashen," I whisper, and he slinks from my hair, pattering along my shoulder before arching his back and stretching with a long yawn. I smile, scratching under his chin, and he responds with a soft purr. "Alright. Show me what you can do."

As if he understands, Ashen leaps from my shoulder, landing deftly on the dock. His body jerks, shoulders and legs kicking out, fur rippling as he grows larger. A charcoal ruff flecked with silver frames his lion's head, and four massive paws pound the damp wood. Then, with a thunderous roar, wings etched with smoke burst from his back. He glances over his shoulder, flapping them as if figuring out how they work. But we will learn together.

I approach slowly, burying my hand in his smoky coat and scratching the top of his head. Ashen melts into my touch, his wispy whiskers twitching with each caress. Carefully, I circle around him and climb onto his back, mindful of where the wings sprout from his shoulders. He allows it, padding his feet on the dock, and I grip handfuls of his mane.

My heart thumps in my chest, my stomach twisted in knots. But I didn't come this far to dwell on fear. I look at Solena, and I see the same doubts mirrored on her face.

"Unafraid," I say firmly.

She nods, a determined glint in her eye. "Unafraid."

With that, she pushes off into the air, crashing into the blur of wings and swords that engulfs the courtyard. I lean into Ashen's ear, surprised when he takes to the sky without me uttering a word. He has become like the creatures of the forest, responding to my thoughts more than my words.

Ashen's wings are magnificent, leaving trails of smoke in the air with each powerful stroke. The battle rages on, and amid the frenzy, it's impossible to discern who holds the advantage. But while the pawns clash, I fixate on the queen.

I tug at Ashen's mane, and he banks left, veering away from the fight and toward the balcony where Lanneth watches. Kaelus kneels at her side, his hand pressed to his neck where Zyphoro's smoke arrow struck. But Lanneth appears unfazed, her focus locked on the turmoil unfolding below.

We charge forward, each beat of my heart punctuated by the loud pops of Mordorin void walking and the clang of their weapons. As we close in, I see Solena stumble on the courtyard, her sword clattering to the ground. A Blade stalks toward her, wings shaking rain loose from his feathers, his sword spinning in hand before he raises it above his head. I tug on Ashen's mane, urging him to bank right.

I won't make it in time.

But I don't have to.

As the Blade's sword falls, a deafening clang rings out when his swing is deflected, crossing with the sword of a Reaper who stands between him and Solena. They strain for a moment, pushing back against each other's strength, but with swift precision, the Reaper disarms him, sending his sword flying across the courtyard with a sharp screech before delivering a sharp elbow to his nose.

The Blade reels back, collapsing with a hard thud while the Reaper removes his helm, tossing it aside as he lifts Solena into his arms. I watch as Orios holds her in a way that would make the stars themselves envy something so beautiful. Solena crumbles against him, and if the last thing I see is two people desperately in love, I feel grateful for the sight.

I grip Ashen's mane, steering him back toward Lanneth, his wings leaving a smoky trail behind us.

Faster.

He pins back his ears, his wings thrashing harder as we barrel toward the queen. A grin creeps to the corner of my mouth as we close the distance. Her back is turned to me. She won't see me coming. I will have her on the ground in surrender before she can react. But then I recoil in horror as her head twists unnaturally, all the way around, her glamor flickering as our eyes meet.

Turn, Ashen!

My command comes too late. Lanneth extends her hand, and a rope of smoke hurtles toward me, lashing around my throat and yanking me from Ashen's back. The constriction pulls me into the air, my fingers clawing desperately, but it tightens further.

Ashen roars, charging toward Lanneth, but she retaliates with a second rope of smoke that lashes out, striking him hard across the back. I watch in horror as he's sent careening through the air until he collides violently with a tower, the impact echoing like thunder. He plummets to the ground, but I can't scream, the rope around my throat stealing my breath.

"Enough, Amara!" Lanneth shrieks, her head twisting back around. "I do not want to hurt you." She pauses, her gaze locking onto mine with an intensity that chills me. "Not until the baby is born. Don't you see? That precious Fae in your belly is the very future of our house. It must be protected at all costs."

Suddenly, a silver blade arcs through the night, slicing through the smoke and severing its hold on me. I begin to fall, the wind rushing from my lungs, but I come to a jarring stop as two strong arms scoop me from the air. I look up into Zyphoro's gray eyes, my breaths coming in desperate rasps.

"Hello, dear," she says, a grin splitting her face. She carries me back to the balcony, and I turn to see Daed facing off against Lanneth, Death Singer glinting ominously at his side.

"How could you?" Lanneth's voice drips with venom as Zyphoro sets me down. "After everything The Father Below has given you. Everything I've done to secure your rule for a thousand years."

She lifts her hand toward Daed's brow, but he turns his head away from her, and I can almost see her heart shatter, confirming she actually has one.

"I loved you like you were my own," she hisses. "And now you turn away from me? For what? A human? She was chosen because she was disposable, but she possessed enough Fae magic to strengthen your heir. Don't tell me you've fallen in love with her, Daedalus."

Daed dismisses Lanneth's questions, which only seem to pain her more. He takes a step back, pointing the tip of Death Singer at Kaelus. "Step down, Father," he states, his voice cold and steady as rain drips along the sharp contours of his face. "And you will be spared."

"You want my crown?" Kaelus gasps, his voice rasping like dry leaves. "You'll have to kill me for it, son."

Daed's shoulders rise and fall as he draws a deep breath. "If that's what it comes to."

"No!" Lanneth screams, her gaze turning to me, revealing her sharpened canine teeth. "He does this for you, but you can't comprehend the monster he is. He knew his duty when you arrived in Baev'kalath. To bed you and put an heir in your human belly, and he succeeded. Now he has brought you home. Can't you see everything is unfolding as *planned*?"

A shiver runs through me, and I turn to Daed, but he shakes his head defiantly.

"She's lying, Amara. That's what she does. She's trying to turn you against me."

"I do not have to try!" Lanneth laughs, throwing her head back with abandon. "Even now, the girl doubts your loyalty. I can see it in her eyes. And you are right to—he is a beast of the void, and you are nothing but meat."

My jaw clenches and I feel like she sees straight into my soul, all my fears and mistrusts laid bare before her to skewer on her fork and sink her teeth into like we're at the table all over again.

"Do not listen, Amara!" Daed yells, desperation lacing his voice. "She is poison."

Zyphoro raises her daggers, directing one toward Lanneth and the other toward Daed. "She is not the only one, brother," she retorts, stepping in front of me as if to shield me from both of them. Her eyes narrow, filled with intensity. "You are no innocent in this. You killed our mother."

"And I have lived with that my entire life," Daed hisses through clenched teeth. "But that is not who I am. Not anymore. Now I am a husband." His gaze locks onto mine, his resolve shining through. "Now I am a father, and I will protect those I love with my life."

Lanneth's laughter fades and I see her glamor flicker between two faces, her magic straining to maintain its mask.

"I gave you the chance to make the right decision of your own free will, Daedalus. But I see you need instruction."

"No," he murmurs, but the defiance in his voice feels frail.

Lanneth extends her hand toward him, her canines elongating as she grins. "You belong to the void, Daedalus. You *always* have. You *always* will."

Her fist clenches, and when Daed's eyes roll over into pitch black, my heart shatters. In an instant, he belongs to her again.

"A shame I am not so easily controlled," Zyphoro snarls, her voice filled with ferocity.

"True. To have you both would lay the world at our feet, not just the Sundered Kingdoms. Had we known there were two, we would have fed your mother more of the void to ensure The Father Below took root in both of you."

Zyphoro shivers, and I see her strength falter. "What did you say?"

Lanneth's smile widens, cruel and triumphant. "You two are arguing over who killed the beautiful and just Queen Veloria when neither of you deserves recognition. *I did it.* I killed the Queen. I cut open her belly and pulled Daed from her before using the same blade to slit her throat. The Father below feasted on what was left. If I hadn't noticed you flailing around inside her, you might have been the second course. I suppose I saved your life. You're welcome."

There are no words in any tongue to describe the way Zyphoro's face contorts. She stands frozen, her dagger hanging limply in her hands, rain streaming over her, masking the moisture pooling in her gray eyes.

"So be at peace with that, Zyphoro," Lanneth taunts. "Before your brother kills you."

Kaelus staggers to his feet, blood seeping between his fingers. "Lanneth. Enough. Don't force them to kill each other. You can tether Daed, and Zyphoro can return to her cage. We have the girl now. It doesn't need to go this far."

"This is what you wanted, Kaelus!" Lanneth screams, her fury resonating in the air. "This is what you asked for. *Power*. Unlimited *power*. I warned you of the cost, and you paid the price willingly. You can't go back now. The Father Below won't allow it."

"I am done with the Father Below," I declare, stepping out from behind Zyphoro. "I've come for your crowns, and you will give them to me. If you do so willingly, I will show mercy."

Lanneth sputters with laughter, the sound growing louder, echoing off the walls. "Silly girl. Don't you see I control your husband? One word from my lips, and he'll crush your windpipe and snap your spine in two."

"No, he won't," I assert, the conviction in my voice stronger than the fear coiling in my gut.

"Really? Why not? Because you carry his child? There are countless ways to hurt you while keeping you both alive until you're ripe," Lanneth hisses.

"No. Because he loves me, and I love him." I approach Daed slowly, willing him to see me through the murky void that surrounds him. I know he's still there, trapped within this darkness. He just needs to hear my voice, and I will guide him back to me.

"Daed," I say, my voice soft but steady. "Can you hear me?"

Zyphoro reaches for my hand to pull me back, but I brush her away. I know what I'm doing.

Standing before him, my heart pounds like a drum, each beat laced with dread. The man I love is trapped behind a veil of shadows, his once vibrant gray eyes now swallowed by the void. Lanneth's sinister influence coils around him, pressing in on us and suffocating the bond we share.

"Daed," I whisper, my voice trembling as I reach out, my fingers brushing against his cheek. "Please, come back to me." But he remains unmoving, a statue of cold indifference, as if my very existence has slipped from his mind.

"Daed!" I plead again, my voice rising above Lanneth's cruel laughter that rings out like a death knell.

"Restrain the princess!" she barks at him, her voice dripping with malice.

Before I can react, Daed's hand moves with unnatural swiftness, seizing my wrist with a grip like iron. Pain shoots through me, and I gasp as fear floods my veins. "Daed, please!" I cry out, desperately trying to reach the man buried within. "It's me! It's Amara!"

His grip tightens, a vice that threatens to crush my bones. My nails dig into my palm, drawing blood, but I don't care. "Husband," I whisper, desperation threading through my words. "I love you."

In that moment, something flickers in his eyes—gray battling against black, a spark of recognition fighting through the darkness. Lanneth's shrieks grow louder, but Daed seems lost in a struggle of his own.

"Enough, Daedalus!" Lanneth commands, her voice a whip crack. "You will obey!"

Suddenly, he tenses, and I hold my breath as a tendril of smoke forms in his hand. He launches it at Lanneth, and the dark projectile slams into her, filling her mouth with a choking cloud.

Her eyes widen in shock, and horror washes over her face as she claws at her throat, gasping for breath. The grip she held over Daed slips, and I feel a rush of hope—*could he truly be breaking free*?

"Daed!" I shout, feeling the swell of emotion rise in my chest. "Fight it! Come back! Welcome the sunrise with me. Please!"

He stumbles, his body taut with struggle, and for a brief second, I see the flicker of his true self behind the shadows. Then he surges forward, collapsing into my arms.

I clutch him tightly, breathless with relief and fear, but the moment shatters as steel thuds onto the balcony. I glance over my shoulder to find a wall of Reapers with Orios at the forefront as Kaelus staggers to his feet.

"Reapers," the king commands. "Secure the prince and princess. Now."

Orios looks at Daed, propped against me, and releases a heavy breath.

"Reapers," he says, "the king and queen are not themselves. Restrain them and await further orders... from Commander Rook."

The Reapers bow their heads, storming toward King Kaelus and hooking him under the arms.

"This is treason!" he booms. "Release me!"

They drag him from the balcony while the others move toward Lanneth, who still tears at her neck to free herself from the smoke clogging her throat. I watch as her glamor flickers, struggling to maintain her mask until it falls away completely, revealing her true face.

"This isn't over," she gasps, smoke oozing from the corners of her mouth. "Baev'kalath will be your tomb."

Daed pulled himself back from the void, but Lanneth is lost to it, her soul forever bound to the abyss. I understand now, more than ever, that she will never stop. It would be so easy to stand by and watch her choke to death right in front of me—but I can't. I thought I could. When I chose to come to Baev'kalath, I even considered killing her myself. But now, as I stare down at this vile, twisted creature of the void, all I feel is pity. A part of me is relieved. Relieved that I haven't let these Fae strip away my humanity, not after everything else they've taken.

"Daed. Release her."

"No!" Zyphoro yells, fury etched on her face. "Kill her! Let this end!"

I shake my head, resolute. "She will be spared to live out her eternal life in the dungeon she kept you in."

Zyphoro clenches her jaw, then spins on her heels, taking to the sky in a flurry of ire.

"Are you sure?" Daed murmurs weakly, doubt flickering in his eyes.

"Yes," I say.

With a flick of his wrist, the smoke dissipates from Lanneth's mouth. She drops to her knees, gasping and spewing tendrils of darkness onto the stone. Just when I think it's over, she wipes her mouth and glares at me.

"Stupid girl," she snarls.

A lash of shadow shoots from her hand. Instinctively, I extend my own hand, halting the onslaught with a pulsing green light emanating from my palm.

"What is that?" Lanneth's expression shifts from rage to confusion. She pours more of her power into her attack, but the light holds strong.

She channels her malice and venom, sweat beads forming on my forehead as my teeth grit in response. Our powers collide, a fierce beam of light morphing from green to black, ignited by a blinding white flare that forces everyone nearby to shield their eyes from the brilliance.

I can feel her energy pushing me backward, but I plant my feet, resolute as an ancient tree. I dig deep within myself, feeling the rune on my neck burn and pulse like a living thing.

As Lanneth pushes to her limits, the inverted crescent on her forehead smokes and sears into her skin. But as I push back, I sense a heat building in the same spot on my forehead. When Lanneth's eyes turn black, I see the symbol of a tree, burnt white into my skin, reflecting at me.

I don't understand how I'm still standing. Her power dwarfs mine; she walks with the void. I've taken a few scrapes, but nothing that should allow me to summon magic of this magnitude.

Then I realize where it comes from.

More magic wells up within me, blossoming from deep inside. The rain no longer drips on my skin; it's absorbed. The lightning and thunder? I claim that too, for they are all part of nature.

I am nature's fury, and I don't need to bleed to hurt her. I carry my pain with me always.

A hard bolt of luminous green light explodes from me, shattering Lanneth's smoke and slamming into her with the force of a hurricane. She is knocked off her feet, screaming as she's flung across the balcony and into the wall.

The light fades to nothing, and I collapse to my knees, gasping for breath. Daed crawls to me, wrapping his arms around me as we lay exhausted in each other's embrace, our heavy breaths mingling in the stillness. Suddenly, the rain stops. The relentless crashing of the ocean and the rumble of thunder fade into silence, and the silver clouds masking the moon dissipate, bathing Baev'kalath in its pale glow.

Cautiously, I trace my fingers over my forehead, relief flooding through me as I find the mark has vanished. But as I lower my hand, I catch sight of faint tendrils of smoke weaving between my fingers before they disappear. Perhaps it was just my imagination. But with a child of smoke and vine growing inside me, who knows what secrets the void holds or how deeply Gygarth's teeth sink into my family.

With Kaelus and Lanneth defeated, Daed and I stand atop the ruins of House Mordorin, armed with a force strong enough to rival the Legion of Saints. The Golden Son's reckoning is inevitable, justice awaiting him as surely as it did the fallen king and queen.

But for now, all I want is to lie in my husband's arms and dare, just once, to envision of a world without pain—a world where battles end, ghosts fade, where we can find peace in each other's embrace and welcome the sunrise together.

CHAPTER 40

K aelus has been mended and confined to his chambers under heavy guard, while Lanneth is dragged up the stairs to nowhere, taken to a room that does not exist. The clang of the iron bars slamming shut reverberates with finality. She is locked away in Zyphoro's cage, a fitting prison for the queen who thought herself invincible.

With Lanneth's power shackled, I feel a weight lift from my chest. The air is no longer thick with her malevolence. The dark shadow that loomed over us is gone. I watch as the last traces of her presence fade from the halls, her laughter silenced, and the hope that took root in me in the Grove seems to grow stronger with each passing day.

Lord Reon has pledged his support, promising to help us bring the Golden Son to his knees. Lady Ilyra of Fyn'Rothar has joined us too, her rogue assassins the deadliest of all Fae houses, and Lord Sarberos of Thal'Morven has committed his frost mages. Together, they form the foundation of something that might actually stand a chance.

But imagine how much stronger we could be if all the houses stood united.

The twins, Vashar and Vasheeth, command the shapeshifters of Jor'Thalas while Lord Horax and his berserkers are near unstoppable on the battlefield.

If only they could be persuaded.

Modok, though—he's beyond saving. Or swaying. I'd be a fool to think otherwise.

The next few days in Baev'kalath are a whirlwind of change. Daed immerses himself with the Reapers and Blades, working to establish a new order among them. While they pledge their loyalty to him, he remains worried that until he is crowned king, some will still resist. The next step is a coronation, but before the storm of politics and planning swallows us whole, we need a moment of calm.

Daed's promise to take me back to Pariseth resurfaces, and I agree without hesitation. Zyphoro is left to command Baev'kalath, while Orios is made Daed's second-in-command, ready to lead the Blades.

With our home in capable hands, we slip into the night, bound for the paradise that waits at the eye of the storm. The moment we land, the sunlight chases away the lingering shadows, scattering the demons that have haunted me for far too long.

The silence here is healing—no metal clashing, no cries of pain. Just the sounds of birds and the gentle rush of the stream. Daed and I sleep for nearly two days, rarely stepping outside as our bodies recover. Even Ashen is exhausted, restricted to his kitten form after so much shifting. He sleeps even longer than Daed and me, his favorite spot at the moment appearing to be the enormous wardrobe in our bedchamber.

When we finally regain our energy, our days are filled with swimming in the cove, getting our hands dirty in the garden, and spending evenings lying on our backs in the long grass, gazing up at the stars. It couldn't be more perfect. I do my best to savor the contentment, pushing aside worries about what lies ahead: The Golden Son and the shadow that Gygarth still casts over my prince.

With Lanneth locked away in her enchanted prison, she can no longer control him, but she was merely a piece in a greater game—a sinister force that still lurks within Baev'kalath. But even with her defeat, her machinations seem to unfold relentlessly. Soon enough, a Mordorin baby will be welcomed into the fortress, just as she planned, while Gygarth's insatiable hunger looms ever larger.

Am I destined to meet my end like Queen Veloria?

Our fates will unfold in their own time, but that time is not tonight.

Tonight, Daed and I hide from the world, dancing to music only we can hear.

Soft moonlight spills through the open balcony, casting gentle shadows across our entwined bodies, his chest bare and smooth beneath my fingertips as I trace his runes and he trembles under my touch. We sway slowly, our movements languid and tender, lost in the quiet sanctuary we've carved out amidst the chaos.

"You are the sunrise in my perpetual night," he whispers. "The dawn breaking through the clouds of my desolation. If you are scared, I will protect you. If you are sick, I will care for you. If you are lost, I will find you. Give me your heart, Amara, and I will be your servant until the end."

Daed's hand rests on my stomach, his touch featherlight as he gazes into my eyes, uncovering a part of me only he knows—a secret space that I allow only him to explore. With his other hand, he cradles my face, leaning down to draw me to his lips. He feels like everything I've ever wanted, and I kiss him with everything I have.

"I am yours, my queen," he whispers, his words stirring a warmth that ripples through every nerve. "Use me as you will until such time as I am spent."

I laugh lightly as he brushes his nose against mine, and I forget all my cares, that mystical balm of his working its magic on my memories, until all I remember is now. All I remember is this. I am a rabbit released from a snare, yet in this moment, I have no desire to run.

Daed guides me to the bed, and as I sink into the silken sheets, the world outside fades into a distant memory. Every touch, every movement between us feels beautifully slow, as if time has released its hold, allowing us to exist in this suspended moment. In the heart of Pariseth, our sanctuary, we have the power to stretch seconds into hours, turning fleeting days into an eternity.

Every brush of his fingers ignites my senses like wildfire. As he leans down, his breath warms my neck, sending shivers cascading down my spine. His lips find my collarbone, trailing soft, fervent kisses that leave a tingling path in their wake.

"Amara," he murmurs against my skin, his voice low and husky, thick with desire. The sound sends a thrill through me as he kisses along my neck, savoring the delicate curve, before descending to my breasts. His mouth finds my nipple, teasing it with gentle flicks of his tongue, coaxing soft gasps from my lips. Each caress sends waves of heat pooling within me, urging me to close the distance, to meld our bodies into one.

I arch my back, pressing against him, craving more of his warmth, more of his essence. His hands glide down my sides, fingers exploring the curves of my body with a mix of tenderness and hunger. When he cups my thighs, a rush of heat floods through me as he pushes my legs apart, exposing myself to him completely.

I can feel his breath hitch as he takes in the sight of me, vulnerable and open before him. As his lips travel lower, he plants soft kisses along my thigh, teasingly close to where I need him most. His tongue flicks out, tasting the delicate skin between my legs, sending shockwaves of pleasure coursing through my entire being.

Then, with a sudden surge of desire, his fingers slip between my legs, finding their way inside me. I gasp, my body instinctively arching toward him, welcoming the sensation as he moves with a skilled, knowing rhythm. His fingers are warm and firm, curling and thrusting in a way that pushes me closer to the edge, while his mouth works its magic, licking and teasing the sensitive skin, heightening the pleasure.

I clutch at the sheets, my nails digging into the fabric as I lose myself in the exquisite feeling of him inside me. Each thrust is both tender and demanding, the dual sensations of his fingers and tongue driving me wild. My breath quickens, and he releases a low moan as he inhales me. All while the world around us blurs into nothingness.

His fingers delve deeper, curling just right. I can feel the tightening knot in my core unraveling, my breath hitching in my throat. My body trembles with anticipation and then, with a final thrust and a flick of his tongue a wave of ecstasy crashes over me like a tidal wave. I cry out, a sound of pure bliss escaping my lips.

He doesn't stop. He rides the waves with me, his fingers continuing their sweet torment, coaxing every last tremor from my body.

"More," I whisper, and he responds with a primal growl, capturing my mouth with his in a fierce kiss that steals the breath from my lungs, his taste blending with my own arousal.

His gaze darkens as he settles between my legs. The weight of his body presses down on me, and my fingers instinctively reach for his length, wrapping around it. I slide my hand along the contours, the smoothness of his skin contrasting sharply with the hard, pulsing warmth that fills my hand.

A low, guttural moan escapes his lips, reverberating through me like a spell. His brow furrows slightly, lips parting as he breathes deeply, the sound of his pleasure intoxicating. He leans into my grasp, his hips instinctively seeking more friction, more contact, and I can feel him throb against my palm.

With a deep breath, I guide him closer, aligning him with my body. The moment he enters me, my breath catches in my throat. He pushes deeper, stretching me, filling me completely, and we both gasp at the sensation. He begins to move within me, setting a rhythm that feels both primal and intimate. Each thrust sends waves of pleasure coursing through us, igniting every nerve ending as we lose ourselves in each other.

As he kisses along my neck and down to my chest, his hands grasp my thighs, pulling me closer to him. I dig my nails into his back, feeling the flex of his muscles beneath my touch as he drives into me. The pressure builds, coiling tighter, and I feel my body responding, ready to shatter under the weight of our pleasure. I wrap my legs around him, pulling him deeper, urging him on, our bodies moving in a rhythm that feels as ancient as the stars.

But before I reach my climax, I shift my position, ignoring Daed's growls of protest as I roll him over. He grins as I straddle him, watching me with a mix of awe and desire, his eyes reflecting the moonlight as they roam over me. With a teasing smile, I begin to move, rocking my hips slowly, savoring the sensation of him filling me once more. Daed's chest shudders with each rise and fall. His hands grip my waist, guiding me as he helps me find the perfect pace, every thrust igniting a fire deep within me.

"Just like that," he murmurs as I sink down on him, his voice barely above a whisper, yet it resonates through me like a melody. I quicken my pace, the heat building again as I lose myself in the moment.

The tension builds higher, an exquisite tightness coiling in my core. I lock my gaze with his, feeling his love and desperation reflected back at me.

As I lean back slightly, pushing myself against him, the pleasure peaks. The world around us dissolves, and in that moment, all I can think about is him—how he feels inside me, how he watches me with those stormy eyes filled with desire. I feel every inch of him, every pulse, and it drives me wild.

"Don't stop, wife," he demands. "Use me."

The gravel of his voice slams into me, and with a final surge, I throw my head back, feeling the wave of ecstasy surge through me, leaving me breathless. At that same moment, I feel Daed tense beneath me, his body responding to my climax as he spills inside me with a deep groan. He grips my hips possessively, grounding me as our pleasure intertwines.

As the waves recede, I collapse against him, my body trembling with aftershocks. Daed wraps his arms around me, holding me close as we both breathe heavily, our hearts racing in unison.

In this sanctuary we've created, we shed our titles of king and queen, Fae and Jewel.

There are no duties to uphold, no responsibilities weighing us down, no sacrifices to haunt us.

We are simply a husband and wife who do not need or want anything but each other.

I cannot recall when I fell asleep in Daed's arms, but the ragged cough of someone clearing their throat jolts me awake.

I bolt upright, and in the moonlight, I see six silhouettes surrounding us. My hand instinctively reaches for Daed, shaking him awake. When his eyes open and he realizes our sanctuary has been invaded, he lunges forward, smoke weaving between his fingers.

"I wouldn't do that, Prince Daedalus," a voice calls from the shadows, the tip of a blade pointed at my throat. "We wouldn't want to make a mess on these fine silk sheets."

Daed clenches his fist, and the smoke dissipates.

"Who are you?" he demands, his voice dangerous. "What do you want?"

The figure steps into the moonlight, revealing a tall, willowy Fae. His green eyes are speckled with gold, and his long blond hair flows like silk ribbons. He clasps his hands at his chest, and I notice his long, curved nails, resembling polished claws—sharp and deadly.

"Anethesis," Daed states, surprise mingling with anger in his tone.

Anethesis bows gracefully. "My Prince. It has been a long time. And Princess Amara, I presume," he adds, his voice dripping with pompous refinement. "A pleasure to meet you, though I regret that it must be under such extreme circumstances."

He wears a flowing sky-blue robe, sheer and light as a summer breeze. Instantly, I recognize the insignia stitched at his breast: a golden ship upon a blue sea, guided by a gust of wind.

"House Ithranor," I mutter, and Anethesis smiles, almost condescendingly.

"Indeed, Princess. I hope the comforts of Pariseth are to your liking. We toiled long and lovingly to create this haven amidst the storm. Is it satisfactory?"

I nod, unsure how to respond. "Yes. It's beautiful."

Anethesis nods as if it were not a question but a statement. "Yes. A shame we have not been able to visit for so long."

Daed's jaw clenches, and he fists the crumpled bed sheets. "What is the meaning of this, Anethesis? How dare you come here unannounced? Get out now before I lose my temper."

Anethesis smiles politely and shakes his head. "I'm sorry, Prince Daedalus, but I cannot do that. We have traveled very far and will not be leaving until we have what we came for."

Daed's eyes narrow, fury radiating from him. "What did you come for?"

Anethesis dips his chin toward me. "The enchanting Jewel of the Tenders."

"You will not touch her!" Daed booms, lunging again. But a sudden, inexplicable blast of wind throws him back onto the bed, pinning his arms taut at his sides. Before I have time to react, another gust ensnares me, dragging me from Daed and suspending me near the balcony.

"Daed!" I scream before an invisible bond clamps over my mouth, muffling my cries.

"I wanted to avoid such ugliness," Anethesis sighs. "But I suppose this was never going to be easy."

The other Fae surrounding the bed move closer as Daed struggles against his bonds, their combined power keeping him pinned down.

"Release her!" he shouts, smoke seeping from his eyes. But Anethesis waggles a disapproving finger.

"There will be none of that, Prince Daedalus, or she will be crushed like spoiled fruit."

With a clenched fist, Anethesis applies pressure on either side of my body, squeezing me tightly and when my eyes widen with shock, Daed relents.

"I will give you anything, just release my wife," Daed pleads, his voice strained.

Anethesis bows appreciatively. "Thank you for your compliance, Prince Daedalus. But that request would best be answered by our ally."

The door of the bedchamber groans open, and all I can do is watch in silence as The Golden Son emerges from the shadows.

Daed's teeth grit, and he jerks his wrists against the ropes of wind that restrain him, his gray eyes burning with rage.

"You look surprised, Prince Daedalus," the Golden Son begins, his hand resting on the hilt of his sword. "I don't blame you. Things have taken an unexpected turn. Who would have thought I wouldn't be alone in my hatred of you? It seems House Ithranor had grievances of their own. Once we sat down and spoke, we realized we had more in common than either of us could have guessed." He circles the bed, his gaze locked on Daed's face. "Crossing the Untold Sea to reach you was always going to be difficult for the Legion, but House Ithranor was more than happy to lend us aid."

"If it's Baev'kalath you want, then fine—take it!" Daed bellows, his voice full of defiance. "Just give me my wife, and we will leave."

"You can keep your miserable rock," the Golden Son laughs mockingly. "But perhaps there is something I could take instead."

"Name it," Daed hisses, his fury palpable.

The Golden Son stalks closer, the moonlight catching the sharply worked edges of his mask. "Release him," he orders the Fae, and with a nod from Anethesis, they withdraw the bonds of air. "Get up," The Golden Son growls, and Daed obeys, though the ire at following commands burns across his face.

When Daed is on his feet, The Golden Son speaks once more. "Now get on your knees."

Daed hesitates, his chest heaving with furious breath, his pride refusing to bend before anyone. But when Anethesis tightens his grip and a muffled cry escapes me, my prince reluctantly drops to the ground, defiance still simmering in his posture.

"Good," The Golden Son says. "Now summon your wings."

Daed furrows his brow. "What?"

"Summon. Your. Wings," The Golden Son repeats tersely, impatience creeping into his voice.

Daed exhales sharply, arching his back as his black wings erupt from his shoulders, magnificent yet now a burden.

The Golden Son nods in approval. "Now, stay still."

In one swift motion, the Golden Son draws his sword from its sheath and slices through Daed's wing, severing it from his shoulder. Daed's howl pierces the air, raw and primal, as the second wing is lopped off, both falling to the floor.

I scream into my bonds as blood streams from the ragged stumps on Daed's back. He drops onto his hands, heaving for breath, and I've never seen him in such agony.

"There," he hisses through clenched teeth. "Now release her."

"Oh, no. That was just for my own amusement," The Golden Son replies coldly. "We will be taking the Jewel with us."

"No!" Daed howls, struggling to his feet, desperation etched on his face. But The Golden Son meets him with a brutal kick to his face, sending him tumbling backward.

I continue to scream against my bonds as The Golden Son approaches. He stalks closer, his eyes roving over my thin nightgown and the goosebumps rising on my skin.

"I'm sorry you had to witness that, Jewel," he murmurs, his voice a smooth, dark caress as his knuckles graze my arm. I jerk away instinctively, but he only grins. "You're shivering. The price of wearing something so... sheer."

I try to scream, but the gag turns it into a muted sound.

The Golden Son tilts his head, studying me with amused curiosity. "Lord Anethesis, it seems the Jewel has something to say. Would you be so kind?"

With a flick of his wrist, Anethesis releases my mouth.

"What was that?" The Golden Son prompts.

I clench my jaw, my voice low and sharp. "Yes, I am cold. So, perhaps you could manage a shred of decency and let me fetch a robe."

His gaze slides over me, lingering before he finally speaks. "Lord Anethesis, should we untie her? Let her get warm?"

"Very well," Anethesis replies, and with another flick of his wrist, the bonds around my wrists are severed, and I am dropped to the ground with a thump.

"But please, make haste, Your Highness. We must depart promptly," Anethesis adds with a weary sigh.

I take a tentative step toward the wardrobe, but The Golden Son blocks my path. "Try anything, and the next thing I take is his head," he warns, his tone icy.

I gulp, battling to keep my expression calm. I refuse to give him the satisfaction of seeing my fear. I reach the wardrobe, flinging the doors open, and glance back at Daed crumpled in the corner, blood streaming down his back and pouring from his nose. Panic rises in my chest as I fumble through the clothes. Finally, my fingers grasp a soft robe, and I swirl it around myself.

"Let me help you with that," The Golden Son says, stepping closer. His blue eyes lock onto mine through his glimmering mask, and I gasp as he takes hold of the robe's strings, yanking them tightly around my waist before knotting them.

"There. Nice and cozy," he says, his voice dripping with mockery.

Daed looks up, his eyes ablaze with fury. He digs his nails into the bed, dragging himself to his feet, but his Fae captors lift him into the air and slam him against the wall with a forceful gust of wind. The back of his head thuds against the stone, and his eyes flutter closed as he drops to the ground, a lifeless heap.

"No!" I scream. "Stop! Let's go. Please! Just leave him alone!"

The Golden Son nods in agreement. "Yes. Time is short. Bind her again. We don't want her changing her mind."

Anethesis twirls his fingers, and my invisible bonds snap back into place, sealing across my mouth and binding my wrists behind my back. With a flick of his wrist, a gust of wind whisks The Golden Son and I into the air, propelling us out of the balcony. The last thing I see is Daed, sprawled in a pool of blood and black feathers, his beautiful wings at his side.

The Ithranor Fae follow, gliding effortlessly on the wind that carries us across Pariseth toward the storm wall. I pray to the Souls that we die trying to break through. Instead, Anethesis extends his hand, and a rush of wind cleaves the wall in two. Beyond it, the raging waves are dotted with a dozen ships, each intricately carved with elaborate figureheads and billowing golden sails and even in the dead of night, they shine.

The Golden Son looks down at me with his piercing blue eyes, and despite my inability to speak or move, I hope my hatred is clear on my face.

"Have you ever ventured to the lands beyond the Untold Sea?" he asks, not bothering to wait for my response. "Me neither. This will be an adventure for both of us."

Once we pass through the wall, Anethesis seals it behind us, erecting a barrier of wind that keeps the pelting rain at bay. When we touch down on the deck, the hundreds of Ithranor Fae summon even more wind, propelling their vessels across the sea faster than any Mordorin can fly.

Despair washes over me as I watch Pariseth fade into the distance, tears streaming down my cheeks, Daed's muffled name escaping my lips.

Aboard the ship, I'm taken below deck and shown to a cabin furnished with the opulence of a palace. Anethesis removes the gag from my mouth but leaves my hands bound.

"I remember what those things are capable of," The Golden Son says, his tone curt. "So let's not take any risks." He glances over his shoulder at Anethesis. "I'll finish this."

Anethesis nods. "Again, I'm terribly sorry it has come to this, Princess Amara. Please, make yourself comfortable."

When he closes the door behind him, I spit at The Golden Son's feet.

"You align yourself with what you hate most. What a hypocrite you've become."

"I aligned myself with whoever would help me get what I want," he snaps, irritation flickering in his eyes.

A shiver runs down my spine, but The Golden Son only laughs. "Don't flatter yourself, Jewel. I've already told you—I have no interest in you, but the Ithranor do. So here you are."

"And what do they want with me?" I grit my teeth, forcing the words out.

"Apparently something you won't want to part with. Do you know what that means?"

I fall silent, a cold surge of fear coursing through my veins. Could they be referring to my baby? But how could they possibly know?

"I have no idea," I reply flatly, trying to guard against the possibility that I might be wrong.

"Well then, I suppose we'll all find out in due time." He strides to the door and pulls it open. "Sleep well. When you awaken, we'll be in a new world, full of possibilities."

With a final slam, he shuts the door behind him, and I crumble onto the bed, barely holding on by a thread. I scramble to the window, peering into the darkness, but there's nothing to see. We are so far from Baev'kalath now that I can't imagine Daed could be anywhere near.

A hollowness aches in my chest, an emptiness I thought had been filled but now feels deeper than ever. Tears flow freely, and I can't help but wonder if they'll ever stop. How did this happen? How could our victory slip through my fingers so quickly, allowing me to win and lose everything? What do the Ithranor want with me, and how long will they keep me hostage in these lands beyond the Untold Sea?

I glance down at my stomach. What will become of my child?

I cry for hours until the tears finally cease, leaving my eyes sore and burning, almost as much as my wrists bound behind my back. I don't sleep. Instead, I watch the sunrise, my thoughts consumed with Daed. What if I never see him again?

The morning sun pours through the window, illuminating the horizon. In the distance, I see the silhouette of land and hear the cries of seabirds. Have we really arrived so quickly?

All I can do now is survive. Not just for myself, but for Daed and his child that I carry. I cast aside my doubts. I *will* see him again. Because I cannot get through the next five minutes if I dare think anything different. I must preserve my strength and keep my wits about me for when he comes. Because he *will* come, and he will exact terrible vengeance on those who have wronged him.

My shoulders ease, and a smile finally finds its way onto my face as I gaze across the sun-dappled sea. A soft purr rings in my ear, and slowly Ashen slips from my hair, pattering across my shoulder before weaving his way onto the bed beside me, curling into a ball.

My poor captors.

I do not think they bargained for a hostage of smoke and vines.

About the Author

Here there be dragons and starships

J.L. Tomlinson is a science fiction and fantasy writer hailing from New Zealand. When not lost in worlds of magic and interstellar adventures, she enjoys reading, exploring spooky things that aren't too scary, and indulging in her love for fried chicken and eavesdropping on people arguing in malls.

Her stories blend the fantastical with the familiar, delivering tales as thrilling as they are heartfelt.

www.ingramcontent.com/pod-product-compliance
Lightning Source LLC
Chambersburg PA
CBHW030805260626
47169CB00001B/199